QUILL & STILL
BOOK I

by Aaron Sofaer

Riverfolk Books

Quill & Still

©2022 Aaron Sofaer

Aaron Sofaer asserts the moral rights to be identified as the author of this book.

This book is protected under the copyright laws of the United States of America. No part of this publication may be reproduced, stored in a retrieval system, or transmitted in any form or by any means, without the prior permission in writing of the publisher. Nor may it be otherwise circulated in any form of binding or cover other than that in which it is published and without a similar condition including this condition being imposed on the subsequent purchaser. Any reproduction or unauthorized use of the material or artwork contained herein is prohibited without the express written permission of the author and publisher.

The scanning, uploading, and distribution of this book without permission is a theft of the author's intellectual property. If you would like to use material from the book (other than for review purposes), please contact queries@riverfolkbooks.com for assistance.

Print and eBook formatting by MadMaxine.
Artwork by Matthias (https://baconstrap.carbonmade.com/).

First published in 2023 by Riverfolk Books.

Riverfolk Books
http://riverfolkbooks.com

This novel is a work of fiction. The names, characters and incidents portrayed in it are the work of the author's imagination. Any resemblance to actual events, locations, or persons, living or dead is purely coincidental.

ACKNOWLEDGEMENTS

This book would not have been possible without the inspiration, aid, or support of the following:

Graydon Saunders, Becky Chambers, and Elizabeth Bear, whose civics inspired me;

Travis Baldree, JollyJupiter, and Alexander Wales, whose stories reminded me that people really will read slice-of-life;

Dr Bret C. Devereaux of A Collection of Unmitigated Pedantry and Dr. Derek Lowe of In The Pipeline, for all of the invaluable insight into history and chemistry respectively which their blogs afforded me;

the author communities of Council of the Eternal Hiatus, The Silver Pen, The Dragoneye Moons, and the Cabal of Many Names for cheering me on, egging me on, and pointing out where I was falling short;

my two eventual editors, eighteen beta readers, various Patreon subscribers, and members of my Discord community who kept loving the story while pointing out errors and inadequacies—bless them all for doing so;

my wife, who kept reminding me that I am in fact allowed to have a hobby, and all of my friends who put up with me being That Kind Of Author;

and the thousands of authors whose stories I've read in my life—because if I hadn't been a reader, I certainly would never have been a writer.

QUILL & STILL

BOOK 1

CHAPTER 1.1 - IN WHICH A WOMAN MEETS A GODDESS

Wandering off the path in the Greek woods might not, in hindsight, have been the most sensible of choices. Compass and map notwithstanding, the trackless wilderness had things that a biochemist was not qualified to deal with. So, following the glimmers of mist along the tiny creek as I hiked upstream towards the tinkling music of a waterfall? Probably not the path of wisdom.

There was no way I wasn't going that way, though. I'm an absolute sucker for the way that morning mist dances as it burns off, and I've never seen a waterfall that I didn't want to stop and admire. And it wasn't like I had somewhere in particular to be or a particular path to take.

It was just me, the woods, a week of vacation, enough food for five days, and enough iodine to purify a month's worth of water. It was my break from the humdrum of what passes for science in academia, from pipettes and flow cytometers and centrifuges; it was my break from exhausted, desperate postdocs trapped in the cycle of abuse and their publish-or-perish PIs.

So of course I walked up-river. Exploring to find the small places of sublime beauty was the whole point of backpacking through the woods.

The quiet snuck up on me. My feet crunching against the leaves and the snap of twigs sounded almost overwhelming as the birdsong, frogs, and other critters faded into silence, and it wasn't long before the only things I could hear were myself and the water. Even so, by the time I noticed the song, I was coming around the bend and could see her through a break in the trees.

She was astonishingly beautiful. I don't know how to convey the extent of it, how to put it into words. Slender, with this incredible Olympic heptathlon physique and stunningly perfect skin, she lounged in the crystal-clear water of the pond with her head and shoulders pillowed on a mossy rock and her arms scratching the lowered heads of two enormous dogs that were lying on the bank in perfect stillness. And that—or the weaponry—should have been a warning sign, but my mental inertia kept my feet going into the clearing, and when I almost tripped over a branch and had to step hard onto the friable ground to keep my balance, her eyes snapped over to me as she reached for one of the javelins at her side.

Hi, I wanted, or maybe should have wanted, to say. *Sorry for disturbing you; I can go. But do you mind if I stay? It's beautiful here, and if I wouldn't be intruding, I'd love to sit by this pond and watch the waterfall. My name's Sophie, and I appreciate your forbearance.*

"Holy shit," I said instead. "Are those your javelins? Because oh my *goddess* do you ever have the arms for them." I blinked a few times, seeing her eyes narrow, and took a very small, careful step backwards, flushed with embarrassment and a sudden nervous fear as her dogs' heads came up. "Sorry, sorry, my mouth gets away from me, you're beautiful and your gods look—I mean your *dogs* look great and I'll just go now."

A moment later, I turned back towards her, away from the impossibly thick brush and the needle-looking spines that barred what was previously a clear path. They ran all the way to the water, and a little more besides; there absolutely was no way I was getting through them, and no way I *got* through them in the first place.

"Or... not, I guess." I tested one of the spines with the tip of my hiking boot, wincing as it went through the leather with ease. "Was there... I *know* there's no way this was like this when I walked through."

"**Approach, child.**"

I'd taken four fast steps towards her by the time my brain caught up. There was an unbelievable degree of command in her voice, and I've always been an absolute sucker for a pretty girl telling me to come nearer to her, so it wasn't the fact that I obeyed that threw me for a loop. It was the fact that I was on unsteady, uneven ground, taking long steps at practically a running speed, and I didn't fall on my face or my ass; and that broke whatever effect it was and I almost slipped, catching an easy smirk on her face.

"Okay, that was weird. This is weird." I looked more closely at her, and at what was strewn around her. Notably missing were things like pants or shoes, footprints, a bag of any sort, or signs of anyone else, along with any collar or mark of ownership on the dogs; present were the dogs, three long javelins with what looked like wickedly pointed tips, an unstrung bow, a shirt, and a horn of a vaguely familiar style.

That, and those two words had been Greek, and okay, I was fluent in Greek, but when I stopped to remember what *words* she used I could hardly recognize them, what with the linguistic drift. So how did I understand her?

I had enough time to perform the shift from looking inquisitive to gaping, along with the obligatory internal *oh*, probably in prelude to an *oh shit*, when she crooked her finger at me. I obediently kept walking forwards, because what else was I going to do? The way out was blocked, and the javelins were within reach of her hand. *That's a tunic, not a shirt*, I thought to myself, uselessly. "I know this is totally rude, but somehow I always thought you'd look older? More, I dunno, late-twenties, at least. Though I guess the myths specifically did describe you as young."

From the look on her face, that was absolutely the wrong thing to say. "**Young?**" The word buzzed in my ear and rippled across the waves, ancient yet somehow understandable, shivering with the feeling of a branch breaking behind you in a quiet forest. The muscles in her right arm—the arm next to the javelins—bunched, and I was fairly sure that my life hung in the balance for a split second before they relaxed. "You have hungry eyes, for someone who thinks I'm *young*."

"Hey, look." I opened my mouth to protest, but then realized that no, actually, I *had* been staring, there was definitely no arguing with that. She was glorious, lithe and powerful, and the water did nothing to hide her slender curves. "I apologize," I said instead. "This is tremendously rude of me. I'd love to look away and appreciate the scenery, but I physically can't, and I don't know why. Is there something I should refer to you by, incidentally? *The Delosi Javelineer* doesn't really roll off the tongue." I used the Greek for it, Dêlias and Aeginaea, as best I could, and her eyes softened a little. I could tell this because while I couldn't look away from her, I could look at whatever *part* of her I wanted; but frankly, her face was so unfairly pretty that that hardly helped.

"You know my name; there a *problem* with it?" Her voice was like honey and also like distilled threat; a personal kind of threat, a *run, so that you can die tired* kind of threat.

"Lady Artemis," I managed to choke out against the sudden pressure. Because this *was* her, I knew that in my bones; I knew it in the sudden thickness of the air, in the way her words reverberated down my spine, in her sublime perfection. I felt it through the cushion of singing calm that threatened to overcome me, and I tasted it in the way my words were being drawn out of me without coming within sight of a filter. "I apologize.

You've been a long-gone myth to us for thousands of years, and I'm not sure what to say. I meant only to avoid giving offense."

And I shouldn't even acknowledge you, a voice inside my head insisted. *The Lord is One*. The mantra had formative decades of repetition giving it weight. I shoved it aside anyway.

Her face twisted as I did so, like she knew what I was thinking. "I know. Manners are manners, aren't they?" Her smile was a thin little quirk of the lips, distant and almost displeased, and she waved lazily at the bank of the pond. "**You may sit and bide for a time.** You've shown enough respect to earn that, so I don't mind letting you appreciate this little piece of the old days before I kill you. Nothing personal, you understand."

"Um. Thanks?"

That felt entirely reasonable, though I knew I should have felt otherwise; and I wasn't inclined to bother her with any metaphysical questions, which was utterly unlike me. I sat down despite those misgivings, for lack of any real alternative. Getting up would be a pain, but I was finally able to take my eyes off of the goddess, and the terrain was *miraculously* comfortable. There was a rock conveniently placed so that I could rest my pack against it and lean back, legs outstretched and butt on a soft patch of moss. I'd sat in chairs—*expensive* chairs—less comfortable than the bank of this pond, I was pretty sure.

And the pond itself and its surroundings were unbelievably pretty, if not worth literally dying to see. The trees and underbrush were vibrant, the water crystal-clear with a bevy of easily visible fish and the occasional lamprey or bivalve where there weren't artistically placed spots of green floating on the water. The trees climbed their way halfway up the stone that defined the far curve of the pond, giving way to mosses as the slope got steeper and the rock got less broken, and those trees leaned out over the water as if posing.

And then there was the waterfall.

The waterfall was, obviously, the *plat de résistance*. It flung itself off the cliff above us, roaring as it hammered down into the pond's depths, spraying rainbows for dozens of feet in every direction. There was a majesty in it, something profound and way beyond my ability to consciously get a grip on, but it was *perfect*. Not too loud, but still thunderous; not so high or with so much volume that I couldn't internalize how big it was, but still coming down from a *cliff*, sheer and tall and grand.

The sublime moment lasted a while, and then I sighed, feeling my attention start to wander. "Hey, Artemis. Goddess of the Hunt, protector of girls and women." I didn't turn my head, instead watching a fish of some kind, probably some kind of brown trout, dart to and fro. "I know there's nothing in your domain that suggests you'd be inclined to do this, and I have no way to propitiate you. But if you're gonna kill me, can you bring my phone to some place that has reception and let it send an email to my mom? Not that she'll believe me, and it's not like my father will let her grieve, unless his influence has waned as fast as he deserves. But I owe her some sort of goodbye. I don't want…" I took a breath, letting it out, a little shakier than I'd have liked. "She's losing her daughter the rest of the way, I don't want her to think I committed suicide."

There was a long silence, long enough that I lost track of the fish I'd been watching. I switched to another fish, a bigger one that looked like it'd taken a shine to another fish, and by that I mean it snapped up the smaller one as food. The movement was explosive, a darting blur of color from a fish whose body barely moved as it shot forward in pursuit of its snack, and I fought down the urge to applaud it for its flawless attack. The ripples of the resulting struggle shattered the stillness of the water's surface, my straight black hair and hawkbill nose refracted into a funhouse mirror of sparkling light and sharp angles.

"So, hey."

I jerked in startlement at her voice, having somehow forgotten that she was there. There was a note of discomfort in her voice. In *Artemis's* voice, that utterly certain part of my gut reminded me—a voice that had just shifted into an almost intimate informality as though the divine weight and distant demeanor had been nothing more than a mask.

"Let's forget about the killing thing, yeah? We're just going to move on. I can't let you go back home because I'm not even supposed to be here, but I can figure something else out, easy as hitting a mark."

My head turned in disbelief. There was a realization written in her new body language, clear as day in her tone and in her crushingly familiar body language: physically a lot looser, with an edge of guilt and shame. "Really? *Really?*"

Artemis sighed. "Oath to my mother, it was an honest mistake, really sorry. And how often do you get that from an Olympian; you wouldn't get it from my brother, okay?" I kept staring at her, now gawking more than upset. "Obviously my bad, explains a lot, let's cut to the chase, skip the in between. We're good, two girls having a bonding moment, just like it never happened, yeah?"

It took me a moment to start my brain back up, and by then my head was in my hands. "Sure. Just… two girls having a bonding moment." I raised my eyes back up to look at her, forcing myself to relax muscles suddenly tense. "What do you mean, though, you *can't* let me go back home?"

"Look, none of us is supposed to be here, okay? You know, epistemic pollution from too many of us having too many shards in the same world. It's nothing I can afford to mess around with, Dad only knows how fate would change, so you… can't go back." The goddess's face had softened, somewhere in saying that, and the disconnect between her cadence and the seriousness of her words kept me from internalizing it for a moment.

Only a moment, though, and then a few things clicked, even if some things didn't—what were *shards*? "We're in some sort of liminal space, right? That's why it's *back*, I can't go back to… to Earth." The thought was momentarily overwhelming, but as I looked at Artemis, it faded in magnitude and relevance. "But a liminal space can connect to *other* places."

"Yeah, that's about it." She sucked in her bottom lip and bit it pensively, in a motion that suddenly trapped about a hundred and ten percent of my attention. "I could still kill you, leave your body where it'll be found. You'd be dead, but closure, I guess. Or I send you on."

"I want to live." The words spilled out of me almost before she'd finished talking. "There's a few people I'll miss, more than a few, but shit, that's better than dead, and they'll get over it, though I still want that message to go out. And I'm sure it'll be more fun than pipetting and running experiments."

"Scientist?"

I nodded at her, and she shrugged, lying back and shifting her hands to scratch the undersides of the dogs' heads. They shifted, too, and I was startled to notice them; what with the subject of conversation and the reality of meeting a goddess, I'd forgotten they existed.

I just about went back to forgetting, about a second later, because the shift had her entire core at least a little bit engaged, and I could and did trace a line of lithe muscle from her hands down her arms and sides to her feet.

"—not all that interested, honestly, but everyone's got interesting things about them, so drop the weight, sit by me and tell me about yourself, yeah?"

"Uh, sure." Not knowing what to say to that, or what to do other than comply, I shrugged out of my pack and slid over. There was another sinfully—or blessedly—comfortable depression in the rock and moss and soil, cradling me as I leaned back in a mimicry of her position, legs outstretched with my feet hanging just over the water. *There's a fucking literal goddess about three inches away from me, and a giant dog that's about as far behind me*, I thought to myself, and I had to fight down a fit of nervous giggles. "Not sure what to say, honestly."

"Work is absolute bullshit and eats all of my emotional energy when I'm not on vacation, so everything is routine; playing a game or reading a book while I exercise is about the most interesting part of my day. And on vacation, well." I looked around, drinking in the sights and sounds, carefully not looking at her. "This, but less so. I'd typically spend anywhere from ten to a hundred hours hiking. Alone, nobody that I'm responsible for, no duties other than to myself. Lose myself in traveling and find places that try to look like this."

"Yeah."

I couldn't help glancing over at her at that point, what with how much contented emotion she put into that one word of reply; and for all that I kept my eyes above her shoulders, there was still probably a whole lot of obvious reaction in my face, forget about my endocrine system. "Not a lot of romance, which is how I like it, and I've been working on getting to a place body-comfort-wise where I could start taking a wider range of folks up on the other side of the coin, which I'm looking—was looking forward to."

"Ugh, modernity." My eyes narrowed at her despite myself, but she just sort of smirked at me, turning a little to make eye contact. "Always caught up in complexes and stuff, I don't know. I'll give us this, we knew that a mortal is always a work in progress, even if that progress is dying, yeah? Fuck who you want, if they want you; use their eyes, if you can't look at yourself."

That got a snort of laughter out of me. "I thought you were supposed to be, like, a *virgin* goddess?"

"I mean, I wasn't *wedded*. Didn't mean I was *dead*, okay? Didn't go for men, still don't, source of some confusion occasionally. It's a rare shard of me that's *that* cold."

"Shard," I murmured. "You've mentioned them twice."

"You've invoked four of mine." Her shrug was loose, but there was a hint of challenge in her eyes. "Been a while since we left, but you knew enough to do that much."

I blanked for a moment—what had I done four times in our conversation? I still had enough of my upbringing and training to cast my mind back to what I'd said, and if it was four times…

"Epithets?" I tilted my head back, regretfully looking away to think more clearly. "It always did fascinate me, the way that every temple, every cult seemed to have its own facet of the gods they worshipped, and each by a different title, a different epithet."

"Not many remember that, not properly."

"I was… looking for something I'd lost, something I couldn't have," I said quietly into the sky. It was something that I'd admitted to myself often enough, but I hadn't verbalized it before. "Something I knew didn't exist, and which was toxic where people thought it did. Safer to explore the farther from relevance it was, and I had friends who loved the stories, loved the scholarship and the civics and the… *aesthetic* of it, priestesses in their cults."

"Well, that's how we broke the world, mostly, not that I should be telling you even that much. Anyway!" She smiled playfully at me as I glanced over, startled. "Let's not take ourselves for too much of a deer-chase. Tell me what kind of life you'd like to be able to live, yeah? Not every world's the same."

"Other than one where I get to hang out with impeccably proportioned women?" The words fell out of my mouth without any involvement of my brain, and by the time I realized what I'd said and started blanching at it, Artemis was laughing.

What with her being a goddess and all, it wasn't a surprise that her laugh was transcendent.

"Uh." I was red in the face, but determined to answer her question anyway. "I'm pretty chill, I guess. I don't want to have to fight." I stopped at that, eyes fixed on the waterfall for some reason. "Like, I know you're the Goddess of the Hunt, or part of you is, and maybe this doesn't make sense to you—" *Right, as if* that's *why I'm not looking at her.* "—but I don't like effort all that much. I resent having to do cardio to stay healthy, I hate running, and I *really* don't want to have to fight."

"Listen, I'm not Ares, alright? I'm not gonna judge you for that. Might not understand, yeah, but won't judge you."

"I appreciate that." I watched the water for a bit longer, gathering my thoughts. "I like being nice to people. I'd like it if society were structured more around being nice. I'd like it if... if I could work on stuff that's interesting, and not work on stuff that's boring just because if I don't, I'll starve to death. Easy access to body-modding magic or shapeshifting, books, friends, and a long life."

"Have to say, can't relate to pretty much any of that, but I can work with it. Not the easiest world to find, but it's not the hardest—and you *are* one of mine in more ways than one. So just lie back and close your eyes, alright? Gonna have to do something with these. Too modern. Nowhere I can send you has this sorta post-industrial style."

I felt a light tug at my shirt, at my pants, and obediently closed my eyes. "There's something to be said for post-industrial," I said, giving voice to my misgivings. "Without my meds, I'm—"

"—Sophie, girl, **what am I?**"

I shuddered in sudden terror at her tone, furious at myself for saying anything. *Of all the people to fucking back-talk, what the* fuck *am I thinking?* "Lady Artemis. Goddess. Please, forgive any insult I may have given; I will entrust myself to your hands."

"Grew a bit careless with your words, you folks did. It's fine, not one for formality, obviously don't do it again. Mind you, most of my family, they might have said that's fair and square, no more debt, we both had a lapse of hospitality, by Dad's laws that makes us even, yeah? Wouldn't feed that logic to my dogs, but *they'd* say it."

I nodded, eyes still closed, shivering as the fear faded into relief. *Theoxenia*, I thought to myself. She'd misstepped, committing a violation of hospitality law, and this was her casually evening the scales; and I'd had the idiocy to imply that she was going to do a bad job of it. Forget that she'd already made more than one error today—that was one thing, but pointing it out? *I was just rude to a member of the Olympian Pantheon and I'm not dead yet. That's my luck for a lifetime.*

"Messages, health, that's details," she continued as if to herself. "Won't send you onwards to a worse life. Magic, with enough structure to guide and enough freedom to discover; adventure if you want it, friends unless you lose 'em, and... nice. I know a place, can't send you with anything they don't have, have to do something about the clothes. Now **relax.**"

I was happy enough to obey, letting the last of the tension bleed out of my body. It was pleasant, and something beyond pleasant; and eventually, I slept.

CHAPTER 1.2 - TO AWAKEN IN A NEW WORLD

Hey you. You're finally awake.

My eyes snapped open wide. The voice was mild, mirthful, and I instantly hated both the voice and its owner.

"Really?" I scowled at the tree trunks just above me and their canopy of leaves *far* above me and glared at the few visible patches of stunningly blue sky. "*Really*? That's what you go with?"

The game had a great deal of crafting, crafting which grants you great power if you use it well. In all places where artisans labor towards mastery, there am I found.

"Well, it got my attention, that's for sure." I started to get to my feet, hands down to split the weight until I was steady, when I noticed that I was up before my fingers brushed the ground. A few seconds later, right around when I realized that my balance was way off, I almost fell flat on my face between one step and the other. I'd made it near enough to one of those titanic tree trunks, though, and I caught myself on it. "That's weird," I muttered. "Am I concussed?"

My half-sister's scales were not balanced. Though this shadow of the memory of my shard's visits here could do only comparatively little, I thought to rectify the matter. You will acclimate in a matter of minutes—do not tarry overlong.

My eyes went wide open, mind whirling. I took a deep breath in, reaching for the calm I'd made such a fundamental part of my personality, and found it ready and waiting; I breathed out, and I was centered enough to prioritize.

Step one: assess. I was, leaving aside useless alternative hypotheses, in a new world. Panic rose at that thought, but less than I thought; I was probably still riding the downswing of an altered state of consciousness from a mixture of work burnout, vacation hiking, and an encounter with a goddess in some sort of liminal space. And speaking of a new world, remembering what Artemis had said about clothes, I looked over myself and started grinning.

I was wearing an entirely new outfit, as practical as it was gorgeously colorful. There was a dark crimson skirt that went down a bit past my knees over luxuriously soft dark red leggings, with what felt like cotton briefs underneath. Contrasting with those, over something not unlike a bra: a shimmery blue shirt, cut at bottom and top both to show a thin blue undershirt of that same amazing cottony cloth. A gray open-fronted coat of what was unmistakably some kind of leather. Boots, barely different from my hiking boots aside from the cords being replaced by buckles; still steel-toed, though these were gray.

Experimentally, I did a spin. The skirt floated up *splendidly*, to my delight.

All in all, it might have been the nicest practical outfit I'd ever worn, but I was going to miss the accessories—no backpack. No pockets, either, but I had a pouch of that same bizarre gray leather; I spilled the contents on my palm, frowning at what they implied about this new world. The paper for the small notebook was rough, and I could feel little striations in it as though from a press of some sort; linen, if I had to guess. Pencils, three of them, sized appropriately for the little notebook, no erasers, and a tiny little knife that was obviously to sharpen them. A square of soft cloth, intricately folded.

More interesting were the eleven coins. Seven small circular ones with a face—crowned, so monarchy was and might still be in play—in profile on both sides, three slightly bigger circular coins with a sword on one side and a crown on the other, and one rectangular coin with a city on one side and three entwined runes or glyphs of some sort on the other. No way to tell which was the obverse versus the reverse, and no way to read the writing around the edge. I was still moderately confident that the crowns, as I'd decided to call them, were the cheapest of the denominations—the other two had complex crenelations around the rim, suggesting that the crowns weren't worth the cost of replication.

Well, that or there was magic preventing forgery, or the monetary system here worked completely differently, but I didn't want to go down those paths quite yet.

No other pouches, no other pockets. I did a deep knee bend and then a squat, falling on my ass when my center of gravity turned out to be all wrong, and I started grinning like an absolute madwoman as I surged back to my feet in one smooth motion.

Nothing hurt. Nothing hurt, and I *really* wanted a mirror, and I had never been so flexible.

"This is phenomenal." I didn't know if I was talking to myself or to the strange voice. Well, not really a strange voice; a combination of process of elimination and his particular interests made it obvious who he was. I bent forwards, touching my toes with my palms; my belly still got in the way a bit, since I thankfully hadn't been magically transformed into someone skinny, but I could *do it*, could rest the heels of my hands on my feet, if I sucked in my gut only just a little.

Then you acknowledge that there is no debt between you and either myself or my sister.

There was a weight to that sentence, one that stole the flipness of my answer right out of my mouth as I shot up to standing. I didn't respond immediately; my mind was whirling with trying to figure out why I'd be owed such a debt and why that would be bad. A moment later, that weight settled onto me like I was a mote of dust under the perception of some eldritch *thing* that could crush me just by the desire to do so.

I'd always read that he was a minor god, barely a member of the core pantheon. Despite that, the impatience of what he'd described as a *shadow of the memory* of his presence outshone Artemis's full-on ire like a magnesium cook-off would have my lab's Bunsen burner.

"Acknowledged," I said hastily, waving my hands in emphasis. "No debts, we're square." The pressure lifted, and my shoulders slumped in relief. "Hey, uh, would it be appropriate to pour one out for you anyway? Like, no debts or anything, and I'm definitely not talking about supplication or worship, just some… grace? Or to, I don't know. Would she like it if I— I'm not a hunter, really, but it's not impossible I'll wind up drawing a bow on a deer or something. I could dedicate my first arrow to her, if she'd appreciate that? And the first work of my hands to you?"

Mortals. There was a wry humor to the voice again. *Grace given and grace returned is the essence of divinity. They will tell you more, where you go; it bears the name Kibosh.* And with that, the presence was gone, and the weird crystalline clarity that was keeping the emotions at bay left with it.

The first scream ripped itself out of my throat, hurled into the canopy of green above me. The next came out as a whimper, and then I was hunched over as my emotions roiled and I tried to hold myself together as best I could, remembering what I'd just been told about not tarrying. It took me a fair while before I could get back on my feet—at least half an hour of pure gibbering, and then a few minutes of cleaning myself up and getting myself in hand again.

I rather wanted to *keep* myself in hand, having gotten myself sorted out. That meant I needed something to do in order to avoid falling back into that emotional pit, so I started a more thorough survey of the area. I was alive, and I was present enough to notice the trees, and that was going to have to do for a while.

The trees in question were... *impressive* wasn't exactly the right word. *Stupefying* was more accurate. I was utterly incapable of evaluating how tall they were; I could see the canopy of leaves, but the scale was all incomprehensible. Taller than the tallest redwood that I'd seen, I was pretty sure, which meant more than a hundred yards; but how much taller, well, I didn't have a clinometer, and maybe what I'd need would be more like a sextant.

Their size wasn't the only thing that drew my eye, though it would have been enough to be wondrous, since even their shorter cousins back home stunned me every time I saw them. These trees had this thing going with them where their leaves had just a little bit of space between them in a narrow ring, and there was something *glinting* up there. It was, it *had to be*, some sort of lensing effect. If I could see a ring of sky over a hundred yards away, no matter how narrow it was, it would have cast a much wider lack-of-shadow at the base of the tree than this did. The wood that it was lighting up was different, too: darker, rougher, and the heat came off of it in palpable waves when I brought my hand near.

It was magical, and I had absolutely no idea why it existed or how even to figure that out, short of... well.

Short of asking someone.

I dragged my eyes away from the forest. Away from the loam and bushes, from the bark and the beetle that caught my eye, iridescent and green. Away from what looked distinctly like a fern but smelled like spearmint, and those were only a few things among many that had caught my eye and nose.

I knew I'd be back soon enough, armed with more knowledge and armored against whatever dangers this part of this world had. And besides, whatever town or city this Kibosh place was, a god was telling me to head there, and I didn't think I was going to find it amidst the trees.

The forest edge was *sharp*. A knife-cut carved a perfect delineation between knee-high grass and tower trees, pruning all the leaves in what initially looked like a straight line but, when I looked again, was perceptibly a gentle arc. I'd been deposited just barely on the forest edge of the border, and had walked a few steps towards the nearest tree; determined to leave and find someone to ask my questions of, I made my way to the edge.

It wasn't all the same height. Bending down to study it more closely, I could tell that the grasses were in clusters, one tall stalk-top rising about six inches higher than the surrounding stalks, and another set of stalks around *that* which were another six inches shorter still. They didn't seem to be razor-sharp or anything, and there was the expected smattering of bugs and grubs and larvae, and even though I didn't recognize any of them in particular they all had more or less the expected bauplan. The only obviously magical thing was that when my hand cast a shadow over the grass, the grass would bristle and *bend* quite noticeably to get as much direct sunlight as possible.

The sheer magical mundanity of it was almost terrifying, and I realized that if I didn't start moving, I'd be sitting down for another, probably longer gibber. *Nothing for it*, I told myself instead; *time to step into the light*.

CHAPTER 1.3 - CIVILIZATION, EVER IN THE DISTANCE

I started itching between the second and third steps.

It wasn't much of an itch, but I'd been rather enjoying the total lack of pain and discomfort. It had been a distinct contrast to my standard aches and pains, what with joints that could only be described as problematic and both tendons and ligaments that were weaker and less tightly coupled than they were supposed to be. Still, startling as it was to get kicked in the metaphorical teeth the moment I stepped out of the trees' shade, I'd probably have noticed it regardless. Maybe not quite as quickly, but by the tenth slow step, I'd taken five breaths, and I was starting to feel the tiniest bit of itching up in my nose.

It was... alarming. I had been noticeably allergic to a lover's house, something that her girlfriend had used as a way to needle me for the brief period before we'd gone our separate, amicable ways. The itch was different from what I would have expected if I'd walked into their—*carpeted, astonishingly*—kitchen, but it wasn't completely different.

If it held true to form, in about fifteen minutes, I was going to feel like my eyes were itching on the inside and I was going to have a definite headache. And given the undercurrent of burning that I was feeling under the itch, *true to form* was going to be only the start of things.

I took a deep breath—no reason not to, it wasn't like shallower breaths were going to save me—and sighed, looking out into the endless-seeming fields of grass. *Probably tarried too long having a freakout and getting distracted by the trees.* On the horizon ahead of me, there was a vague blur rising out of the fields; the town, probably, and if it had any kind of wall, that would explain the sort of uniformity of appearance it had from this distance.

From this distance? Well. I couldn't exactly *assume* that the planet I was on had the same curvature as the Earth, but if I assumed both that and that I was looking at a palisade that was in the vicinity of ten feet, I was about three miles away. Not a particularly comfortable distance to traverse feeling like I was, much less how I would be feeling shortly, but far from impossible.

Besides, I had been bid by a god, the god who'd dropped me somewhere with my joints all fixed up. No sense in getting all paranoid about whether I should take the obvious route at that point.

May it be your will, Lord our God, I took a moment to pray, *that you lead my steps towards peace and health.*

The irony of it all—a prayer for safe travels made to a God whose worship I'd walked away from so long ago, about a journey involving two members of the Greek Pantheon—was not lost on me. I did it anyway, without being sure why, and focused on putting one foot in front of the other.

Things... proceeded. I knew, intellectually, that three miles was less than an hour's easy walk, but walking in discomfort through the trackless grass meant that I lost all sense of time and place. The itch that had settled across every inch of my exposed skin felt like it was taking root and spreading; my lungs burned, and I found myself wiping my eyes clear of rheum over and over again as I cast my eye around the grasslands. There were some brilliantly colored birds gliding on thermals above me, and those kept me distracted for long minutes as I tried to figure out whether it was just a matter of angles and distance that made their wings look odd.

Most of my focus, though, went towards pushing myself as hard as I could to keep my pace up and prevent my walk from turning into a trudge.

Around the time when I was starting to lose that fight, when my steps kept slowing and I was catching myself picking at the hard, scaly patches on my skin, I heard—or maybe *felt*—a skirling, harmonized piping sound, something high and playful over a drone. It was like someone had combined a pan flute and a bagpipe, and something about it sunk into my brain and let my limbs move more freely. The discomfort dimmed, my eyes and sinuses cleared, and I looked in grateful interest over towards where the music was coming from.

It was a goatherd, or possibly a shepherd. They waved at me, sitting, of all things, sidesaddle on what looked like a particularly shaggy-fronted pony, pan pipes lifted to their lips with the sleeves of their brilliantly colorful robes pulled back and tied off to stay out of the way. They had a hat with a short frontal brim and a long, floppy back, dyed in browns and reds, and their baggy pants billowed in a breeze that I definitely wasn't feeling. There was, yes, a pouch of some sort on the near side of the pipes, so it *was* a combination of bagpipes and pan pipes—I tried to cultivate the feeling of vindication, because maybe that, too, would distract me from the itch.

It was unlikely, but hope was a better habit than despair. In the meantime, I waved back. I'd never been the type to be rude to kids, even if the wind on my hand and arm when I gestured felt like knives.

The animals they were herding—caprines with back-swept horns and not a whole lot of fur, most of them shoulder-high on the pony-mounted kid—grazed their way through the plains at a slow amble. I caught glimpses of a few dogs, or what I thought were probably dogs, chivvying stragglers along; they were nigh-invisible in the grass, calling out in barks and showing themselves in jumps. One of them was particularly hard to spot, given that the dog in question didn't seem to be physical so much as a sometimes-coalesced, sometimes-disparate cloud of angles and lines; it said something about how impatient I was to get to my destination and hopefully get the itching taken care of that I just didn't *care*.

Even after I lost sight of the kid on the other side of a small hill, I could still hear the pipes. Their music sank into my muscles and tendons, into my joints and ligaments, into my skin and mucous membranes and eyes. The notes felt like they were entering a battle as a third side, isolating the strife from *me*; it was like I had a shield, a tenuous and porous shield but a shield nonetheless, against the discomfort.

It let me pick the pace back up to something more reasonable. Three, maybe four miles per hour—the pace I'd intended to keep up, the pace I'd fallen off of disappointingly quickly. One foot in front of the other, maintaining as much momentum as I could, I made it to the gates before I even realized I was getting close to them.

It wasn't anything like a commotion. There had *been* a commotion, I realized belatedly; I'd heard, but not paid attention to, people shouting and calling out to me in what sounded like two different languages, one full of sibilants and front-of-the-mouth vowels and another packed with gutturals and clicks, neither of which I recognized in the slightest. But by the time I got to the walls of the village, my wrists and hands were back to being on fire with itching and I was back to blinking fluid out of my eyes constantly. Distracted, the only thing I really noticed was that everything was orderly and quiet, with someone who was probably a guard—the spear was suggestive—beckoning for me to follow.

Score one for, if not the universality of some gestures, then some degree of parallel evolution. Probably.

I tried to pay attention to the guard and to where I was going, but my attention wound up just cycling between all of the different discomforts I was feeling and the alien sounds of the languages the people around me were speaking. Before I knew it, I was three rooms into a building and trying to figure out whether the walls of the building were painted, exceptionally well mortared, or one seamless expanse of stone, and I belatedly registered that the guard had stopped.

My eyes were captured by the circle of blue squiggly rune-like things on the ground, with a tall cylinder of that same shade of blue projected up from the stone. It was like a hologram, translucent and solid-looking at the same time—and at a gesture, I stepped into it.

I grunted inelegantly in relief, with a sound more suitable to being punched than anything else. It wasn't exactly freedom from pain, but the *itching* was gone, and my ability to think through and around the rest of the discomforts increased at the same time.

"**[Lesser Communication]**."

The words cut off my train of thought before my brain had so much as worked through the relief of not being in quite as much pain. It was a woman saying it, but the words had *weight*, weight like I had heard when Artemis commanded me to approach her a lifetime ago, or alternatively, some hours ago. A weight of smoothed stone and deep foundations; a weight that bracketed it in my mind to separate it from mere speech. She, the woman who'd spoken, flopped casually into a chair—*okay, there's a chair there, why didn't I see that before?*—and the man whose wrist her hand had been on straightened, facing me across the light-blue haze of the magic cylinder.

He had a sheaf of papers in his hands, and he glanced down at them one last time in a gesture that was familiar to me; he was about to say something that was rehearsed, but not rehearsed *enough* that he had it fully memorized.

"Please be aware that the Skill being used to communicate," he began, startling me by speaking in perfect English, "permits precisely one sentence, and that sentence is being used to provide you with medical and integrative information, in the former case so that you may be informed before we act and in the latter so that you may be informed and either grant or not grant consent, and the information is as follows: we will be momentarily casting a spell of biological adaptation, without which you will be dead due, among other things—" I felt my lungs burning sympathetically, but he somehow showed no sign of being out of breath. "—to incompatibilities in your digestive system between your home and this world, and which requires your awareness rather than your consent; and you have the option of a spell of integration, which will supplant your known extra-planar languages as well as providing you with access to the empowerment of the Stolen Flame, and which you may signal the acceptance of, a choice I strongly recommend, by ringing the bell on my desk before leaving the room. **[Biological Adaptation]**."

It took me a long, timeless moment to realize what had just happened, that he'd done another one of those *spells* that echoed in that same command voice. It might have taken minutes; I spent them vomiting my guts out into a suspiciously convenient bucket, a bucket that slowly glowed brighter and brighter blue as I filled it.

After a subjective eternity, a wash of almost comfortable frigidity swept through me. The stink, the copious former contents of my stomach, and what felt like a few layers of skin up through my throat and mouth *disappeared*, along with the urge to, or so it felt, voluminously piss my intestines out my ass.

I quite literally collapsed with relief.

The bucket was a dull steel-gray when I managed to get up again, and the light blue cylinder around me was gone. So were the itching and the burning, and after a nearby cloth was applied to my eyes and nose—in that order, always in that order—I felt at least two thirds human again.

The room was simple. I could even look around and pay attention to it now, and I took a moment to study it for what it implied. Hardwood floor, not shiny but not overly scratched up; more of those seamless stone walls, with corkboards overflowing with paper covered in a dense, flowing script that looked like it was written right-to-left. There were a couple of armor stands with what looked like multiple layers of a bunch of stuff and a weapon stand with a couple of swords, some strips of cloth, some spiked maces, a couple of satchels, and some shields; they probably would have told me a lot about how they fought, if I knew anything about pre-modern warfare. Or warfare at all, really, other than what I'd picked up from video games. Which… wasn't much. Neither Celeste nor Fallout: New Vegas was exactly a historical primer.

I didn't have to think about my decision all that much; I wouldn't have been sent there if I weren't supposed to take the offer. I walked over to the desk—wincing as I barked my shin on the bucket in passing—and noted that where the man was sitting was the *little* desk in front, not the big desk back in the corner where the woman was.

He had the bell out, the one that would signify my acceptance. He'd very obviously shifted some paperwork to make space for it while he worked on something with intent focus, pencil—unmistakably a pencil, which meant they had some kind of graphite processing—scratching away. He paused in his writing to grab a knife, whittled off a few shavings to sharpen the pencil, and then noticed me standing at the desk.

He cocked an eyebrow and, smiling, I hit the little lever on the side of the bell. It chimed, and he nodded in obvious contentment, smiling back at me. He called something out to the woman in back in yet another language, neither the sibilant one nor the guttural one but rather one that sounded like he had a mouth full of potatoes, and she looked up from her own writing and smirked at me.

"**[System Integration: Kingdom of Shem, Duchy of Aluf, Dungeon Village of Kibosh]**," they intoned together without any preamble, and my world went black.

CHAPTER 1.4 - POSSESSED OF A CERTAIN STRUCTURE

Welcome, Traveler. System Initialization Commencing.
The Theurgist's System Welcomes You.
Current Maintainers: Archmages Ashaf, Kosem, and Yidani

Unique Identifier Registered:
36ee483b94f99ef87c536d8e4101567f
Name and Identity Registered: *Sophie Nadash, Adult Female, 39 Years of Age.*
Method of Travel Registered: *Divine Intervention (Artemis, Olympian Pantheon)*
Location of Integration: *Kibosh (Dungeon Village) | Aluf (Duchy) | Shem (Kingdom)*
Languages Supplanted: *English, Mandarin, Spanish, Greek, Hebrew*
Languages Provided: *Shemmai (Modern), Shemmai (Ancient/Liturgical), Koshe, Qatn, Sylvan*

BEHOLD! Your Divine Flame Enkindles!

"What. The fuck."

My field of view had gone black like a canned slide transition, followed by green lettering scrolling rapidly in front of my eyes. Once I'd finished reading a line, it faded, and line by line I read through the words on display. It didn't take long, and then I was looking around the room again.

"Seems like a clean Integration, ma'am."

"Formality, James? Really?"

"Felt appropriate to put our best foot forward, I suppose."

My mind idly followed their banter, and I hissed out a breath full of a thousand different emotions. "What the *actual fuck*?" I spun around, looking at first the woman—jotting down notes on some parchment, by the looks of it—and then at the man, and my jaw dropped.

He had one hand thrust out towards me, and there were dense circles of runes surrounding it. They rotated slowly around his wrist, three rings of them, looking like the most absolutely, amazingly magical user interface I'd ever seen. His other hand was poking and prodding at them, spinning them around and zooming in and out.

Stunned and delighted, I walked over to his desk, his hand still tracking me.

"Miss Nadash." His voice was a mellow baritone, in that uncanny range where a voice doesn't sound high and doesn't sound low. Smooth, compassionate, and still professional; this was a man who spoke to people for a living. "My apologies for the indignities of the past few moments; I thought it best to do things by the book, as it were. It is my pleasure to be the first to welcome you to the Kingdom of Shem! My name is James Morei, and I am the Clerk Administrator for Kibosh. On behalf of Their Graces, the Duke and Duchess of Aluf, I am at your service. No doubt you have many questions."

His pause was a clear signal that it was my turn to talk, so I stopped just gawping at him. "I'd say you have no idea, but you… probably do, don't you?"

"Actually, Miss, you're the first Traveler we've seen in Kibosh since its founding, some hundred and thirteen years ago. There was one other in the Duchy during that time, but he was within the Kingdom for no more than a fortnight before his departure."

"You're over a hundred years old?" I took another look at him. He was remarkably well-preserved even for a man of sixty, never mind a hundred. Dark brown hair, a faint facial shadow only beginning to go gray, barely any wrinkles other than a few smile lines, skin on his hands free of blotching and not drawn tight against the bones; everything about him suggested a man in his forties.

"I was appointed Underclerk here as part of the initial expedition to investigate the Dungeon and build a base camp. I'm nearly two hundred, Miss Nadash." He smiled at my stunned expression. "The Theurgist was displeased with the Gods for many things, but the dearth of our time in the world was writ large on his list. All are granted, in their very first Tier, an Attribute which we do not understand, even now—"

"Doctrine." The woman's voice cut calmly across James's more engaged mellowness. "James is a faithful adherent of the Church of a Thousand Faiths, like every other good Clerk; what he's saying isn't so much wrong as a Gods-blinded technicality. We *do* understand what the Longevity Attribute *does*—and as for why the Theurgist made it, it wasn't to empower other people to live well, century after century. He wanted to be eternal, that's all. It was the Shemmai who took the Flame and quantized it, parceled it out to empower everyone. *Clerks*, the lot of us."

There was no rancor in James's face as he looked over at the woman, smiling fondly. "Miss Nadash, forgive me. I should not preach at you; there is far too much to discuss. Know this to be Captain Meredith Morei, and be known by her in turn."

Gears turned briefly in my head, but between that smile and the shared last name, along with the absolute lack of any visual similarity... "Married? Assuming marriage is a thing here."

"I have that divine honor."

"He puts up with me, it's true. Nadash—Sophie?"

I responded to her measuring look with one of my own, and decided that yes, I was fine with informality. "Sophie is fine... Meredith."

"Good. Excellent. Welcome, and suchlike." She punctuated the words with wide slashes across the scroll of parchment she'd been writing on, using an embossed quill that had a feather which glowed a gorgeous amber-red. "James, mind the time. Make sure she's introduced to Kelly with enough time to tour before Levali opens for dinner."

"Kelly?" James raised an eyebrow at his wife, adopting a distinctly dubious face which she didn't look up to see. I could see her smile anyway, a narrow kind of smirk, which suggested she was well aware of his expression. "Not to criticize or doubt you, dear."

"Out with it, *dear*."

"Kelly had the settling of Mattathias. Ellana—"

Meredith cut him off. "Ellana is *one hundred and eighty-seven years old*, James. Ask the girl how old she is."

There was a beat of silence, and James sighed and leaned backwards in his chair. "Sophie, if you don't mind—"

"I'm thirty-nine."

He boggled at me for a bit, and Meredith's smirk got a fair bit more smug.

"To be clear," I elaborated into the silence, "I hit puberty at twelve years old, which was right in the expected range, a year being the span of time in which our planet orbited the sun. Gestation of a baby takes a woman nine—" I stopped, not finding the word I was searching for. "It takes three quarters of a year. Two and a quarter seasons? We had a one-twelfth of a year measure." I didn't have the *word* anymore, and it suddenly hit me that I wasn't speaking *English* anymore. I couldn't remember what it sounded like or think in it. This was Shemmai, and it was a language I knew intimately and deeply, and *I didn't know English anymore.*

"—are identical, so the good Captain is correct. It had... entirely slipped my mind, but of course, if I surprised you with my own... excuse me for a moment." He stood, glancing at me and then at his wife. "Dearest?"

"Go," Meredith grunted. She made two more flourished strokes with her quill and then put it away, by which time James was already out the door. "He's going to go get Kelly. Listen, sun's past zenith, so I'll make this quick. Welcome to the Kingdom of Shem. We have magic and friendly people. It's nice here, and there's no power on the continent that we won't break to keep it that way. Kibosh has two refectories for a hundred seventy-three people, that includes you. We're a Standard Plan village, so the basics all come outta taxes and Dungeon fees. We've got, notionally, two-fifty houses plus shop-houses and the workshop lofts—that's more houses than we got people, even if every herder slept every night inside the walls. Kelly'll help get you settled and give you more details. But that ain't what you want to know.

"What you want to know is what the *fuck* that voice was when you Integrated. Yeah?"

"Huh." I blinked a few times, processing her rapid stream of facts. "Actually, it was writing, not a voice. Theurgist's System, Divine Flame, maintainers and identifiers, all of it written down."

"Eh, not unknown. Must come from a literate culture, not an oral tradition. Make sure to tell Kelly that. So! C'mere, stand up, feet at about your shoulders wide, hands flat on my desk, and look me in the eyes."

I shrugged, standing—just *standing*, no need to be careful, goodness it was nice to have functioning joints—and walking over. She *tsk*'d quietly, glaring at the desk from her chair, and my hands shifted to a more natural, relaxed position as the desk itself sank down a few inches.

"Breathe in," she said once my eyes were on hers, and I breathed with her. "Hold. Breathe out. That's your cadence. Breathe in for five heartbeats, hold for five, breathe out for five. Again." I breathed with her again, and she nodded, not breaking eye contact. Something had grown intense in her gaze, drawing me in, and I successfully resisted the urge to scratch my nose. "Again. Now, open your mouth. Your breath in through your nose is cold; your breath out through your mouth is hot. Your breath in is *coldness*; your breath out is *heat*. Your body is an engine, one which takes in the air and transmutes it; your body is a furnace, one which imparts its heat on the air."

My body was, in fact, a furnace—I might have been a chemist, but I knew that much biology. Her hands were on my hands, lightly pressing them into the desk, and her eyes were startlingly close to mine, and I was breathing just as she said.

"Just like you, a furnace, impart heat onto the air you transmute, the Gods dole out grace to us as we transmute ourselves. The Theurgist stole a piece of that grace, that divinity, and named it the Flame. Call it Divine or Stolen, it doesn't matter; it lives inside you, a furnace that transmutes the mundane work of your hands into the sublime. It lives in your mind, where your brain processes inputs into understanding that your hands are on my desk; it lives in your mind, where the soup in your skull turns physics and biology into *perceiving* that my hands are on yours. It lives in your mind, where what hits your eyes becomes more than just light, and becomes *real*."

I was transfixed. Part of me, a part of me that was getting quieter by the word, was disdainful and scornful. The rest of me was doing its best to throw all skepticism to the winds. I had just had a run-in with a goddess, been sent to a new world, chatted with a god, and had my face rubbed in the fact that magic was real here—skepticism could wait till I had some answers.

"Breathe in. The Flame lives where the mind imparts meaning to the world, and just as you can hear my words and breathe as I bid you, you can see those words and touch the System. Hold. Feel the engine of change that is the body, feel the connection the body has to the mind. Breathe out. It's a *nothing* step from there to touch the connection the mind has to the System, and through its layer of abstraction to the Flame itself.

"**[Command]**. Reach out, and touch it; and then, *having changed nothing*, return to me."

The words washed me away like a flood, and I *reached out and touched it*.

You Gaze Upon Your Divine Flame!

They Shall Know You By This Name: *Sophie Nadash*
These Are The Years Of Your Life: *39*
Your Levels of Elevation Upon The Road To Apotheosis: *Worker 10 (Apex, First Tier)*
Neither Dreams Nor Aspirations Have You Selected To Guide Your Paths
In These Skills, You Embody Excellence: *Learn, Read, Study*
Bestowed Upon You Are These Attributes: *Hale*
Discovery Begins As You Rise Upon The Paths Towards Divinity
Your Skein Of Fate Records These Deeds: *World Traveler, Godtouched*

Your Path Reaches For Fulfillment; Grasp Your Future, And Rise!

I surfaced from the trance, gasping for air. My mouth was dry, and I was sitting in a chair in front of Captain Meredith's desk; seconds had passed, maybe a minute, but I was pretty sure that it hadn't been any longer than that.

"Wow. That was... *something*, alright."

"Wouldn't know." Meredith huffed out a breath, running a finger across her forehead. "Now. Got an important question for you. Ya need to answer it *immediately*, no thinking, no hesitating, or this is gonna take a while longer. Understand?"

"Sure?" My mind spun a little, trying to think of all the possible questions she could ask. Most of them, naturally, were embarrassing. "Go for it."

"*What color is my hair?*"

"Black and blue, like so black it *looks* like it's got blue highlights." My response came immediately, as she'd ordered, and I shook my head a few times afterwards. There was a *feeling*, a reaching out with my mind to touch something, like I was a bridge between that feeling of touching the System and my visual cortex. As soon as I noticed it, it broke, and I suddenly couldn't remember what color her hair was—I only knew what I'd called it. "Wow, that's trippy as *shit*."

"Seeing. Or Observe, or Inspection, whatever you wind up fucking getting. Your first Skill unlock in your new home, congratulations, throw yourself a party. Alright! We're done here. Go on, out the door, down the corridor, turn left at the end, head for the sunlight." She stared at me for a beat, hand reaching for a quill, as I blinked in stupefaction. "Well?"

"I still have—"

"—a lotta fucking questions, I'm sure, but that's for Kelly and my husband. You touched the System on purpose there; you can do it again, you're set." She glared at me, but I had the impression she *wanted* me to push, so I stayed put. "Fine. Fine! One question. *One*."

Words caught in my throat. The first thing I was going to ask could absolutely wait; I *knew* it could wait, because the answer to why I couldn't hold a picture of what she *looked like* in my head wasn't actually important. *What does any of that mean* would also have to wait, since it could be answered by other people. *Why the fuck do I have Levels* could also wait—and besides, far be it for *Sophie Nadash, Laboratory Technician III* to get hung up on that. So if I had only one question, and I didn't have enough context to know what a good question for Meredith *specifically* was… "What's the one piece of advice I need most, that I'm least likely to get from anyone else?"

Her eyes gleamed. "Some people think that only the tip of the spear is important, and they're wrong. Whatever you're gonna do, *don't take a combat Class*. Out of shape, a flincher, missing the disposition, got no training; walk that road, and I'll be filling out forms about how ya died before next season's out."

I grimaced at that, laughter threatening to bubble out of me. "I hear you loud and clear, Captain. Thank you for your time."

She grunted, attention returning to the scroll she'd pushed aside for my hands, and I made my way out her office's door.

CHAPTER 1.5 - WHERE A FRIEND MIGHT GUIDE YOU

As implicitly promised, James Morei was waiting outside for me. With him was a *stunningly* pretty girl who looked like she was in her mid-twenties—which apparently meant absolutely nothing, if James was almost two hundred years old—and a basket whose odor made me realize that I was *ravenously* hungry.

"Sophie, be known to Kelly Avara. Kelly, be known to Sophie Nadash." James beamed beatifically at the both of us. "We know full well the costs of magic, and you bore the brunt of a grand working upon your body today."

"I heard that we had someone new. A *Traveler*." Kelly's eyes sparkled down at me as she smiled, and I momentarily forgot about the food. She had a voice to die for, a clear soprano that rang like a bell and was totally unfair in conjunction with her looks—I'd have killed for her curves, once upon a time. "Soon as James here let me know I had the duty, I grabbed you a walk-basket! It's from Levali's, so it's probably Keldren who cooked it." I reflexively held my hand out to shake hers, which in hindsight was *obviously* the kind of cultural artifact that wouldn't carry over to a different world, and I almost fumbled the handoff when she handed me the basket. "And you have no idea what that means! So eat, *eat*, we can walk and talk."

"Sure. I…" I looked down at the basket. There was a layer of dumplings on a cloth, and I popped one of them in my mouth with, if not trepidation, a bit of caution. My eyes went wide, and I chewed hastily, swallowing a little bit too early and shoving another dumpling into my maw.

"They're good, aren't they!" Kelly nodded excitedly at me, head bobbing up and down as she swayed from side to side. "Keldren does the mants! Well, I know that Hitz calls them *mantou*, but Keldren says mants. Anyway, I always make sure that if I'm doing something that calls for a walk-basket, it's on a Levali day. I swear he can make a hundred kinds of dumplings; these are just my favorites. Anyway, today is—"

"Kelly, not to interrupt," James murmured quietly, quietly enough that I almost didn't hear him, "but I did do a fair bit of magic myself, and I would like to avail myself of Thesha's hospitality."

Another dumpling fell to my hunger, and I missed what else he said to her. She nodded at him, pushing at him playfully while laughing. "Go, go! Get yourself a bespoke meal. You had to cast, poor James!"

"Sophie." He ignored the shoves, smiling genially at me. "You are welcome here. This is the Kingdom of Shem; here, we do our best to ensure that all flourish. Be a good First Friend to her, Kelly; call on me for whatever help is needed. And mind that you—"

"James." He winced genuinely at the barbed sweetness in her voice, and her next shove had more force to it and less playfulness.

"My apologies, Kelly. I leave her in your hands." With that, and a nod at me, he turned right—his right, my left—and started walking down the road.

I looked at them, him moving in the direction she'd been pushing him and her with her hands propped on her hips and staring at him. I swallowed, managing to savor the bright flavors of citrus and the tang of the juices that exploded out of the dumpling in my mouth, then mustered my courage. "First Friend, huh?" I raised an eyebrow at her, voice definitely not nervous at needing to make a good first impression. "That sounds like it has capital letters."

"It does. It's my *job*—to be your friend, advocate, assistant, guide, and more." Kelly gestured to a bench a few steps away. "And speaking of my job! I forgot to get you some water, which means the walking has to wait a moment. Sit down! I'll be right back, okay?"

"Sure, sure." I bit down on another dumpling, sitting down and watching her take off at a quite respectable run. She looked fantastic doing it, multicolored skirts hitched up around her hips to show off bright teal tights or leggings that tucked into boots very much like mine. I watched shamelessly, grinning, until she turned and was no longer in sight.

I blinked a few times, popping another dumpling into my mouth. *Only a few left*, I thought to myself, then shrugged. It was the first moment I'd had since I stepped out of the forest that was genuinely relaxed, and I looked around in curiosity at the... village square, almost certainly.

The sun was getting low in the sky but still brilliant and warm, maybe four-ish if it was—ah, not *summer*, not in Shem; that was a Qatn word, a word in the tradertalk pidgin of the continent. Growth, it was the time of

Growth. The season of renewal was past, and we were in the season of striving, which was split into Planting, Growth, and Harvest. Next would come the season of quiet, split into Frost, Ease, and Anticipation, and then it would be back to renewal: Thaw, Rebirth, and Festival.

I took a deep breath, trying to stay calm and think clearly. I could work with this; the important part was that I had an intuitive understanding of the timekeeping of wherever I lived. It wasn't important that I pointlessly remember the names of the year's subdivision we used where I'd lived until now. At least they still had hours and days, here! At least I *knew* some of this stuff after whatever the fuck the Divine Flame, or whatever it was called—

I shook my head sharply, pulling myself out of the mounting panic attack. Needing an external focus for my thoughts, I turned my attention back to my surroundings. There were two buildings on the square, one facing the other, and I was sitting on a bench right in front of one. It was very obviously the administrative building and military headquarters, given that it had contained the office of both the Clerk Administrator and the Captain of the Guard, and it was connected to a series of low buildings surrounded by stables and practice grounds. It also abutted the wall of the village, which seemed... weird, like the square-wave stone of the parapets was somehow not in the right shape.

I put that aside. I was not, after all, an expert on fortifications, not in the slightest, so I was just projecting expectations from medieval Europe onto a fantasy world like an idiot.

There was a ring road to my left and right that went around the village parallel to the wall, and they both terminated into the square. Past the practice grounds and stables that lined the walls, there were two sets of five two-story houses, each spread out around a central vegetable garden. Each house was connected at the rooftops with slender, arching walkways to the other houses in their set and to the next set over. Some of those sets were then connected by more of the same, slightly wider, walkways to open areas on the wall, which might have been why it looked so odd.

The ground around the grassy square in front of me was... cobbled? I kicked at it idly, humming. If it was cobblestone, it was remarkably smooth and evenly mortared, but that seemed entirely possible, especially with magic. *Call it cobbled for now.* The ground, then, was cobbled, and the four corners of the square had three trees each which reached at least twenty feet high. They weren't exactly like the titanic nearly-redwoods that I'd seen in the forest, more mundane and narrower proportionally, but they were clearly kin to them and it was oddly reassuring to see them.

The building behind me was made of a light gray stone, textured and weathered. It looked like it had black mortar between the blocks—but it wasn't mortar, on closer inspection, just decoration that highlighted the structural seamlessness of the construction. The colors had to be a deliberate contrast against the building in front of me, which had the colors reversed.

Dark gray stone with white mortar, and it was indisputably a library, because it was quite literally shaped like an open book facing the square. The spine rose higher than the pages, each page represented by an outthrust wing of the building with big, clear windows that showed a cozy-looking chair and side table.

There was someone at one of those chairs, leaning back with a book in hand, and something unknotted in me to see it. I took a deep breath of air that tasted of crystalline purity and stretched up, left, right, and down, spreading my knees a little to accommodate my belly as I touched the ground. It was remarkably quiet—not silent, but in that almost suburban way where the main noise was coming from children, whether at play or, at least in one case, wailing nearby that they weren't thirsty. *Kanja* was thirsty, whatever that meant.

I ate the last dumpling, and right on cue, Kelly came around the corner with a large bag bouncing at her hip. Its design was odd, with two straps that were both over her opposite shoulder, both crossing across—ah. *Those*, I thought to myself, *are shoulder straps. She's just wearing it like a cross-body bag. How excellent.*

I was still grinning as she ran over and stopped in front of me, pulling a waterskin out of her bag. "Here! Did you miss me?"

"Atrociously," I lied smoothly. "My life wasn't complete without your water. I mean, you."

"Flatterer." She handed me the waterskin and I twisted the cap on its spigot, pulling it off in a motion that felt practiced but which I'd never done before. "I got you a standard kit. Two three-quart skins, a three-quart insulated canteen, some odds and ends. Left a bedroll at Levali's—she'll put you up for the night tonight—along with a couple sets of underclothes that looked like they'd fit and, you know. Soap, a washcloth—"

"How much is this going to cost me?" I was still blinking at her exuberance after the relief of the water, both to quench my thirst and to wash down the remains of the dumplings, but I had to interrupt her. "I didn't anticipate... all of this."

"Right, of course, you wouldn't know. Matti, he was Shemmai—" *from the Kingdom of Shem*, I knew that to mean— "so... right." She put her hands together in front of her face, pressing her palms into each other, and took a deep breath.

From the Kingdom of Shem. I mentally flinched at how the fact was just in my head like I'd grown up speaking the language. There was a different inflection that would have meant he was *culturally* Shemmai, and a third one that would have referred to the ancient, liturgical form of the language named Shemmai and would imply she was calling him old-fashioned; and at that point, I managed to pull my mind out of its spiraling before I crashed. She was waiting for me, and I nodded at her.

"This is free," she said simply. "We won't, *can't*, charge you for the basic necessities of life—it's bad policy, it's cruel, and almost everything you're getting is either bulk production or apprentice work. One person's contribution to society, *your* contribution to society, is just... so much higher than a few waterskins. So we count the cost in the time it takes for you to settle in, the time that it takes for you to find your way in our world. Even with someone like Matti, someone who's established in a trade and came with a wagon, it took him a season to really get out of the city in his heart and settle into village life. James is probably thinking that if you're happy and thriving a year from now, I did my job."

"Your job, which is... First Friend."

She wrinkled her nose, a momentary frown crossing her face. "Sophie, I know you're probably overwhelmed and that's only going to get worse, but you already asked that." Her voice was quiet but intense, and her bubbliness was absent from her voice. "Yes, that is my job. To be the friend you need so that you can build a better life. To help you navigate a community you're a stranger to, with mores you have no way to know and manners you won't recognize. And this is proof of that." Her voice got a little bit more energetic as she waved at the basket next to me on the bench and at the waterskin, now nearly empty, in my hand. "Would you have known that you could go to the day's public refectory and get a walk-basket? No. Would you have known that you can get a standard kit for free, as someone new to the village? That there's a bunch of kits stored in Rise and none in Fall? No!

"You don't know the laws, you don't know the Breach Protocols. You don't know what it means that we're a Dungeon Village, that it practically defines our economy. You don't know who to ask questions to, even when you know to ask them. You don't even know that there's another layer of mants under the cloth!"

She paused, triumphantly, and I obediently pulled away the cloth that I thought was at the bottom of the basket. There was indeed a second, smaller layer of the mants there, and I started laughing quietly.

Taking a deep breath, I made myself stop before my quiet laughter became uncontrolled hysterics. "Okay," I said after a moment. "And how do you feel about that? Because I know how *I* feel about having a stunningly pretty girl compelled to be friends with me; specifically, I am very not okay with people having to spend time with me who don't want to."

"Oh! You think I'm pretty?" She batted her eyelashes at me, trying for a simpering air, but it lasted about half a second before she started breaking into giggles. "Sophie, first off, I'm older than you are. Wherever you're from, they didn't treat you right." She reached out, tracing a line across my brow, face suddenly serious; I didn't feel the slightest urge to flinch, which was nice and new. "And second? I love new people. I love meeting them, I love helping them, I love being friends with them. It's…"

I waited to see if she was going to resume after trailing off, then tapped her on the shoulder. "It's what?"

"Nothing." She smiled sheepishly at me. "Come on, let's walk."

"Come on. Are we friends or what?"

She shot me a shocked, almost betrayed look, and then threw her head back, laughing. Dropping unceremoniously onto the bench next to me, she leaned her back against my side, and I waited patiently until her laughter faded into chuckles. "I'm going to like you or loathe you, Sophie. Listen, I wasn't lonely as a kid, this isn't me trying to rectify my trauma or atone for misdeeds." Her weight and warmth shifted off of me right around when I was going to extricate myself, and I turned in time to catch her smile turn soft. "I think it's important work, and I like stories. I'm not supposed to have a selfish motive, but even after twenty years of this I still like stories, and being your friend is going to mean hearing them, and maybe telling some of mine."

"*Maybe* telling some of yours?" I grinned back at her as she giggled. They were absolutely delightful, top-tier as giggles went. Not some delicate chiming sound, these—her giggles had a snicker to them, they had depth and resonance, and it made the joy she was showing feel so much more real.

"If you think you can be my friend without dishing all your embarrassing details, you've got another think coming."

"Sealed!" She grabbed my hand, putting my palm against hers around shoulder height. "This is how we seal a bargain. Not a business bargain, and not one that calls for a God to witness, but a personal one; a promise, if it's reciprocal. We push like *this*."

I pressed back, thinking rapidly. "Is that related to the thing where you put your palms together and took a deep breath?"

She nodded, a sort of quick triple-nod with small head motions. "Yes! We hand the moment to our future self, our self two moments from now. Then we take a moment and we breathe, because we don't have to deal with it; and we give that breath to our future self too, who pays us back by doing what needs to be done."

"Where I come from, we pinky swear. We lock our pinkie fingers together like this—" I demonstrated, feeling embarrassed, but she went along with it with such obvious joy that it was infectious— "and we move our hands up and down like we're shaking hands, which probably doesn't exist in your culture, and we make the agreement that way. I think it's supposed to signify vulnerability or something."

"Pinkie swearing." She nodded slowly, then nodded again, faster. "That doesn't make any less sense than how we do it! Now come on, I have to show you around town before it's dinner time, now that your food's all gone!"

I looked down and realized that, somewhere in the middle of that conversation, I had eaten the second layer of dumplings. Shifting from the pinkie swear to holding my hand, she pulled me up to my feet. Laughing, following her as she practically skipped towards the ring road, I allowed myself to be dragged along in her wake.

CHAPTER 1.6 - TO INDULGE A BOUNDLESS CURIOSITY

"So, I totally have about a thousand burning questions for you," I told my guide as she pulled me towards the road.

"Only a thousand?"

"A thousand *burning* questions," I protested. "There's no need to smirk at me like that! The number of merely smoldering questions I have are countless, a stream of primordial curiosity that only the end of the universe can extinguish."

Kelly nodded, the two of us stopping so that she could give that proper consideration. "I accept this," she eventually said with utmost seriousness. "I could already tell you were that type, after all."

"I don't know if I just got complimented or insulted."

"Yes."

Her contemplative face broke a moment later, and she burst into an absolutely delightful set of giggles. I shook my head, choosing not to make a pretense of being affronted—I was already enjoying bantering with her, but I didn't know how well body language would translate. I'd seen some similarity, but I'd definitely seen some differences to offset that.

It seemed best, given that, to avoid putting on a front of offense over a core of joy for humor's sake.

"It's elemental curiosity, by the way."

"Huh?"

"Curiosity is elemental, not primordial." Kelly shrugged at me, grinning. "I don't totally understand the difference, because the lies-for-kids definition is, like, ninety-nine percent of the way to true as far as usefulness goes."

I raised an eyebrow at her. "And?"

"Primordial means it's inherent to the universe, elemental means it's imputed. Entropy's primordial, striving is elemental."

"Where's it get messy?"

"What's the difference between Yelem and the planet we're standing on?"

I paused at that, standing with her on the road. *They know what planets are*, I thought to myself idly, *and that we're on one. Also, we're on a planet—that wasn't guaranteed.* "Am I right in guessing that Yelem's the name? Because if so, it's the difference between *air* and a mix of gasses."

"A name," she confirmed. "Anyway! Questions and answers. The first thing is—"

"—why and how Meredith has all of her details unnoticeable?" I blinked up at the stunningly clear sky, grinning as my thoughts poured forth. "What do Skills and Attributes mean? What's Elevation, and why am I an apex? What are these trees called, and are they like the ones in the woods? What was up with the odd rings of sky over there? How does magic work? Can *you* do magic, and when do I learn how?"

"Um." Kelly's jaw worked for a moment, and then she visibly reset herself. "Okay, all of your questions are valid and interesting—"

"—that's not anywhere *near* all of my questions, just for the record—"

"—but! There are a bunch of things I need to cover before I give answers to those."

I pouted involuntarily, doubling down on it once I realized what I was doing. "At least the one about whether you can do magic?"

"Not to the level of a proper mage," she said after a moment and a sigh. "I mean, I can do magic, yes! But when you're living in a village with someone who pulls a second house out of the bedrock just to see whether the textures should contrast or complement, and then he settles them both back into the ground because it's not like anyone needs the houses and now he *knows*—" Kelly stopped herself, shaking her head. "That's *new*, wow."

I stared at her. "I'm guessing you were the friend who needed a new place, but uh, a *house*? Just pulled out of the bedrock, casually? Also, what's the thing that's new?"

"You!" She beamed at me brightly, and I smiled back in equally bright confusion. "You're what's new. See, I have some Skills that let me relate to people," she explained. "But sometimes it can be a bit much."

I let that pass—I wasn't *that* prone to rambling, was I? "Okay, but seriously, a house? Pulled out of bedrock?"

"Come on." She nodded towards the side of the road nearer the wall, and her voice dropped lower, no longer carrying. "Kibosh is lucky to have Kan and Ketana as the senior members of our Stone Team. I won't pretend every village has someone who can do, well, what I *think* we're about to see."

"Okay, you have my attention," I murmured, drifting towards the side of the road and matching Kelly's lack of volume. A man and a woman stood in the middle of the empty lot we were next to, and I nodded in their direction. "I'm guessing these two folks are Kan and Ketana?"

"There's three, actually. It's hard to even see Junior of Stone Kibosh—that's their title, they don't go by a name. I don't actually know why, it would be rude to ask, right? So just Junior, or a little more formally, Junior Stone. But not just Stone, because that's not *technically* proper."

"Junior Stone," I murmured. "Got it."

I didn't, not really. For one thing, I didn't see a third person anywhere, and it wasn't like there was somewhere to hide in the flat, empty lot where Kelly and I were looking. For another, that seemed... *antisocial*, jokes about not wanting to be perceived aside. But it wasn't any of my business. What *was* my business was that the folks a hundred feet away from us were Doing Something, and it was going to be magical and—

The ground cut me off by rumbling under us, a shaking that was audible but somehow didn't disrupt our footing at all.

"This is why I brought you this way," Kelly said softly. "And why I wanted us to get moving, even though there are things I technically should have gone over before we did anything else. We won't be able to do more than watch them bring it up, it's not safe to get close, but..."

"No intruding on an active worksite," I agreed. "At least *some* things are familiar."

The two mages standing on the unremarkable dirt were facing away from us, so all I could see of them was brown clothes with gray trim and a crenellation pattern done in white. They didn't *do* anything impressive or eye-catching, nor were they wreathed in light or power. They just sat down smoothly next to each other, holding hands and leaning their shoulders against each other fractionally.

I heard an indistinct murmur—like the voice of a faraway announcer on a loudspeaker—and stone started to bubble up and pool around the Stone Team as though it was being squeezed out of the ground. The stone *moved*, once those pools had reached a certain size; three narrow pillars rose, lifting the geomancers out of the way as a thousand-square-foot palm settled into smoothness and became a floor.

With the Stone Team out of the way, mottled gray-and-white hands formed before thrusting outwards and upwards, the fingers fusing and flowing into and around each other. Rocks followed them from below the ground and from the soil around them, melting into the streams of building-in-progress. The walls rose, thickening and merging, and they began to reach for each other like hands steepling as they passed the pillars and the mages sitting on them.

The texture smoothed out and openings appeared for windows. The roof acquired corrugation and a rakish asymmetry, the front acquired a door flanked by pillars, and embellishments—vague at this distance—shifted into existence. Finally, the surface of the stone on the outside twisted in on itself, forming a fresco of woodgrain and bark on a massive scale.

It couldn't have been more than a couple of minutes, and the only sound had been that initial murmur and a faint humming that I'd more felt than heard. *A couple of minutes*, I thought to myself dimly, *and there's a two-story house, a gorgeous one. One that looks like it was grown out of wood and then transmuted into stone, and I can't unsee that even though I literally watched it get made—extruded from the ground and then molded like clay.*

Kelly's hands clapping thunderously together snapped me out of my reverie. "Alright," she said briskly. "So, Sophie! We have some things we actually *need* to cover sooner rather than later, but I didn't want to miss the opportunity to show you *that*. So!"

"Bwuh," I responded eloquently.

"Um. Are you... okay?"

Am I okay? I could ask myself the question, but my mind was a swamp of questions so thick I couldn't get a single one to manifest... until I could, and then the questions overwhelmed any verbal filter I might have had through the pressure of their sheer endlessness.

"What *was* that? Is not hearing any sort of invocation the difference between magic and Skills? Are all of your houses built like that, is *everyone* that capable, how long did they have to study to do that? Can you—no, you said you couldn't, that you weren't a *proper mage*, but what does that actually mean, what *can* you do?"

I looked towards the road, face falling when I realized that I had been rambling into an awkward silence. Kelly was staring at me with... indecision? She shook her head as if to clear it, pressing her palms together in that gesture she'd shown me earlier. A moment later, as I started to walk towards her, she nodded firmly as her previous good humor reasserted itself on her face.

"I know it's a lot," she said gently, "and yes, I will answer *all* of your questions as best I can, but there's something actually urgent to talk about. Now. Do you trust me to do my job?"

I blinked at her a few times. "... yes?" I thought about it a bit more, then shrugged. "Other than not having much choice about it, yes, I do. I mean, you've been doing this a while, right? And you brought me to see this. This is... this was..." I stumbled over whatever I'd been trying to say, the thoughts draining out of my head.

"So trust me to know what I'm doing. Trust me when I say that there's something we need to go over, and let me get us back on-path instead of us getting lost in the trackless grass. Okay?" She sounded more like she was trying to convince herself than me, but I nodded anyway. "So! There's too much to possibly explain everything on your first day, and I do want to make sure you're not late to the first seating. But, um. This should have been the *very first* thing. And technically, the Captain should have covered it, but I know she doesn't, and that's *my* cover for bringing you here to see this first. Do you know what a siren sounds like? The warning kind?"

"Yeah, actually." It wasn't the most pleasant of memories. I acknowledged that fact even as I let those recollections flow through me and away, distracting myself by following the woodgrain-in-stone of the new house's walls. "I'm... familiar with them. I'm familiar with more than one kind of siren, but yes, that includes the warning kind."

"Good! Now, this is important. If you hear a warning siren—you can't possibly mistake it for anything else, it's five-toned and it wallops you with a metaphysical fish of *this is a warning siren* in the cognition—*and* you get an intrusive System message of any kind? If you're with me, you get *to* me, and get skin-to-skin contact, don't even stop to read the message." She grabbed my hands, gently, startling me with her intensity. "I'll teleport us both outside the walls. If you're not near me, you run. Don't grab anything that'll slow you down, don't slow down to grab anything. *Run*, and if someone calls *outgoing*, you get to them and get skin-to-skin contact. That's your Breach Protocol, for if the dungeon decides to kill us all and the Delvers are incompetent enough to let it try." Her eyes bore into mine, utterly serious. "Do you understand, Sophie?"

I swallowed, my throat suddenly dry. "Yeah."

"Can you tell me in your own words?"

"Intrusive notification plus a warning siren means a Breach. The siren's impossible to confuse with anything else. If you're around, I grab your hands, you get us out of there; if you're not, I bail, book it to the nearest gate or the nearest teleporting ride out of the village."

"Okay. Good." She spun on her heels, but not before I saw a welter of emotions cross her face, upset and relief written in her expression and body language. "Just so you know, there's no chance it'll actually happen. The Delvers here do their jobs and the dungeon hasn't ever had a deviation. We do a siren drill once a year, but those don't have the System message so there's no risk of confusing them and we won't see one for at least a season regardless."

She paused for a moment and then stepped back, letting my hands go as though she was surprised to be holding them. We stood a moment, looking at each other awkwardly, and then she spun around and pointed back towards the gate and its guard-and-administration building that we'd met at.

"You asked about the trees," she said briskly. "The ones that are planted around the southern open, which more formally we call Tome Square or just Tome, those are called redwoods if you're a city girl. Here, they call these trees greatwoods and the ones in the Forest, or at least in *this* part of the Forest that's technically the Southern Conflux Remnant Edgewood, are called titanwoods. Those are the ones with the light-lensing magic you're asking about, and it's to harden, heat, and dehydrate a ring of their trunk just deep enough to keep out pests and parasites."

"That sounds… like it's a really good thing I didn't stick my hand in there."

"We'd have regrown your hand when you got here," she reassured me. "It would have made things complicated, though, because James would have had to get Rafa or Veil to take care of it before Integration, but after you made the decision."

"Rafa or Veil?"

"Respectively, the village's healer and the Pillar for the Thousand. Which, segue!"

Kelly flashed a megawatt grin at me and pointed westwards along the ring road with a thumb. I obediently followed her, and she almost reached for my hand to pull me along before visibly deciding that gesturing was more important.

"Kibosh is a Dungeon Village—a village built on top of a growing dungeon, one that we delve just enough to control its growth—that's built to the Standard Plan. That means we're built looking in, with the dungeon and primary fortifications in the middle and the Five Pillars around that: Hall of the Thousand, Delving Guild, Tower—of the Arcane, but nobody *says* that—which is also the Guild of Mages, Hall of Writ, and Guild of Crafts. The gates are at the four cardinals, and they have names for what's in front of them: Tome in the south, Hammer in the north, Rise in the east for Levali's refectory, Fall in the west for Thesha's."

"Okay, that's a lot of names to hit me with in a row." I rubbed my temples as though that were going to help with the headache I was anticipating. "Most of them I can *probably* infer by context, at least sort of. Tome has got to be that library, refectories are… communal dining halls, and Hammer is probably some sort of crafting district, associated with the Guild of Crafts? But even with the magical language proficiency, there's a whole lot of things that *Writ* can mean."

"Right on all counts, and yes! It does mean a lot of things! But in this context, it's… administration, law, policy, logistics. It's all the stuff that Clerks deal with, it's everything that generates or consumes paperwork. And almost none of it actually happens at Writ proper, because Clerk Administrator Morei is *James*, and who's going to tell him he can't share space with Meredith? And *she* cares about being in the guardhouse, so the Clerk Administrator takes a desk in the Guard Captain's office."

"I can't relate in the slightest, but that's adorable anyway."

"That's pretty much what everyone thinks, when anyone stops to think about it, which is basically never because they've been doing that since before Kibosh formally existed. Anyway! Where was I… gates, Rise, Fall, refectories. Right! So, the outer ring—that's the ring road and everything between it and the wall—is broken up into those four areas. And where we were was pretty quiet, right? That's because in the mornings, Tome is pretty busy with the littles all either running around out here or studying around the Library, but then after lunch they mostly stick to their quints. Or they nap, or it's someone else's quint, but this is when everyone gardens."

"Which explains the sounds, I guess." I'd mostly tuned out the sounds of children sometime during the dumpling-eating process, but I was noticing them again, now that she'd mentioned them. They sounded… happy, a little wild in that way that children are at the best of times.

I'd often felt like you could tell a lot about how a society was structured by how their kids behaved, and thus far I was tentatively pleased with what I was hearing.

"The thing about Tome in the afternoons," she continued, "is that it's not really where anyone is. Most of the Guard's out patrolling, littles are all elsewhere, and folks studying aren't all that loud. Now, Rise and Fall, even leaving aside the coming and going on meals and hauling and cooking, plus visitors at Fall and the herder-folk taking care of themselves and each other at Rise? That's where we've got the shop-houses, and Hammer has the workshops and craft-houses."

"Shop-houses, workshops, craft-houses, refectories." I rubbed my temples, momentarily surprised that I *didn't* have a headache. "All built by the Stone Team? Like that house we just saw?"

"Something bigger than a house takes more time; it's more than eight times as hard to double the volume. But they've been doing this for a lot longer than I've been alive! So yeah, all built by the Stone Team. The enchantments, too—and even with them, Hammer's *loud*, workshop-loud we call it. Loudest in the morning, since that's when the biggest, hardest work is done, you know? Well, I mean, you might not, obviously."

"Yeah, I really don't." I shrugged. "I'd usually have done my work in the afternoons, if I'd had a choice. Not that I ever did; I'd say experiments were scheduled for other peoples' convenience, not mine, if their lives hadn't sucked even worse than mine. At least I didn't get asked to work extra hours, once I made clear they'd have to pay me for it like the law mandated; the others, the students and scholars and anyone else who… wasn't me, I guess, they all kept putting in ten-hour, twelve-hour days, sometimes more. All the way up the chain, too, to be fair."

"That's…" Kelly had stopped in the road again, and she was staring at me with an expression of confusion on her face. "That seems short-sighted? Unless James missed something when he said that you and I were born just as human as each other?"

"Oh, no, it's totally short-sighted. Was short-sighted. And abusive, and exploitative." I closed my eyes for a moment, feeling again that mental itch of knowing that there was more to be done than I could ever get done, that I was *behind* on my duties, always, no matter what. "Let's not talk about that," I said quietly, and Kelly nodded slowly. "Anyway," I continued after a moment, trying to fill the sudden awkward silence, "what do you mean by *born* just as human? That's pretty specific wording. And how many of these quints are there—I'm guessing that's the word for those five-house clusters around the communal garden? Am I going to be expected to help with the gardening? Because let me assure you, I have a black thumb. Plants that other people swore were indestructible and immortal died aplenty under my care."

She snickered in that charmingly inelegant way of hers. "Alright. Let's walk and talk, and I'll try to answer a few of your questions between the things we really need to cover."

CHAPTER 1.7 - QUESTIONS ANSWERED BIRTH QUESTIONS ANEW

"So, gardening."

Kelly had taken us towards one of the quints, the clusters of five little—well, more like medium-sized—houses in the outer ring. They were placed around a garden bigger than any of the houses, with a bewildering array of vegetables and herbs growing in a chaotic tangle that no doubt involved words like soil, balance, support, and mutualism.

It was beautiful, and I would absolutely ruin it the moment my fingers got involved.

"Even if you live in a quint, you don't *have* to garden," she reassured me with a poorly-hidden snicker. "It's maybe two out of five adults and about half of the children who like it well enough to take it as a responsibility. As to how many there are?" She scratched the back of her head with one hand, scrunching up her face a little. "Most folks who like some distance wind up taking a shop-house instead of trying to live alone in a quint, but there's a few. But by and large it's kin to a quint, like they say, and we've got twelve of them with all five houses being lived in. Two of those are palmer quints—that's when it's not a family living in any of the five. Friends, usually, or cheerful strangers who don't like too much distance."

"And that's with how many people again? A hundred and..."

Kelly shrugged. "I don't know the exact number. More than a hundred seventy, less than a hundred eighty? Also, some of the herd-families don't stay in one town more than a season, they run the ring, they call it. Makes it hard to keep track, 'cause it's not the same ones every time. Four out'a the five full quints in Fall are herd-families, along with two out of the three part-full ones."

"That's... fifty-five houses, plus, what, another fifteen? And that's in Fall."

I studied the houses again. Each of them was about a thousand square feet in footprint, with the central vegetable garden being about another thousand, maybe a bit less than that of actual growing space since it wasn't exactly a grid and there were places to sit and gather. Who knew how much produce that was when magic got involved? There was so much *greenery* in the village; it had only just started to sink in how different the vibe was going to be, how I wouldn't be going back to the stench of even a relatively nice city. And all of the *space*...

"Seventy houses on the west side of the village," I finally said. "You said there's another at least thirty-seven or so in Rise. A hundred and seven *houses* with less than twice that in people?"

"We're a young village. Herders came here with the founding before even the first of the crafting types, but most others, like my folks, came less than a hundred years ago. And folks like their space; even when you're partnered, even if you're sleeping together every night, you might have your own house in the quint until you've littles to be minding together."

"Every question answered," I grumbled good-naturedly, "leaves me with *several* more. Alright. Lots of houses because the Stone Team can just conjure up a house in a day, people like a little space, it's like living alone but not, fine. You mentioned shop-houses and craft-houses?"

"There's fewer of those." She started walking again, and as we came around a bend in the road and passed one more set of houses, I saw the first of the larger buildings.

I'd seen glimpses of them, since the buildings of Kibosh weren't exactly abutting each other, but they were more impressive seen properly. On the inside of the ring road, there were moderately sized shops with signs hanging out front and wide, floor-to-ceiling windows. Most of the signs were blank, buildings vacant, but there was one with books, sheaves of paper, and little cylinders that might have been scroll cases. They had between two and three times the footprint of the houses, with a second story that was obviously—

"Folks live up top, in the 'house' bit of the shop-house," Kelly said, gesturing at the nearest of the vacant stores, "and have their shop and sometimes workspace on the ground floor. Storage in the basement, sometimes a *lot* of storage! And some folks also take a bit of the green for working space, but not all, 'cause not every trade is suited to that and not everyone likes working in the sun."

"And across the road is the... you called it a refectory?" It was a rhetorical question, given the smells of cooking and the first idle people I'd seen thus far lounging on benches outside the structure. They looked our way with undisguised curiosity, but they just exchanged nods with Kelly and didn't approach. "Herb garden behind it, looks like. What're the two side buildings?"

"Travelers' house and stables." She sounded pleased for some reason. "One in Rise, one in Fall. We hardly ever get anyone, though, so mostly Fall stable—that's this one—gets used for sick or laboring shoats, or once in a long while one of the dogs, and they'll put up herder folk who are here on some kind of formal business. Ponies go either way, but the shoats don't tend to get along with the big horses, so those go to Rise along with most visitors."

We meandered in companionable silence for a bit, Kelly giving me some time to digest what she'd said so far. It gave me the opportunity to look more closely at the construction of the shops, which seemed to be structurally identical to every other building I'd seen in the village. I was pretty sure I couldn't even appreciate how impressive it all was, given how long Kelly'd said the Stone Team had been accruing mastery in their profession, but it was still... well, *magical* was almost too on the nose.

Everything was made of smooth, amber stone with a bunch of veining and speckles on it. The guardhouse and library mimicked smooth blocks of it mortared together, and the house I'd seen being built had looked like petrified wood. The shops, instead of playing games with form and composition, boasted seamless stonework with subtle ornamental patterns.

They ranged from a tessellation of triangles whose straight lines seemed to curve in elegant arcs to artistic renditions of scribal tools as mundane as a desk and a blotter. They somehow managed to make a shavings-bin for pencils look elegant, which seemed an almost obscene act of artistic braggadocio.

I'd seen a fair few things in the past day, including a literal goddess in her grove, so this wasn't exactly the *most* awe-inspiring sight, but it was almost... no, it was *absolutely* more impressive for its mundanity. This was magic not just put to the making of a quiet, small village's houses or to a single superlative structure. It was an *across-the-board*, *artistic* use of it, the practice of spending your effort and energy in making the facade of every single home and store an expression of beauty and creativity. Even the road had to have layers of magic that were subtler than just the obvious—it looked like stone, but there was a little bit of give in it, just enough to make walking more comfortable. It practically reached up to cradle my stride, and it made for the best footing I'd ever walked on.

"How much does one of these cost, anyway?" I didn't know how to ask the question gracefully, so I just made myself break the silence with it, carefully not looking at her. "A place to stay in one of the... the quints, one of these shop-and-house combos, one of those craft-houses you were talking about? I have a little money—" I had a *totally unknown* amount of money, in fact, and I needed to fix the unknown part of that statement— "but I have no idea what kind of situation I'm in, financially."

"Oh, that." Her voice was... wry, mostly, and a little apologetic. "I mean, not that we wouldn't have gotten around to this eventually, but there's so much to tell you! So, let's see, we already talked about how the Stone Team takes care of the *structure*, right, but if you want something special from Hammer, sometimes you'll need to pay to queue-jump, or cover materials? And obviously there's things you can only get on consignment, and *that's* coin on your shoulders. If it's for a business, well, you'll be eligible for a loan, and that's a whole thing we'll talk about later, but it's usually not a problem to get what you need. Nobody wants you to fail just 'cause you don't have the right equipment."

"Okay, but how much does the Stone Team cost, which raises these houses from the ground?" I looked over at her, grimacing. "I mean, you seem nice and all, but these are *really* more house than I was expecting a village to have. I don't know what I should be expecting to pay for rent or maintenance, taxes, services, or whatever else is inevitably going to mount up. Shit, I didn't even ask whether I'm going to owe any money for the biology magic and System integration!"

She glanced back at me, a flash of surprise and then guilt crossing her face as my heartrate spiked with a sudden wash of anxiety. "Right, you're a Traveler, you wouldn't know. Adaptation and Integration are... well, the books call Integration a *divine* intercession, though it's always seemed more arcane to me. Anyway, nobody tithes to the Flame except through striving, which isn't exactly an accounted cost."

"An accounted cost?"

"It's the cost that wouldn't have been paid otherwise—if you're making a road anyway, the accounted cost to someone using it is only the change in maintenance." She waved at the ring road, raising an eyebrow at me, and I nodded slowly. "Anyway, that's Integration. Adaptation is free by policy because the cost of it is, I mean, it's not *trivial*, but for someone like James it's an extra meal and a heavier dinner. Doing the accounting would be worth more than the cost. Not to mention that even the corners of Alqar farthest from Zuqeh's grace aren't going to try to squeeze you for a contract you didn't negotiate—he's not the most powerful of Gods, but the Thousand looks after its own, you know?"

I stared at her, blinking. "That... makes sense," I said hesitantly. "I don't suppose that means that since the Stone Team is building houses just to experiment with, I shouldn't expect to pay much in the way of rent, then?"

"I'm not sure what you mean?"

Kelly had a quizzical expression on her face, and her body language was... confused, mostly, and a little bit offended. I was *fairly* sure there wasn't a linguistic misstep going on, since the Shemmai we were speaking had a word for rent that felt like it had the right connotations—though the almost-identical Ancient Shemmai word didn't, I realized.

That word was for offerings you owed the gods above and beyond the value you received, with gods who demanded that as a rule being derided as *rent-seekers*, which was momentarily distracting in its bizarre hilarity. Sylvan literally didn't have the word; the closest you could get in Sylvan was the upkeep you owed to your environment in order to maintain its health, and that wasn't much different from the Shemmai word *upkeep*, which it seemed cognate with—a loanword, possibly.

Koshe had a broader word for rent which covered the fee you paid to someone who owned a *thing* in exchange for the right to temporarily use it, and some related words that expanded on it. Qatn, the tradertalk pidgin that I could expect foreign visitors to know... sort of did, too, if you accepted *taxes that you owed a private individual* to be a form of rent—that was a weird concept, but Qatn felt like a weird language.

All in all, given that Modern Shemmai had a word for rent that meant exactly what I was asking about—the cost to make routine use of a structure or plot of land—I wasn't sure why Kelly was so confused.

I shook my head out of my reverie, grateful that she'd waited for my thoughts to finish wandering. "Well, I mean, I don't own the house," I began, "or whatever I wind up using and living in. So where I came from, I'd expect to pay, maybe seasonally, for the right to use the house and the land it's on? Which the owner theoretically uses for repairs and upgrades, but mostly just takes as profit?"

"I know what rent is, you don't have to patronize me." She rolled her eyes at me, imperfectly burying a flash of genuine hurt beneath humor. "But why would you be paying rent? The village manages the land, and if anyone *owns* it, it's the Kingdom itself, since a person owning land just doesn't make any sense at all."

"Koshe has separate words for rent-as-upkeep-of-the-Commons as compared to rent-paid-to-a-land-owner," I pointed out absently, head spinning at the idea that I was going to be living *rent free* in one of the houses I was seeing.

"And you're the first person I've had in my charge who knows a single word of it, because there isn't a Low Road within a hundred miles," Kelly said, with a very familiar *why do you even know that piece of trivia* face. "Come on. Let's sit for a bit, now that you've seen a little bit of the village, and we can talk about the rest of the most important stuff."

CHAPTER 1.8 - DUES BOTH CIVIC AND DIVINE

"So, the most important stuff." Kelly, my guide—my First Friend, which was apparently her job title—put her hands on her knees and leaned back. Frowning up at the brilliant blue sky above Kibosh, she hummed tunelessly for a long moment.

"The most important stuff," I prompted her as patiently as I could manage. "Like food and shelter?"

"Sure, let's start with that! Food's easy, anyway. That building? It's the Fall refectory, also just called Fall." She pointed to the west of us, across the plaza where we'd sat down on a bench. "Both refectories do breakfast, but for lunch and dinner it'll be one of them doing two communal seatings and the other will do bespoke meals for coin."

"How much is—"

"Economics is on the *tomorrow* list," Kelly said firmly. "Today is the tour, mostly, and some absolute basics, so that you get a sense of *place*, which gives you a framework to slide the details into. So! Communal refectory meals are free, and so are walk-boxes, but it's impolite and also just unkind to not make it there by second seating at the latest."

"Throws off the timing of cleanup," I guessed, "and there's a social component?"

"Exactly! Anyway, there's this thing called *sundrage*, which is absolutely not a word but it's a legal term that comes from sundries. Basically—" Kelly waited a beat, and her face fell when I didn't react. "I forgot, you don't get why that's a pun. Sorry, I'll explain that at some point, but not right now! Anyway, to qualify as even a village, a place has to be able to fulfill the obligations of sundrage, which means feeding everyone, housing them, that kind of thing. The village taxes the economic activity of residents and Delvers, and that money goes to pay the Stone Team, everyone who works in the refectory, the Guard, and everyone else who works *for the village*, which is… about two in ten right now."

"Two in ten, but the ratio will go down as the village grows?" She nodded affirmatively at my guess, beaming a delightful, delighted smile at me that warmed me to my toes. "I have to admit, though, I'm actually really curious about and distracted by the Koshe thing. Why is it so different from Shemmai, why are the *concepts* so different? For that matter, why did the System pick it as a language to swap in if it's so irrelevant?"

"How many languages did you—no, Kelly, *focus*. At least *one of us* needs to stay focused." I almost giggled at the fierce glare she fixed upon herself, but managed to stifle it in time not to risk any ire. "Sophie, Koshe is the language of a nation—a set of nations, really—that is located quite far underground and is, in fact, *not* the Kingdom of Shem. They aren't Shemmai, but while that means I'm not surprised their language is different on account of their culture being different, it also means that I haven't actually studied their culture."

"Oh." I blinked, processing that. "I... expected a way weirder answer than that, somehow. That makes sense."

"Great! So, now that you're not distracted: *sundrage*. Food at the refectory, housing courtesy of the Stone Team, furnishings and basic goods courtesy of the fact that people need to make practice pieces or indulge in their hobbies and it's not economical to ship 'em for sale. Access to services and facilities like the Library, physical security, the village supplies all the things that you *can't* do without."

"Do you not have to, like, defray the capital costs of building—wait, no, with the Stone Team just... pulling buildings out of the ground, there aren't really *capital* costs, are there? No scarcity of housing, but do you not, like, charge for bigger or better houses?"

"If you need a bigger house," Kelly said with a shrug, "ask Kan or Ketana to make you a bigger house. Remember, they're always experimenting and practicing, and if they were so busy they didn't have free time to help you with something, how could they possibly deal with an emergency? A city will charge for location preference, if there's too many people who want to live somewhere specific, but charging people for the costless, productive use of surplus is bad policy *and* an inefficient way of collecting taxes!"

"Your enthusiasm warms my heart," I said unthinkingly, which was true—she'd warmed up to the subject and had barely stopped herself at the beginning of a rant, and I could very much tell. My reward was another one of her beaming grins, and my brain stuttered as a result. "I don't think I've remembered to say thanks yet? So, um, thank you for your help. I know it's your job, but that doesn't mean I'm not grateful."

"You're quite welcome," she said with an odd smirk. "I *like* my job, and I like helping people. Also, I'm even more sure than James is that this'll be a job worthy of a Feat, and that's always nice—for the challenge, but also because of the experience."

"A Feat? I can *hear* the capital letter you put there. And come to think of it, I had a couple of those myself."

Kelly closed her eyes for a moment, taking a deep breath before raising her face to the sky and blowing it out. "Okay, so, this is one of those topics that runs away with you, but Feats are ways that the Divine Flame, acting through the System that the Kingdom of Shem built and which the Archmages maintain, recognizes you doing something *unusually* impressive."

"The System." My eyes narrowed. "I thought you meant experience in the sense of, like, to experience something. But you mean a quantized measure of progression along a path of increasing power, don't you? This seems… tawdry, especially since I've seen it a hundred times in games. But it makes at least some sense, I guess—always felt like every hobby and job was trying to put a number on how good or how senior you were, from belts to certifications."

"The books say that every Traveler is surprised we have it all quantized." Kelly shrugged at the thought. "Shem's had continuity of governance and internal peace for a thousand years. The Clerks probably have a hundred million peoples' work and progress on record."

"I'm familiar with the effects of a thousand years of commentary," I agreed with a forced blandness. "It's a lot of overthinking, and a lot of cruft."

"And there's some of that too, and we can get into it *later*, if you really want to, because it's way too much for your first day. For now, just trust me when I say that steps in power are discrete, the advancement upon them is known, and the records are *extensive*."

"Okay. So, we… prioritize, I guess?" Her face broke into a smug cheerfulness, and I snorted. "Yeah, okay, I ask a lot of questions about totally unimportant things, but I was really curious about the trees!"

"Absolutely. Trees, very important."

It was kind of offensive how thoroughly she was cheering me up just with that smirk of hers, but I let the snickering chuckle show through anyway. "So, what's the plan, then?"

"We've spent long enough that the charted path, the thing the book says we *should* do, doesn't make much sense, and it assumes you show up in the morning anyway. Personally, I usually want to know about what I'm doing *next*, so... around the ring road, and between your questions I'll tell you about dinner, introduce you to a few people?"

"Honestly, I'd rather hear about what my next meaningful or major decision is going to be, and what I need to know about it. Not," I said quickly, "that I think social interaction and eating food isn't meaningful. But I'm not going to be able to do much about my social habits in one evening, and I'll eat whatever is on offer. So... the next big thing."

"Your Class tier-up." Her response came instantly, and with complete confidence. "There's no *way* you're not at the apex of First Tier, you're twice the age we are when we take our first Class after Worker."

"I have Worker at... apex, the System said, yeah."

"Then you're eligible to tier up to Second Tier, if you have Classes unlocked, which you will, and if you don't, we're all here to help. In a long-term way, that's gonna define your Path, as far as the Flame goes—it's not just that you get Classes, the Flame will help you walk your Path to become who you want to be." Her smile didn't go away, but with how intent her voice was, I found myself taking things more seriously all of a sudden. "Plus, that'll give you a second Attribute, *and* you'll get a second Class when you have your new first Class at 10 again. By which I mean *level* ten, the tenth step up the stairs—discrete, which they all are."

"I'm familiar with... with levels and experience. And it somehow makes *sense*, because you've gotten it all quantized," I muttered. I should, in hindsight, have recognized what I'd seen in those first moments of my Integration—a database entry or dossier of some sort, not just a set of random information. I'd just been... overwhelmed, really. "I can't believe she did this, sent me to a place like this—I left civil service Grades behind to go somewhere with whatever Tiers are. But uh, level 10 *again*?"

"Tiering up resets your level and raises your level targets by five—Second Tier means you hit apex at fifteen. Anyway! That's not just your first big decision; it's the biggest, in a way. I mean, it's not like it locks you into what you're doing forever, that would be *awful*, but..."

"But it's big."

Kelly nodded, and then spent a moment opening and closing her mouth, visibly trying to decide on what to say. "What kind of life," she eventually asked, "do you want to live?"

I giggled at that, and giggled harder at her inquisitive look. The look developed a pout, and I raised my hands in surrender. "No! No, not the puppy-eyes! It's just that, um. The goddess who sent me here asked me that question before sending me here, more or less?"

"You were sent here by a *Goddess*?"

"Yes?" She was boggling at me, and for all that I had no real reason to be embarrassed—other than my lingering feelings around polytheism being *real*—I felt myself going red in the face. "What? How else was I supposed to get here? Get hit by a truck?"

"I know for a *fact*," she said with the first display of negative emotion I'd seen on her, "that you haven't been to the Thousand, and that would have been the *very first* place we'd have gone if you'd told me that. And in fact, it is where we are going *now*." She made a tapping gesture towards my forehead, and I flinched from it instinctively, even though she was nowhere near making contact.

I didn't quite fall off the bench, and she didn't seem to notice She rose, and I didn't; that, she definitely noticed.

"Sophie, this is not a joke. Grace given is grace returned, as the Gods say; when they are *involved*, they have *expectations*. And one of those is that when they act, we take note and show our gratitude in the appropriate ways, using the appropriate forms. Because we do *not* want to be rude."

Something about her tone and what seemed like *nervousness* on her face and in her body language had me standing—grudgingly, made more grudging by almost twisting my foot somehow as I got up—as Kelly set off towards a path that ran inwards between two quints. "I don't understand. He said that we were square, no debts owed! And I offered to pour one out for him—"

"That's nice, but *walk*—"

"—and he said," I continued, standing there and glaring at her interruption, "that *grace given is grace returned* like you just mentioned! I thought that meant I could focus on my life until it was time to, like, do something meaningful—like dedicating a craft—"

"Sophie, *please*."

The layers of emotions in that single word brought my words to a dead halt. Displeasure and anger, I was used to, and certainly impatience; a plaintive worry, though? Genuine hurt? That cut through my defenses like they weren't there, slid right past all of my armor and habits and history.

Noticing the anger led to letting it bleed out, flowing through me and leaving only a cold lump in my stomach behind, and I sighed as I walked up to her.

"Sorry," I said quietly. "That was rude of me. I shouldn't yell."

"Thousands Abounding, Sophie, I didn't expect you to be this oxheaded, since you *know* you're new to here." There was a slowly fading anger written in the lines of her body, and I could tell that it was the remnant of a genuine, if fleeting, fury; tension all the way down from her neck to her balled fists, head slightly ducked, face scrunched and skin the tiniest bit blotchy with redness. "But just… walk with me, and you can finish that thought? It'll take us some minutes."

"Sure." I took a deep breath, letting half of it out as we started walking slowly down the path, heading deeper into the village. "I did say I'd trust your judgment when you say we have something to go over. Might as well trust you when you say we have something we should do, too." That got me a weak grin, not that mine was any stronger. "I just don't like doing… meaningless, performative shit, I guess. Really feels like a waste of time. For me *and* for whoever I'm doing it for."

Kelly nodded slowly, making thinking noises and rubbing her forehead. "I don't understand how this is even a question for you. She said to you—no, wait, you said *he*, is this Goddess fluid or of multiple presentations?"

"No, that was her brother, or half-brother, I guess—"

"*Two*. Travelers!" She sighed, shaking her head. "I'm sorry. I cut you off."

"It…" I started to say *it doesn't matter*, but it did, actually, in at least one sense the phrase could be taken, and possibly in the other, too. "She's titled the Goddess of the Hunt, and a bunch of other things. Protector of women and girls, that sort of thing. Her brother, half-brother, is a crafting god. He… rebuilt me, I guess, or they both did."

"And yet you—I mean, you have the *words*—ah, no, that's not the way." She stopped walking, going from rubbing her head to running her hands through her hair. "Did you ever live with anyone? A lover, a friend?"

"No." She raised an eyebrow at me, which I took to mean a request to elaborate. "I got a room of my own at the… academy, surrounded by strangers who didn't know me. When I left and enrolled in my apprenticeship of advanced studies—" there really wasn't any better term for it, not in any of the languages I now knew— "I got another room of my own, an even smaller one, and then when that ended and I began my professional life, I saw no reason to lose my privacy."

"There is something we call the habit of grace." She started moving again, steps slow as she spoke, like she was lost in thought. Her voice was a lot more formal than it had been before, like she was paraphrasing a paper or something. "It is the habit of gratitude, in a sense; to thank each other, to show appreciation, even for those things which are duties or which are routine and mundane. We see each other through this, acknowledge the time and effort that goes into all the deeds of the day.

"So too do we speak to the Gods. We return their grace by showing grace of our own. That is the meaning of the phrase this God of Crafts spoke. The alternative is a Theurgist's Path; to take as though those things are your due, as though the habit of gratitude is unimportant."

"Huh." I mulled on that for a bit, matching her pace and probably her level of distraction. "Still seems a bit performative. Why should—I mean, it *is* our due, in a sense? My job is something I owe my due diligence to in return for the money it owes me, consideration is something we all owe each other. If I lived with someone and we were splitting chores, I'd owe it to her to, I dunno, sweep the floors, and she'd owe it to me to clean the bathroom. I wouldn't want the, like, performance of being thanked; I'd want her to do her share of the work."

We were both quiet for a little while as we walked, approaching the vegetable gardens I'd seen from the road. "It isn't really about the other person, or about what you're thanking them for," Kelly finally replied. "The habit of grace is about *you*, because how you act changes how you are. Kindness, gratitude, respect, consideration; we practice them so that they're more a part of us."

"Sounds like prayer, and that rankles something fierce," I said, voice soft. "You sound like the teachers I'd had when I was a kid, all full of talk about how prayer isn't just about God, it's about me and the community as a whole. An obligation that I owe someone for them doing what they said they'd do, what they owed? I don't like it. But thanks for telling me anyway."

"You're welcome! How easily grace comes to you."

She beamed at me suddenly and I spluttered, some of my dour mood leaving me. "That wasn't—I didn't—hey! Rude. Rude!"

"Come on. Let's get to the Thousand so that we can make it back in time to eat. And Sophie?"

"Yeah?"

"Thank you for listening. Eventually."

Her smile took some of the sting out of her words, but only some of it, and I swallowed through a bit of thickness in my throat. "You're welcome. And I'm sorry."

She nodded at that and sped up, and I followed obediently in her wake.

CHAPTER 1.9 - MINDFUL OF DIVINITY'S DUES

We walked in an almost companionable silence for a bit, which I recognized was a kindness I didn't entirely deserve. I'd tried to follow up with a more genuine apology, but she refused it; she'd hear my gratitude after we visited the Thousand, she said, and that was that.

It gave me an opportunity to just... look around, at least. And there was a lot to look at, even in our relatively short walk—gardens full of trellised beans with various vegetables growing under them, rows of root vegetables, fruit bushes, and a scattering of fruiting trees. Even the open ground between the quints and the building ahead, about a hundred feet of uncountably many kinds of ground-cover mosses, vines, and inch-high grasses, was fascinating.

Shame I wasn't in a state of mind to fully appreciate it.

The Hall of the Thousand was a modestly sized building, relative to its name. Compressing the sacred dignity of a cathedral into just two stories, the structure was another seamless, intricately carved edifice of stone. The decorations were stunning enough to break me out of my funk; veins of what initially seemed to be dark-red wood wound their way across the otherwise immaculately white walls, curling and curling inwards in fractal patterns that seemed to be actively wrapping themselves around triangular windows, ones that shimmered with intricate geometric designs in uncountably many colors. What seemed like wood turned out to be another kind of stone, so seamlessly integrated into the other stone that I couldn't see a single seam or join even from inches away, and from up close I could see that the intricate detailings were glowing subtly, visible—if barely—even in the sun of the late afternoon.

The Hall—the Thousand, rather, based on what Kelly had called it—was set into a wall, less beautiful than the building but just as impressive. It was just taller than the roof that it transitioned smoothly into, and it curved gently for a bit towards our left before running straight for a while and curving again to meld into a second building maybe a few hundred feet away, too far for me to be able to distinguish much in the way of detail.

It probably did the same thing on the other side; I'd caught glimpses of another wall there, but with our angle of approach, we weren't seeing much of it.

There were three doors along the east side of the building, and five along the south side. The path we were on split and re-combined in a looping, swirling pattern as it approached the building, and I followed Kelly as we stuck carefully to the seamless stone. It was just wide enough that the two of us could have walked side by side, but I hung back a couple of steps behind her, not wanting to crowd her in case some tension was lingering—my own hesitation to walk by her side might have been involved in making that decision, but it wasn't the only factor.

The door she led us to opened at her touch, swinging soundlessly open in its six-foot-wide span despite its hefty width and solid stone construction. But marvelous as that was—and that mass of stone moving with such fluid, silent ease *was* marvelous—once I stepped inside, all thought of it fled my mind.

The Hall of the Thousand was a hall of mirrors, and something more.

I took a weak step forward, and then another. There was a mat of sorts just one more step ahead, and I finished closing the distance haltingly, looking around in wonder and no small amount of terror. Kelly was nowhere to be found, and everything about the space was utterly impossible, from its vast size to the indescribable singing chimes that filled it softly, to the physical and emotional pressure of nine hundred and ninety-nine pairs of eyes noticing me as the attention of just shy of a thousand entities vaster than I could comprehend fell onto me.

In a moment that lasted an eternity, nearly all of them studied me as much or as little as they intended and dismissed me from their sight. Some of them were not so kind, observing me with some degree of curiosity, an observation that threatened to both utterly define and utterly annihilate me, and that was fine, for certain definitions of fine.

Two of them looked upon me and *knew* me, and the weight of their regard crushed down on me.

They all looked upon me from faces that I knew, faces that were mine. Down to the clothing we wore, the body type, the lines of their faces, every mirror but one superficially reflected me. It didn't help or confuse matters in the slightest, though; these were the faces of gods, and they had simply borrowed mine in order to avoid breaking me. The sole exception was Artemis, who bore the face I had known her by in that forest glade, beautiful and wild and both cruel and kind.

She drew back her bow, or perhaps her javelin; she breathed in the cool forest air, whistling sharply to her hounds. She was a study in a hundred different motions simultaneously, every facet of that single aspect of divinity laid out before my eyes, and my knees threatened to buckle under me as I forced myself to remain standing.

Thank you, I tried to say, but there was no mortal speech in that place. I formed the thought more deliberately instead, making of it an encapsulated, self-contained thing, a mental construct, an abstraction made real in the mind. *Thank you, Lady Artemis*, it said, and I dutifully offered it up as prayer, feeling the thing coalesce and drift away with something like the same feeling I'd gotten interacting with the System.

I was prepared to be chastised, to be corrected. I had, after all, erred; when Kelly had told me that I should pay my respects, it took her mixture of pleading and gently beating me over the head with the *you're-clueless* bat for me to come here. And if it was the expected ritual, I knew that the penalty for disrespecting it could be anything from forgiveness to my death, based on the capricious stories of the ancient pantheons I'd grown up with and the equally capricious people who worshiped them.

Her indifferent dismissal, almost but not quite a judgment that what I'd just offered wasn't worth her notice, was worse than I had expected. Her attention, the manifestation of her presence, had in it a proportion of disappointment that was as a droplet is to an ocean, but for a moment I was drowning in it.

I tasted it, and knew what my failure was, how much of the past day I had taken for granted. I needed to do better than rote politeness and begrudged duty for a new start, one where I'd be hale, hale for centuries in a place of beauty and joy. I saw the future, an abstract representation of what might come to pass, and it was beautiful—and I craved it, and I was filled with the magnitude of how much kinder the possibilities I was suddenly faced with were. Breathing deep, I began anew; not a single thought, not an encapsulated message driven by duty, but an open mind and an open… heart, for lack of a better word.

Thank you, Lady and Lord, Artemis and Hephaestus. I felt both their attentions on me now, a physical weight that threatened to drive me to my knees. He'd been there all along, and had just been so much more subtle, so much less obvious about his presence that I'd *guessed*. Exulting in having guessed right, I bent my knees, bowing shallowly, and then straightened—respect, rather than obeisance. *For what you've done for me today, I'll sing your praises, Lady and Lord; in word and deed, now and in days to come, I'll inhabit the generosity you've shown. Thank you for leading me to peace, and granting me this opportunity to reach for a better life, for gladness and ease.*

The words came easily, but they always had. It'd been seventeen years since I'd prayed, but that wasn't enough to erase the previous twenty-two. Still, the words, despite my best meditative efforts, weren't entirely heartfelt.

Twenty-two might not erase seventeen, but it leaves its share of scars. And the twenty-two before that were screaming at me from within my spine—there was *one* God, those years insisted, and He commanded that we have no other gods beside Him, that no other might infringe upon His eternal Presence.

If only He had bothered existing, if only those loudest in their devotion to Him hadn't been the first to turn on me, I might have cared more; if only He had bothered existing, I might never have stepped off the path. As it was, I found it within myself to draw on a decade and more of the pagans and witches I'd disproportionately found myself spending time with, and on the old stories I'd gone to in order to try to fill a hole in my life shaped like divinity and like scholarship… and applied those, inevitably, to what I'd known best.

Lord and Lady, I resumed, relieved and amused that I could tell they understood and didn't care that I'd gotten distracted. *You rescued me from the life I had trapped myself in, and forbore to levy on me the punishments you might have; and instead, you blessed me with health and well-being and a chance at a better life, to a hundred and twenty or threefold that and beyond.*

It didn't even take much adapting, with most of the concepts of the prayer I'd dutifully mouthed applying comfortably to this new one, old words repurposed to more heartfelt use. In this new language, for this day, they were no longer ash in my mouth.

Mostly.

Lady and Lord, you have granted me favor in excess of my desserts, I have traveled far by your hand, and if here I live and love and learn, and travel no farther, may my deeds find favor in your eyes.

May the Eternal bless you, *Artemis Prostatêria,* protector of women and girls, who sees in me a woman made in your image. And bless you also, *Hêphaistos Klytotekhnês,* artisan of all crafts and handiworks, bringer of light, who safeguards my body.

Blessed are you, Lady and Lord, who hear this prayer.

The names, the *epithets*, came to me as naturally as breathing, as naturally as remembering an old friend. But there was something... missing, and I felt it when I paused. Something expectant, like I was forgetting the last verse of a song, like I was missing one particular—ah. I hesitated for a moment, then remembered something Kelly had said, and began before I could second-guess myself.

It was only proper. After all, I actually *had* something to be thankful for and somewhere to address that gratitude.

Bless you, abounding gods in your multitude; and bless me also, whom you have remade, and sustained, and enabled to reach this day.

Their attention lifted from me with a blended sort of contentment, less even than the disappointment that had crushed me earlier. It still elated me beyond measure, flowing through me and leaving no true memory in its wake, only an intellectual understanding of what I'd felt.

I knew this to be a mercy, and still wept for it.

When I opened my eyes, Artemis was gone. She'd left behind an *understanding*, a fragment of knowledge that seeped into my... my soul, for lack of a better word. It was a whisper-quiet slice of an idle thought from just one of her thousand facets, but it hollowed me out as it moved through me nonetheless. It took long moments for sense to return to me enough to put what it said into words, and it was this: that she wasn't displeased, and she understood exactly how uncommunicated expectations could lead to those expectations not being met; that she had enjoyed that time in that place by the woods, and if I chose to dedicate my first arrow of every hunt to her until I made a perfect shot, well, that was up to me.

Grace and something almost like companionship, rather than supplication or worship. I won't claim to have been a genius, but I wasn't such an idiot that I'd ignore a hint like that.

Hephaestus was still there when I pulled myself back together. His presence was different from hers; where she was a facet of an unbelievably vast power, and still overwhelming regardless, he was a breath of fire and a swing of a hammer, a strike of a chisel and the scrape of a saw. All at once, they would be suffocating, a deafening clamor alongside a malodorous mélange of glues, paints, pigments, and sulfur. But they came one at a time, one fading into the other, and he didn't speak or wash away my self with a tidal wave of concepts so much as imbue each strike and stroke with meaning.

A flaw in iron, a flaw in glass, a flaw in wood. What are you?

I breathed in a ragged breath, awareness starting to trickle into my body. I'd sat down at some point, cross-legged, and my legs were sending pins and needles up to my brain, as were my fingers. I pushed all of that aside and attended to the sound of the forge, listening to the epiphanies it contained.

Flaws in materials differed per material. Hephaestus, especially under the epithets he was… inhabiting, or manifesting as… was a god of *craft*, of artisans, of masterworks, so he wasn't suggesting that an uneven cast iron pan is still largely fine, an imperfect glass can still be drunk out of. To him, a flawed piece of wood was not something that you incorporated into your construction somewhere hidden, where the weakness wasn't a structural problem; you cut it down, maybe, if the grain permitted and you could get something smaller but now perfect, or you disposed of it. You certainly didn't befriend it, or *her* in this case, because we were talking about *me*, and I'd read quite a few stories in which an Olympian did, in fact, become friends with a mortal.

Not wood, then. A flawed piece of glass could be re-melted, if you got to it early enough and there weren't too many additives; iron, through fluxes and other means, could be purified in the working without returning to formlessness.

That metaphor, it occurred to me, didn't seem like it had much in the way of *continuity* for the glass.

I'm a bunch of coping mechanisms in a trenchcoat, I composed with a casual dryness of humor that surprised even me, *trying to reforge myself in mind and body to be better. I'd like to think I'm iron, Hêphaistos Ærgastír.*

There was, in the air from the bellows, a note of approval. It takes fire to change, because it's fire that makes us malleable; but it takes more than that. It takes work and time and help, and you need more than fire. You need… whatever the equivalent of adding carbon is, and quenching, and around then was when I realized that the moment was gone, and the mirrors were dark in the Hall of the Thousand.

I stood, marveling at the ease with which I could move, and promptly lost my footing as the mat shifted out from under my feet. Laughing at myself, brushing the momentary pain off my hands, I stepped out into the light with a quiet contentment and a thrumming sense of purpose.

CHAPTER 1.10 - AFFLICTED BY A TERRIBLE JOY

I stepped out of the Hall of the Thousand into the light of the setting sun.

"Sophie. That—"

I interrupted her by hugging her, arms snaking up her back to feel the sudden tension at her shoulder blades, the moderate expanse of my belly squishing up against her. "Kelly," I announced into her shoulder, "I am not, at any point in this year to come, going to appreciate you enough. You are beautiful and kind and gracious, and I would be lost without you."

"I... wow, okay. That's nice to hear." Her arms came around me, and I sank into the embrace contentedly. "Did they... speak to you?"

Is this something they told you to do, I understood her as saying, and I giggled. "Did you know," I said in lieu of answering, "that a single cell of yeast contains tens of millions of molecules of proteins?"

"... no. Sophie, are you okay?"

"It's a system so incredibly complex we don't understand it. We can't even understand the *smallest example* of a cell, not really. It's a chaotic soup that exists in this state of dynamic equilibrium—two equilibria, actually, one inside it and one at the membrane that separates it from the outside." I blinked a few times, smiling so wide my face felt like it was going to break in two. "I didn't think Shemmai would have the word for equilibrium. Or membrane."

"The word for a state of balance is thousands of years old and predates *Ancient* Shemmai, and 'membrane' we know through one of the Gods of Life, I don't remember which. Sophie, look me in the eyes for a second?"

I lifted my head from its comfortable perch, grinning at her and meeting her gaze. "I have no idea how much of an understanding of any of the fields of natural philosophy you have. *Science*. That's another word in Koshe that you don't have an equivalent of. But that's more than I'd expected!"

"Sophie." Kelly grabbed my jaw in one of her hands, moving my head to the left and right. I let her; she was still hugging me with the other arm, and everything was fine. "Sophie, your eyes are forge-flame. Did you—no, obviously you spoke to a God, you've got the biggest case of Godtouch I've seen in my *life*, I need to write this down tonight and then check the Library tomorrow. *How long* did you speak to those Gods of yours?"

"They're not *my* gods, silly." I thought about that for a moment. "Maybe I'm one of their mortals, though? I'm not sure I'm ready to commit the other way around. I mean, after a few thousand repetitions of *Hear, O Brethren, the Lord is our God, the Lord is One*, it's a little hard to—I'm babbling. Is this euphoria? What's Godtouch?"

"Sophie, yes, you're babbling. How long—"

"I'm so sorry, I'm just so happy and this world is so beautiful—"

"It's fine, you're adorable, actually." She paused after saying that, then nodded briskly. "Yes! That's exactly what this is. Also worrying!"

"Ah. Um. Um!" I was blushing furiously, and back to burying my face in her shoulder. "I don't know what you mean by *how long*. I walked in there, and I took three steps forward surrounded by the mirrors and the music, and then…" She made a circling motion with her hand, which I interpreted as *keep talking*. She had a smile that had layers and I couldn't read them, but it was a smile, so things were clearly okay. "I don't know? I don't know! It wasn't words. It was expectations and feelings and they were shadows of their shadows. If you hold a grain of sand, did you touch the beach? Do you *have* beaches in Shem? I mean, the language—"

"Yes, Sophie, we have beaches in Shem. Two hours, which explains a lot about why you're one with the clouds! Come on, let's get you to dinner."

She let me keep an arm around her waist, and I reveled in the feeling of touch. I felt like my body and mind alike were boneless, without a single piece of tension; I felt like I could dance, like I could sing. "I hope I turn out to be iron," I heard myself saying, not paying much attention to my words, snickering in anticipation of the pun I was about to make. "I don't like being cut down. I don't wanna be Procrustes's guest! Annealing sounds way hotter. Oh! That works in Shemmai! That's great."

"I am *definitely* going to have to spend some time in the Library tomorrow." Kelly was practically muttering, presumably stupefied by the glory of my sense of humor, a thought which had me giggling all over again. "What was that about iron?"

"He was all sorts of things, one at a time, but not like he was changing. More like I was seeing a different part of him, like he was a… a 3-sphere, a sphere drawn in one more spatial axis of measurement—hey! That's a word that you're missing! And Koshe doesn't have it either!"

"Keep walking, Sophie. You can keep talking, just keep walking."

I had in fact stopped walking. I started again, putting my arm around her waist once more instead of gesticulating with it. Her hip bumped against mine every few steps, which was fantastic. "I can smell so many things I don't recognize. I didn't realize it until now, how many new things I'm smelling! I smelled the forge-fire, kinda, it's more like feeling the heat but there's some smell. Not like the glue, not like the paint. They all said different things to me. They? He? He was all of them, they were him. Of him."

"We call it *communing*." Kelly grabbed my shoulder to keep me on the path when I failed to notice it curving, splitting around a patch of vines. "I mean, *usually* it takes a bunch of getting ready and then a bunch of meditating to connect like that with a God, but maybe *usually* doesn't apply to Travelers!"

"Huh." I blinked a few times, intending to process the difference between our experiences and give it careful consideration. "What kind of fruits are those on that tree?"

Kelly didn't answer for a bit, and when I looked over at her, she was shaking her head slowly, shoulders going up and down in what might have been suppressed laughter. "It's a triple citrus," she eventually said. "We have bushes, too, but they're single-variant. The triples usually have lemons, limes, and oranges."

"I think the translation is giving me the same word for different fruits," I complained, beaming in joy. "Those don't smell like what I expect. Oh! Did you know that most people think the smells are because of—" I paused, groaning. "You don't have anything close to that word! Well, you do have chirality. But the chiral mirrors aren't a big enough portion of the smell to make the difference! Instead, the difference is that Earth's limes have a smell that's like a kind of tree, lemons have citral—hey! You have that word!"

"Ye—oh! I don't know that word."

"That's okay! I mean, I only know it because I looked it up when I got into an argument about why the different citruses smell different. It turns out it's weird because food smells and perfume smells are really different!"

"Is this what you're like when you're drunk?" We'd gone far enough down the path that there wasn't any more curving and splitting, so Kelly took her hand off my elbow, which was terrible. "The books say that Godtouch is like being drunk, for some people, but you aren't unsteady on your feet and your eyes can focus."

"Oh, no, no. When I'm drunk I'm a lot more, I can stay, I'm less *everywhere*, you know?" I gave it some thought, entire seconds of it, managing the titanic feat of not getting distracted. "Not that I ever let myself get more than tipsy, but no. This is more like when I got fucked, like *really* properly fucked. Oh shit."

I tried to take my hand away from her waist to bury my face in both my hands, but it wouldn't move, so I just buried it in just one hand, feeling the embarrassed heat flooding my face. Kelly was giggling, or snickering, or both, and *wow* she had a nice giggle, but did anyone have a *bad* laugh?

Okay, first off, yes, Dan had an awful laugh, forced and fake, and second, I can't believe I just said that. "I'm sorry," I babbled. "That was too much. I shouldn't have said that, that's mortifying, I'm mortified. Totally inappropriate of me, please forget that happened."

"Hmmm." Kelly squeezed my hand into her side with her elbow—which explained why I couldn't reclaim it, for that matter—and made probably performative thinking noises. "Nope! Gonna keep that one for blackmail, or maybe for deciding which guys to introduce you to, not that there's a whole lot of choice. Mostly just the Delvers, actually!"

"Girls, actually." I flushed even harder at her quirked eyebrow, but it wasn't... *judgey*, it was just curious and a little confused, and definitely not intrigued—I wasn't even *entertaining* that thought. "I don't do—I'm not attracted to guys. Boys, they're fine to be friends with, but for sex? The whole masculine thing, just zero interest.

"No, I like girls. Women, isn't it weird to call girls who are adults girls? But I identify as one? Anyway, I'm gay, gay, *homosexuelle*, oh wow, that's Sylvan!" I giggled at that. "It's like, uh, that other language I used to know! Oh, and fluid is good too, I just don't like *men*. I mean, sexually. They can be fine as people. I'm going to shut up now."

Kelly looked over at me, still not releasing my hand—not that I was making more than a token effort to free myself—and smirked. She didn't say anything, and I waited a perceptual eternity for her to.

Why isn't she saying anything?

"Counting the seconds," she said with an even wider smirk, and I realized belatedly that I'd said that thought out loud.

"This is so embarrassing. I haven't been this embarrassed since I was a student, wandering in the desert by trying to squeeze hedonism in between classes and research as an Academy aspirant. And you probably don't have that saying but that's okay because it comes from a passage in a book where the actual situation is *completely different*!"

"That doesn't sound like a very effective way to be hedonistic!"

"You're giggling at me. I'm being ridiculous! Why are you giggling at me?"

"Because you're being ridiculous." She beamed at me, and I had to stop in my tracks to have a fit of giggles right back at her.

She was nice enough to make sure I didn't fall, which was definitely appropriate, since my giggle fit was all her fault.

"I got high on—on something you don't have, it was a plant, it made me want—nope nope, no, uh, it had twenty-one carbon atoms, thirty of hydrogen, and two of oxy—hey! You have the same elements! You have the periodic table!"

Kelly's voice went a bit more serious, and she let my hand go. "The Thousand could not have decreed the Edict Against Subatomics otherwise."

"Ooookay, that's something for me to ask about *later*. A lot of somethings for me to ask about later."

"Yeah." Her voice lost its seriousness, and I saw her eyes twinkle at me out of the corner of my vision. "And what did it make you want? Just asking for blackmail purposes."

"I—hey! No fair! That," I spluttered, "is proprietary information and I am embarrassed enough. And mortified. Did I mention mortified? And embarrassed? But I can't *stop*, and everything feels so good, including talking and every emotion in the world, and the sunlight even though it's fading and all the smells and you. I don't know how you're tolerating this! Or me, actually."

"Sophie." Her voice was gentle, soothing, and oddly formal. "You are in an altered state of consciousness due to Godtouch, of all things. I would never lie to you, so I won't say that this is an inherently *holy* state, since we would describe it as a side effect of the divine rather than the purpose, but… we call it *Godtouch* for a reason. I joke, but nobody will hold what you say tonight against you; or at least, I certainly won't, because that would be… sacrilege."

"Wow, that's really convenient for me personally." I tried to relax onto her shoulder dramatically, but we were still walking, so instead I almost fell over and she had to catch me again. "You know, there's a passage in the holy books of the faith I grew up in where someone accuses God of sacrilege? As a bargaining tactic! And God obviously approves, and isn't that great?"

"Now *that*," she said with a more focused curiosity, "is a story you'll have to tell me some other day."

"Really?"

"Yeah." She smiled at me, not a broad grin or anything, just a genuine, honest smile that warmed me down to my toes. "Not tonight. Not in the refectory, even for the second sitting. But I love new stories."

"Oh fuck." We'd somehow reached the end of the path, and the refectory was *right there*; I hadn't even noticed us passing the quints we'd walked between. I took in a deep breath, the smell of food shooting straight down my spine to make my stomach clench and growl audibly. "Oh *fuck* I'm hungry, apparently."

"Really? I hadn't heard anything of the sort."

I giggled at that, leaning on Kelly for stability for a moment until my stomach gurgled again. Laughing even harder, I propelled myself off of her, and we walked together towards the smell of the food.

CHAPTER 1.II - AS A FIRST DAY TURNS TO NIGHT

Dinner was some sort of bean stew. I could practically taste it just from the smell once we walked in the door, the aroma filling what felt like my entire sensorium.

The euphoric high—and it had *definitely* been that—was fading fast, and it left me with weak muscles and a wobbly lack of balance. After I slammed the side of my arm into the doorframe trying to avoid falling over, Kelly kept a hand under my armpit for stability, and it worked well enough. I didn't fall again, at least, until she guided me to a bench and I more or less collapsed onto it.

I dimly heard someone commenting, with casual words but a viciously waspish tone, that it was certainly unusual for someone to be so late to the seating. Kelly's entire body tensed up, her hand squeezing my arm like a stress ball, but her voice was steady and kind as she said something about yadda yadda Hall of the Thousand blah blah Godtouch, but I wasn't listening.

I couldn't listen. It was a physical impossibility, because someone had shown up and slid a large bowl in front of me, along with a flat wooden plate of sorts that looked like a cheeseboard with a very small hollow. There was a loaf of bread on it, brown and crusted and smelling like God had decided to prove the existence of the World To Come, and I had a piece of it in my mouth before I'd really registered my own intent to move.

It tasted even better than it smelled. There was a hint of sourness, a bit of acid, but mostly it was salt and carbs and a butter that was definitely the most flavorful butter I'd had in my life. I had to force myself to slow down enough to chew and swallow instead of choking on it, but I was *absolutely* a grown-ass adult of thirty-nine, and not a two-year-old, so I managed.

I still somehow choked on the spoonful of stew I followed it down with, coughing with my mouth closed by dint of long habit, but it barely slowed me down.

The stew was almost as good as the bread. It wasn't complex, not by any measure, but it was hearty. Beans, mostly, with something very much like cabbage and a dead ringer for eggplant, salted somewhat less than I'd usually go for and spiced with a bunch of flavors I didn't recognize and a couple that I *did*. Bay leaves and rosemary were distinct, and these were absolutely those, and that raised a bunch of questions that could definitely be answered later.

My spoon clinked against the bottom of an empty bowl about a moment later, and I looked at it in stupefaction. I mopped up the last of the stew—and, belatedly, the drips of butter from the loaf—with my last hunk of bread, chasing it down with the last of a large mug of water, and sighed in relief.

"Welcome, young lady. How good of you to join us."

I looked over at the speaker, across the table and one seat to my right. I'd had only the briefest of moments to take in the surroundings, to look around. Now I needed to hold a conversation—a conversation with a stranger, which I'd always been taught should be seen as an opportunity to make a friend. A shame, then, that I recognized her voice, now with that waspish tone hidden under thin graciousness; a shame I could see the twist in Kelly's lips where she sat next to the woman, see the crease between her brows.

Also probably a shame that I was so exhausted I could barely register her as a person, much less really notice anything about her. Still, I'd dated a girl from the South; I could do politeness in social combat with… not the best of 'em, but I wasn't the worst.

"Thank you. This has been… I don't have words for how nice this place seems. I don't know how I haven't started disbelieving it, honestly. It's absolutely the kind of thing that I'd expect to have a dark hidden secret, like Kelly's going to harvest my o-*oh*—" I tried and utterly failed to stifle a yawn, blinking back tears with how deep it had been and wincing as my jaw muscles screamed. "Excuse me, it's been a long day. Like she's going to harvest my organs—"

"As your *friend?*"

"—once I've been here a year and a day." I winked at her, smirking a little. "I would *never* accuse you of planning to betray me during your First Friend tenure! So yes, it's been *very* good to have joined you. Miss…"

I could see that my politeness had just scored a direct hit, because I heard someone audibly snicker on the other side of me and I could see Kelly's eyes light up. It got a brief death-glare out of the woman, which vanished into a tight smile that did a respectable job of pretending to be kind, judged on an extremely sleepy curve. "Matron Zeva. And what is your name, child?"

"A pleasure to meet you, Matron. You can call me… Doctor Nadash?" I frowned at the table, breaking eye contact without thinking about it. "Not Professor; I didn't teach, I did research. I got the *language*, but I didn't get enough Shemmai cultural context. Help me out here, someone?"

"A Doctor might teach, but the essence of the word is singularity." The voice came from my left, and I turned to see an absolute titan of a man with an astonishing light baritone voice, dressed in a mix of deep browns and slate grays. "One so wise in their field that there is no-one they might not teach; one so brilliant that they forge a new path of light through the shadows of ignorance. Scholar Nadash, I am Kan; Stone Shaper, Engineer, and Quilter."

"And father of four children." The words came with an eye roll from the woman across from him. She was *tiny*, not just by comparison with him but entirely; he had to be well over six feet tall, and she probably wouldn't have broken five feet on her tiptoes. "Yes, yes, three aren't *children* anymore, but we will never stop being their parents. Ketana; I met this lunkhead in Kaffar more than two hundred years ago. Stone Shaper, Geomancer, Clerk."

"I am so—" I yawned again, hearing my jaw crack and pop. There was something tickling at my brain about them or about their introductions, something I was missing or forgetting. "Mrrm. Good to meet you. So sorry, but I really doubt I'll remember your names tomorrow. Won't forget the food, though. It was—wait, Quilter?" I blinked at him owlishly.

"Indeed, esteemed Scholar. I—"

"No way, nuh uh." I shook my head at him. "I am too tired to be *esteemed Scholar* to you. Call me Sophie… uh, Ken?"

"Kan." His smile didn't budge, so probably he wasn't offended. "As a hobby, it has served me well. One can, of course, create more end-products more efficiently, but mine are made suited to the person and place."

"That sounds nice." I felt compelled to add something more, engage with him, and after a few moments, a memory struck me. "Oh! I had a neat quilt when I was a kid. It was, um, generational? A lot of layers and patches of clothes that got worn out. It was… it was always my favorite."

Ketana caught what I had let slip. "Was?"

I didn't look at Ketana, couldn't look at her, no matter how soft and gentle her voice was. "It, uh. Went to someone else."

"It's not so bad, when something nice goes to another child, or to a grandchild."

I managed to drag my eyes off of the wood of the table enough to look at Matron whatever-her-name-was, who probably wasn't even intending to be hurtful this time. "It went," I said to her, like the two of us were the only people in the room, "to the boy my father adopted to replace me, when who I was became incompatible with his faith."

There was, blessedly, silence after that. Kelly reached over the table to put her hand over mine, which I appreciated, and I slumped forward a bit to lean on my other arm. Conversation started up again eventually, and so did some kind of dessert, which I ate without tasting it or even knowing what it was. Someone slid the remnants of a couple of loaves over to me along with another bowl some time later, and I ate again, feeling the hollowness in my stomach finally fade into contentment as I relaxed into the renewed buzz of quiet conversation.

It was… nice. Nobody was expecting me to contribute or be involved, nobody was expecting me to be social or even particularly present. At the same time, the sound of voices in friendly chatter was soothing, and I dozed off, letting the ambiance soak in. Kelly's arm under my armpit drew me out of that stupor, and I found myself being gently urged up.

"—need to wake up enough to walk, Sophie. Wake up enough to walk, Sophie, please, we need to clear out so they can clean and go home. I actually, literally can't carry you, you're heavier than I am and I'm not particularly strong, Kan, Kan! Over here, please help. Take her up?"

"She lodges in the travel rooms?"

"For tonight. She hasn't chosen a Path, and we wouldn't have time to get her settled in anyways."

"Very well. Sophie, unless you should ask otherwise, I will undertake to transport you to your temporary home for the night."

I murmured something vaguely positive. The table was comfortable enough, but okay, it made sense that I couldn't sleep there—they couldn't clean under my face. But just a *little* bit of a rest and I could walk—or I could be lifted; he was warm and his clothes were soft and his carry was utterly steady, and I regretted briefly that I wasn't into guys because that would have made it *really* nice.

There was a flight of stairs, taken with barely any jostling and a little bit of sway, and then a short corridor or something. There was a door, and a doorway that I was very carefully maneuvered through, and a mattress, maybe this was a *bed*, way better than sleeping in a chair with my face prevented from planting onto a table only by my hands.

I stirred closer to wakefulness when someone started undoing the buckles on my boots, feeling the sharpness of the release, like they were ski-boot buckles. They drew something heavy over me once that was done, fluffy and smelling of something vaguely treelike. "Quilt," I managed to say. "Kan?"

"Yeah." Kelly's voice. "He made this quilt. He makes all our quilts."

"Nice quilt." I smiled beatifically at the ceiling, or roof, or whatever was up there; my eyes were far too closed to tell. "Good night."

If Kelly said anything in response, I didn't hear it, or didn't remember it.

I floated, instead. The waves rocked me, rising into the sky and falling gently into the depths, as I rode the peaks and troughs on a soft wind.

Everything was in motion, and everything was still. I wasn't alone, and the sun and moon were high in the sky, light and light's reflection, and the tree that swam beside us whispered with its branches a name I couldn't hear or understand.

The man behind me and to the right was so thin, so very thin, but he had such fluffy wings, and I saw them slowly beating. I kept my eyes forward, though, and my hand where it was busy, and he muttered at me. *This is crock*, he said, and I giggled at him and replied, and he touched me on the forehead with the tip of his finger that pierced me through the spleen for some reason.

Pick a Class tomorrow, he said as everything faded, or maybe I said it, or the girl behind me did. *Or don't, what do I know, I'm just a God.*

And if I dreamed further that night, I didn't remember it upon waking.

CHAPTER 2.1 - A SIMPLE SOLUTION TO THE MALUS OF HUNGER

When I woke up the next morning, drifting out of slumber in warm contentment, I was alone.

I was almost ashamed at how relieved this made me. Almost, and not at all; gratitude waged a short and overwhelming war against shame, victorious in a matter of heartbeats. The sun was shining through the window, every bit of me was perfectly warm without any of me being overheated, and I was more perfectly rested than I ever remembered being. I was mystified by the dream I'd had, both more coherent than I'd ever experienced and still totally incomprehensible, and I could hear people in the hallway chattering in Shemmai, distant and muted.

I was in another world.

It would be a lie to say that hadn't sunk in. From the moment I'd woken up after Artemis's transport of me, I'd believed it. But it was sinking in *again*, now that I'd woken up in a strange room, sleeping on what I'd thought was a mattress but was actually something like a tatami mat. Poking at it, I could tell that it was only two, maybe two and a half inches tall, but it had been more comfortable than any bed I'd slept on.

There was an itch to that thought, a percolating warmth in my mind that urged *here, touch this*. I recognized the connection, the bridge to the Theurgist's System I'd been inducted into the day before. Following the mental—or spiritual, possibly—patterns that Captain Meredith had walked me through, I touched it, smiling in anticipation of its ridiculousness.

Your Divine Flame Wakens With You!

Behold These Boons And Rejoice: *Traveler's Rest*
As Boons, So Too Are Maluses: *Hunger (Moderate)*
New Skills Enter Your Repertoire: *See, Inquire*

> Divinities Have Left Their Mark Upon You: *Artemis (Least), Hephaestus (Minor)*
> The World Trembles, For Your Feats Grow: *Godtouched*

Live. Change. Grow. Transcend.

"Huh." I blinked at that a few times. Meredith *had* said something about how I'd unlocked a Skill from seeing her hair color, that black so deep it seemed blue, which had presumably been obscured by some magical effect. Maybe I could get more information about them, or about… well, nearly everything there had *something* I was curious about.

Nothing for it but to try, I reasoned, and built a packet of thought as though I were back in the Hall of the Thousand, praying to the gods.

Dear Divine Flame, or Theurgist's System. What benefits does the Boon "Traveler's Rest" confer?

I released it, guiding it to the bridge in my mind that led to the System. It made it there, encapsulated in an act of willpower, but then it… *popped*, for lack of a better word, the words spilling back into my mind with a sense that nothing had received it.

Well, I thought to myself, *that was worth trying. On with the day! What to do next…*

What to do next, I decided, was getting up. The mat I'd slept on was barely higher than the floor, so that was easily enough done; shoes, shoe buckles, and then I rose smoothly to my feet from the floor without a single pang of pain or crackle-crunch of joints.

"Bless you, Hephaestus of the Forge," I murmured, "for the grace that renewed my body. Blessed are you, who reforges the flesh."

"Taken to grace so quickly?"

"*Ayah*! Warn a girl!" I glared at Kelly from where I'd fallen flat on my ass. "I don't know how you snuck up to the door like that, but don't!"

"That's Qatn, right? What's it mean?" She just about bounced on her feet, emanating a ridiculous degree of good cheer. "Ooh, ooh! I know! I bet it means 'It's good to see you, Kelly! I am up and ready to start the day!' Did I guess right?"

"Wow." I tried to glare at her, but I was giggling, which probably detracted from the effect. "You sure woke up and chose violence today."

"Travelers and your funny sayings." She held out a hand to help me up, and then looked disappointed when I rocked forward onto my knees and then smoothly stood without help. "What did that Qatn word mean? I recognize it but don't remember it."

"It's just an expression of surprise." I momentarily regretted not taking her hand, so I went in for a hug on impulse.

"*Ayah!*" She hugged me back, squeaking in surprise. "Was that right?"

"Close enough." Her accent wasn't amazing, but it wasn't *bad*, despite the fact that there wasn't much in the way of trade between Shem and other countries. "I apparently am hungry enough to have a Malus on my Status. I don't know why I think that's so funny."

"Maybe you're silly when you're hungry?"

"Prob—"

"But not as silly as when you've got Godtouch."

I leaned against the wall and buried my face in my hands, groaning. "Gods, *literally*, spare me."

"Sophie, like I said yesterday, it would be ridiculous for anyone to hold that against you." She caught my eye as I lifted my head, smiling reassuringly. "I mean, it's not called *Godtouch* for nothing! I wasn't joking! Holding that against you really would be getting mad at the Gods, it's screaming at the lightning!"

"And people here… don't get mad at storms."

"It's a saying." She huffed dramatically, folding her hands across her chest.

"So people *are* going to hold it against me." I squinted at her, then hazarded a guess. "Specifically, Elder Whatever-Her-Name-Was is going to hold it against me."

"She absolutely is!" Kelly beamed at me and started walking down the hallway. I followed her, muttering darkly in her wake. "She'd find something to dislike you for anyway," she said after a moment. "She always does. This way, it's something that nobody can agree with. A couple other people, too. But… four, maximum."

I nodded at that, and we walked in silence for a bit. Not for very long; the hallway was short, or at least the room I'd stayed in was close to the stairs. Only about fifteen feet of stone, with tapestries on the walls for beautification and rugs on the floor to cushion our steps.

Well, the tapestries also cushioned me when I accidentally rammed my elbow into a wall after I more or less tripped over my own feet, but that probably wasn't their primary purpose. Temperature mediation, maybe, since I seemed to remember something about stone being awkward to build with because of that? But they were definitely gorgeous, covered with abstract geometric patterns in a riot of brilliantly saturated colors.

I'd had one rug that could have *maybe* competed with the least of what was so casually displayed here. It had been an heirloom from my great-grandmother of blessed memory, whom I'd met when I was too young to form memories; it was the only thing she'd bequeathed specifically to me.

My mother got it into my hands after my father, may every ugliness of the world be a magnet to his eyes, had disinherited me—disowned, really, though even that was understated. It might well have been the first and only open act of defiance she'd engaged in, made in a calculated—and desperate—bid to remain part of my life, even clandestinely.

I smiled at the tapestries, feeling a bittersweet joy. I didn't know what Artemis had told her, and I might never know, but I found myself content to trust and look to my future.

"Sorry, what?" I realized belatedly that Kelly had said something while I wasn't paying attention, and turned to her. "Say that again, I wasn't listening."

"I *said*," she said, smirking, "that you seemed lost in thought. Also, in the way!"

"Oh shit, sorry." I stepped to the side, letting the person behind me pass. The corridor was wide, but I'd been in the exact middle of it, and the stairs were a bit narrower than the hallway. "Yeah, lost in thought."

That got me a contented grunt as they passed me. "Happens. Traveler, Avara. Morning light's blessing."

"Sunshine on your crops, Farmer." Kelly sounded a lot more formal and respectful than I'd heard her be before. She touched my arm lightly as I made to follow them down the stairs, shaking her head minutely. "They don't like having people behind them. Don't crowd them, okay?"

"Sure." I kept my voice to the same murmur that she was using. "Sounds like a history?"

"Probably. But don't ask! It's rude, and they're really nice in their own way." She hesitated. "They're not Shemmai. I don't know where they're from, but they *specifically* came to the newest, smallest village, okay? Tethanne, she was one of the village's First Friends until she died—"

"May her memory be a blessing," I added automatically, as she drew a circle over her heart with her thumb.

"—and she had the settling of them, and *she* said," and Kelly's voice dropped even lower, "that they were moving from a *different* outer ring village, one that'd grown too big for them. That they're like a calmness in a pond which un-ripples any thrown stone. They just go by Farmer, no other name, and they bring in six hundred bushels of grain a year, mostly wheat and barley."

"Sovereign power bless them, that's a *lot*." I did a bit of quick mental math. "They feed the entire village?"

"In grain, and only about half of us." She made a side-to-side gesture with her hand. "We don't just live off bread."

As if on cue, my stomach gurgled loudly, and I flushed a little, laughing with Kelly's giggles. "Speaking of. You said something about breakfast!"

"If you're done walking the Darkness!" She headed down the stairs, and I followed in her wake.

"Okay. That one, you're going to have to explain to me."

"Well, the world is a sphere surrounded by nothingness." The stairs were even, with enough tread to have perfect footing. Fully enclosed, they had grab-rails on both sides, though they were a little lower than ideal, possibly for children to use more easily. "I know that sounds crazy! But it's true. And out there in the Darkness, there's just nothing, no mana, nowhere to stand, so *walking* it—you're laughing."

"We call it, uh, *space*, which I guess is the old word for volume. Sorry, I should have stopped you, instead of letting you flounder."

"Well." She stepped out into the main hall we'd eaten dinner in the night before, hands pressed together, and took a deep breath. "That was rude," she said after a moment.

"But funny."

"But funny!"

She was grinning, and I was snickering, and then the smell of the food hit and my stomach growled loud. "Right. Food?"

"Food." She nodded at me, then pointed to the long trestle tables against the back wall of the hall. They were in a sort of broken u-shape, starting at the wall and jutting outwards with the same food on the outside and inside of both sides. "It's Thesha's day to do breakfast *sittings*, but for breakfast there's always help-yourself where there aren't sittings. They'll do bespoke lunch and dinner here for a crown, today, and then switch back over.

"A crown for a meal is a lot, it should be five scepters, half a crown, but that's how much goes to tax in a village. And anyway, it's not actually great to have a lot of people eating bespoke, since that means more consignment and *that* means outflow. We're hardly poor, but we don't collect much tax in coin except from the Delvers and merchants, and most of *that* goes to Tower and Writ."

"Wow. That's... a lot that I don't know how to unpack." We'd kept walking while she talked, making progress towards the food. "Ten scepters to the crown. What else is there?"

"Ten crowns to a balance, ten balances to a city, a hundred cities to a world. That's Shemmai coinage—modern Shemmai coinage, nobody uses the old weights anymore—but everyone has different coinages under a world, so it's just a city or a balance but it's a *Shemmai* world, or just a Shem. Then there's a thousand worlds to a God, but I don't think Shem has a God's worth of coin circulating. Deshanna or Sudh might, they're a *lot* bigger."

"Got it." I didn't, not really, because the practical value of coinage depended on a huge number of factors like how it was set and whether or to what extent there was international exchange, but that was enough information that I could construct a very vague sense for how much my eleven coins were worth. "Do we just... how do we do this?"

She'd marched us up to the nearest of the tables, one of the two that abutted the wall. Reaching over to the wall, she grabbed a handle I hadn't noticed and slid a panel down, revealing utensils and dishes. "Grab a plate!"

"Huh. Neat." *Stops it from getting knocked over*, I thought to myself, and followed her lead. New food, cooked in new ways, on the level of the dinner I'd had last night, and this morning I might be able to actually appreciate it?

I took a deep breath, closing my eyes for just a moment to better appreciate the aromas.

My new life was going to be *good*.

CHAPTER 2.2 - OF BLESSINGS AND BREAKFASTS

Not knowing what most of the kinds of food on offer were, and egged on by Kelly's encouragement, I went for one of everything.

I'd had to go back for a tray, on which I balanced a second plate and two bowls. Nobody seemed to bat an eye at that, despite the immensity of what I'd taken, which suggested Kelly wasn't playing a prank on me when she practically ordered me to get more food for myself.

"The adaptive magic and System Integration is still at work," she said by way of explanation as we walked towards the front of the hall. There were five smallish tables, three of them empty, each with space for six people—eight if they were willing to get cozy, which one family obviously was. "The books—I checked this morning, before you were awake—say that… actually, what the books said is too technical to explain quickly." She shrugged, and I looked over to see an expression of distinct embarrassment on her face. "Um. The spells are still eating your fuel, and also you can't make as much fuel from the food you eat until something really small that lives in you finishes changing?"

"That's… fascinating, but just so you know, I do know enough biology to be aware of the role that my gut bacteria play in digestion." I smirked at her blush, and then was distracted from my distraction when I recognized one of the two people at the table we were approaching. "Hi! We've met, but I absolutely don't remember your name. Good morning!"

"If the Traveler says so."

The gravity and gravitas he'd injected into his tone had me snickering as I sat down across from him, Kelly plopping inelegantly into her chair. "Something tells me that's not the colloquialism here."

"I am Kan." His voice was even more amazing than I'd remembered, now that I was fully present to hear it, and his smile was reassuring and kind. "This is Kanatan, my youngest."

"Is *good morning* what they say where you're from, Scholar, Na… Nadesh?"

"Nadash, but *really*, call me Sophie, and yeah, it is." I smiled down at the kid—seven years old, at a guess—who was at the head of the table, between me and Kan. "What do *you* say?"

"Um." He paused, sort of shrinking into himself under our scrutiny. It took him a moment—and me switching my attention performatively to the food and giving him some space—to collect himself, and then words spilled out of him in a rush. "My name is Kanatan because that's like my momma's name and my daddy's name, and we say *morning's joy* but that's short for *may the morning be a joy* and is it true that you were sent here by a God and you're Godtouched—are you staying? Is that too much like work-talk, everyone says before you eat breakfast isn't time for work talk, but Tana said that Kibosh is way too quiet for anyone to want to stay, but momma and daddy have been the Stone Team here for*ever*, so I think it's just cause *her* momma—"

"Whoa, kiddo, slow down." I grinned at him. "Hi, Kanatan. Morning's joy; it's nice to meet you. I was sent here by a sort of protector-huntress goddess, and her half-brother helped; he's a god of craft, of making the best things you possibly can."

"*Wow.*"

"As for staying here?" I shrugged, and cut myself a slice of something that looked like sausage. "I think—" I popped it into my mouth, then closed my eyes and had to suppress a moan. *Holy of holies, blessed is the name of the God Above Gods.* I chewed, swallowed, and had to resist immediately shoving more food into my face in an uninhibited rush. "I don't see why I would ever leave."

"We are quite lucky indeed that Levali has chosen to reside here, and it will delight her to hear such joy. Thesha, as well, come the morrow." Kan smiled at me. "We have only just now sat down ourselves, and it being your meal with us in full wit, is it within your traditions to offer a grace to the Gods, as it is within our own traditions?"

I flushed, a reflexive refusal stalling on my tongue. *No, dumbass,* I told myself, *you will not be ruled by your scars.* "Yeah," I managed, forcing myself not to slump or plant my face in my hands.

I didn't quite keep my voice level, and it shook a little bit in time with my racing heart, but you can't have everything.

I looked around the table at the three others, thinking rapidly. "Arguably," I said, "I have no reason to believe that the bread here contains the grains my religion of origin specified. But it's *bread*, and the language supplantation gave me the same words; wheat, barley, oats, rye and—okay actually I don't have a word for that one, but it was an old version of wheat, basically.

"But more to the point, I'm…" *I'm having a crisis of faith* seemed like both an exaggeration and an over-simplification. I hadn't *had* a faith since my early twenties, I was just full of cultural detritus that was unable to cope with the idea… "I'm having trouble reconciling my upbringing with the whole grace given, grace returned thing. Do I direct it at them, or at one of them, or just vaguely *around*?"

"You know," started Kelly, and then she paused. When I raised an eyebrow at her, glad for the reprieve, she snorted and shook her head. "I can't believe that *I'm* saying this to *you*, but you know, between what you said of those two, I doubt any of them has a domain that calls for meal-grace."

I stared at her, boggling, until what she'd said sank in. "Well, shit. I just kind of had a panic attack over nothing, then, because yeah, grain and bread and both, separately, are in the domains of different gods. Well. Okay, then, back to the wellspring of my youth we go." I took a deep breath, and grabbed my bread from my plate, fluffy and buttery and covered in honey and cheese. "So, there's a lot of stuff on my plate, and blessings are pretty specific.

"There's a blessing for fruit, and a blessing for root vegetables, and you get the idea. But conveniently, the blessing for bread is sort of a catchall; if there's bread, you say the blessing on bread, and there you go. So!" I held the bread up in the air, and reached for a state of… if not the sublime belief that my father—may his memory be a blessing, and with all due haste—kept talking about, then a state of hoping that if there *was* some supreme sovereign, that hypothetical entity might not be a complete asshole.

I pushed that hope, a prayer and a tiny bit of connection, along that same bridge as the System, and sang. "Bless you, God, ruler of the universe, who brings forth bread from the soil."

There was a bit of quiet when I was finished, in which I got a round of contemplative nods. I bit into my bread, eyes more or less rolling back in my head—the flavors were almost too powerful that early in the morning, just skating on the edge of being overwhelmingly strong. The System connection was starting to sort of mentally itch, but I pushed it aside, because my stomach had now gotten the message that it was mealtime, and I was absolutely not going to be dissuaded from filling it.

We all tore into our food, the others with not all that much less gusto than I was exhibiting. I had a dozen different foods that were passingly familiar, recognizably similar to the foods whose names from Earth they had occupied the semantic space of, and a half dozen that weren't. I worked my way through the first category first—potatoes, eggs, something between oatmeal and porridge, the bread, sausage, and more—and then started more carefully tasting the novel ones.

While I filled my stomach with food, I alternated between the five different kinds of juice, the water, and the milk. I'd partially filled some glasses at Kelly's urging—well, I'd poured a full glass of water; hydration was serious business—and got the absolute culinary surprise of my life when I sipped what looked like grape juice and had my entire mouth go dust-dry.

Amidst the raucous laughter of the rest of the table, I washed it down with a substantial amount of water. Snickering, red in the face, I saluted Kelly for the indignity she'd inflicted on me.

Giggling in that utterly infectious, totally unselfconscious way of hers, Kelly showed me the expected way to dilute it. The recipe was one part of what I was inclined to call cranberry juice—if cranberry juice had been maybe twice as acidic—to two parts each of an apple juice that tasted nothing like apples, a pear juice that for all I knew might have been Earth pears, and the juice of a fruit they called *silphan*. The resultant cocktail was sweet and tart in equal measure, and somehow reminded me of the taste of mango while tasting nothing like it.

That turned out to not be the only culinary trap on my plate, but I was forewarned of all the others by the fact that none of my three meal-mates could keep a straight face. Well, Kan probably *could*, but he wasn't; Kelly, on the other hand, was visibly trying and utterly failing.

The others loosened up as we ate. Kanatan was excitable to the point of babbling, but—with the occasional reminder—was conscientious about letting others have a turn to talk. Mostly he wanted to hear from me, but he took time between questions to tell me about his cohort, which led to *me* asking questions. Hearing about the cultural mores around childbirth was fascinating; the herder-folk who lived mostly in and around the outlying Shemmai villages—like Kibosh—had the custom of hundred-year marriages, after which if you wanted to stay together you'd get married again, and in each of those marriages you'd have two kids.

Those kids would be close together in age, and the whole village—or your greater social circle, for socially traditional folks in a larger town—would time their kids more or less together, so there was a single cohort that was within about ten years of each other. It didn't work perfectly, since people came and left, so you'd generally have two cohorts in a century.

Kibosh had twenty-seven kids, which seemed both a lot and not very many to me. Kelly fell over herself explaining that the reason the ratio was so high was that adults tended to leave for somewhere more exciting, which meant basically anywhere, and from that I could infer that at least for Shem, a ratio of about fifteen percent *was* high.

Kan, in turn, told me a bunch of stuff about the Stone Team, and I managed to keep the awe and astonishment mostly out of my voice as I asked follow-up questions. The three of them—Kan, Ketana, and Junior of Stone, whom I'd forgotten about—were governmental employees, working directly for the village. They maintained all of the buildings, roads, and defenses, other than three. The Hall of the Thousand, as I might have already guessed, maintained itself; but along with that, the Tower was raised and maintained by the magic of those who lived and worked there and the Guild of Crafts was worked on by those who were members there as a sort of building-scale showcase of their skills.

When I asked him if that wasn't rather a lot of responsibility for one team of three people, he chuckled jovially and gave one of those not-smug not-smirks that was very much a smirk and almost intolerably smug. Stone, he pointed out, was durable to work with even before you started getting magic involved; a structure would go decades before it needed any work at all, and that work would take less time than the tea, whatever that meant.

That made a lot of sense, given what I'd seen the day before—if he and Ketana could make a house in a day, a few hundred buildings would be trivial for them to maintain.

By the time that conversation was over, I'd moved on from the familiar foods to tasting new things, things that I had absolutely no frame of reference for. There was a tremendously sour fruit that I nearly choked on, and which Kanatan happily ate the rest of when he was done laughing, and then immediately afterwards there was something that looked vaguely like a leafy green but tasted utterly bizarre, sticky and almost like a tart powder as I chewed it. I followed those two with another drink of the undiluted cranberry juice, just to see the delighted good humor on the kid's face, and as the juice *fizzed* in my mouth I felt the pressure and itch of the System bridge redouble, spiking painfully.

Explaining the dramatic wince and hiss of pain I'd just given got me sidelong, confused looks as both Kelly and Kan fell over themselves explaining that as we weren't in a critical situation, it was *entirely* appropriate to *commune*, as they put it, with my System.

Kelly wasn't satisfied with my agreement and acceptance with that. With the implicit threat of her otherwise being pointedly disappointed, she extracted a promise from me to tell her immediately if I was suffering from any major pains or discomfort. If it weren't for Hephaestus's gift, that would be a joke; but as it was, it was quite possible that every ache and every pain was noteworthy—so I agreed, and only then did I reach out to that mental bridge.

Your Divine Flame Deepens In Hue!

In Your Heart, One Faith Rings True: *Pantheism*
To Him, Your Fathers Looked, And Their Fathers Before Them: *YHVH*
The Paths Before You Grow In Number: *Class Unlocked (Apprentice Alchemist)*
And Lo, Upon Your Boons Is This Added: *Hearty Breakfast, Strong Foundation*
These Maluses, Vanquished, Have Faded: *Hunger (Moderate)*
Behold, The Injuries Of Your Experimentation: *Chemical Burn (Least) (Tongue)*

In Every Experience, Our World Grows Brighter

In hindsight, I thought to myself, *I should maybe have paid more attention to the mental tingling.*

CHAPTER 2.3 - SUBJECT TO DOCTORS AND LAWS

Chemical Burn, Least, Tongue. I wonder what that—*ow.* "Ow, ow, ow. Ow! Fuck!"

"Sophie?" I heard a scrape as a chair was moved, and then a thump as the chair—Kelly's presumably—hit the floor. I couldn't see anything; my eyes were full of tears. "Sophie, what's wrong?"

"Burns," I slurred, tongue feeling swollen and ashy. "Water." I reached out, touching a glass, but I didn't know if it was the *water* glass, and apparently I guessed wrong, because someone pushed my hand to a different glass. I swirled a mouthful of water, grabbed another glass, spat, and did it again, and then winced as I realized what I'd just done.

"What just happened? Are you okay?"

I grabbed a napkin and rubbed at my eyes, sighing. "I'm fine, I'm fine. Pantheism, though?" I looked up and over at Kelly, who was sort of hovering over my shoulder. It took some careful effort to speak with decent diction, but my tongue was already going from raw burning to numbness and tingling. "Admittedly, that blessed lens grinder wrote words that burn with truth, but still."

"Sophie." Kelly folded her arms across her stomach, glaring at me and pointedly ignoring my theological tangent. "What did we *just* talk about?"

"I *am* fine!" I grimaced, then sighed, waggling my tongue around in my mouth. *Huh, mostly numb, like the nerves got shut down. But it still moves right.* "I did, however, just unlock the Apprentice Alchemist Class by giving my tongue whatever 'Chemical Burn, Least' means. Turns out the *hello, pay attention to me* from the System was an alert after I made the bad call to combine those greens and the undiluted juice."

There was a moment of stupefied silence, like people couldn't figure out whether to yell at me or laugh. I broke it by starting to snicker at my own trivial misfortune, and the mood lightened.

"Miss Avara, I do believe that we have identified a possible first Class in Scholar Nadash's Path."

"You're laughing at me." I glare at Kan without any heat. "You can keep a poker face all you like, but I *know* you're laughing at me."

He inclined his head in a gesture of acknowledgement. "The good Scholar possesses the wisdom of her station."

"Jerk."

He chuckled, breaking his stoic expression, and the last bits of tension around the table broke as we all laughed with him.

Footsteps sounded, alerting me to someone's approach. I turned, getting ready to say hello, but Kelly beat me to it. "Rafa! You have impeccable timing."

The woman walking over to us snorted. "It's a refectory, not the Thousand. So what if I'm around?" Her voice was acerbic and pointed, but I could swear there was a deliberate kindly twinkle in her eyes. It went well with her whole aesthetic; her face was a mass of wrinkles, and overall she looked at least as old as the matron I'd met the previous night. "Call me Rafa. Herbalist and Healer."

"A pleasure to—"

"Yeah yeah, what'd you do, catalyze a reaction inside your face? Look here." She grabbed my jaw with her left hand, gently but firmly, and waggled it side to side. "No bone damage, no muscular atrophy. Open up."

"Uh." I looked at her dubiously, and opened my mouth despite my misgivings.

"Hm." She tilted my head to one side, then the other, and performed a series of seemingly random checks, tapping my teeth and poking the inside of my cheek. She avoided touching my tongue at all, but she got a wince when she brusquely ran a finger across my upper palate, and that got another contemplative sound.

Eventually, she let go, glowering at me, and I raised an eyebrow at her. "Well?" I kept my voice level, or at least tried to.

"What the fuck is wrong with you?"

"*Excuse* you, what? I had no way of knowing—"

"Not that. Obviously you didn't know the egg-greens would react with the cranberry juice. *Those* idiots should have known, but that's on them. **[Suppress Affliction]. [Hasten Recovery]**." She glared at them for a moment as the echoes of structured power in her voice faded, then turned back to me. Her eyes narrowed, trapping mine, as the pain blessedly—or magically—faded into nothingness. "That burn should have been qualified as Minor at *least* in your System. If you've got a habit of self-harm, you go to the Clerk *right now* and tell him you need to see someone qualified to handle that. **[Healer's Orders]**."

"Peace!" I waved her off, sighing and relaxing back into the chair. *Amazing how much it sucks to go back to hurting, even for a moment*, I thought to myself wryly. "I had chronic pain. Ligaments and joints, mostly. Maybe my scale is just off from that—I was never the self-harming sort."

I hadn't felt any sort of magical influence or compulsion from any of those ringing invocations that the world had trembled to hear. I had the feeling, though, that if I *had* been... if I'd had a history of self-harm, if that was why my pain scale was broken, I'd be marching off without another word.

Rot my eyes, I might have done that just from the tone of her voice, no magic needed.

"Hmph." Rafa glared at the chair which Kelly had, hastening to my distressed side, upended. My First Friend got the hint and scurried over to pick it up, holding it for the doctor to drop heavily into. "You get that taken care of? I'm hearing a past tense."

"Yeah. Got fixed up a fair bit by one of the gods involved in sending me here—"

"*Travelers*." She made it sound like a swear word, and I grinned. So did she, a moment later.

"—and I got Hale for an Attribute when I... initialized? Or at least, that's what my System wrote. So hopefully that'll help too."

"Mmm." She didn't seem particularly displeased at that. "They tell you much about the road to power we use, the one some damn fool built a while back?"

Everyone around us looked mildly horrified, but I found myself snickering. "My *Divine Flame*," I said with deliberate and mildly sardonic emphasis, "hasn't really been the subject of much conversation. It sure is something, though. Incredibly bombastic."

"Hmph." Rafa looked over at Kelly, lips thin and jaws tense, as though she was fighting to avoid saying something. "Orthodox approach, I suppose," she eventually muttered.

"I'm not Tethanne, ma'am," the First Friend replied with an odd mix of heat and primness. "Call it by the books if you want, it's in the books for a reason."

"More in the books than there should be. Still, I suppose she's not a child." Rafa stood up, and I recognized the way she held the edge of the table in doing so, the careful way she made sure not to put torsion on her joints. "I'll leave you to it."

We let her go in silence. She walked steadily towards the other table, rejoining a conversation there, and none of us spoke until she sat back down.

"Well." Kelly wore a grimace like she'd bitten into a tomato she thought would be good and it'd turned out to be mealy, but her voice was level and cheerful.

That's how she sounds when she's forcing cheer, I noted to myself in passing, and nodded to her. "Well."

"That… was Rafa. She's…" She hesitated, then forged ahead. "She's someone to listen to, about anything she says, no matter what it is. Even when she just, you know, hints, I'm gonna listen to her! Anyway. Right! Kan, Kanatan. You don't have to stay if you don't wanna. This is basic stuff, and it might be boring."

Kan looked at his kid, tilting his head a little. The boy in question squirmed in his chair, obviously conflicted or stuck between conflicting… I couldn't tell, really. Desires, priorities, obligations, something along those lines.

"Miss Kelly and Miss Sophie are really fun," he finally said, "but I wanna go play with Tino."

"And where, young man, are you going to meet Tino?"

I could hear the eyeroll like a clarion call. "Tome, dad. Mamma Savata is gonna be there with him and Zak all morning, 'cause Tino sleeps better with the training noise, I've told you this."

"So you have, so you have." Kan's smugness was palpable to me, but probably not to his son. Sometimes that was a fine line; other times, not so much. "Off you go, then. We won't be at Fall for lunch, since we're doing road work, so if you need—"

"—anything, I talk to Pat," Kanatan said in an impatient singsong. "And if Pat isn't there I talk to Clerk James or Captain Meredith, or I wait in the Library and be gentle with the books."

He slid out of his chair and then paused to look over his shoulder, almost sheepishly. Kan gave him a nod, and he shot off at an eerily familiar not-quite-run, not-quite-walk.

Some things never change, I thought to myself with a smile. "So, what now?"

"Now," Kelly said firmly, "we talk about the Law."

I gave her a skeptical look. "Like, the normative rules of behavior enforced by the State through the threat of coercive force?"

She made a face. "No, important as that might be, that's mortal business, and if you transgress, it's a matter for the Captain or Writ. Besides, it's a *way* longer conversation than we could possibly have time for!" She shook her head. "For Shemmai lay-law, what we call civic or civil law, I mean, obviously I'll help, but that's the whole body of law! It's tomes and tomes!"

"Lay-law." My eyes narrowed in thought. "So, the Law, presumably capitalized, is something related to the Gods of the Thousand?"

"Exactly. Okay. This is going to be kinda weird and a little scary, probably, and I can't tell you, I can only show you. Ready? Trust me?"

She grinned at me, and I grinned back sheepishly, flushing a little for no particular reason and thinking about the day before. "Yeah, do it."

"Okay. And after this, we're gonna talk about Classes and Paths! And about your System and how you can work with it instead of just... we're gonna talk about that stuff." It was her turn to look sheepish as she deliberately reigned herself in, but her eyes retained a spark of excitement; it was pretty obvious what she was more looking forward to. "So, the Law. I'm gonna skip the history lesson; let's just say for now the Divine part of the Divine Flame is a real thing, and anyone with a System gets a connection to the Law through it. Right?

"Right. So, um." She blinked a few times. "You haven't set a Path yet, much less picked a Class, right?" At my nod, her shoulders settled in a movement of relief. "Okay, I was a little worried about you having done some Path stuff. That makes this easy! *Really* easy. Because... so, a Class is a step towards divinity, right?

"It's a transcension of the mundane, of who you were as a mortal. It's a confirmation of who you are, rising, and movement towards apotheosis. But Classes can be specific, and Skills can be narrow, and Paths might be inconvenient. Wouldn't it be easier if you could *make* someone be useful to society? If you had a child, and you could make sure they picked *right*—"

That tickling pressure poked at me, and I opened up in dutiful fulfillment of my earlier promise to Kelly. Time itself felt like it was stretching, and there was a weight, a *gaze* boring into me. "Stop." The word tore itself out of my mouth. "Stop, I got it, this is awkward and weird."

It was an eerie *certainty* like nothing I'd ever experienced, a knowledge coming from outside of my mind that left no room for doubt or questioning. It was almost entirely foreign to me—I'd never been a person of particular faith—but it sang of that same purity and clarity of knowledge I'd come into over years of struggling.

It wasn't exactly the same, though. My knowledge that I, as a woman, was utterly uninterested in men, attracted almost exclusively to other women? That came from within, from the same place as my uncertainties and my curiosities and sense of wonder. This was an *external* intrusive thought, something that had a meta-tag in a sense I couldn't describe in words.

It wasn't incompatible with my own beliefs, the ones I had come to through my life and my experiences, but it was distinct. This was my System bridge talking, in a way. It was conveying that I needed this conversation to *end*, because Kelly was right in a lot of respects—fuck, I worked my ass off to convince my niece to minor instead of majoring in music comp—but what she proposed was *wrong*, it was a *violation*.

"That was fast!" Kelly looked triumphant, for all the sympathy in her voice. "The Edict of Paths. The choices we make in the System are ours and ours alone. You can teach, you can advise, but anything that narrows someone's agency? Nope! 'Cause the road the Theurgist charted is personal."

"That was kinda trippy and unpleasant. It feels like I have a notional headache, like someone flipped the headache switch but there's no actual *symptoms* of it. It's weird as shit."

"I know!" Now the sympathy was on her face, crowding out the triumph. "But the good news is that you'll never violate the Law by accident, and now you understand why."

"Because I get an alert if I even think about it? And the downside is that that's because the gods are literally reading my mind."

"Might we otherwise suppose otherwise?" I had forgotten that Kan was even still around, what with the weight of what'd just happened. I quirked an eyebrow at him, and he shook his head. "You are right to rebuke me, Scholar Nadash. To repeat myself in such a manner is atrocious wordsmithing; I should have asked whether *in the absence of the Law* we might suppose otherwise."

"You're kind of ridiculous." That got me a smirk and a nod, and I sighed. "But you're right. There's no point in worrying about literal deities knowing what I'm thinking; they have better shit to do than thought-police me, and I can't do anything about it anyway."

Kelly coughed. "That's not *really* true, you know?" I cocked my head inquisitively at her, and she grimaced. "Well, I mean, there's no Law against Theurgy. It's within our remit to try to usurp the Gods, or ascend to join them. If you oppose the Law, you can walk that Path, and try to change things."

For a moment, all I could do was boggle at her. "Um. *What?*"

"He—the Theurgist—stole the Divine Flame in the first place, and we know for sure that, um…" She looked at Kan imploringly. "Kan, do you know how many Ascenders there were? Like, for sure, confirmed, one hundred percent?"

"Thoroughly attested and with neither divine nor mortal disagreement? Seven, within the Time of Light. That is one of the many ways," he explained to me in an aside, holding one finger up meaningfully in a gesture I had no context for, "we refer to the years since the creation of his System. Years since the inception of structured magic, since the defined road to apotheosis.

"Their names and deeds are known to Shem by Shemmai attestations, these seven, and these are they: Eichan, who strives; Naga, who defies; Emmna, the shield; Basathon, who builds; Shei Maham, whose wilds overtake desolation; Li Li Deshta of the crossroads; and Theophania, the spark of sudden insight."

In Kan's resonant baritone, those names were an invocation, a prayer. It rang in the silence after his words, and it felt almost wrong to disrupt it.

"Well! Thanks, Kan!" Kelly broke the mood with cheerful insouciance. "Okay. Moving on—"

"Wait, we're just going to move on from that?"

"Sophie, please." Kelly smirked at me. "As much as I love history, we should talk about the present. Time's a-wastin!"

"Talk about the—time's a-wast—oh *fuck* you." I stuck my tongue out at her like a girl a third my age. "This morning, *I'm* not the one going on wild tangents, and you know it."

"Your System," she said, pointedly ignoring me except to smirk wider, "is in a lot of ways a little personal God. It responds to prayer, and it's smart enough to listen."

I stopped good-naturedly seething at her to consider that. "Back in the Thousand, I formed little mental packets of… words, concepts, and intentions, and sent them deliberately on. I can do that and ask my System to tone it down a little?"

At Kelly's nod and her expectant, level look, I settled myself down and thought for a moment. I honestly found the extravagant enthusiasm of the text I'd been reading rather charming, but it wasn't... *efficient*, and I wanted a way to get the most relevant bits in an easily digestible form.

Existing or unchanged information in a compressed form, I thought to myself, mentally building it into a construct. *You can go ham with new things and major changes, unless they're time-critical.* I sealed it off and, with a nudge and an odd, fluttery sense of anticipation, I let it drift towards my mental bridge. A moment later, the world faded, and I looked at my first deliberate iteration of what I might call my Status Report.

CHAPTER 2.4 - DESCRIBING CLASSICAL CONSTRAINTS

You can go ham with new things and major changes, I'd said to my System; but I'd asked for anything that didn't change to be in a compressed form.

My System, proving Kelly's advice to be spot-on, delivered.

Your Divine Flame Shapes Itself To Your Will!

You Are: *Sophie Nadash | 39 | Kibosh, Shem*
You Cleave To: *Pantheism (Faith), YHVH (Culture)*
You Look To: *Artemis (Least), Hephaestus (Minor)*
Your Skills: *Learn, Read, Study, See, Inquire*
Languages Provided: *Shemmai (Modern), Shemmai (Ancient/Liturgical), Koshe, Qatn, Sylvan*
Classes and Attributes: *Worker (10/10) | Hale*
Feats: *World Traveler, Godtouched*
Your Future: *No Path; Requirements Met for 21 Classes*
Your Boons: *Traveler's Rest, Hearty Breakfast, Strong Foundation, Hasten Recovery*
Behold! Look Ye Upon Your Maluses, Which Number Naught!
In These Matters You Approach Mastery Ever More Closely: *System Communion*

It wasn't perfect, I thought to myself, grinning. The writing was… well, it was serviceable, but unstructured, and it didn't make great use of the available space. But it was a written representation on an imaginary page, displayed without ever touching my eyes; did it actually *matter* whether it took more vertical space than needed?

Well, I supposed I was something of a perfectionist in craft, which went fantastically well with my terminal incompetence at graphic design. So yeah, it mattered, but this would do for the time being—and the *important* part was that I had been able to change it. *I've played Skyrim,* I thought to myself wryly. *I shouldn't be surprised that mods make a big difference. Not that this makes me take it any more seriously.*

That being done, there was something of an open question, wasn't there? That dream from the night before, and what Kelly had told me about my next major step... I focused, finding the exercise easier, the System somehow closer to hand. *Remove all combat Classes from consideration, please, and display Classes that I meet the requirements for.*

Your Divine Flame Answers Your Query!

And Lo, These Apprenticeships Are Earth Most Fertile For Mundane And Sublime Alike: *Alchemist, Druid, Clerk, Examiner, Agent, Singer, Cyclist, Cleaner, Artisan, Explorer*
Connection Comes Through These Respectable Journeyman Professions: *Scribe, Traveler, Student of the Law, Mathematician, Cook, Scientist, Hedonist*
Surpass All Ordinary Expectations And Find Balance Through Your Expertise As: *Technician*

Choose, And Transcend Mere Mortal Bounds

"Huh." I tried to say it levelly, but my hands were clenched on the table, and I was shaking in a way that I was pretty sure was visible. "That's. A thing."

"Sophie?" Kelly was at my side, and she put a hand on one of my hands as though to still it. "What's wrong?"

"There's..." I took a deep breath, imagining my anger flowing through me and away. It helped a little. "There's a Class option that's very upsetting."

"I—"

"It's from a gendered language, you see." I interrupted her without caring about the rudeness, speaking more to the air than to anyone in particular. "It's a predecessor to being a theologian and sage, a community leader and cantor, a judge and counselor. The option I'm being offered,

Student of the Law, is Ancient Shemmai and it's a masculine word, just like it was in my native language. There wasn't a word for a woman who takes that position, not really, because the feminine version meant the learned one's *wife*, and my community of origin didn't permit women to take the leadership positions."

"Oh."

The pain in Kelly's voice… helped. So did her hand on mine, and the fact that she'd so instantly recognized that I wasn't okay and moved to comfort me. "I'm not going to take it," I said bluntly. "It's a part of who I am, a huge part, and I once thought it was my vocation. But I'm not going to take it." *And it's not even the right word*, I almost said in a fit of absolute pettiness. *It should be Laws, plural, because it's in the liturgical tongue.*

"Okay." Her voice was calm and kind, and so very nice. "Nobody is ever going to tell you to take a Class or not take a Class. Let's strike that one off the list. What else do you have, by category?"

"Ten that are Apprenticeships, six others at Journeyman, and one… my System was ambiguously wordy." I quoted them all what the words had been, and the stunned look on Kelly's face did a lot to cheer me up. I could tell the difference between different kinds of disbelief, and this was definitely the *you must be cheating* kind. "There a problem with this?"

"Sophie…"

"As words appear to be failing my compatriot and dear friend," Kan interjected, "perhaps I might interject on her behalf: *what* Class are you being offered which dwells within the Realm of Balance, and might I also ask, has she been so good as to explain the implications of such a thing?"

"She hasn't, and it's Technician," I said slowly. "It's… I don't know if you know the word? It's someone who maintains the systems others build and design, or who executes plans that others have written. It was my profession, and I was very good at it." I looked at them levelly, forcing my shoulders to go down, to relax. "I'm not wasting a new start by going back to it."

"Then it's off the table." Her words weren't heated or firm. They were just… calm, quietly certain, like she was making a totally banal observation. It was a tone of voice suited for saying *that ocean is large* or *the community for that game has toxic elements*. "Do you want an explanation of why that kind of Class as an evolution of Worker is surprising, or would you rather move on?"

"I..." I stopped myself from saying *let's move on* or possibly *I want to leave, and stop talking about this*. I flashed back to a skeletally thin figure with slow-beating wings, and his... advice, or command, or exasperated complaint; I had no idea how to interpret it. "Explain it, please. And thank you for your patience and understanding."

I did my best to make that last compelling and true. It came out closer to the target than I'd expected, and by Kelly's smile and the tension easing in Kan's wrists, it was the right thing to say.

"I began my career," Kan said contemplatively, "as an Apprentice Stone Shaper. My wife began hers as an Initiate Mage. These were the fruits of our maturity: our Class Evolutions from Worker, which is the near-universal Tier One Class and arises out of what we consider the Zeroth-Tier Child. In these, we were in the first Realm, that of growth, of Earth—mundane mortals in whom were seeds that could become wonders."

"By seeds," Kelly interjected, "he means that it's a growth stage. School after your schooling."

"From these, I became a Stone Shaper," Kan continued on as if Kelly hadn't interrupted, "and Ketana became a Geomancer; and upon reaching Level 10 in those Classes, we grew further. Our second Classes came to us, respectively Engineer and Stone Shaper. In time, so did our third, in which we kept with custom and departed from the domain of what we had.

"Those of Shem who grow with more than the expected diligence develop and refine themselves to transcend the second Realm, that of Connection. At the peak of mortality, such Shemmai hope to dwell within one of the three Destinies—Glory, Balance, and Eternity."

He paused, looking at me as if to gauge whether I was listening. I wanted to yell at him that he was using ten words where one would do, that I had other things to be doing. I wanted to snap at him to get to the point, to explain why this *mattered*.

I did neither of these things. Instead, I nodded at him, and he continued.

"We grow greater as we do this. As we rise, we gain Attributes, such as mine of *Attuned* and *Rooted*; and had I begun in the second Realm, they would have been stronger. Though... I would have struggled to learn the use of them, as it is the quintessence of the Earth that is *growth* and the quintessence of Connection is to begin to truly *wield*. This is the purpose of the Theurgist's creation: to be a path towards perfection of intent and Self, just as experience becomes perfection of execution."

"That's what *you* think is the purpose of the System and the Divine Flame." Kelly jumped in with a reproving, almost scolding look. "And last I remember, the scholarship still disagreed with you."

"I am," Kan sniffed, "simplifying."

I couldn't help laughing at that, and after a moment Kan gave a sheepish shrug. "Simplifying, huh," I said, still snickering, and his expression set me off again. "Sorry, sorry, I'll be good."

"The *relevant* factor," Kan continued reprovingly, "is this: as you grow more powerful, your Skills and Attributes will manifest differently or change outright. They will demand more understanding from you even as they become more…" Kan snapped his fingers together a few times, frowning. "More magical. Easier to use, yes, but demanding mastery, empowering you to act and *be* rather than to *learn*. And so, to begin in the Realm of Connection is to declare yourself as moving past the study of the art and of life in its trivial forms. To begin in the Realm of Balance, then, would be to declare yourself as no longer a student of your Self and your place in the world."

"So if I start with a Class in the second… *Realm*," I said slowly, trying to think past the absurdity, "I'm, let's say, ahead of the curve as far as raw power goes, but it's a harder road, because I'm aligning myself or whatever more with using what I have instead of growing and learning. Less hand-holding, less structure—or different structure? And even more so if I started doing Balance things, it sounds like. Because I knew exactly what my place was—I was a cog, laboring for other peoples' benefit."

I took in their nods and their understanding expressions and straightened my back against the chair while they waited patiently.

"I'd be great at it," I said after spending a moment collecting myself. "I did it for a decade. Inhabited and exemplified it. Okay. It's still struck."

"There is no—"

"Kelly, I *know* there's no need to justify it to you. I'm justifying it to *myself*, just out loud." I gave her a side-eye, then cracked a weak grin. Like I'd just given her permission to, which I guess I had, she giggled, and Kan sighed in mock exasperation. "Anyway, like I was saying, I had this rule, this principle. Got a better option? Don't hype the bad choice. Just strike it, and don't come back.

"It's different if you have only bad options, or only good options. But *fuck* going back for Technician, even if I could be a better Technician than I could be a Scribe or whatever. I want to… create, to design, to be independent. To do things for *myself*. So, yeah! That's the most... me-iconic two down. What's next?"

"We categorize what other options you have." Kelly's voice was suddenly fully confident and assured, like we were finally on solid ground again. "What were your other choices?"

Smiling at her burst of professionalism, I told her, and she took on a thoughtful mien that looked practiced. *And maybe it is practiced*, I thought to myself, smiling.

"Now we break it down by categories. Static versus traveling? In Kibosh, leaving for the wilds, or a city—or at least a town? Creation, study, or... services?" She frowned. "Writ, Crafts, or Tower, I guess."

"Static, and staying in Kibosh." That didn't require any real thought. "Leaving aside that this is where I was *sent*, and I have no reason to think I was sent in anything but good faith? I want to relax and make connections, to just sort of chill out and work at my own pace in a context that supports that. I want to have a routine that I fill with the fantastical, and it seems really nice here. I like the people, I like the village itself, and it's... convivial. And even if I could make friends anywhere, I like the ones I've already made *here*."

For some reason, that made her blush, which I was counting as a definite victory. "And for the last? You can just pick one to take out, if you don't want to pick one to settle on."

"Drop the services, I guess?" I shrugged at her raised eyebrow. "I don't know. I liked singing as a *hobby* well enough. I just don't think I would want to do it as my main thing. I want to be *making* something, or doing something genuinely constructive. And yeah, clerkly stuff could qualify as that, but being a cog again..."

Kan and Kelly traded a look, and she frowned a little, lost in thought. It was a good look on her, which was tremendously unfair; when I frowned it inevitably became a scowl or a sullen glower, but on her it was just this cute look of concentration.

"We should keep all of Hammer and Crafts in contention for now." She traded looks with Kan, and shook her head when he did something subtle with his body language that I didn't understand. "Don't be silly. Artisan, right off the flare! She doesn't need anything else to take up a trade."

"Much of Hammer is not suitable for the requirements Scholar Nadash has provided."

"Well, sure. But we're not talking about setting her up as a blacksmith, and anyway, we have one, *and* an apprentice, and she doesn't need strikers."

"All those involved in leathers and fabrics are one step in a chain. These, we should—"

"—not bother with, because she wants to work at her own pace." Kelly waved a hand dismissively. "And she wants to work on her own, so that double rules out the Stone Team. Triple, because you're fully staffed."

"No such thing exists, and it would do us credit to have an apprentice." Kan's grin was distinctly impish. "However, you are without a doubt correct with regard to the other two reasons."

I sat there and half-listened, tuning out their banter. As much as I wanted to pay attention to them, as much as it was heartwarming to hear them take my preferences so very seriously, it was hard to follow. They were going exhaustively through a list of dozens of professions, and most of the reasons they wouldn't work out were either obvious or incomprehensible.

Kibosh already had two carpenters and an apprentice, which was one more carpenter than the village needed. A brewer was part of an extensive production line and getting me qualified for a Journeyman slot would take months. The village simply didn't have the demand to support a jeweler, and a business that relied on shipping goods to cities—as distinct from the nearest towns, which were much closer—wasn't appropriate for a Traveler. The list went on.

"Alright." Kelly's voice jolted me out of my reverie, where I'd been meditating and trying to draw closer to my point of connection with the System. "That's that side of the list. Glass, alchemy, inscription, enchanting, herbalism. Nothing in Delve, nothing in the Thousand, you've ruled out Writ. Tower… well, I guess enchanting is already a little bit Tower."

"It is not certain that she may grasp the flow of mana and shift it."

"Stitch it! Doesn't matter, this is my first pass. There's all the Magus lines, obviously, and the divination stuff, and whatever *Scientist* means. Is that another Koshe word?"

"She speaks Koshe?"

"Yes, I speak Koshe," I interjected, rejoining the conversation. "And yes, it's another Koshe word. No divination, I both find it ridiculous and hate the very idea of prophecy."

"Struck! And last, Mathematician. Eight Classes, plus maybe Tower stuff. Unless you want to change one of your other constraints, this is what you're looking at. For most of them, you wouldn't even need a real apprenticeship, you could just jump into making your own decisions after a few days…"

"Wait, how's that? I've never done any glassblowing, much less enchanting. If I could do it in a few days, why would any kid growing out of Worker bother with—" I cut myself off. Kan had already *told me* the answer to that question, and I hated it when I found myself asking for a repeat answer.

Kelly gave me a thoroughly unimpressed look, which was perfectly fair. "You're already Artisan-qualified and have twenty years on that kid. Maybe you can't handle the heat, but if you feel like you really want it, we get you the Class and you'll get either an Attribute or a Skill that'll make it work. But that kid? That kid doesn't have the focus and broad base to pull it off, and then they'll be stuck with a job that expects more of them than they can deliver."

"Okay, that's… okay." I gave her a sideways look, narrowing my eyes. *And that hypothetical kid wouldn't have your help*, I thought to myself, but I didn't say it—Shem might have had dedicated helpers for new professionals for all I knew, and it didn't matter. "So, if the crafting is through Artisan, the herbalism stuff I guess is through Druid. That doesn't feel right, but okay, I'll take your word for it."

"Good! Because now," Kelly said with a wide, toothy smile, "I bet you're tired of listening to us talk, and you want to *do* something."

I paused, looking at her with some suspicion. "You're not wrong," I responded dryly. "No offense."

"Kartom can't test you this morning, he's busy. We don't have reagents, you don't know how to channel—if you even can—and we can't ask someone to teach you glassblowing or herbalism, not till this afternoon. So what do you say we borrow a workspace and do some alchemy?"

CHAPTER 2.5 - IN HAMMER DID HITZ A WAREHOUSE RUN

Borrowing a lab meant, in this case, heading to the north of town—to Hammer, where the warehouses and loud crafts were. And while we walked, we talked, going back over the list of Classes to winnow it further.

"The thing is," I mused out loud, "I want to *create*, right? That's the whole—it's a big part of the reason why I'm not taking Technician."

"A creative endeavor." Kan's rolling baritone was smug, and I glanced over at Kelly to see her sticking her tongue out at him. "Ah, my friend, be not so discomposed."

"Scribe and Librarian, struck. You were right." Her eyes flickered to me, then went back doggedly forwards. "I got all caught up with the relaxed and intellectual and didn't keep the other stuff in mind."

"So with Herbalist struck—" I had rapidly come to that conclusion, based on how lethal wandering into the Forest could be— "that leaves Mathematician, *Scientist*, and some crafting stuff? Plus anything totally magical."

"Yeah. And we can't really have you try most of them this morning, like I said, but alchemy? Alchemy, we can just borrow Hitz's lab for."

Kan stopped in his tracks at that—I almost ran into him, it was so abrupt—and turned to stare at Kelly. "Just borrow Hitz's lab."

"Yeah!"

He boggled at her as she kept walking. "*Just* borrow Hitz's lab. *Hitz's*."

"Come on, Kan! We aren't made of time."

We picked up the pace as he muttered under his breath, something rapid and venomous in a language I didn't understand. I paid him no attention; we were approaching a muted cacophony of industry, and even the sounds of it were fascinating.

The hammering of metal was the loudest of it, but it was far from the end-all. Between the *tink-TANG-TANG-TANG-TANG* of the strike pattern—Kelly informed me cheerfully that the lighter sound was the blacksmith herself, and the louder ones were her two strikers—there was a roaring wind from what she called Forge Row that provided a three-toned drone as a backstop to the clear day.

Underneath, layered atop, and competing with that, there was a whole range of other noise. Saws, shouting, some sort of work song coming from younger voices in response to a cadence from an older voice, two different high-pitched grinding wheels, and the snapping of fabrics in the wind, shockingly loud for what it was, formed an astonishing din.

And yet, according to Kan, this was a pale shadow of what the noise could be. The enchantments that the village maintained in the vicinity of Hammer, he explained, dropped the sound levels by up to sixty decibels, for the loudest of them.

Unfathomably louder, those strikers hammering on metal would have been otherwise—six unbelievable orders of magnitude. I couldn't comprehend it on a gut level, but that was fine. I appreciated it, and made a mental note to praise whoever was responsible.

"Every one of these is technically a standard workshop, but they can make whatever changes they want. See that?" Kelly pointed to a building, slate-gray like every other building in Hammer, each with windows at the tops of the walls that ran the entire length but were only about six inches tall. "That's the Stone Team's place."

"Entirely unchanged from its fundamental design," Kan noted, "and in respect to venerable tradition, a showcase for our subtler talents."

He wasn't kidding. Those gray walls were absolutely covered with incredibly fine ornamentation, done in a variety of high relief styles. There were intricate geometric patterns, murals of people—presumably the Stone Team—erecting buildings, fractal curlicues, and more.

"I have no idea how to evaluate it. It's very impressive to this Traveler," I reassured him solemnly, "and I'm sure you're a very good stone team."

That got an almost startled laugh out of him, mood fully restored, and an uninhibited giggle out of Kelly. "As you can see," she managed in the midst of her laughter, "all the other workshops are plainer, but changed. Make some guesses!"

"Glassblower's workshop." I pointed to the next workshop down, keeping my voice totally serious. "If I have the right of it, what with the glass being blown outside, and the pieces left to cool."

"I'll allow," Kelly retorted haughtily, "as you might be right in that regard."

"The next two are both working with wood, but uh, there's a barrel above one of the doors and there isn't above the other." It wasn't a sign with a barrel on it; it was simply a barrel, about three feet tall, that looked like it had been pushed into the stone of the building a few inches and left to just sit there. "Cooper and carpenter?"

"Cooper and carpenter. And then the other carpenter! Sure, they could share a workshop, but we have plenty of them!"

I grinned, as much at Kelly's enthusiasm as at anything else, and we kept walking.

The variety of work being done was overwhelming, and we didn't have time for me to linger a while at every building. Kelly was on a mission; she took us briskly past the carpenters and the brewer, past the blacksmith and the leatherworker and the tanner. There were a few other workshops that I didn't quite catch or parse, and then we were at her destination.

"Hitz! Hitz, open up!"

The door she was banging on was inlaid with a simple drawing of a building, with a wagon and a few people out front. 'Dynamic Storage' was written near the top, and there was a subtle brick-like pattern running along the bottom of the walls, but otherwise the entire structure was starkly plain.

"Hitz! I got *business* and we gotta get it done so I can get–"

The stomping of a heavy tread cut her off, and she waited with a sudden shift to patience. The door slid open, disappearing into the wall, smooth and nearly silent in apparent defiance of the nature of stone, and I gawked.

Everyone I'd seen in Kibosh had been in perfect health, hale and hearty, with even the Matron moving with a surety that belied her age. Hitz, though, assuming this was Hitz, was scarred to shit. They stood with a leg that terminated at the knee and had a blueish metal prosthetic at the end, and their scalp was burned and blackened in long streaks where their dark brown hair didn't grow.

That prosthetic scraped across the stone as its wearer stepped forwards, eyes narrowing into something like a glower. "Like what you see?"

"Morning's joy," Kelly interjected hastily. "Sophie, this is Hitz, they're Kandashi born. They have a… problem that stops them from getting healed, okay? Hitz, Sophie. She's a Traveler, I like her, please be nice."

Their face was drawn in a scowl, but I was pretty sure that was just, well, how their face was, with the sharp angles drawn sharper by the ridges of scar tissue. "Honestly," I said with a grin, "the pinpoint burns on your arms are a cool look, the prosthetic is gorgeous, and I've always kinda dug muscles with scar tissue."

"Really." Their single-word, grunted sentence was a masterclass in skepticism, and I grinned wider.

"I'm almost entirely into women, but if that weren't true, I'd wait to kick you out of bed till the morning. Even with the grease fire scars. That must have hurt like a motherfucker. Sorry if I stared rudely."

Their grunt this time had more of a note of amusement. I was, conveniently, entirely telling the truth, and I recognized what kind of person they were immediately. Proud of their life and the road they'd walked, they were the type to treat their scars like trophies and memories.

"Hitz." Kelly sounded like she thought this was tremendously awkward, and I shared an eyeroll with the Kandashi, making a mental note that I should learn what that meant. "We need to borrow your alchemy workshop. Sophie needs to. The real one, she's not an apprentice. She's, uh, *Mumki*?"

"She know the fuck anything is? Or gonna shatter it all?"

"I know to use the round bottom flasks on the distillation rig's flame, if that's what you're asking." I smiled thinly at them, something deliberately about halfway to a sneer and halfway to picking a fight. "What's that word you just used?"

"A Rank. Expert?" They shot a look at Kelly, amused and derisive. "Shitter, System, different words."

"Shitter?" I squinted. "You having me on?"

There was something almost smirk-like in their eyes. "Same *Shita*."

"The Theurgist's System," Kelly interjected smoothly, "shows up differently in every place that it's present in. Kandashi have a different society, and… well, a language that's nothing like Shemmai. *Shita* is their name for it, and their Rank is something like our Realms, kinda."

"Hey, listen." I glanced inside the door, and then frowned. I couldn't… *see* anything, my eyes were just sliding off the space inside the doorway. It itched in my head, itched with a feeling like I was remembering something that hadn't happened yet. Whatever the itch was, though, what I *was* remembering had more to do with Hitz's choice of words. "Ironically," I continued after a moment, trying to get myself back on track, "I desperately need to take a shit. Can I come in and use your toilet?"

Kelly's eyes went wide, and she started to say something. Hitz beat her to it, though, with a grunted laugh and a wave towards the door. "Integration? Go. Rightmost path."

I walked in, moving with purpose. Kelly was half-explaining and half-apologizing behind me, going into some depth about the gut microbiota thing she'd assumed I wouldn't understand while Hitz made amused noises that I'm pretty sure was them leading her on. The explanation made perfect sense—no sense in wasting the energy to fully reformulate my innards when they could just kill it all off and replace it with a seed colony—and I made a mental note to actually get the whole explanation at some point, but my gut was informing me that its consequences were upon me.

Those consequences had me striding through a disorienting magical doorway.

I wasn't sure exactly what I was doing in the moment of stepping through the threshold. I had a flash of being able to see where I was about to step, but it was an *array* of different places I was about to step.

Rightmost path. Between the thought and the moment my foot hit the polished wood floors of every next step I could potentially take, I touched something through the System, feeling a sense of connection to my surroundings. It let me choose, or chose for me, or something; my foot touched down on wood, in a cavernous and entirely empty warehouse about ten times the size of the outside of Hitz's building.

The world spun momentarily, but there was no nausea, and everything snapped into place without any residue of dizziness. There was, I saw, a door in the right-side wall about five feet ahead of me, and I booked it.

It was… unpleasant. The best that could be said for it was that the seats were comfortable, there was no chance of missing the target, and there was neither residue nor smell. Actually, there were a *lot* of upsides to taking a shit somewhere with magical toilets, but there was still the major downside of, well, the kinds of bowel movements you get when your GI tract has gotten annihilated.

I need to up my diligence about hydration, I thought to myself with deliberate good humor.

My first time using a toilet in Kibosh had been in the middle of the night, mazed by sleep, confusion, and an emotional crash. This time I could appreciate the craft that went into it, the sheer level of aesthetic diligence that went into a *toilet* in a *warehouse*, and I put the thought aside because I just didn't feel like processing that thought.

Sure, shoving stuff aside like that was a terrible idea, but I could always gibber later. Eventually. When I didn't have someone standing around waiting for me to be done with my attendance to nature's call.

The enchantments—or spells, or whatever they were—left not only the bowl I was sitting over but also *me* without any residue, cleaner than the most thorough bidet without so much as a square of toilet paper. There was a similar setup for my hands off on the wall, a space delineated by two right-angled brackets in opposite corners of a notional square; I stuck my hands in the space, and after a few moments of a mild tickle and a less-mild itch they were clean and sanitary.

Bless you, Lord our God, yadda yadda, who commands us with respect to the not-exactly-washing of our hands, I thought to myself wryly.

Then I shoved that aside, too. Reconstructing the traditions of my mother and father—and their mothers and fathers before them, to the hundredth generation and beyond—would have to wait its turn.

The door on the way out was exactly where it ought to be, and led to the outside without any shenanigans. Hitz was gone, and Kelly was waiting for me with an impatience that she probably thought was well-disguised and a concerned, compassionate mien that was either genuine or *incredibly* well-constructed.

"Everything's settled. Come on!" She grabbed me by the arm, half-dragging me back towards the door. "We're gonna make something! It's going to be *great,* no matter what we make."

I let her guide me back to the spatial distortion, trying to suppress my awareness of how it felt to have her arm wrapped around mine.

A moment later, any such thought fled my body as I stepped into wonderland.

CHAPTER 2.6 - A HEAVEN TO JABIRIANS

Hitz's lab was a thing of vast, awe-inspiring beauty.

Well, a thing of beauty to me, who grew up on mad scientists with equally mad cackling.

The entryway opened into a room that was easily a thousand square feet of contiguous space, with a half-dozen doorways scattered around. Huge, fragrant ropes of what seemed to be herbs and flowers hung down from the ceiling—a ceiling that might have been fifteen feet high—and more were growing in pots that ran along the sides of the building. Sunlight streamed in through tall windows, and the air was suffused with a sourceless light that illuminated everything without casting a single shadow.

And what a sight everything was.

I walked forward, entranced, towards what was obviously the primary distillation area. There were seven columns there, each with an entire supporting framework of pipes, additional entry points for gasses and liquids, condensers of all kinds, and what looked like aeration chambers; each also had a bunch of reaction chambers where who-knows-what would happen.

I could trace the plausible path of one subsection, but only one subsection. A vat of something would be distilled, boiling and fractionating into five different gaseous outputs even as a liquid trickled through a filter of some sort. I didn't actually remember enough about continuous fractionating columns to be able to make guesses about what that implied about the composition, which I'd made a habit of terrifying people by doing, but the piping was obvious enough, and most of those pipes went to other parts of the whole.

Two didn't. One of them went to a condenser and then to where a flask would clearly sit. The other would blow—that was clearly a blower of some sort, though its mechanism wasn't clear—over a series of flattish trays and then through a liquid of some sort. After that, the liquid would drop into a chamber where something would be steadily added via a geared funnel, and the gas would continue on into a circular tank.

That was just one section—the smallest, *simplest* section of this spectacular arrangement of machinery. All in all, it took up hundreds and hundreds of square feet—maybe thousands—and it called to me on a primal level.

Look at this, I thought to myself, grinning ear to ear. *You'd think I was transported to another world or something.*

Kelly's hand touched my elbow, and I turned to see a soft, hungry smile on her face. It was like a revelation, the way her smile made me feel and what it revealed about *her*, and she saw my recognition in the same moment I made the connection. There'd been a word for it, a word I no longer had, but I recognized the look of someone finding joy in my own happiness.

"Glad you've trusted me so far?"

I didn't know what to say to that. Specifically, there were too many things I could say to that, and I fought a half-dozen responses that were too flip or didn't seem right, trying to figure out how I actually felt. She gave me the time, not rushing me, just standing there with her hand on my elbow and smiling.

"You said that you love new people, new stories," I began eventually. I hesitated, but she nodded at me to continue, so I did. "I'm not asking this to brag, but that means me, it means the world that shaped me, it means the moments we'll share. Right? And it's not just about a love of novelty for its own sake, which I'm guessing is… unusual, here in Kibosh. You love it in people, too."

Something dark flashed across her expression, and her body language tensed up and then relaxed again in the span of a moment. Her smile was flatter, though, and I regretted the social distress I'd caused even though I'd needed to ask. "Yeah. It… doesn't sit right with some folks, socially."

"Then thank you." I held her eye, feeling my smile continue to stretch my face. In the end, it didn't matter all that much *why* she was so determined to do a good job, did it? "Really. Thank you."

She looked at me blankly for a moment as I smiled. "For what?"

"Kindness, dedication, some degree of respect. Honesty. Being a person worth trusting. That sort of thing." I was joking, but I wasn't joking, and there were important conversations we had to have, but they could wait. "For loving novelty, for helping me out, for smiling like that at me."

She punched me lightly in the side, only flushing a little bit. "We don't use Hitz's rig," she said, deliberately changing the subject. "Obviously. We don't *touch* any of this, nothing in this part of the room. They do consignment stuff, some sorta thing they don't talk about much that takes, well, all of this. Us, we use that stuff."

I followed where she was pointing to a corner that was clearly set up for experiments. It was spacious, by comparison with the labs I was used to working with, and I could immediately start picking out salient details. "That's still a lot," I said with a quiet glee. "I've worked a lot of time in places less equipped."

Shelving, both wire and solid wood, separated it from the rest of the warehouse. They formed walls at about chest height, delineating a space without blocking line of sight, and there weren't any of the hanging herb-bunches in that area. Nor were there in a dozen feet of the shelving; there wasn't anything, just stone... with visible scorch-marks and spots where acid might have dissolved parts of the floor.

"It's not what you'll have starting out. Don't get too attached, okay?" She started following me; I hadn't even realized until I heard her footsteps behind me that I'd been walking slowly towards the workspace. "I know the basics better than this stuff, but I have some Skills that'll help. Learning, finding, using, the works. Anything we use up or break, we do paperwork, get it replaced; Hitz is doing me a favor here."

"Burners," I noted serenely, pointing. "Hot plates. Heat-grips, those are obviously for heating up the thing they're holding, but I don't know how they'll actually work. Mortar and pestle, but it's not in use, judging by the dust; three things that are obviously automated grinders of some sort, *those* are being used. Drip pans, gloves, goggles, masks. Bottles and flasks and vials, eleven different markings of glass tubing—diameter, length, types of joins, shape, could be anything. A cauldron, a small vat, both of them have a bunch of complicated stuff that looks like magic machinery. Scales, flat panel thingies that are next to the scales, a whole shelf labeled *reagents*.

"Off the top of my head, I don't see... tongs, secondary containment, something for air purification? No fume hood. Paper and pencil? I can use mine, but we need to write down anything we use, right?"

"Air purifiers, air filtering... **[A Friend in Need, Fulfilled]**," Kelly whispered, and a familiar shiver ran through the world. She set down the basket she'd been carrying, a basket I hadn't even noticed until it hit the table with an audible *wham*. Then she walked, eyes half-lidded, towards a box labeled *cyclers*. "I guess they're in here!"

I followed as she opened the box, shaking my head. "That seems like a helluva... Skill?"

"It's a Feat-Skill," she said absently. She pulled out what looked like a T-shaped pipe with a parabolic dish on each of the short ends. "What *is* this?"

"A cycler, I guess. You don't know, huh?" I tilted my head quizzically, peering at it. "The long end of the thing obviously plugs into or joins with another pipe, but what are the dishes?"

"I can look it up!" She grinned at me and pointed to a set of boxes on the end, near a wide table. "Reference books! But at least now we know that this is what we use for the air."

"What's in the basket?" I glanced in one of the boxes, marked *I Can't Believe I Kept This Shit*. It had a set of glass, ceramic, and metal alembics in it, spotless despite the box's title. They looked functional enough, and my eyes passed over them, dismissing them as irrelevant to our needs.

"Food," Kelly said. I was confused for a split second before realizing she was answering a question I'd asked just a moment ago. *The basket, right.* "It's a double double. Four meals' worth of work-food; two for two each. We gotta bring the basket back, they're pretty heavily enchanted."

I took a deep breath, looking around with my hands on my hips, taking it all in again. "Alright. This is... a lot."

It really was. Shelves filled with boxes, clear containers, or unpacked equipment took up all the separating walls of the experiment nook. Two large tables and three small ones filled most of the center, and there was a series of posts with hooks and pipes whose purposes I didn't understand yet. There were clamps mounted on the sides of the tables, ones with interesting fasteners that looked like they tightened onto—*ahah*.

"I think those glass cubes are probably what I'm supposed to use for experimental containment. Never thought I'd miss having a fume hood, because this seems... not optimal! They go in the clamps, so that they're secured, and there's other clamps for flasks, probably. Tongs, tongs. I'm sure we'll find tongs."

"There's an index." She'd drifted over to the boxes of books, pulling one out and setting it on the table. She opened it and flipped through a couple of pages, smiling. "It's sorted by... actually, there's two of them. One of them's by function, the other's by where it is." Apparently on instinct, she flipped again to the end of the book, nodding to herself. "Not two, three—at the end there's another index, alphabetical order and page numbers."

"So that we can look something up that we've seen, or we can find something by name or by function."

"There's a recipe set, too." She held up another book, waiting for me to take it from her hands. "This one's got the Journeyman's Basic Set for alchemy in it, the stuff that every professional alchemist can make."

I paged through the book absently, noting the level of detail and rigor of the recipes. They didn't have a whole lot in the way of context or safety information, but they were absolutely meticulous in the ingredients, measurements, and methods. *Is there… ah, yeah. Good.* I smiled at the end-notes for one of the experiments, seeing the same level of care lavished on storage and cleanup of the end-products and intermediates.

I put the book down on one of the smaller tables. "This is great documentation." I shook my head, impressed, and walked over to the reagents. Glancing through the beautifully labeled jars, I could feel a mental itch coming on that I hadn't felt in years and years. "You know what I want to do instead of just staring at all this equipment?"

"I couldn't possibly guess."

For a moment, butter wouldn't have melted in her mouth, she was so performative in her naivete. She lost it a second later, grinning impishly. *She has dimples*, I thought to myself. *I knew that, but forgot it. How totally unfair.*

Well, I'd allow it.

"I want," I said grandly, drawing myself up to my full height and stretching, "to engage in a radical act, an act to mark a fundamental change from the life I once lived. I want to stride boldly into one of my possible futures and indulge in *creation*, and also maybe in some joy and delight and highly tedious detail-oriented planning and execution.

"I want, in short," I pronounced, pausing dramatically and flaring out my coat, "to do some alchemy."

CHAPTER 2.7 - INSPIRATION; AN ACT OF CREATION

The usual way of things, when someone started working on a new trade in Shem, was to follow the well-trod path. I was, to my own surprise, rather disinclined to do so.

"We have detailed, easy-to-follow instructions for all the Basic Set's potions, you know."

"I know." I picked out six containers based on their labels, three of them jars and three of them vials, trying to work through the notation system in my head. "Acids and bases, I get. But there's something else on the labels, too. Weak, strong, and a third category?" I put them carefully, carrying them one at a time in each hand, on the nearby table.

"I have no idea! Sophie, *among* the things we have instructions for are potions that'll unlock your Alchemist Class at Journeyman Rank, right?"

"Yeah." I grinned at the mortar and pestle. They were so quaint, and so charming, and I was absolutely not going to waste my time with them. Instead, I grabbed two of the automated-looking grinders; I'd use one for acids, I expected, and one for bases. One more thing to look up in the books. "Did you figure out how the cyclers work?"

"It's got two mana inputs. One's a setter for what the air should be, did that. The other makes one of these dishes suck in air that has anything in it that shouldn't be. Air like what we want comes out the other dish, everything else goes down the tube."

"Great. Okay, these posts and tubes are obviously for that. I think. Can you confirm that, and then if it's the case, set up, let's see." I glanced around, trying to intuit the design intent of the space. "The layout of the posts suggests we want two cyclers on the far side of the table from me and one on each side?"

"Yes, but, *Sophie!*"

I grinned at the jar I found, the one that had exactly what I was looking for. *Now, to find the flask again that I'd seen…* "Kelly, do you know where we had those flasks with the center reservoir, the one where pulling the pin dumps the contents out into the mix?"

"West wall, third shelf from the left, second row. But Sophie, can you just tell me *why*?"

"I dunno." Her memory was exactly right, and I made my way back to the table with a couple of them, humming to myself. "I guess I just want to start out doing something creative instead of following directions. It's the path I want to follow, right? To be a creator, not a technician."

"Oh." Kelly's frown cleared, and the whining note in her voice vanished. "Oh! Okay. That makes sense, and I'm sorry you had to tell me again. What do you need me to do?"

I nodded at the table and the tools that were on it. "The bits of dandelion seeds—conveniently, whether or not they're the same dandelion seeds as where I came from, the labels say they have the same reactivity—need to be as finely ground as possible. So do the lemon seeds, but use the other grinder, absolutely no cross-contamination. They go into the reservoirs for these flasks. Can you deal with that while I handle the rest of the prep for this experiment?"

"On it!" The contented joy in Kelly's voice went a long way to reassuring me that I could, in fact, use her as an additional pair of hands, which was nice. "Why as finely ground as we can?"

"The finer it's ground, the more surface area it has per volume."

It took a moment, but without any further prompting her face lit up with the epiphany. "And more surface area means the powder will touch more of... whatever it's touching."

"Yeah. It'll react faster."

That was enough for her, so I went on bustling around, resorting to the index and finally finding what I was pretty sure was an atomizer nozzle: a rubber bulb and tube mounted on a ring, where the ring had a wire clamp that would secure it to the top of the flasks I'd picked out.

"This," I told Kelly absently as I fiddled with the clamp, "creates a low-pressure zone that forces liquid up into the gas stream and disperses it as droplets. At least, if the laws of fluid dynamics are the same here as they were back home. So it's going to aerosolize whatever liquid is in this flask, and that'll spray into *this*, which—and I checked—has an airtight seal with the atomizer tube. A closed system, no backspray."

"And the powder goes in the liquid, 'cause you wouldn't have me grinding these otherwise."

"Yep! Hmm. I need a... ugh. I can't believe I'm saying this." I grinned despite my words. "Where am I going to find some kind of pipette?"

"West wall, leftmost shelf, third row." She grunted with effort, the grinder bucking against her with a sudden growl as she put her full body weight into it. She turned it off instantly, presumably cutting a mana feed or something, and started clamping it onto the table with a sheepish expression. "Um. Yeah. That's where you'll find the hand stuff."

"Thanks!"

There was, wonderfully, a sort of magical whiteboard. I picked up something halfway between a stylus and a very fancy pen and wrote out a few bits of nonsense, enjoying the richness of the color and the total lack of odor or residue.

There were two black bars, one each running along the top and the left, and I stroked my finger down one of them; as I did so, it erased the content aligned with my finger, confirming my hypothesis. *More like a magical etch-a-sketch*, I thought to myself, and got back to work. The stoichiometry of the reactions needed figuring out, and that meant the chemical reference books, yet another boon from Kelly's magical insight as to where things were.

When I stopped to self-check, I found, to my surprise and Kelly's lack thereof, that my hands were shaking. I took a break to take care of that—finished one side of the basket without even noticing what it was, sent her for a drink refill, attended nature's call, that sort of thing. That meant losing context—and besides, best practices were universal—so I wrote out a quick checklist on the whiteboard, and had Kelly take a look at it.

That cross-check caught a hilarious oversight: we'd set up the cyclers, but hadn't done anything with their exhaust pipes. Once we were done laughing about that, I rolled a small drum over to each of them and figured out pretty readily how the gaskets worked and how to check the seal with the hand pump. Mental math and a quick check of the books had the maximum pressure of the drums at about ten thousand times what the reaction could even theoretically produce if it were completely converted to gas, but when Kelly *checked with me* about it, bless her, I walked her through the math anyway.

Accidentally catching my foot on nothing in particular resulted in a confirmation that slamming my hip into one of the drums didn't budge it, so I checked off the mental box labeled *drums are properly secured* and tried to ignore the forming bruise.

I knew the chemistry of it suggested that there shouldn't be more than trace amounts of excess gas, and all the byproducts should be mundane and largely benign. I didn't much care; I've always felt like the act of skimping on safety procedures is what causes the hazard, and I wasn't going to start cutting corners now. At least the glassware here was effectively impossible to break by dropping it, or by catching my foot on the floor and accidentally hurling it for that matter, so that wasn't something I had to worry about.

I still wasn't sure about the question of byproducts even after reading through what information there was in the books. They didn't have exact molecular composition, and there was some variance in the reported data that was a bit excessive, so I spent some time being a bit more thorough. I calculated the maximum plausible pressure, cross-checking to make sure the flask—and the atomizer, and the lid with the last-ditch valve—could plausibly handle the reaction, and then just to be sure looked up the pressure capacity of the different components in yet another book.

Eventually, after some time at the whiteboard, I had a decent ballpark of the molecular proportions I wanted, and I wasn't actually going for *perfection*. The scale needed adjustment, which was tricky until Kelly found some magical calibration weights for me; and after some back and forth with volume versus mass I confirmed that the density measurements in the book and the purity-and-ratio labels on the bottles were all correct as far as I could measure them.

Of course, we then learned that the flat panels next to the scales were magical scales, but at least we knew how the mechanical scales were calibrated.

Two kinds of seeds, ground to a fine powder. Two remarkably non-toxic liquids, given how volatile their fumes were, one actually used in a wide variety of cooking. One oil extract, something theoretically usable for cooking but which would be an incredibly bad idea. A dozen pieces of equipment. All of it was carefully positioned and secured; every upcoming step was planned and written down.

Nothing we were using was irreplaceable. Still, I was careful to make sure that nothing was in a position to break; this was someone else's gear, someone else's lab, and just because most of the stuff we were using was actually super basic didn't mean we shouldn't be respectful.

It was time.

I was very—excessively, by most peoples' standards—careful about the remaining bits of work, that tiny fraction which was intended to be the so-called *actual* experiment. Flask secured to the table, protective equipment on, I painstakingly pipetted the suspension of oleoresin in its respective liquids into first one vessel and then the other. The pipettes went into the magical cleaning bucket, and the jars of reagents were wiped down, resealed, and put back on the shelves.

Kelly had long since gotten the powders into their respective cylinders, and she slid them into place at the top of the flasks with a frown. That frown—and the fact that everything was ready and I'd want to do a last check anyway—was reason enough to pause, and I caught her eye with a raised eyebrow.

"I don't think this is going to work." Her voice was uncertain, and her frown intensified as she spoke.

"What's not going to work? The reaction itself? That would be an interesting result in its own right, I wouldn't exactly complain. Be confused, sure, but not complain."

"No, not that." Kelly smiled at me, but the frown came back a moment later. "I think this just isn't enough."

"Not enough, like…"

"I'm not sure this'll do what you need for Alchemist, instead of what you already have. I mean, 'cause… look at this." She waved a hand at the experimental apparatus, a pin-pull away from… from whatever was going to happen.

"What about it?"

"It's apprentice level, this. Designing it, sure?" Her voice grew in confidence as she spoke, and she almost started to gesture before remembering where she was. She put her hands on her hips instead, shaking her head. "There's no *magic* in it, and no spark, and I know for a *fact* you're not making this up as you go along, you're doing something you already know about. Sophie, honey, this is an Expert Technician at work, not an Alchemist."

I flinched at her words, hands opening and clenching. I discarded the first three or so things that came across my mind to say, had a moment of thankfulness that I hadn't had anything in my hands, and closed my eyes for a moment. I let a range of emotions flow through me, mostly the fear of stasis and the paralysis of not believing the status quo can ever change; and then I opened my eyes.

"You're right." I smiled at her, which was hard at first and then grew much easier when she smiled back.

"So what are you gonna do about it?"

"Simple." I did my best to infuse my voice with a cocky certainty to match the question in hers. I was well aware of how short I fell in the attempt, but just trying to do it made me feel better, shifting my mood a little bit towards that feeling. "I'll improvise an addition. Something with spark. Something *magical*."

Her grin gleamed, hard and challenging. "Show me."

I walked the line of reagents, trying to clear my mind. I knew I didn't want to mess with my delivery mechanism or the storage; those would *work*, and I wasn't coming up with any brilliant insights about that. I needed something that I could add to what I already had, something that would elevate it to an act of creation from, yes, a largely rote recreation of something I knew.

Hephaestus, paragon of the Forge, I prayed as I walked. Words flowed from my heart, a plea and offering in one, and I felt the pressure of perception and knew that someone—or something—was listening. *God of craft and artisanship, of excellence in its own right. You helped me reforge my body; help me now forge a new path and transcend who I was. I dedicate the fires of my eventual workspace to you, should it have such, and ask for your blessing.*

Hermes, herald and messenger, guide and trickster. Thrice-Greatest, the mystical chemistry which is alchemy lies within your domain. To you I dedicate vial and flask, pipette and retort. Let my every potion be worthy in your eyes; bless me, if you will, and help me find once more that spark which drove me. Help me find within myself the act of creation.

I reached the end of the line and started back again, and about two thirds of the way something twigged in the back of my head, a little nudge from the System bridge plus something I couldn't identify, and the feeling of being perceived faded. I backtracked a few steps, looking for what had triggered the feeling, and my eyes landed on a jar of dust.

Perfect.

"I have no idea how much of this to use," I murmured to myself. "What a novel experience."

"Not very much!"

Kelly's voice sounded from just over my shoulder, and I yelped, the jar slipping from my fingers as I startled. I tried to catch it, which only imparted some spin on it, and reflexively leapt backwards with a flinch as it impacted the floor.

"Good thing those are tough." With the adrenaline spiking, my hands shook a little as I squatted down to pick up the jar. "Please don't do that."

"Got it. Breathe; you're okay, and it's okay. The glass is very tough and everything is fine."

Part of me wanted to get mad at her soothing tone, but most of me was too busy trying to follow her excellent advice. I took the deep breaths I needed, standing up and walking back over to the work bench where we had everything rigged. "Not very much, you said?"

"It's strong, even if it's common enough to be in the basics."

I frowned at that, and went, inevitably, to the books. The description had some measurements in terms of power, but all I remembered is that I vaguely wanted something on the order of 85,000 candela. That conversion wasn't particularly hard to do, and I wound up with about a milligram of the luminous dust added into the mix on each of the flasks.

I also set up a transparent, blast-proof safety shield mounted on the table. Secondary containment never hurt anyone, and lack of it certainly had hurt me in the past.

"Creation," I said grandly, waving at the experiment-in-waiting. "Magic!"

"Yeah. Magic! I mean, literally." Kelly frowned at the dust mix. "My Skills aren't giving me any feedback about whether this is going to work."

"But you don't have one about whether it *won't*, right?" She nodded, and I savored the nervous flutter in my stomach. It was a rather new feeling. *The first of many*, I told myself. *Wondering whether something I created will turn out okay*. "Alright. Technician shit or not, safety first. Goggles, gloves, and mask?"

"Goggles and gloves and mask. Bucket of sand, at hand!"

"Cyclers prepped? Everything bolted down?"

"Cyclers prepped. We've got steelglass to hide behind, and nothing is going to move."

I looked over at the checklist on the whiteboard and then at my lab assistant and maybe friend, her eyes crinkling with an eagerness and anticipation that matched my own.

Reaching over with one hand, my other hand holding the rubber bulb, I firmly yanked the pin out. Dust billowed into the liquid blend at the bottom of the flask, and the world stood still.

CHAPTER 2.8 - THROUGH DEEDS AND JOYS ARE PATHS OPENED

An injection cylinder was largely what it said on the tin: you pulled the pin, and the air compressed by the motion propelled the contents of the cylinder.

In this case, the contents were a careful mix of some astonishingly acidic lemon seeds, ground into powder and mixed with what was labeled simply as *luminous dust*. What they were reacting so rapidly with was in turn a mix of capsicum oleoresin and a highly basic cleaning liquid, and the results were exactly as I'd predicted.

The reaction frothed up almost immediately as the acid-base reaction turned citric acid and *something* into carbon dioxide, water, and something I vaguely remembered as being a food additive—well, assuming the chemistry of lemons was the same here. The resulting turbulence did a great job getting the rest of the dust in contact with the liquid, and the entire mixture turned into a churning, pressurized cloud.

A *glowing* cloud, glinting and scintillating in every color of the rainbow.

I allowed myself one manic half-giggle, half-cackle on my first pump of the atomizer. The moment it compressed, though, I was all business, watching the mist spray out in a narrow, powerful jet that splattered all over the inside of the primary containment. There was a beam of light that, in defiance of all physics, seemed to be spraying out with the mist—it refracted partially off of the inner surface of the glass in exactly the places that the spray did, spray-painting the inside of the containment vessel in translucent rainbows.

Not all of the light refracted, though. It was hitting glass, after all; enough passed through the vessel to cast a brilliant spotlight on the stone wall. It cast a narrow pinpoint which looked like it had all the concentrated light from a flashlight more powerful than anything I'd ever touched. I pumped again as it started to fade, grinning broadly as it brightened back up.

I pumped it a third time and a sense of distraction flooded me, a demand for my attention from that immaterial connection to the System I'd been calling my bridge.

"Kelly. You have the baton?"

"I... what?"

"System's calling. Take over the experiment, or at least make sure it doesn't break."

"Yes! Yes, yes, I've got it!" She didn't push me aside—which was good; I'd have been *mad* about that—but she all but leapt to grab the pump and run her fingers along the sides of the flask. "This is great and I'll be fine and have fun, now go!"

I snickered, stepping away and making sure nothing was out of place or unsecured. Leaving her to enjoy a moment of mad science, I crossed the room to a bench near the ramp, well away from the experiment. Even keeping my attention on walking that far was difficult, but one foot went in front of the other until I sat down. Only then did I let the connection snap into place, and the words washed over me.

Your Divine Flame Is Enriched!

The Designs Of Your Mind Lead To Insights: *Brightly Burning Mist Potion (Discovery)*

Behold, The Feats Of Your Legend Increase: *Advanced Creation*

Those Who Perform Feats, Grow By Leaps And Bounds: **[Compounding Intuition]**

The World Observes Your Skills, And Confirms Them: *Nothing Left to Chance, Chemical Calculation, Mechanisms*

Your Gaze Locks Upon Your Future: *Mystical Chemist (Path Chosen)*

Lo, A Step Upon Your Path Clarifies: *Classes Unlocked (Alchemist, Chemist, Novice Sacred Artisan)*

Word, Deed, Offering; These Gods Hear Your Prayer: *Hermes (Aspect: Trismegistus), Hephaestus; Dedication Accepted (Primary: Hermes, Secondary: Hephaestus)*

Divinity's Journey Beckons: Class [Alchemist] Matches Your Path! Make Your Choice!

> <Review Path (Mystical Chemist)>
> <Evolve [Worker] Into [Alchemist]>
> <Awaken, To Return In Due Course>

I felt the flow of the words stop, and paused for a moment to assess what the options felt like. I didn't want to make a hasty choice, and it didn't *feel* like this was a one-time offer. There was a sense of patience to the moment, an idea bubbling up through my head that of course I could choose to awaken and then return here, wherever here was, whenever I so chose.

I needed that. As tempting as it was to keep diving into this path, as incredibly curious as I was to find out more about my Path-with-a-capital-P, I had left Kelly in a room with an active experiment. I had left a *complete novice*, someone with absolutely no training, in a room with an ongoing experiment that paired volatile chemicals with magical reagents.

I didn't think anything bad had happened or would happen, but it was still at least a little bit irresponsible of me.

I took a deep, entirely imaginary breath, and deliberately shaped my thoughts into the mental act of choosing to awaken.

Sensation, memory, and the memory of sensation flooded back into my awareness. Like a fog clearing from my mind, like a flash of recollection, I *knew* that in the approximately two minutes that had passed, very little had happened other than Kelly somehow turning the lights off—the windows were dark, too—amidst her escalating laughter. It had started as a delighted giggle and passed, in short order, into more of a maniacal cackle, and when I looked over, she was only just starting to wind down.

The once-translucent layers of light that'd painted the inside of the glass had run and melded, blending and dripping even as the glass itself had gone gray and opaque with heat. I could see that just fine, despite the warehouse's lights being turned off, just as I could see *Kelly* rather clearly; the wall, after all, was glowing, the air near it visibly hazy from the heat. Kelly wasn't pumping the atomizer anymore. Standing behind the bench at a respectful distance, hands clasped behind her back, she was bobbing her head and swaying her hips as though dancing. I stared, mesmerized for a long moment by the combination of that and her still-diminishing maniacal laugh—and then I rose, transferring my attention to first the discolored flask and then the glowing wall.

"That looks verging on the edge of unsafe." I nodded at the flask, smiling happily in the alchemical afterglow. "You stopped in good time, though?"

"Soon as the clouding started in the glass, 'cause I was worried about what that meant for, I dunno... anything?"

"That was the right call." I put as much praise into my voice as I could, drawing on memories of hapless undergraduate interns. "The clouding meant that it was going to absorb more of the heat, and it had already started affecting the structure. No telling what was going to happen then, and we weren't as well set up for the flask exploding as I'd like."

Kelly was silent for a long moment, and I looked over at her, raising an eyebrow. She seemed lost in thought, and I let her be as I double-checked the state of the ditch-valve—something, some twitchy but contented instinct in me, was telling me that this incredibly resilient bit of the apparatus had been the most likely single point of failure, and it looked fine after the experiment.

I made to walk towards the wall, but stopped after a couple of steps, whistling in surprise at the radiant heat coming off of the stone. "You know," I murmured, "I hadn't thought about what it means that this is glowing enough to light up the experiment nook. I just assumed it was fine and you'd, I dunno, turned on some mood lighting."

"It is fine! Also, don't touch it, it's burning hot. I'd say that was the other reason I stopped, but." Kelly giggled, a little watery and a little exhausted. "I was... having fun."

"As is proper." I couldn't stop looking at the wall, watching it shift just ever so slightly, deforming. The centerpoint of the radiant glow was an angry red, and the stone there was *dripping onto the floor*. "I don't know why I'm not worried about the fact that the wall is melting. Is that going to, like, be a problem?"

"Nope!"

I turned to look at her, raising an eyebrow in my best unamused-supervisor face. I held it for about a half second before I started snickering, just long enough for her to plant her face in her hands. "Sorry, sorry. That was just too funny."

"Mean, *mean*!" She walked up to me, bumping my hip with hers and giving the emphatic lie to the petulant whine in her voice. "I guess it was a little funny."

"So why exactly is this not going to be a problem?"

"Well, I mean, it's not gonna make the building fall down, right? And the Stone Team can just fix it real quick tomorrow, or Kan can just do it himself, 'cause that's easy peasy. Little job, barely a breath in and breath out.

"And he'll *want* to, 'cause he won't believe us! That stone doesn't melt easy. The floors, that's one thing, they're tiles, that part of the floor will have some scorching and nobody'll be surprised. The walls? The wall's *bonded*, it's supposed to split the heat across tens of feet. I've never seen something like this."

"Brightly Burning Mist." I clasped my hands behind my back in a conscious mimicry of her earlier pose, stretching and enjoying the lack of pain in my shoulders. She'd carefully not answered whether she was a budding pyromaniac who was going to violate lab safety procedures in a fit of fiery fun, but she hadn't done so this time. "I guess that's a fair name. It'll light a whole lot on fire."

"Two doubles. Overlap." Kelly and I spun around, startled witless—or at least, I was—by Hitz's voice. Prosthetic notwithstanding, they'd walked up to a few feet away from us; they stumped over, every step loud. "Clever. Journeyman potion. Base of five?"

"Hitz! Maybe that's why I wasn't worried," I said absently. "You were around. But base of five, doubles, overlap… you're gonna—Kelly, *you're* gonna have to explain that to me, sorry Hitz, don't mean to impose. Maybe while we break this down?"

"While we… oh, Thousands. Shiuai bless, I lost track of the time!" Kelly grabbed my elbow, effortlessly spinning me around to face the ramp. "We're gonna be late for second sitting! We can't miss it, we *can't*, well, I mean, we can, obviously, but we *shouldn't*, not after getting that big of a basket, Thesha would have *words* for me. But as long as you get there as fast as you can, it'll be fine."

"Kelly, we can't just leave—"

"I'll take care of it. You need to *go*." Her voice was emphatic, intense—worryingly so, until she took a deep breath and visibly calmed. "It's a social thing, nobody's going to get mad at you but they'll *feel* taken for granted even if they know you don't *know*. I already vented the leftovers into the ditch-valve and neutralized it with the sand. I'll put the other flask in a hardbox and put *that* in a drum, leave the cyclers running with enough mana for a day, and catch up, I might even beat you there. But go, take the ring road through Tome. Make a good impression!"

I started walking, stripping off my protective equipment. "Make sure nothing's near the drum, point the flask at a wall." Gloves, goggles, and mask went onto the bench I'd been sitting on. "And anything with residue—"

"—goes into an autoclave, I'll be fine! Mother hen that you are! If I'm not sure about something, *Hitz* is here!"

I hesitated one brief moment at the threshold of the ramp. It wasn't that I didn't *trust* Kelly, it was that… well, that I didn't trust her, in my professional sort of way. But I needed to trust her in *her* professional sort of way, and I *absolutely* trusted Hitz despite not seeing them at work, and Kelly was telling me right now that I needed to make haste to the refectory on the other side of the village.

Besides, that little voice in my head, the one that had identified the ditch-valve as being the weakest link, was absolutely silent. And if I couldn't trust what I thought was my new Skill, well, the other reasons were still salient.

Hitz nodded at me as I dithered, and that was enough.

I ran.

I'd never been much of a runner. The joints would have precluded it even if I'd enjoyed it otherwise, but I really didn't. It wasn't even the pain of it, since an exercise bike or a hard hike wasn't any less inclined to make my muscles burn; it was the tedium.

Maybe it'd have been different if I liked listening to stories.

Running around the arc of the ring road in Kibosh was a revelation. The motion sang in my body, and I felt every beat of my heart as though it were pumping diluted glory through my arteries and veins. My boots were wrong for this, but it didn't matter; every step propelled me forwards, and the sheer clarity of the air was such a joy as to fill my mind.

A scattering of people—from their shops or on their walks, from their work or from where they gardened—cheered me on or heckled me in turn. *Go, girl, go* and *now kiddo, that's why we leave on time* spurred me on equally, my breath going short as I laughed. A shout from a reedy figure of middle age and indeterminate gender rang out, a clarion call of **[Arcane Endurance (Lesser)]** resounding across my world, and the burn that had started to grow faded.

Now almost sprinting, I passed through Tome, the library on my right and the combined administrative center and guardhouse on my left. I heard laughter that was recognizably Meredith's and caught a glimpse of a waving James. I waved back at him and ran on.

I passed into the quints near Fall, lungs starting to burn as I slowed down. The light of the noon sun and its reflections was almost blinding, and I didn't see the oh-so-helpful woman who called out in heavily accented—but perfectly comprehensible—Shemmai. I waved to her, not really processing what she was saying, and in return she incanted one short, catastrophic phrase.

[Benison: Swift Movement]. She called it out to the endless plains, to the spirit of the dogs and the traditions of the herders, and the power swept around me and propelled me forwards.

I couldn't see well enough, and I wasn't prepared. I made it three steps, three vast, bounding steps, before my left foot caught on the end of the path. It didn't matter how little the toes dug into the soil, at that speed; I sailed, gracelessly airborne, for a split second.

When I slammed back into the ground face-first, it was in shocked silence and two flares of pain, in no small amount of shock and a strangely bright lucidity.

That, I thought to myself, *is some bruised ribs and a fucked-up nose.*

And then the shouting started, and the apologies, and the laughter; but at least the only one laughing was me.

CHAPTER 2.9 - LUNCH, AND THOSE WHO ARRANGE IT

My dramatic pratfall, the result of someone's kindly attempt to get me to the refectory faster, was hilarious—to me, at least.

That might have been shock, but it might not have been. I'd always been the type to laugh at myself when I did clumsy things, possibly because the alternative was to be laughed at while I wept, hissed in pain, or picked up the pieces. At least if I laughed, the logic went, people were more inclined to help me clean up; and so it became a habit, and at some point I internalized that actually, I was just a slapstick comedy character and it really *was* funny.

The herder woman who'd given me the good-intentioned benison was a stocky woman in flowing, crimson-and-blue robes that failed to hide her muscles and graceful movements. She introduced herself as Rael, and extracted a promise from me to not tell Rafa just what had happened. I emphatically so swore, and the murmur of **[Healing Wind]** poured through my mouth and nose, wiping away the pain with a tangible and audible shifting of cartilage and flesh. It did nothing for the blood—which I could feel crusting on my face—or the dirt, but it was enough that when I took a full, deep breath, there wasn't a hint of pain.

Rael was right behind me heading into the refectory, which I hadn't realized until the eyes of a dozen people shifted from me to her.

"Sorry 'bout this, Thesha, all of ya." Her accent was thicker than it had been when she'd talked to me, like she was playing it up. "Don't get too mad, but I sorta gave the girl a tumble by accident. Girl was makin' good time, I tried to help."

"Rael." That was Rafa, sitting at a table about a third of the way down the hall. Her voice effortlessly carried her mix of disappointment and rough humor. "You make more work for me?"

I glanced back at Rael, wondering why she'd even asked me not to tell Rafa about it if she was going to just… do that herself. Rael caught my eye and winked, just enough for me to tell, and my brain skipped back to what she'd said.

"She fixed me up, ma'am." I grinned at the healer, letting her see how abashed I felt. "Actually, it was really fun for the three steps or so I lasted before I wiped out."

"You!" Heavy, fast footsteps heralded a middle-aged woman whom I tentatively identified as Thesha on the basis of her apron and general air of total local authority. I'd have read her as in her sixties on Earth, but she had a face composed of smile lines and crow's feet *here*, so she was… in her second century, at a minimum.

And maybe her eyes were crinkled in humor, but her mouth was drawn in a scowl.

"Auntie, this is Sophie," Rael said hastily. "She's—"

"I know who Sophie is. Traveler, she is." She drawled it with a hint of a dipthong, sounding more like she was saying *trayvlah* than anything else. Hands on her hips, she held the scowl until Rael raised her hands in surrender.

"I'll just—"

"Sit *down*, Rael. I'll bet you used a Skill to heal her up. Were you thinking you'd tough out the price? Go out muzzy-headed tomorrow when something might come from the Forest?"

Rael winced. "I have travel-bread and some of last harvest's—I mean, no. Thank you, Auntie." She backtracked smoothly, smoother than her awkward words suggested, and made haste to sit.

"She's being kind," I murmured softly, "but I really wasn't going to make it on time, no matter what she's implied."

"I didn't get to run a refectory by being an idiot, girl," Thesha said, rolling her eyes at me. "It's about having an excuse to not judge. Nobody gonna be mad at Rael, 'cause nobody *else* is that big of an idiot either; but nobody gets to be mad at *you*, because she's covering for ya. Now sit yourself on down and eat. **[All Things In Their Proper Place]**."

Just like that, once the rippling wave of the Skill invocation faded, the cracking, crusted feeling on my face vanished. With it went every bit of itch or discomfort due to sweat, dirt, or grime. I touched my hair, which was suddenly *perfect*, neither too oily nor too dry, and noted carefully the way that Thesha's shoulders stiffened and one breath caught in her lungs.

Only one breath, though, and then she was unchanged except for a narrowed pair of eyes.

"Thank you, ma'am." I wanted to bow, or hug her, or *something*. Instead, as she chuckled and strode away, I followed her orders and made my way to the nearest table. Sitting down, I nodded to the people who made space for me—a man, two women, and a kid—and made sure that my face was set to a grateful smile rather than my resting glare-face.

"Zenith's blaze, Miss Nadash." The older of the two women spoke first, a motherly figure with callused hands and waist-length hair gone white. Everyone else echoed the words in her wake, absently, as they attended to the last of their food.

She was waiting for me to say something, and I reddened a little as I realized I was being rude by not reciprocating. "Zenith's blaze, ma'am. Please, call me Sophie."

"Theodora." She smiled at me, setting me at ease with her warmth and the kindness in her eyes. "How are you finding your first days in Kibosh?"

"Honestly, I'm still a little in disbelief." I grinned a little weakly at her, my stomach growling as the odor of everyone else's food wafted over to me. "Everyone's so *ridiculously* nice, your society is a dream, and the food is phenomenal."

"Thesha's a blessing to us all, may her name ring across the grasses for a thousand years." Theodora seemed utterly serious at that, for all that she was still smiling. "Levali, too, even if she isn't blood and bone to us wandering folk."

I was saved from having to respond to that by the arrival of my food. It was an enormous bowl of a dense soup, almost homogeneous, thick enough that I could almost imagine eating it with a fork instead of a spoon. There were more familiar flavors in there, though it occurred to me that I couldn't trust my memory—did the language supplantation include a substitution of flavors? My old languages had been taken away and replaced with new ones—had my memories of what fenugreek tasted like been changed, to match another world's herb?

I shoved the thought aside. *Fenugreek*, I thought to myself gamely, blowing across the wide, shallow bowl of the spoon. *Ginger, black pepper, salt, vinegar, aliums, chickpeas, and some kind of grain. Beans of some sort, dairy.* There were more flavors than that, but I couldn't recognize them; it all blended into a heavenly, creamy flavor.

I ate rapidly, half-listening to the table's conversations as I did. I lacked the context to make sense of the names and events, but they were talking about their herds and their duties. They compared different grazing grounds, the speeds of this name or that name, distances from the town or the Forest or other place-names I didn't recognize, and more. The kid sitting across the table from me listened intently, every now and then asking a question and getting another question in response.

It was, I realized, a puzzle of sorts. The endurance of the herd attendants—dogs and children, I was fairly sure—and the paths of the two Guard patrols were given, but the community had its own guard force. Those were a quick-reaction force, if I understood correctly, with the time they needed to arrive at any trouble determined by the resilience and strength of any given herd and the Skills and fighting strength of its attendants.

They weren't so much trying to find an optimal solution as just kibitzing. The actual schedule for the next weeks was the responsibility of a woman named Eymee, their Plainsheart—title or Class, I wasn't sure. The griping around the table was good-natured, the complaints of people who knew their concerns had been heard and a sensible set of decisions had been made regardless, and I relaxed into the mood.

It gave me some time to look around, at least, and I did so with undisguised curiosity. My table-mates were in the same style of sorta-robes that Rael was wearing, flowing garments in rich blues and greens, but my attention didn't stay on the *people* for very long. Thesha's refectory, as Kelly reminded me the Fall dining hall was called, was both exactly the same and totally different from Levali's, and I was fascinated by the implications.

The building's construction was identical, as was the basic internal layout. Same doors, same tables, both in the same places; same windows, same storage mechanisms for dishes. The people were different, though, and far fewer in number than I'd seen at dinner, rowdier and speaking with a pronounced accent whose implications I lacked the social context to understand.

Most strikingly, the decor was wild and gorgeous. Each wall was a beautifully executed mural of nature in one of four different biomes, and the flocks of Kibosh's herders roamed across them all: adults, children, dogs, shoats, and more ruminants that I only vaguely recognized.

There was a mountain wrapped around the entrance to the east, rugged slopes with deep canyons and tenuous carved paths working their way up the steepest faces. To the west was a forest that was recognizably the same forest I'd arrived in, only it had shadows with sharp glimmering angles and they didn't get the mosses right, or—more likely—the mosses were different in that area. An ocean sent its waves crashing into the jagged teeth of the low cliffs to my south, and on the north wall a rolling range of grassland hills sprawled into the distance.

Well, it was probably some specific kind of grassland, but even if this new world of mine had Earth-like biomes, I didn't actually know that much about ecology. The difference between savannah, prairie, and steppe was... something about rainfall, I was pretty sure? If it was a difference between different lengths of hydrocarbon chains, though, then I'd be good to go.

Come to think of it, I'd also be good to go if the question was a matter of how many nitro groups you could stuff into one molecule. That came from having friends into experimental unstable—read: wildly, uncontrollably explosive—chemistry; not something I'd touch even with a ten-foot pole and a blast shield between me and the fume hood. So, a different kind of *go*, one that involved sprinting.

I was about two thirds of the way through the bowl of soup when Kelly arrived. I caught her voice, a quiet protest against a firmer tone from Thesha, but not her words. Still, it was clear she was getting scolded good-naturedly for *something*, and I shook my head with a smile at the sheer domesticity of it all. When she approached a few minutes later, it was with two of the soup bowls in her hands and a relieved smile.

"Zenith's blaze, Mama Dora. Jannea, Annok, Tino." They nodded at her with a murmur of *Avara* and *Kelly*, making space for both the bowls—one to go down in front of me to keep my current one company and the other for herself. "Thanks."

"You look like shit, Kel," the enormous man—presumably Annok—said bluntly. "Do I need to call someone over?"

I heard her choking and glanced over to see her sputtering into a napkin. "No, Thousands *no*." She cleared her throat, taking a deep sip of soup. "I'm a little drawn, is all. Skill-use, a lot of it, but it was important. Thesha knows, I swear."

Annok nodded at that, looking entirely satisfied, and went back to his food. Jannea looked up, head cocked to the side and eyes suddenly locked onto me, and I saw an odd sense of calculation supplant her earlier disinterest. "You're the Traveler," she said softly. "I didn't realize."

"Yeah. First days in Kibosh and all. You're Jannea? Kelly mentioned that you're a painter, said it in a tone that suggests she thinks well of you." I turned to the kid, smiling at him. "And that makes you Tino. A friend of Kanatan's, I think? If I'm getting his name right."

"Yes, ma'am." Tino's voice was quiet—not exactly shy, just soft and reserved. It was a big contrast to how he'd been just a few moments ago, but then I supposed he'd been interacting with people he *knew* a few moments before, not a stranger.

I mimicked Jannea as she finished her soup, tilting the bowl to drink from a notch in the side and using a piece of flatbread that I hadn't noticed to mop up the dregs. Tino didn't seem inclined to say anything else, despite the conversational lull, so I busied myself with switching out my bowl and digging into my second serving.

This bowl had the same soup, but there were strips of meat and bits of something crunchy scattered across the top of it. The crunchy bits were nothing I recognized, but the meat was *powerful*, somewhere halfway between mutton and goat—shoat, probably. It was spicy enough to make my eyes water and my nose start running after a single bite, but the soup was even thicker with cream or butter than my first bowl.

It worked out, even if I wound up getting passed an extra napkin by a faintly smiling Jannea. *Maybe she's warming up to me based on my suffering*, I thought to myself wryly, but that was fine, because even if the smile looked forced, there was empathy in the gesture and something like kindness in her eyes.

Everything was fine, my food was delicious, and I was perfectly willing to focus on eating and let Kelly carry my side of the conversation for a while.

CHAPTER 2.10 - TO GLIMPSE UNCOUNTABLY MANY FUTURES

Jannea didn't say anything to me after our short exchange, but I noticed her glances, like she was judging or evaluating something about me. I ignored them and alternated between rapid spoonfuls of soup and blowing my nose, while Kelly tried and failed to draw her into a conversation about where she was planning to go after her apparently imminent departure from the village.

"In-ring, to the cities," she said eventually, as Kelly's probing became more blatant. "Different paints, different styles. Good for growth. Tayir tiered, village'll be fine. Avara, anything you need, anything the Traveler needs that ain't standard, you got a week."

That had Kelly's jaw snapping closed and ended the conversation, for whatever reason. "I don't really have any aesthetic sense," I offered, and Jannea's face fell momentarily before it went back to a distracted neutral amid a long moment of silence.

"Well." I stared at the empty bowls in front of me, feeling like I was one or two bites from being unpleasantly overstuffed. "This was… good. And necessary."

"I'll take care of your stuff. Why don't you—"

"Kelly, I feel like I can bus my own—"

"—take a look at your Paths?" She cut me off as if I hadn't spoken, which was reasonable, since I'd cut her off in the first place. "I know you didn't take long enough to do it, and I can see you're still sitting on the cusp."

"I… you're right that I haven't taken the plunge, but how did you— magic, right." I sighed over-dramatically, half laughing at myself and half performing.

"I wouldn't be much of a First Friend if I didn't have my ways." She tapped the side of her jaw twice with a finger, a gesture I recognized but still didn't understand. "Take your time. It's compressed, and nobody will mind. Won't tell you not to take the leap, but remember we haven't seen if you can take a Class from Tower, and nobody here's gonna *interrogate* you."

She levied a mock-glare on our lunch companions, and the folks around the table nodded, Tino doing so only belatedly. He did a terrible job hiding his curiosity, but the others made a show of going back to discussing things among themselves as Kelly got up, bowls and spoons in hand.

Apropos of my earlier thoughts, I wrote out in my mind, *I want to limit the all-out ham to two things at most—still only changes or new stuff. Try to condense things a bit more, and give me an indication for if I can get more information about something. That said, I think it's time to do the thing. Path Review, please.*

I focused on the idea of wrapping up the words in a nice neat bundle, and then on the idea of that bundle drifting inwards, heading somewhere with slow purpose. It connected more easily than previously, and I felt, distantly, an emotional warmth as though someone—or some*thing*, since it didn't feel human—were reaching out to offer a hand clasp.

The world faded slowly into darkness as green lettering wrote itself across the notional vision of my mind's eye.

Green lettering on black, like a throwback to my days writing code on a computer lab's terminal, filled my mind. Unlike other times I'd seen my System's reports, though, there was something flickering in the background. Everywhere I looked, there were ghost-images at the corners of my eyes, outlines of people in burn-in that disappeared when I tried to focus on them.

Stymied, still curious, I attended to the text instead.

You Consult With Your Divine Flame!

Current Path: *Mystical Chemist*

Behold, Your Paths Unfold Before Your Eyes!

My vision, the vision of my mind's eye in this System trance, shattered into a million pieces. Each of those pieces was a bit of the future, a node in a colossal web. Distant, dim ones linked to others, brighter and nearer. From there, they linked to brighter ones still, in a pattern that was... *ah.*

It wasn't a web. It was an immense tree diagram, with thousands upon thousands of pieces of possibility leading to fewer and fewer pieces as they grew in power.

I looked at one, willing it to come into focus, to help me understand. *Apprentice Artisan*, this very distant one was. I saw myself working a different trade every day, handling odd jobs for everyone under the sun. It was pleasant and interesting, varied and useful, but it didn't have any focus or any feeling of mastery in it. But what it led into…

Artisan was more of the same, a thousand different tasks, done with skill and competence. But at the same distance, at the same Tier—and this was a certainty, though I didn't know how I knew, which left me with additional questions—was another Class, *Fusion Artisan*. This one blended the skills and talents of a dozen different trades, fluidly applying one to another to transcend each individual trade. *Artisan of All Trades* did much the same, and a multitude of engineering-themed Classes rose out of each Artisan like a set of fine, overlapping gears.

I basked in an uncountable stream of potential futures. Each of them was a glimpse of what I could be, were I to make those particular choices, walk that particular path. And for all that I gloried in seeing them, they were not *comfortable* ones—the periphery was a mosaic of shattered lives, of misery and stagnation.

Without the spark, without the hunger to embody my Class and become the paragon of it, there wasn't another advancement. The Technicians mostly crumbled from the burnout, so many of the Druids died a thousand ways in the wild or ran from the dangers, and all the Runeworkers and Scribes set aside the tedious work to live a life of quiet ease until old age claimed them.

But even on the edges of my vision, there was more than one Path that grew to the fourth level of that vast array of possibilities, becoming so bright in its radiance that I couldn't look at the shards directly. *Student of the Law* grew into a community leader, a powerful woman who radiated the safety and comfort of home across a village that grew into more: a font of philosophy, law, and theology. One *Mathematician* learned to see the way the future might unfold from studying the past and present; a *Hedonist* gave herself to those who wanted someone to *experience* something—art, cuisine, writing, theory, and more—until she could twist her perspective, until she could live any moment through fresh eyes or jaded ones with equal ease.

A *Clerk* became a multiply-connected node of forms, a *Locus of Processes*. A *Scientist* challenged every theory and belief, becoming a *Spark of Truth* or a *Breaker of Myths*. An *Agent* matched people to each other and needs to surplus, becoming a *Matchmaker* or a *Logistics Expert*.

Examiner, judge, cook, and more, all on the fringes or in the distance. There were a lot of blank ones, maybe as much as a quarter of them, representing directions I could go that I didn't know about, but even as it was… the visions of all these paths I could follow—all of the Sophies I could be—spun before my eyes, and I drank them in until I could wait no longer.

I took a deep breath and looked at the ones that took up the center.

I leaned against a wall, arms crossed, half-glowering and half-smiling at a fractionating column. Liquid dripped from a half-dozen condensers into an elegant array of piping, each taking liquid to a different flask. From there, they were heated or cooled, were mixed with other liquids or had gasses bubbled through them, and eventually found their way into flasks that slid out into racks when they were filled just-so.

My mind's eye blinked, and the image changed, and changed again.

Dressed in full protective gear—protective gear that glowed and whispered of each airborne molecule it ate—I painstakingly let two drops of a sizzling green liquid fall into a flask that was half-full of thick bits of resin suspended in an amber fluid. I immediately slid the tray the flask was on into place, and moments later thick purple smoke bubbled out of the flask. Three seconds later, it shattered in an explosion that rocked the thick primary containment vessel, spiderwebbing it and releasing vapor into the secondary that hissed and bubbled at the glass.

Sleeves rolled up to my shoulders, I worked side by side with a seven-foot-tall woman with utterly implausible musculature as we pushed at the vat on rollers until it slammed into place, shaking the piping it was now locked onto. The primer in it churned as the heat kicked in and the stirring rods began to move, and soon a precise stream of ingredients was pouring into it. We switched to the other vat, rolling it out; with a grunt of effort, it slid cleanly into the output system, and the thousand flasks for that batch's healing potions started filling.

It was… glorious. I wanted more; I wanted to see a thousand slices of these futures, live those lives by proxy. I wanted to dwell in those moments and grow even more amazing, more that awesome figure I was in that shard.

Mystic Alchemist. Alchemist of Volatility. Production Alchemist. And those were only the start of it, just three possible paths through the third Tier; I couldn't see where those lives would take me, but I could get a sense of how many directions they could go, and how far.

It felt like they went to the ends of the world and beyond.

Alright, System. As excited as I was, my mental writing went cursive, all loops and curves with an illuminated capital at the beginning of every sentence. *A lot of those paths you picked for me look great. Amazing, excellent, an undisguised blessing. But let's wake me up now without picking one, because due diligence is what it is.*

I folded it into a letter, sealing it in wax with the swooping, sweeping SN that I'd gotten a seal for, back when being Sophie Nadash was new and my continued studies hadn't ground the whimsy out of me. And then I sent the letter onwards and inwards, and it slid into a place that I still could neither see nor touch but which was closer than ever.

Your Divine Flame Heeds Your Will!
Class Evolution Remains Available.

When I came to, looking around at the world again, I was alone at the table. I was fairly confident it had only been a few minutes, but the others had been done with their food for a bit. That suggested that they'd been sticking around mostly or entirely for social reasons; I didn't know whether I'd been rude by sitting down there, but I could ask Kelly that later.

Speaking of Kelly...

"—yes, ma'am," my First Friend was saying to Thesha, nodding rapidly as the refectory manager considered her levelly.

"Nice girl. Good attitude. Shoulda brought her by this morning."

"Auntie, I—"

"C'mere, Traveler."

Between Thesha's expectant look and the command in her voice, there definitely wasn't any mistaking that as optional. I walked over to them—they were just a few steps away, obviously deliberate on their part—and grinned sheepishly. "Hey Kelly. Ma'am. Didn't mean to eavesdrop."

"Didn't figure you were." Thesha squinted at me, frowning, and I felt a tickle of something, like a warm but slightly itchy blanket being wrapped around me. It was familiar and considerate and not entirely comfortable; if

I'd had to put a name to it, it would have been *Grandmother-in-Law's Gaze*. "Hm. Not as bad as all that."

"Like I said, Auntie—"

"Girl, you got air between those ears? Did I use a word like *negligence*, or did I say we shoulda had a conversation? Ain't my job to go through books looking for nutritional tables. That, I shoulda heard from you. Sure, standard is *fine*, won't kill her to eat standard, but if she's eating for two at a sitting, it's easier to plan for it, especially if you're both getting baskets on top of that."

"Auntie, I just didn't want to—"

An utter stillness rippled out from Thesha, and my heart skipped a beat as her eyes flared in a mix of indignation, anger, and disbelief—and more emotions, but I couldn't parse them out. "Kelly Avara, you were *not* about to say you didn't want to put me to bother." Kelly's breathing went shallow, almost panicked, as Thesha's tone sharpened with every word. "The day I need a girl not even in her century to make decisions for me 'bout my refectory is the day after I'm given up to the Forest and its crows."

"Yes ma'am," Kelly whispered into the silence. The rest of the refectory was visibly carrying on in the background, but we couldn't hear even the slightest sound from the room. "I mean, no ma'am."

"I expect this'un will want to rest this afternoon, and you'll be at Tome. You can bring me a copy of the Adaptation Summary."

"Yes, ma'am."

"Thesha, ma'am," I broke in quietly, fighting the urge to step up to Kelly's side in support. "I've been running her ragged and going against all her best practices and protocols. It's my fault as much as it's Kelly's that she didn't have time to talk to you about what's best for me to eat or how much I'm eating."

I was going to say something else, but the look she gave me drove it out of my head. For a moment there was nobody in the universe but the two of us, and nothing about me that she didn't see.

And then the effect faded, and the sounds of the refectory kicked back in as the bubble of silence faded with it.

"You two go on and get this girl some rest," Thesha said in a carrying voice. "See that you both eat—this here's your basket, mind you don't forget it. And tell that Morei girl I say she was right to pass over Ellana this time."

The dismissal was unambiguous, and we nigh-on fled the building, almost euphoric in our reprieve.

CHAPTER 2.11 - VILLAGE GOSSIP ON THE MOVE

Escaping the refectory with some fraction of our dignity intact, we walked in silence for a bit, heading counter-clockwise around the ring road from Fall.

"That lady," I said reverentially, breaking the silence, "is absolutely *goals*."

"Not that I don't disagree…"

I glanced over at Kelly to see her raising an eyebrow at me. "Did you notice that when she scolded you, it was in a bubble of silence, and when she praised you, it was publicly? Thesha literally ordered you to go tell Meredith that she thinks you're doing a good job."

"I… huh."

"You're blushing."

She stuck her tongue out at me, blushing harder. "Nothing wrong with having an emotion. Thesha, what she says means a lot."

"Speaking of Thesha. If I understood right, this is a full meal for the two of us, on top of lunch and dinner?" I pointed to the basket Kelly was carrying, and she nodded, obviously grateful for the change of topic.

"Full meal for a heavy work-day. Your body's still doing all kinds of magic, and also you're not digesting as much as you will be."

"And you're running a bunch of Skills to… keep up? Keep ahead of me? Keep me pointed in the right direction?"

"All of that." Her face and body language were completely open as she started ticking things off on her fingers, like she couldn't imagine why she might hold anything back. "**[Intuit the Happy Path]** is the most draining one, that's a Feat-Skill." The words came with the usual shiver of the world, though I could taste or feel something about it, something like a whisper of a better future. "And there's more, obviously.

"I've got a Skill to understand your language better, body and words both, and a Skill to let you understand mine better. One to—well, you already know about Friend in Need, that one's actually the most draining *in the moment*, but I'm not using it constantly. Then there are Skills I lean on to help me remember stuff, keep a plan straight, learn faster, be better at what you need me to do, that sort of thing."

"Huh." We walked in silence while I chewed on that for a while. "So you're eating, what, five standard meals a day? And I'm eating eight? How long is that *eight* going to last?"

"Baseline, two more days, and then it'll taper like a cliff, Thousand willing and the grasses don't burn. Five meals on your fifth day here, then down to whatever your new baseline's going to be. But!" Kelly turned her head as she picked up the pace, smirking at me. "You're gonna need more than baseline, once you Class up from Worker. Every level's got changes to your body and soul, and the same with every Skill you pick up, improve, evolve, or fuse. And all that takes fuel!

"At a guess, you're gonna be eating like this for three more days, not two, and you won't taper nearly as hard." She shrugged. "That's just my guess. Probably won't be less, might be more."

"Huh." The amount of food they'd been shoveling into me—and the amount they expected to *keep* feeding me—put a vastly different spin on the food situation in the village, especially given that I was being fed for free. "How do they raise enough meat-animals for the amount of meat I've been eating? Even just this basket was... kind of a lot, contextually."

"Well, there's a few things. Rakin grow about a pound a day on two pounds of feed, 'cause of at least three thousand years of breeding programs before Shem even existed, and they're kid-work, it's so little handling. That's for feed-fed, but we got wild-fed fish that do maybe a half pound a day and about half that for cote-birds, but they keep the weeds and bugs down something fierce."

"That's—what the *shit*, a bird that grows by a couple pounds a week?"

"Uh-huh! That's mostly post-System breeding." We started rounding a curve, Tome—or at least the administrative gatehouse—coming into sight. "Magic isn't much good for making more *meat*, but it can sure make meat last and not go bad and stretch the meat without stretching the taste, so that helps. Hunters sometimes bring in game, herders sometimes bring in some of that and some of what attacks 'em, and adventurers chip in once in a while if there's a monster that's edible."

"That... makes sense."

We walked in silence for a bit, and as if that was the cue, suddenly what must have been a social bubble around us disappeared. I had been noticing people speaking to one another with a careless ease that suggested both a lack of haste and years of familiarity, but now a few of them hailed me as we passed.

They did it with a kind sincerity that suggested that to them, every stranger was a potential friend. Kelly chatted back, trading mostly friendly gossip and also the occasional jibe; I exchanged names, forgetting theirs immediately and half-worrying that they'd remember mine.

Tome, the south end of the village—so named because of the library and the administrative work being done in the guardhouse—was full of life. Kelly had said there were twenty-seven children in Kibosh, and I didn't think there were quite that many around, but there were definitely more than a dozen. If I guessed the demographics right, maybe all of the children who weren't visible were with the herds or napping; I hadn't forgotten the one kid with the pipes, on my fateful and excruciating walk.

Most of the older children sprinted across the green spaces and wove around trees, playing some sort of complex game of tag or hide-and-seek. Meanwhile, the younger ones rested, wandered, or played quietly, in one case by carefully plucking out a single blade of grass, giving it a tentative lick, and then moving on to the next blade.

All of this was under the benignly watchful eyes of a few adults, lounging about with an almost entirely casual air of neglect. It didn't escape me, though, that while they were performatively unconcerned with the children who were running around towards the road and Tome's square, they kept a much closer eye on the ones who were closer to the guardhouse and the squad of probably-soldiers training there under the just-after-noon sun.

One of those, a kid who looked to be somewhere in the vicinity of three years old, approached me with rapid, determined steps. I caught one of the minders, a man of such unremarkable and mundane appearance that I was absolutely certain there was something supernatural involved, rising as if to intervene; when I stopped and squatted down, he sat back down.

"*Khulu, son of Matsdaku and Tmula,*" he murmured across the distance. I nodded at him gratefully, though with no idea how he'd done that, and turned to make eye contact with Khulu.

"I have a bird," he said without preamble, ignoring Kelly entirely. He drew out the vowel, *buuuuuuuurd*. "It's big. Really big."

"Really." I gave him my best serious, considering face, fighting not to giggle. After a moment, I nodded. "It's good to have a big bird."

"Her name is Kanja. She's awake now, but she'll be sleeping soon. Do you have a bird?"

"No." I shook my head slowly. "I did have a shark. It was blue and soft, and I would hug it when I was sad, and also sometimes when I was happy. Do you hug Kanja?"

"Sometimes." He stared at me, unblinking, and I waited patiently. "Kanja likes to eat worms," he eventually added. "Chomp!"

"That sounds like a good thing for a bird to do."

"Chomp!" He held his arms out, bringing one palm smacking into the other fist in a pretty respectable chomping motion. He did it again, harder, getting a louder smack but losing some of the clarity of the gesture. "Sharks chomp too! Why did you hug your shark?"

"I liked to think that when I hugged it, I was hugging everyone else who had ever hugged a shark like it."

He gave that serious consideration, then nodded—though whether he'd understood or discarded it as too confusing to care about, I had no idea. "Okay. Bye, shark-lady! I'm a message runner now!"

I watched him run off at a remarkable speed, letting the delight and bemusement show on my face now that he wasn't looking at me. Rising, I turned to see the man who'd sent that murmur smiling at me, chuckling softly. I nodded at him, shrugging a little and grinning a lot, and got back to walking.

"How did you…"

I turned to look at Kelly, who was boggling at me. "Little kids are fun when you can give them back," I said. I was grinning, which was only possible because of her expression. "I had a few niblings, before I… left, and some of my eventual friends had kids around."

That seemed to satisfy her, even if she obviously remained baffled, and she was content to chat with those we passed as we left Tome behind and I let my memories of what I'd long ago lost fade back out of mental sight. While we walked, she gossiped in a steady stream about seemingly every single person in the village, and almost none of it registered.

One thing did, because as my steps went from striding to plodding, she apologized repeatedly for how far we were having to walk. Apparently she'd picked my house—and it really wasn't sinking in that I would have *my own house*, a house that was also my own storefront and my own workshop, all rent-free—specifically to avoid being near the town's herbalist.

The woman—the Home Herbalist, as her Tier Three Class—was apparently a busybody. Worse, she was a woman with strong opinions about how other people should live and do their jobs, which involved not making any changes to the tried-and-true old practices

"She's more than three hundred years old, which, well, that's *old*, 'cause even three Classes near the top of Third hardly gets you halfway through that century." Kelly had handed me the basket so that she could gesticulate wildly as she talked, and I'd almost fumbled it—it was *heavy*, and she'd swung it around like it weighed nothing. "She came from an old, *old* herder family. Took some sort of Class in Animal Husbandry, then went Herbalist; she's almost the first-line doctor for the animals."

"Almost?"

"Eh, families, they have their own remedies, sometimes their own magic and Skills." She shrugged. "They figure it's always better to be able to deal with something in-round, right, just in case you need to deal with it on the move?"

"That… you mentioned that they're sort of semi-nomadic, right? So that makes sense. But what's special about this particular old lady?"

"Well, Kenna, she lives in a quint, y'know?"

"No, Kelly, I *don't* know." I poked her under the ribs with my free hand, eliciting a squeak and a flailing of hands but not, I noted, her moving farther away from me. "What does it mean that she lives in a quint?"

"Well, she's an herbalist, and that's a shopkeeping profession, 'cause she sells what she makes, and she needs a workshop cause some of it is processed, right? So nowadays she'd be living on the second floor of the shop and using the basement for a workshop, just like you're gonna at least for a while. But no, she lives in a quint and does business through the local agent, which nobody's done for like two hundred years."

"Huh."

"Anyway, Kenna, Herbalist Kenna, if she weren't from a herding family she'd be Matron Kenna but they really don't do titles like that, it's not like being closer to her is going to mean an easier time getting her herbs or something, since she only goes through the agent."

"Uh huh."

"She'd just be coming round to try to convince you to move to a quint 'cause you apparently can't integrate properly and *join the community* without living exactly like she does, which everyone knows is shoatshit, almost everyone who works a shop-trade lives off-quint."

I stifled a yawn, narrowing my focus to not shambling or stumbling. "Right."

"And it's not like the bugbears are gonna come eat you for living there; they only eat children who hide under the bed."

"That's very convenient for the parents."

"... oh, you *were* listening?"

"Not really." I smiled at her as best I could, failing to stifle another yawn. "I just have a really good yes-dear reflex with a cache, trained by decades of awkward relationship moments and experience with toddlers. Like I guess you saw."

She blinked a few times, processing what I'd said. "We're almost to Rise, and your house isn't much further than that towards Hammer. Let's get you into a bed so you can rest a bit, I'll go to Tome and Fall and be back before you know I'm gone, and then we can see Kartom after we eat some more food."

"I love this idea." I smiled at the road, keeping one foot going after another as a wave of sleepiness crashed down on me. I had no idea who or what Kartom was, and I couldn't find it in me to care. "I don't know if it's food coma or the magic stuff or what, but I love this idea."

"That's because it's my idea. And my ideas?"

I knew she was grinning smugly at me from the happy lilt in her voice. On the basis that it would get me a nap and on no other basis, I decided to humor her. "What about your ideas?"

"They're the best ideas."

I couldn't argue with that. Bless her, I certainly didn't *want* to argue with that. Not while we walked, not while I staggered up the stairs in my new home, and not when she brushed the hair out of my face as I fell asleep.

CHAPTER 2.12 - AFTER A NAP, A TOUR

Waking up was disorienting, to an even higher degree than I'd been used to.

Wisps of dreams slipped through my fingers as I reached for them, meaning fading as I came into lucidity. I was left with the feeling of having *known* what I'd been dreaming of, left with the certainty that for a fleeting moment I'd remembered. Remembered that bits and pieces had retroactively slotted themselves together into an incoherent whole, remembered that emotions had filled my sleeping mind that drove them to do so.

There was a terror in it, to some degree. Knowing that I'd known them so vividly was a reminder of the frailty of my memory, and my eventual dissolution; it was a reminder that even the greatest died, that even the sharpest lost their edge.

All in all, it was comforting in its familiarity in a strange and new land.

I had absolutely no memory of what my new digs—home, workshop, and shop all in one—looked like, or how it was laid out. Still, the bathroom was obvious from this vantage, and I could figure out everything else once I was done staggering to the toilet.

Enchanted bathroom, check. I grinned to myself, enjoying the novelty of it; I knew my expectations would recalibrate eventually, but the casual miracles that were Kibosh's toilets were bringing me a great deal of joy. The thought chased the last of the fog from my mind, and by the time my ablutions were completed, I felt like I could handle being awake again.

The sunlight helped. One wall of my room was mostly window, from well over my head down to knee level; and the bathroom had some kind of light-well in the ceiling which was bright out of proportion to its area.

My room led to a short hallway, and I paused there to contemplate my new home. It was a version of the single-piece stone construction I'd seen elsewhere, almost entirely plain, with a ceiling about nine feet high and a hallway that—at five feet from wall to wall—felt wider than it really had to be. The stone of the flooring was subtly textured for a better grip, but it was definitely *stone*, and uncomfortably hard against my socks; I had a dim recollection of leaving my shoes at the entryway, and made a note that I'd have to get slippers or rugs.

Illuminated as they were by a sourceless, soft light that left no shadows, I could see that the walls were textured too, but for looks rather than feel. They had an almost-invisible pebbling that both softened the severity of their plainness and emphasized a thin line of black stone about a foot above the floor. It did a decent job breaking up the otherwise uniform slate-gray color, and there was an odd depth to it, like the black had other shades of black hiding inside. *Another thing to add to the list of questions*, I told myself, and given how often I'd be seeing it I might even remember.

There were three rooms, and I stared blankly at the one across the hallway from mine. It was a mirror of my own room in every way, from the position of the bathroom to the sleeping pad, though the pad was in a deep purple with red trim rather than the pastel blues with white and pink trim of mine. Well, that and the fact that mine had been slept in and hers—

I pivoted away and opened the door to the third room, shoving the thought aside and reminding myself not to make assumptions. There was... nothing, absolutely nothing in there. *Remarkably* nothing; the room was a rectangle just as perfectly clean as the other two, but it was utterly bare. More windows and bigger than the other two, though, and they were already substantial in size; between the three of them, well, I didn't have a great grasp for space estimation, but the condo I'd lived in was a bit over a thousand square feet, and these put together were way beyond that.

My stomach growled at me before I could get sidetracked with finding something to measure with, prompting me to actually notice the smell I'd been ignoring in favor of looking around. A tantalizing aroma was coming from a basket I'd overlooked, sitting just outside my room. It turned out to be some absolutely glorious little wraps of some sort, and my brain went momentarily blank with anticipation when I opened the lid.

I forced myself to study the food and savor it as I ate, instead of just scarfing it down like I had at lunch. Yesterday's basket had been full of dumplings, some of them filled with meat and some with soft vegetables, and that had been delicious in a familiar way. This was meat that had been marinated in some sort of vinegar-based sauce, wrapped in bread alongside crunchy vegetables, and it was no less amazing, if strikingly strange. The bread was soft and sour, with just enough bite to offset its chewiness, and the meat was falling-apart tender and ridiculously flavorful.

The basket was split into two halves across the center, and I steadily ate my way through layer after layer of the cylinders of glorious food on one side. They'd been considerate enough to fill the waterskin at one end of it, and I greedily drank down about a pint of water in three long, all-consuming pulls. Food that I'd been in too much of a rush to chew properly—my best efforts to the contrary notwithstanding—worked its way down my throat with an urge to hiccup, successfully suppressed, and I reveled in the refreshing citrus taste they'd cut the water with.

I had to force myself to stop once I'd finished half of what was present. It wasn't that I was still hungry; it was that it was delicious, and I wasn't *full*.

I stopped anyway. Kelly needed her share.

"Afternoon's contentment!"

I spun around, startled by Kelly's voice. She'd ascended the stairs without my noticing and was leaning against a wall, smirking at me with a sparkle in her eyes. It took me a moment to still my racing heart and get my voice to come out level, but I was, for some reason, smiling about it. "I guess that's the equivalent of *morning's joy* for this time of day?"

"Yep!" She pushed herself off the wall, grabbing me by the elbow that had the basket. "Come on! Let's go downstairs! I'm excited, are you excited?"

I popped another roll into my mouth, chewing deliberately as I walked with theatrical slowness towards the stairs. "Extremely," I said once I'd swallowed. "I've never been so excited to ask someone a question, and that question is this: what are the other equivalents? I can guess that zenith's blaze is for noon."

"Sophie!" Kelly grabbed at my arm to try to speed me up, playing at a tone halfway between whining and scandalized. It would have been more effective if she'd stuck to one or the other, or if she'd been able to stop herself from smiling; as it was, she barely avoided giggling, and I knew for a fact she was strong enough to pull me off my feet, even if she'd said she couldn't carry me.

"It's an important question! Is it *evening's post-dinner sleep coma*?"

"Evening's ease." She sounded surprised. "Night's slumber, howl's caution."

"Huh." I set my pace back to normal as I went down the stairs, appreciating the railing even if it was a little lower than I was used to. "Kinda weird that my guess was so close to right."

"It's probably 'cause of the System swapping out your languages, right?"

"I guess. I've got *some* idiomatic stuff, at least."

We descended the stairs the rest of the way in silence, mine thoughtful and hers expectant. My whistle of surprise when we got to the bottom was enough to get her giggling, which was rather the point; but it was genuine, if a little exaggerated.

The ground floor of… of *my house*, astonishing as those words seemed, was about three thousand square feet in footprint and had a high ceiling, maybe ten feet or so. Rectangular, almost entirely empty, and made of that same stone in the same pattern, it had a staircase leading up, a staircase leading down, a counter in the center, and a tremendous feeling of potential.

There were little notches in the walls at regular intervals whose purpose was unclear to me, and hooks in the ceiling that I expected would serve to hang things from. Gloriously, along every wall there were windows that ran from about two feet off the ground to about two feet away from the ceiling, with only short stretches of stone between them. The afternoon sun shone through and lit the room with a warm glow, and my face hurt from how hard I was smiling.

"Windows aren't any less sturdy than the walls, most times." Kelly rapped on one of the windows as if to demonstrate. "But if you're *trying* to break one, it'll pop right out, 'cause… well, you can probably guess."

I absolutely could. "Toxic gas potion shatters between you and the door. Oops!"

That got a snicker out of her. "Happened once, someone figured out how to modify the enchantment, modification went into the book, Standard Plan adopted it. Anyway! Come on! You think this is where we're heading? Let's see the workshop, 'cause *that* is the whole point of this place, right?"

"Let's."

This time, I led the way down the ramp—not another set of stairs, as I'd initially thought, just a ramp made to *look* like stairs for whatever reason, which seemed like a horrible idea and which needed to be changed as soon as humanly possible. Kelly followed in my wake, vibrating with a barely suppressed anticipation and glee, and for a moment I was worried that her expectations would set an unattainable bar.

That didn't, as it turned out, happen.

The basement was a two-part workshop with twelve-foot-high ceilings and very familiar shelving units serving as a wall between the two areas. Along the very top of the outside walls, there were angled light-wells that brought in a surprisingly substantial amount of light from the outside and showed a bit of blue sky.

That was only the tertiary illumination, though. The walls themselves glowed, and a swirling pattern of orbs glowed a couple of feet down from the ceiling, hanging on silver threads that were thin enough it took effort to see them.

"I like that it has the same herb hooks as Hitz's did," I said, gliding forwards. "It gives a nice witchy atmosphere, especially given how low stuff will hang. The cauldron will be a bit much, though, won't it? Even if I go Alchemist, it's hardly a controlled reaction chamber."

"Y'know it doesn't work to say that while you're grinning like that, right?"

"Oh, you noticed." My face hurt from smiling, but it seemed like everywhere I'd been today, there had been something new to marvel at. "This could be great, once it's stocked. And it's already so beautiful."

It was largely bare, which only made the cauldron stand out more. It was in the center of the main workspace, with a large table and two small tables bracketing it on three sides. Close enough to reach, but far enough away not to be crowded, and there were gaps I could pass through; on a hunch, I bumped a table with my hip, and it failed to budge at all.

"Anchors at the bottom of the legs," Kelly said, pointing. "They bind the legs to the stone, unbind if you twist. Same thing with the cauldron supports. They're iron, not steel, but I'd break before they would. I dunno what this is, though, on the table."

I snorted, looking at the apparatus on the tabletop. A round flask covered by a cap, and a tube heading down from that cap to a much smaller glass chamber? I recognized that, alright. "It's an alembic," I informed her. "Timeless, by which I mean the basic design was five thousand years old when we invented fractionating distillation."

She giggled, which was tremendously rewarding for such a feeble joke. "How does it work?"

"This big flask is a retort. Well, technically most of this assembly *put together* is a retort; the flask is actually the *cucurbit*. We put a liquid in here, see, through the tap on the top—the head is on top of it, we'd have to disassemble this to fill it up." I wiggled the round bulb that capped the large flask, waiting until Kelly spotted the intake valve and making a note to myself that one of the words I'd used wasn't in Shemmai. "Then we put it on a burner, which there isn't one here, and vapor condenses on the glass of the head. The condensate flows down through the tubing into the receiver, and we've got distillate."

"Got it." She nodded slowly, studying the alembic and running a finger across its parts. "I'm gonna have a lot to learn. I mean, if you take up alchemy as a Class. And if you don't, you're still getting the workshop, you could still do it as a hobby."

"Yeah." I stared at the alembic, wondering how long I'd be using it. "I'll teach you what I can, if we wind up doing this and you want to help. Then again, wherever I wind up, I'll have a lot to learn." I turned to grin at her. "You'll probably be teaching me too, right?"

She had her hands on her hips, leveling an almost entirely mock glare at me. "*If* I want to help? Sophie. Helping you is literally my job and the core tenet of my Class."

I nodded, grinning wider. "Then no matter what I pick, we'll teach each other as we go. And speaking of which." I gestured around the room, which had nothing left that we hadn't seen. "Where do we go now?"

"The Tower." She nodded at the ramp, letting me precede her up it. "We'll bring you by Kartom, he's Tower Senior here right now. Introduce you, and have him test you for magic and see if you have any other Class choices we haven't considered."

CHAPTER 2.13 - A WALK IS A GREAT TIME FOR CIVICS LESSONS

Magic.

I'd always loved the aesthetic of magic, when it was done well, for a very biased version of *well*. There was always a sense of power to it, this idea that by communing with or manipulating an aspect of the universe more fundamental than mere physics, you could break all the rules, but that wasn't even the main draw.

It was the sense of *wonder*, the grandness of it and emotional connection. Even when magic was a matter of mathematics and diagrams and an eldritch intellect beyond the ken of mortals, there was still a wonder to it, at least in my mind.

I dwelled on that as we walked. It wasn't particularly late in the afternoon, which meant I'd only had a short nap but I felt wonderfully refreshed; no doubt the result of some enchantment or another, maybe from the house or from the quilt I'd wrapped myself in.

Kan declined to comment.

He'd been waiting outside, much to my surprise. He made some excuse about having too little to do until the Stone Team went out for their next job, but the casual ease of his banter with Kelly told a different story, one of genuine friendship. They had a kind of social intimacy that let them poke fun at each other and find a shared joy in it, and enough of a history that it was laced with in-jokes; and I was momentarily jealous.

And then, as naturally as breathing, Kelly drew me into it. She giggled at my jokes and was quietly sympathetic after gently prying into bits of my own history, and pretended not to notice when even just that little bit of empathy from her had me fumbling for words.

She changed the subject instead, and we talked about civics.

"With Kibosh, specifically, everything revolves around the dungeon and what we pull out of it, even if almost nobody interacts with it directly." She'd taken up something of a lecturing mode, one which she'd *definitely* practiced. "We sell goods on to Hayir, the nearest town, sure; some of those raw, some of those finished. But there wouldn't be a Kibosh if someone up the chain in Writ hadn't said to old Mararie, 'We're expanding the bubble on the Forest side, go put the kibosh on this dungeon'. So we have the dungeon, and we have the Forest, and we tax folks on extraction and on the value-add work that they export."

I giggled, finally making a connection that I'd been wondering about for almost a full day now. "That's why the village is called Kibosh, huh?"

Kelly beamed at me in response, nodding. "Captain Meredith and her sense of humor—she wasn't Captain then, not until James became Clerk Administrator, but she was around and her name stuck. Anyway, we have a dungeon in balance, like everyone wants to have. It's growing at a rate we can handle matching, and we're not exploiting it so hard it goes to war. We get condensate and crystals—mana condensate, mana crystals—out of it, the monsters have monster parts somehow, there's a hundred different things growing down there that are useful in some way or another, and its tunnels run way underground and under a *lot* of ground, which is useful somehow for geomantic divination."

"Useful somehow, monster parts somehow?" I lifted an eyebrow at her. "Just somehow?"

"Yes. Somehow." She looked at me with performatively narrowed eyes. "If you want to know more about the *how* of the ore or whatever, ask a Geomancer or a Diviner. Like Ketana!"

"The *monster parts*, as Miss Avara calls them, are formed through a conversion of mana to organic matter which I admit I do not fully comprehend." Kan adopted a baffled, *I'm so ignorant* air that was just as performative as Kelly's pretensions to umbrage. "My understanding is there is an initial seed of material, which is often acquired through leavings and scavenging of the surroundings. From there, the dungeon performs growth by duplication and by manipulation of the matter itself. Mana is well-suited, in terms of efficiency, to recombining materials into higher-energy states through a variety of means akin to…"

I waited awkwardly after he trailed off, not sure if he was going to start up again. Eventually, I got tired of his more genuinely perplexed face. "Akin to?"

"I hesitate to confess such a thing, but I do not recall the term of art. Quite an embarrassing turn, after making pretensions of a lack of understanding!" He smiled at me sheepishly. "It is a thing which changes the shape of small biological components without itself being consumed in the process, through entirely physical means."

"Enzymes. They're biological catalysts, presumably you're talking about enzymes."

"Yes! My gratitude. Through both these and magical equivalents, base matter becomes nobler, and matter undertakes a transformation into something more, no longer purely mundane. These are tremendously valuable, rare, and a primary purpose of a Dungeon Village such as Kibosh."

We walked in silence for a bit. We were taking a path much like the one Kelly and I had used to reach the Hall of the Thousand, and it was… quiet, quiet and charming. We could hear the sounds of children at play from the south, past the Library, and the sounds of industry from Hammer to the north; but it was distant, muted, and the trees were thick between us and them.

"Thousand, Writ, Delve, Craft, Tower." Kelly broke the silence right around when it was starting to get awkward, at least for me. "We've been to the Hall, so I don't need to tell you anything about that. Writ is civil administration and *usually* the Guard, but Captain Meredith set up in the Gatehouse back before the old Captain-Administrator's Path went to completion." She and Kan both drew a circle over their hearts, a gesture I'd seen her do before.

"The Hall of Writ is largely a matter of contracts, in a village such as ours. Even so, all but the archival of them is done in what it pleases Kelly to name the Gatehouse, though properly it is nothing but the guardhouse at Tome's gate." Kan's eyes flickered away from me and then back, a gesture whose meaning I wasn't sure I was following; possibly an indication he had some history there. "There are few enough adjudications that our assigned Judge of Inquiry visits only at need. For routine matters? Writ numbers only these: an accountant of taxes and fees, for all that he would be better suited to Clerkship, and one Clerk-Adjutant who assists both the Clerk Administrator—who acts as well as the village headsman—and the Captain.

"In a township, these would be only the beginnings of their needs; an adjudicator who is secondary to a Judge of Inquiry, a place in the Judge's regular circuit for matters of sufficient weight, and entire teams who organize all manners of matters. But a township has fifty-fold our population." He broke off at that, as if not sure what else there is to say.

"So," I said awkwardly into the silence, "Delve?"

"Delve!" Kelly picked up the thread, and Kan nodded at me gratefully. "Every Adventurer reports to the Delving Guild, but it's not just them. Delve is responsible for the fortifications of the village. All of them, not just the ones around the dungeon; the skyroads, the outer walls, the attritional spaces and paths." She waved at the woven patterns of the stone path beneath our feet, and the thick greenery between each curve. "Like these!

"They also have a part of handling external security, but that's *mostly* a Guard thing. Adventurers will go into the Forest to fight for training, or they'll shadow one of the patrols—there's two—just to have something to do in their downtime, but they don't have direct taskings unless there's too much going on for the Captain to handle."

"The Guild of Crafts, you should consider a loose sectoral organization. They are not a Guild, properly speaking; such a thing is a voluntary association which pools resources and knowledge, at the cost of some measure of independence and profits. They are instead… hm. Are you familiar with the term 'union'?"

"Intimately." I grinned at Kan. "I have fond memories of the unionization fights we won against the Academy's administration. The number of laws they violated was motivational, even if it didn't get them in any trouble."

"They… I must admit a lack of understanding."

"She doesn't come from the nicest place," Kelly interjected calmly. "Let's leave it be for now, unless you particularly want to talk about it, Sophie?"

"No." I did, kind of; but way more than I wanted to rant about the bullshit I'd had to put up with to people for whom that would be sacrilege and travesty, I wanted to know more about *here*. "So it's an automatic sectoral bargaining unit, or a set of them for the various trades? And skill share, and advice, and legal consultation, and whatnot?"

"And more than that. Like, the Guilds—as opposed to the Guild of Crafts—will have a representative there, in a village like ours it's just one person who represents all the thousands of Guilds, and they're the person for consignments, for patent bounties, they talk to you about how wonderful joining one of the Guilds would be for you, that kind of stuff."

"I have no idea what a bunch of that means, but sure. And then… Tower? Which is the civic institution, as opposed to *the* Tower, which is the building."

"Exactly." Kelly nodded a few times, head bobbing. We'd diverged from the path we'd used to get to the Thousand, and we were now passing it, going northwards. "They handle everything mage-y. They're the pillar that has the most overlap with the others—Stone Team reports to both Tower and Crafts and works *for* Delve on the fortifications, and anyone who's a Delver and does mage-y things balances Tower and Delve."

"Mage-y, huh."

She *harrumphed* at me, and we both giggled. "Teamsters are actually the most split, 'cause they work with Writ, Crafts, *and* Tower, since even if they're not mages of any sort they carry magical goods, and sometimes Delve too. And there's some Writ-Tower folks, like a Weather Diviner, 'cause farming's actually Writ, along with herbalists and miners and, uh. Lumberjacks? Clay?" She shrugged. "I could look it up, obviously, it's in the Basic Books.

"And Copyists are Writ-Tower, 'cause all the book duplication is magic and the Library is under Writ. And technically, *technically*, every pillar head is a village councilor and that means they're also under Writ, but that's only for when they act *as* that. And not everyone is obviously under a pillar, like a merchant or the food broker or the refectories and travel houses, so they all fall under Writ."

I nodded slowly, trying to keep up. "So Writ is the catchall. What's the, uh, Basic Books you mentioned?"

"It's the thousand books every Library has to have in order to be, like, a Library instead of just a library." She spoke deliberately, and I could hear the capitalization in her voice. "You can't have a System-interfacing councilor or village head unless you qualify as a municipality, in Shem, and one of those qualifications is having a Library."

"Five hundred are the basic books of reference," Kan said sonorously and with deliberate drama. "Five hundred are the basic books of learning. These, any true Library must have; and also five hundred books of learning or reference which are not within the Basics, and five hundred of… no pedagogical value in particular." He leaned in, stage-whispering. "Leisure-reading. Often romances or adventures of a lurid nature."

I sniggered dramatically, grinning. "Sounds like I'm going to have to pay it a visit. It looks cozy, anyway," I added more seriously. "A nice place to curl up with a book."

"What Miss Avara has failed to disclose, perhaps as a result of it not being in her immediate experience, is that our professions and endeavors are more entwined than even this." Kan inclined his head to Kelly, who tilted her head back at him in curiosity. "The smithing team is just so: a team, bound by not merely shared intent but by contracts. Smith, strikers, and apprentice on the bellows; this is the minimal team, and those contracts are within the remit of the Hall of Writ.

"But who purchases these weapons? An enchanter, whose magic is a facet of the Tower; the Guard, who serve the Writ; an adventurer, who looks to the Delving Guild? And who provides the charcoal—if carbon levels are not managed with magic, as is traditional, and heat likewise—and the ores? These, too, are mediated by contracts, and the involvement of magic, and the sources are as diverse a realm as the road leads."

"As diverse as the road leads." I frowned, picking that apart. "Which is everywhere?"

Kan nodded. "And so entwined, we seek to be gracious and look to the duties which need completion rather than the jurisdictions they are performed in. And when such practices fail?"

He looked at Kelly, and she looked at me, rolling her eyes in mild exasperation. "Then it's James's problem, or if whoever's having an issue thinks he can't rule cleanly, it goes to the councilors, and they decide as five. And if whoever's having the issue thinks *they* ruled wrong, they can appeal to the Duchy, which I think has almost never happened."

"Twice."

"Twice, whatever, almost never!" Her voice bright, she clapped her hands together. "Anyway! We're here. Civics lesson over. Time for magic!"

CHAPTER 2.14 - MEETING THE WIZARD IN THE TOWER

Kelly's words rang in the air, and as they hung there the gates of the Tower of the Arcane, the Guild of Mages, swung open dramatically.

We paused to take it all in, but not for long; there just wasn't all that much to see. The wall flowed into a semicircular building that was—as far as I could tell—exactly the same height as the Hall of the Thousand, with a different set of geometric patterns in the wood-and-stone design. If not for that and the different shape, they might as well have been the same building, which was apparently a deliberate part of their design.

No pillar was more important or valuable than the others, Kan had said in an offhand manner, so each pillar was constructed to be precisely as grand as the others.

The first floor of the inside wasn't any more impressive than the outside, just a big open chamber with stairs leading up and down and a balcony with a row of doors. No furniture, no decoration other than the construction itself. It said a lot about my disinclination to be impressed by architecture that I could even think that, I supposed—I could recognize that what I was seeing would have been a simply stupefying level of artistry and craft back on Earth, it just wasn't making all that much of an impression.

I felt distantly bad about that, like it was a personal failing, but I was who I was. I felt much the same about the wizard waiting for us up on the balcony, for that matter; both that he was unimpressive, and that I should be ashamed of my mind leaping to that observation.

There was no doubt about the wizard bit. He was wearing a loose, wrap-around robe in dark gray and silver, embroidered with what looked like runes in turquoise and teal, and he had an almost offensively meager scraggly beard that was trying far too hard to lend him some bit of dignity. I might have expected him to be a little pudgy, just on the basis of a desk job kind of aesthetic, but instead he was scarecrow-thin and gangly.

Contrasted with Kan's sleek, slate-gray tunic and pants, my own skirt and shirts under a stylish coat, or Kelly's outfit with her dark blue breeches over bright blue leggings and a wine-red top under a black jacket? The wizard simply looked ridiculous.

He did, however, have impeccably perfect skin—not a spot of acne, though there was a weird tinge to his paleness—and three floating orbs around his shoulders that were inscribed with runic glyphs so dense they blurred into each other, along with a floating stylus of some sort that was inscribing glyphs into a fourth orb. So that was cool.

"Avara." His voice was awful, too; reedy and distracted, with nearly no resonance or carry. "I assume this is the Traveler, and you're here to have me test her."

"Afternoon's contentment, Kartom." Kelly smiled at him, brilliant and joyful. "Any interesting news? Has the Thrice Destiny adjudication ruled?"

"… afternoon's contentment, Kelly." He sighed, sitting down on thin air and becoming visibly more present in the moment at hand. "No, the Crown is trying to hurry it along, but the panel deadlocked *again* on which interpretation of the Integration Principle should rule, because *of course* they did."

"At this point, I guess that makes sense. I mean, it's the controlling principle of the whole challenge, in a way."

He sniffed derisively, getting up from his invisible air-chair to start pacing. "It's ridiculous. A farce. Even if the panel rules for the challenge, the Crown will rule for Thrice Destiny on the appeal. The Queen has made that abundantly clear."

"And is not that sufficient reason for the panel to deliberate and make the best possible ruling?" Kan strode up the ramp to the balcony, arms out. "Is not, then, the true purpose of this adjudication to make a show of the independence of the adjudicator?"

"Hmph." The wizard—Kartom—met Kan halfway, and they hugged in a familiar way. "I am content to leave *politics* to the rest of the family."

"They're brothers, aren't they," I murmured. "That's hilarious."

"Yep!" I hadn't looked at Kelly, but she obviously heard me. "Same cohort, even. Kartom is nice, he's just… focused."

"I can see the resemblance," I murmured. "I hadn't really looked, but they have that same sort of grayish undertone to their skin, don't they? Kan just wears clothes that contrast with it, but Kartom doesn't bother."

"And there's the way they talk."

"And there's the way they talk."

Above us, Kan's voice was getting accusatory, and I tuned back in out of not-exactly-prurient curiosity. "—and Mother would be disappointed. You know this to be true, deny it to yourself though you may; I refuse to hear otherwise."

"I am far too close to a breakthrough to lose ground by leaving the Tower. The spell structure cannot—"

"—cannot be left alone or it will destabilize, I *know*, Karo. But how will you feed the spell if you do not eat?"

"My apprentice is more than capable of feeding the diagram; she is not yet capable of stabilizing it." Kartom gave another one of those derisive sniffs. "And before you ask or invoke our mother's specter for the purpose, *yes*, I am sleeping, but the stabilization requires the presence of a suitable anchor."

The two of them lapsed into silence as Kelly half-led, half-pulled me up the ramp. "You're ridiculous, Kartom. Extra-dimensional brain the size of a Hall, but you can't see the obvious solution." She poked Kan under the ribs, smirking. "Expected *you* to think of it, though."

Kartom's eyes narrowed in something like distaste. "Enlighten me, then, Avara."

"Have your apprentice—good decision, by the way! I know you fought not to have one for the last decade, but I'm glad you have help—get a walk-box from Levali for meals." His mouth opened, but she lifted a finger and tapped him on the lips, cutting him off. "I know what you're about to say; Levali's not gonna be okay with it. Which, normally she wouldn't! But.

"*But*." She paused for dramatic effect. "The cold-orb she uses in one of her fridges is down past the sustainable threshold for Keldren's throughput."

"You are in no doubt as to this," he said after a moment. "How?"

"Oh, you know me, I talk to people." She smiled one of those brilliant smiles of hers, the eye-catching ones that set her eyes to sparkling. "They have fifty gallons of dairy that need purifying, and Levali can handle the input into the orb for now, but—"

"—not for more than a season, due to the cascade failure effect in the design." Kartom grimaced. "It pains me to take even so little time as that away from this work."

"When should I tell her you'll have it ready?"

"Hmph." He frowned at Kelly absently, but I could tell his attention was elsewhere. "Thirteen days at the ambient rate."

"And if you get the baskets, that's… I have no idea, actually! How fast can you metabolize food into usable mana?"

"For aspected mana? A week. I am no Archmage, to shatter the limits of the Ownership Principle."

"My brother," Kan said, cutting in, "forgets a small matter; a cold-orb requires no aspected mana. Four hours to fully metabolize such carbohydrates as bread, longer for other foods."

Kartom scowled, nodding. "A third the efficacy, a third the efficiency, but it can be done."

"And the orb pattern is rated for a freezer!" Kelly's voice was brighter and cheerier than ever. "So will it still be inside the, whatever, parameters?" At Kan's and Kartom's nods, she clapped her hands together in satisfaction. "Great! I'll tell Shuli while you test Sophie."

I stared at her as she strode off down the balcony, momentarily stupefied. Something felt hollow as she walked briskly away, like the departure of her cheerfulness and energy was leaving a void behind.

Unwilling to entertain that line of thought further, I turned to Kartom. "I have," I admitted without a trace of shame, "very little idea what you three were talking about. I mean, I was able to infer a few things, but *wow* am I missing a whole body of civic life and magical theory that I'd need in order to actually *understand* it."

"Quite." He smirked, leaving it at that, and I snickered in genuine appreciation of his jab. It obviously wasn't the reaction he was expecting, and he sort of spun on his heel and headed down the hall to a different door than the one Kelly was now going through. "Well?" He paused, calling out over his shoulder. "You waste all of our time with hesitation. Follow me."

"Following you as now directed," I announced gamely—and loudly, just to make the point clear that he hadn't, in fact, given me any such indication beforehand.

That got a snicker out of Kan, who waved me onwards. I wasn't super excited about that, since I knew him and didn't know his brother, but I figured that Kelly wasn't going to do me dirty by leaving me with an asshole.

Or, well, with someone who was more-than-superficially an asshole, and if she *was* the kind of person to do that, I was kinda screwed anyway.

I shoved that thought aside for later, to go along with the other worries and the growing sense that I was going to be having a medium-tier freakout *real soon*, and followed Kartom through his door.

His office, which this obviously was, was oddly familiar. I'd seen a thousand offices like it before—cluttered but not messy, with each thing in its own place according to a filing strategy that made perfect sense to him and *only* to him. There was a narrow desk along one wall and a wider one perpendicular to it, the narrow desk covered in haphazard piles of wood and metal and the wider one covered in paper, orbs, a dozen kinds of styluses, and a heap of what looked like broken glass.

There was a chair behind that, the only chair visible in the room that wasn't covered with stuff, and he waved me to it, preemptively sitting on another one of his air-chairs as if he expected me to object.

"How much has Miss Avara explained to you about this?"

"Basically nothing." I made note of the respectful tone and form of address; it was interesting that he used it only when she wasn't around. "Just that I'd be getting tested to see if I could qualify for a magic-using Class in short order, and if so, what Classes might suit."

"Adequate." He rifled through a pouch—one of five identical pouches—hanging from a hook on the wall. "I presume you have not so qualified?"

"Nope." I had specifically asked Kelly about whether a few of them counted; her reassurance that none did was a relief, given my lack of inclination to take the Classes in question.

"Take these." He handed me two sticks, each with a clear grip in the center and with a bulbous shape on each end. "Squeeze them with enough force to activate the muscles of your arm. There will be an unpleasant sensation; endure it."

I squinted at him, tempted to demand more of an explanation than that, but forbore and squeezed as instructed. "Shit, you're not kidding. This itches." It wasn't a physical itch, either; it was an itch at my System bridge, like there was a metaphysical grain of sand in my eye.

Kartom seemed entirely unaffected by my expression of discomfort. "There will be a new, differently unpleasant sensation in a moment. Continue gripping those, and attempt to invoke your Divine—your *System*."

The grain of sand was gone. In its place was a distance, like my System was just out of reach. I focused on the mental bridge, on trying to replicate the feeling I'd gotten when Meredith had guided me to activate it. It was like trying to grab something that was multiple feet away; I was stuck wishing for telekinesis.

"Enough. Return them."

"Huh? Oh." He had his hand out, and I carefully put the two sticks, whatever they were, back in his hands. "That was weird. Felt like I just… couldn't touch it, couldn't reach far enough."

"Yes, well." He shoved the sticks back into the pouch, then stood up. "We have spent enough of my time, necessary though this was. Avara!"

"I was definitely not listening in or snooping!" Kelly stuck her head into the room, grinning. "But since I'm coincidentally here, there's no reason for you not to tell me!"

"Nothing." She cocked her head at him, and he scowled. "No affinities," he clarified. "No projection, no manipulation, no sensorium.

"She is not, and never will be, qualified for any Class that interfaces with any magical energies."

CHAPTER 2.15 - WINNOWING DOWN TO THE LAST OF THEM

Not, and never will be, qualified for any Class that interfaces with any magical energies.

I waited a moment for that to sink in, mulling over it deliberately. It wasn't making much of an impact, and I wasn't sure why, but giving it a few more seconds didn't seem to be triggering some sort of revelation.

"Okay," I finally said. "So we're done here?"

"This—you—"

"How—"

"Sophie." Kelly's voice cut across the stammering of the two men, Kan having come within hearing range at some point. "It's okay to be upset, and to say so, if you are. I know you were excited about maybe getting to do magic stuff! Don't, like, bottle it in, okay?"

"It's fine." I stood up from my chair, careful not to grab for the desk to stabilize myself—I didn't want to knock anything over, and the stack of broken glass was way too close to the edge for comfort. It wasn't fine, obviously; it's just that my reaction was muted, like I'd known this was going to happen.

It ached, sure. But after my career? Oh, the budget can't support a cost-of-living increase, ignore the seven-figure bonuses going out to the admins. Oh, we don't think the lab really needs a scientist, we're not reapplying for that grant; oh, you know, everyone else is *leaning in* to get these experiments done, we need you to come in on the weekend, we need you to cancel your holiday plans, I'm sorry that your PTO won't roll over but this is *important*, we need you to step up.

Obviously I wasn't going to get magic. Obviously I wasn't going to be a wizard. I should have known that going in, and it shouldn't have hurt even this small, muted amount.

I pushed the thoughts aside, along with my self-awareness and introspection. "Are we done here?"

"Sophie, honey..."

"I didn't actually expect to get anything magical." I shrugged at her, and then at the other two. "I mean, it would have been neat, but I'm about as un-magical a person as there is, really. The most magical thing I've ever done in my life was get mistaken for a man by a goddess, who felt bad enough about that—and her violation of her father's hospitality rules—to send me here."

Even Kartom winced at that one, which, well, fair, I probably shouldn't have said that, and it wasn't entirely fair to Artemis. "Kan suggested you were something of a scholar," he said primly. "It would be reasonable to be... discomposed that a Class such as Arcane Researcher is barred to you."

"I'm not sure anyone survives..." I forced a little smile, searching for the words; the fact that they didn't *have* the words was maybe a point in favor of where I'd landed up. "I'm not sure if anyone's fundamental curiosity survives being an Academy researcher, where I'm from. If it isn't ripped out of you by abuse, it's ground out of you by stress and a dozen different pressures. All I want to do at this point is be comfortable and find my future on my own terms. And have some friends," I added, preempting whatever reaction Kelly was obviously queueing up.

"Well." Kartom sighed, holding out a hand to the side. A piece of paper from his narrow desk flew to his hand, and I watched with intent curiosity as letters wrote themselves on it in a neat, readable cursive. "It would, of course, be inappropriate were I to endeavor to convince you that you should..."

Kan quirked an eyebrow at Kartom as the wizard trailed off. "Should regret the circumstances?"

"That." He sniffed, but his heart obviously wasn't in the derision. "Avara. That paper contains the list of known Tower-affiliated Journeyman-Rank Classes she might nonetheless qualify for in less than a season. You may see yourselves out."

Kelly waited patiently as he turned to walk back into his office. He took one step, and then turned around with a sheepish expression.

"Ah. And, ah." He coughed. "Thank you. For alerting me to the matter with Levali's enchantments. You are a credit to your training, and a valued friend."

"We all look out for each other," she said softly. "And for the village. Everyone wins, here."

He nodded, clearly content to let her have the last word, and the door closed behind him. It felt like it carried a sort of emphasis, like the quiet *thunk* was a sign; there was a pressure urging us on, and I didn't fight it.

We started walking. I didn't really know where we were going, but I could just follow Kelly—and then I realized, belatedly, that there was a conversation happening and that I should be listening.

"—already have, Scroll Mage is a combatant, I thought I told him to rule those out, but obviously I didn't, he'd have listened." Kelly shook the paper dramatically as we walked out the Tower's door. "Assistant? At Journeyman, really? And... oh, come on, I don't even want to waste my time saying that one out loud."

I giggled at that, and at how she was obviously torn between getting mad and laughing herself. "That bad?"

"Test Subject! I didn't even know that was a Class! Why would he even write that down! *Wizards.*" She said the last word as though it were a curse, grinning. "Golemancer is out, unlocking it in less than a year would mean taking a contract in exchange for the unlock. That leaves... huh."

I waited a couple seconds, but she didn't say anything, just wrinkled her face at the paper. "Well? Gonna leave me in suspense?"

"Sorry, it's just... Runeworker, okay, I bet you could manage that. Binder, you're obviously literate, we'd have to summon something friendly enough to consent to the right binding, and that's a bunch of constraints—completely one-sided, for one thing, the only thing you'd be offering is the mundane parts of being bound here. That's not too unreasonable though, since there's no end of minor spirits who'd jump at the chance, the *real* downside being that the chance of personality bleed-through is more like a certainty. But *Ritualist*?

"The next Ritual is, like, Ease! That's in two and a half seasons! Unless there's something that people haven't been telling me." She stopped in her tracks, staring suddenly at Kan. "And it is *very* unusual that there's something that people haven't been telling me. Especially if it's something that affects what Class my friend and charge can unlock."

"If there is a Ritual being conducted early, I am not aware of it." Kan had a thin smile, an expression much flintier—*heh, flintier, for the Stone Team guy*—than what I'd seen on his face before. "My brother is not prone to mistakes, nor imprecise speech. Even less so is he prone to japes. And yet, I am not aware of such a Ritual."

"I hate to interrupt," I said pleasantly and entirely unconvincingly, "but does it matter?" They both looked at me, having probably forgotten that I was there. "It doesn't sound like Ritualist suits me regardless, and I am absolutely not doing Binder. So that just leaves, uh, Runeworker? For the only Tower-specific thing I have to consider?"

"You're right, sorry, I just..." Kelly pressed her hands together, taking a deep breath. She let it out a moment later, and nodded briskly. "That's my problem to go figure out, and has nothing to do with you."

"Except that we're friends."

She looked at me with a surprised expression, which, fair; I'd just surprised myself, too. It took about three seconds for it to melt into delight. "Except that we're friends," she said softly.

I breathed in like I was going to pull in the affirmation of that face she was making through my lungs. "Um," I managed with astounding coherence, and then mentally shook myself. "But like you said, later? Let me know if you wind up finding out something hilarious or need to rage in my direction?"

"Right. For now, this. You! My job!" She waved the paper in the air and started walking briskly, Kan and I following her along a path that led towards the south. "Mathematician, *Scientist*, Alchemist, and Tower Classes. We strike Enchanter, Inscriber, and Runeworker, now that we know you can't manipulate mana. They all need either magical ingredients or mana infusions."

"Were you not opposed to longer-term contracts and some decades of commitment to a Guild, we might yet suggest it. This, no doubt, is why they were enumerated." Kan's voice was distant, but despite his obvious distraction he was still managing to project kindness and consideration.

"She could do Runeworker by rote, even without infusions, and use an ambient focusing array." Kelly's voice made clear that this was a pro-forma objection. "Not a creative endeavor at all, though."

"Struck, then, for the same reason as Scribe," I say firmly in response to that, and they both nod. "Strike Mathematician. I did enough stats work back where I came from. I have absolutely no desire to yet again be the person telling other people that no, what they want can't be done with the resources they're allocating. Or, even more fun, that what they want to do won't have the effects they're claiming in order to justify the project."

They both winced at that, which suggested they were familiar—at least in theory—with that pattern. It felt bad to be cheered up by that; the attitude was, of course, the source of tremendous failures of public policy, but it was *relatable*. I needed a few things that were relatable.

Bonus points if they were relatable things I could complain about.

"Glasswork. How do you feel about glasswork, Sophie? Casting, blowing?"

"I am absolutely hopeless at doing crafts with any artistic merit." I managed to keep the bitterness out of my voice. Mostly. "Even when I have clear instructions, or a strong mental image of how I want it to look, or a pattern to match. Absolutely fucking hopeless. I could ruin a stencil project."

"That rules out painting, too." Kan raised an eyebrow at Kelly wordlessly, and she tapped the side of her jaw with a finger twice, smiling. "With Jannea looking to her future…"

"Jannea's apprentice becomes the new primary painter, and looks for a new apprentice?"

Kelly nodded at me. "Tayir. That's Jannea's apprentice's name," she clarified when I gave her a baffled look.

"Okay." I didn't bother faking embarrassment; I didn't even remember when I had heard the name, assuming I had. "So since I'm definitely not going to try to become a painter, what with my abysmal talents in the domain, that leaves… *Scientist* and Alchemist."

"Tell me about *Scientist*! All I know is that the word's Koshe, and that you already have the option open."

I had, thankfully, an answer already on hand for that. It had been an obvious question. "Kinda like a Natural Philosopher, but not exactly. That implies more a sort of observational, try to find plausible answers sort of vibe; your Natural Philosophers, semantically, *look for* answers. *Science* is about trying to find ways to prove the answers wrong, as a technique for determining what is real."

"Scientist." Kelly put a Shemmai spin on it, pronunciation-wise, and it felt like something clicked in place, a sense of *rightness* with the word. *I guess the lexicon just grew by one. System-mediated languages; now that's magic!* "Scientist, okay. Well?"

I opened my mouth to say something like *absolutely not*, and then closed it. This wasn't something to be knee-jerk or reflexive about, and I owed myself—and Kelly, and everyone else who was going out of their way to help me—better than that. This wasn't a decision to make in one day, even, and I'd have insisted on sleeping on it were it not for... well, the dream was sticking with me, like it was more than just a dream.

I mulled it over while we walked, rolling it around in my head. We were passing the houses when I spoke again, questions bubbling to the surface of my thought process.

"Ultimately," I said eventually, "I think the problem with Scientist is a sort of microcosm, or maybe a synthesis, of the problems with all the other Classes. How am I going to gather observations? How am I going to perform experiments? There's a ton of ways that magic could be changing how the world functions, and I can't sense it. Can I build... detectors? How hard and expensive would that even be?"

"Some of those aren't a problem. I mean, there's no reason you can't shadow people, you just wouldn't get experience from having *their* Class, you know? But... experiments and detectors." Kelly's excitement turned pensive. "I'm not sure. I haven't looked a lot into whether there's ways for someone without *any* metaphysical perception to integrate an external one, and experimentation is expensive by definition. So, it's something that's just a drain on earnings, I mean, it's traditional to have one as your third, maybe second Class, but as your first?"

"My brother's thoughts notwithstanding," Kan interjected smoothly, "I should think that such an endeavor would be blessed by the Tower, or perhaps—if you preferred it—by the Hall of Writ. My concern is that such a commitment would take you far from here in short order, when you have said you wish to stay."

"Alright." Knowing that it was an option for the future was... useful. "I gotta admit, there is something in me that's waking up, that little spark that drove me to study biology and chemistry in the first place. But specifically delving into the mysteries of the universe... it just doesn't sound *practical* at this point? If I want to... rest, I guess. Stay somewhere quiet and small."

They didn't answer, giving me space to work through it. I could study the mundane sciences here, and figure out how they worked observationally and experimentally in ways that didn't involve any measurement or detection of mana, sure. But other people were no doubt already doing that, and possibly doing that *better* than I could. They had money and backing and teams, and I wasn't actually a special intellectual hero brought here to save them from ignorance.

It had its appeal. It resonated with fond memories from childhood, before my studies and the publication grind and the utter tedium of actually running experiments had burned out all of my curiosity. But there was a flame in me that I'd lit that morning, and for all my dedication to due diligence, I knew I'd been spinning my wheels until I made the inevitable choice to follow it.

"A new start," I said quietly.

Kelly stopped in the middle of the path, turning to look at me. "So?"

"Let's, um." The intensity in her gaze hit me, and I stuttered a little. "Yeah." I grinned at her, re-engaging my brain. "Looks like I'm going to be an Alchemist."

Her sudden squeal reverberated in my eardrums, and she launched herself at me, wrapping me in a tight hug. "Yay! I'm glad you made that choice."

I hugged her back, for lack of any other idea for what to do or say. It might have stung, were it not for how glorious it felt to rest my head on her shoulder and feel the way her hands shifted along my back, feel the way her muscles shifted under my hands. "Thanks for the vote of confidence," I managed, grinning.

"Help to make the call, confidence once you do, and help by your side. It's what I'm here for."

And there was nothing to say to that—nothing to do but to start walking again, still grinning, visions of Hitz's warehouse with its swoopy tubing and distillation columns filling my mind.

CHAPTER 2.16 - OMINOUSLY, JUDICIAL PROCEEDINGS OUT OF NOWHERE

I didn't say much as we walked, content to listen to Kelly and Kan gossip good-naturedly. I wasn't even sure where we were going; it was a beautiful day, I was in friendly company that had no expectations of me, and I was content to enjoy the moment.

Our destination wound up being Tome, or specifically the administrative guardhouse. Kan peeled off as we approached, and I followed Kelly in as the silence between us grew more serious. The beauty of the day waned in my attention, and by the time we got there my mind was on alchemy, paperwork, and… responsibilities, maybe. Duties, debts and obligations.

James and two strangers—well, people I hadn't been introduced to yet; I hardly knew even Kelly—were waiting for us in a meeting room. It was across from the office I'd met James and Meredith in, a day ago and a lifetime ago, and for some reason I glanced into the office and caught a glimpse of Meredith looking at me. She nodded once, reassuringly, and then the door swung shut and I turned to face the music.

"Miss Nadash. Miss Avara. You have arrived in good time." James's baritone was still that smooth, comforting voice that had been honed to a soothing gleam. He smiled at me, impeccably the professional bureaucrat from the neatness of his dark brown hair to the ink spots on two of his fingers. "As this is a Ducal proceeding, there will be a formal record, which will enter into the Archives. Please, sit."

The chair he pointed to was stark, a plain and unpainted wood, uninteresting to the eye. That was in line with the rest of the room; the chairs, table, walls, floor, and ceiling were all utterly unadorned except for a seal on the wall facing the door. The seal was a blue circle with a yellow rim; a black line cut through it horizontally, with a city in white growing downwards from the center line and a set of triangles that I was pretty sure represented scales took up most of the upper half.

I sat, not sure what to expect. The chair, at least, was comfortable, and Kelly was beaming at me from the seat she'd just taken, so whatever was going to happen was presumably not a bad thing.

Come to think of it, all four of them were smiling at me, though the two I didn't know went instantly serious the moment James opened his mouth.

"I am James Morei, Clerk Administrator for the Village of Kibosh, a Dungeon Village within the bounds of the Shemmai Duchy of Aluf. With us here are Sophie Nadash, a Gods-transported Traveler and presumptive Scholar who arrived yesterday; Kelly Avara, resident of Kibosh and Scholar Nadash's appointed First Friend; Jonathan Mishka, whose banking and investment remit on behalf of the Duchy includes our village; and Judge Tala Fatei, whose Inquiry Circuit includes our village.

"The purpose of this Inquiry is to determine the degree, kind, and timeline of the support that the Duchy will invest into Scholar Nadash's intent to pursue a Path of Alchemy, and whether she enters into that Path with full intent and having a full awareness of her other options." He paused, and I felt like my heart was starting to beat again after momentarily stopping. "Judge Fatei, I would like to request that this Inquiry be sealed to casual access."

"Granted. Let it be that this record is made available only to those with a direct interest." She turned to me, eyes intent. Her voice was a low, firm alto, with some decent commanding resonance. It suited her, somehow, and suited the sheer gravity of her presence now that she was in business mode—a presence made only stronger by the intricate steel-gray braided hair that swayed as her head turned, and by the lines of age that creased her face. "This, for Scholar Nadash's edification, includes such people as are employed or studying for positions in administration, law, fiscal matters, or social support. It also includes those in the industries which directly relate to your chosen profession.

"There are more stringent degrees of sealing available, but this is the degree which was requested by Administrator Morei. If you have any concerns or objections, please voice them. It is both our collective duty and my vocation to ensure that all the results of this Inquiry benefit all parties."

I shook my head immediately. "I have an enormous number of questions, but almost none of them are immediately relevant. I would like to know if there's a title I'm supposed to call you, though."

"Your Honor is appropriate, or Judge Fatei." There was a very pleased note in her voice; apparently that was a good question, or maybe my response was a good response as a whole. "Will everyone else please state their preferred forms of address for the record?"

"Technically, I should be asking you to call me Advisor Mishka. But please, I would much prefer Jonathan." The man's voice was ludicrous, a deep thrumming bass completely at odds with his diminutive stature. It brimmed with energy, at least, which mirrored the twitching of his fingers as though he were barely stopping himself from tapping and fidgeting, as though he yearned to straighten the simple, perfectly pressed clothes that hung askew on his gangly frame.

"Likewise, rather than Administrator Morei, please call me James."

"Kelly."

I paused for a moment, thinking. *What do I want them to call me*? "While it's kind of James to offer," I said slowly, "I don't feel entirely comfortable claiming the title of Scholar here, no matter what my experience was back home. In formal settings I've usually wanted to be called Miss Nadash, but I'd be uncomfortable going by my last name with people who've asked me to use their first names. So... Sophie, I guess."

"Thank you." Judge Fatei smiled at me, and something about that expression started unknotting the tension in my stomach and back. "May all the Gods of Justice bless this Inquiry and grant Their grace to these proceedings." She said it like a formula, but also with a certain amount of earnestness, and she paused for a moment of quiet. "Jonathan, I believe that as a Traveler new to Shem, Sophie would benefit from a description of the standard terms and some degree of context."

"Yes, of course!" He pressed his hands together, taking a deep breath. Letting it out, he began reciting a clearly prepared speech in an excited tone, eyes sparkling. "Welcome to Yelem, and to the Kingdom of Shem, Sophie. Kelly has spoken with me about your home of origin, and I want to make sure that we're on the same page with regards to baseline expectations.

"Shem, as a matter of policy, requires all Duchies to provide the basic necessities to all citizens at no charge. The Duchy of Aluf interprets this as a responsibility devolving to municipalities, where relevant; as such, the Village of Kibosh has the duty to ensure your free access to standard housing, food, educational resources, appropriate medical care, and opportunities to walk the Path of the Thousand. None of this is a real imposition. In order to qualify as an accredited municipality, Kibosh must already be in a position to fulfill this duty at effectively zero marginal cost. Follow me so far?"

"Yeah." It was one thing to hear this kind of thing informally from Kelly; to have this land on me in one batch of information-dump in a setting this official was... really something. *Definitely not in Kansas anymore*, I thought to myself with a suppressed grin. *It's not exactly fully automated luxury space communism, but there isn't a place on Earth that could have made that boast.* "I follow so far, and I'm surprised and impressed."

"Thank you, Sophie, we all appreciate that." Jonathan flashed a bright, genuine smile, hands going wide to emphasize it. "So! I'm told that you, with help from Kelly, advice from a member of the Stone Team by the name of Kan, and likewise advice tendered to you by Captain Meredith Morei, have made a decision with regard to your choice of Class. That Class is Alchemist, at Journeyman Rank and without any qualifications, whose Path Review you have, I am informed, completed to your satisfaction. I'm also told that you have a strong desire to stay in Kibosh, access to travel and support elsewhere notwithstanding. Is that accurate?"

"I... yeah, I guess."

I was trying to suppress my frown, trying to just go with the flow—I had a decade and a half of doing that in performance reviews and job interviews, after all—but my discomfort was apparently visible. There was a shuffling of bodies and attention, and a narrow look from Judge Fatei.

"Sophie," she said with a gentleness that took me off-guard, "please elaborate. It's important that the record be as close to truth as possible, and not merely comprised of true statements."

"Okay." I shoved away the emotional reaction I was having, that it wasn't in fact okay. "Then I want to add that Kartom, whom I met today, tested me for magical aptitudes, and apparently I have literally none, zero, nothing. No ability at all to sense or control mana. That... helped narrow things down a lot." I tried to keep my tone level, but I was apparently more disappointed than I was letting on even to myself, and my voice quavered a little. "And also I don't know how you know this already, or in time to have shown up, since I made the decision *on my way here*."

"I'm on the Circuit." Judge Fatei smiled at me. "I was already here, Sophie, as I am once a season; I expect to depart in two or three days."

"I, on the other hand, received a message from an acquaintance here yesterday afternoon, and left this morning!" Jonathan grinned brilliantly at me. "I might have made less haste if Judge Fatei weren't here, but I might not have. With regards to Kartom, noted. I'm glad you mentioned that; Kelly had told me you'd met him, but I hadn't realized that he'd helped in the winnowing.

"Speaking for Their Graces, I have to point out that Kibosh is a Dungeon Village without an alchemist engaged in the manufacture of general-use potions, which means that the village is importing such potions as a cash expenditure. These see routine use, both in the economically central business of delving and in the Guard's maintenance of public safety. Since the Basic Set is price-fixed, the village is taking a loss—due to transportation expenses—on the vast majority of potions consumed, which is a meaningful reduction to the net earnings of the village and therefore to the taxes Their Graces collect. However!"

Jonathan's face lost its smile, and he looked slowly around the room at everyone else at the table. There was something meaningful in that look, something that had Kelly's hackles up and everyone else more alert, like we were finally getting to the real meat of things.

"Useful," he continued bluntly once he'd stared everyone down, "is not the same as necessary. Your background, I'm told, has lent you the opportunity to begin your Second Tier within the Destinies, the third of the Realms. I am aware that it's a path you don't want to follow, but you are absolutely capable of choosing from a wider range of Classes, and potentially more Classes within the Destinies, as you are today." He paused, folding his fingers together, then unfolding them and refolding them into a different configuration. "Why the rush?"

"Uh." I searched for a polite way to say it, failed to find one, and then shrugged. "Well, I mean, what else am I gonna do? I'm not even qualified to do manual labor here. I've got to do *something*, right?"

"I'm concerned that I might have been unclear." Jonathan's face was a rictus of utter seriousness. "Supporting a new resident who wants to do nothing more than curl up with a book of fiction had better not be a hardship to the village."

James cut in smoothly. "It is absolutely not any such thing. You have clearly had a difficult time in your early adulthood, in your world of origin; we would be quite content to be your home, with no expectations other than that you rest and heal."

"I…" I stopped, at a loss for words. I wasn't sure why I was internally rebelling so hard against what they were saying, and I had a feeling that it would take more time to unpack that than I had available. "I hear you," I said after a long moment. "I don't think I could handle that for very long, especially if I don't have a concrete goal in mind, which I wouldn't. I have… cultural hangups around the idea."

"Even so. You could take a series of non-binding apprenticeships, enter a directed course of study, or author a testament of your world of origin. What drives you to take up a Class on your second day here, and why Alchemist in particular?"

My mind flashed over to the dream I'd had the night before, to the emaciated man with the fluffy wings and the advice I'd heard, though I didn't know from whom. Was that… *no*. I didn't know where the certainty came from, but my desire to move forwards with this wasn't primarily because of a dream, no matter how eerie or compelling. That had been *advice*, not mind control—advice that I agreed with, but only that. The desire was… well. I *knew* what it was.

"There are a lot of mystical traditions where I come from," I said slowly. "Some of them were religious, and I belonged in some respects to one of those, but some of them were… esoteric, I guess, esoteric ways of understanding the world. And none of them were true, as far as anyone could tell, but alchemy was in a lot of ways the foundation on which modern chemistry was built, and I always found it compelling and fascinating. Not just as a chemist, but also as a person who struggled to find something to… replace, I guess, the tradition that I fell out of.

"That's the more serious aspect, I guess. The other side of the coin is that it's… beautiful? I went into chemistry not exactly *expecting* swoopy tubing and fizzing liquid in beakers, but inspired by that. Instead, I wound up as a glorified technician in a biology lab, pipetting ten thousand precise droplets for… well, for tedious steps in the pursuit of hypotheses that often were either nonsense, pointless, or insupportable. And in all three cases, the expectation was—it doesn't matter.

"I wanted swoopy tubing and fizzy liquids." I couldn't keep the bitterness out of my voice, but I *could* leaven it with an honest note of hope and yearning. Empirically could, since I *was*. "I wanted to find better ways of doing simple, useful things that had useful outcomes. I felt like chemistry and biology were both *magic*, and even more so when they intersected; an enzyme mechanically reconfigures things to catalyze a reaction, how *ridiculously amazing* is that?

"Alchemy is the actual thing I was looking for." I was talking too emphatically, too loudly, too fast. I didn't care, couldn't stop myself as the words poured out, as I unburdened myself of something I hadn't previously been able to put in words even to myself. "Alchemy is the esoteric version of chemistry, the mystical art that I wanted chemistry to be. Alchemy is distillation columns and vapor condensers. So yeah, I know that I can do whatever I want. I know that if I spend a few weeks, a few months, I could unlock more options, ones I haven't even thought of. I bet if I spent a decade and a half at it, I could even unlock an Alchemy Class that's the equivalent to the Technician one I'm rejecting.

"I just don't want to." I stopped suddenly, not knowing what else to say. I put my palms together, in an intentional mimicry of the breathing thing Kelly had told me about; I breathed in, passed the breath to my future self, and breathed out. "I don't want to spin my wheels for years, spend the next years of my life studying like I'm at the academy again. I can't, I just can't. I'm excited and eager about the opportunity to do this, and the fact that it'll be genuinely useful is a huge bonus, and I don't want to waste time, and I don't want to sit around and second-guess myself into a doubt spiral. I wanted to get started; I want to take the Class *tonight*."

The room was quiet in the aftermath of my… answer, ramble, rant, possibly all of those. Kelly's eyes were shining, and both she and James were beaming in delight; Jonathan looked serenely content, and even Judge Fatei looked approving.

"Your Honor," Jonathan said softly, "as the representative for Their Graces, I am fully satisfied with Sophie's answer."

"Thank you, Jonathan. Kelly? James?"

"Judge Fatei—"

"Your Honor—"

The two of them spoke over each other, and Kelly nodded to James, ceding the floor. "Your Honor, the Village of Kibosh is prepared and eager to move forwards with supporting Sophie's chosen profession," he said firmly.

"Judge Fatei, I'm absolutely, totally, completely happy about this."

"Then as there are no objections to Sophie Nadash, Traveler, pursuing her intent to unlock and take the Class of Alchemist as quickly as possible, nor are there any objections to her taking up residence in Kibosh as that profession… Jonathan?"

"Thank you, Your Honor." He leaned forward in his chair, making eye contact with me, energy almost literally sparkling in his eyes and body language. "Let's get to the details."

CHAPTER 2.17 - IN WHICH WE ARE ALL SHOCKED TO EXPERIENCE MORE CIVICS

"Let's get to the details."

I felt a deep unease at the words from a lifetime of being hit with problems in the small print. I more than half expected Jonathan's smile to turn sharkish, for the gleam in his eyes to turn predatory.

"No, first she needs to know where we stand, 'cause she doesn't." Kelly interrupted Jonathan ruthlessly, leaning forward. She'd been quiet so far in the meeting, and her sudden assertiveness took me by surprise. "The short version is that for this part, Judge Fatei is here to make sure everything is legal and fair, and James is here to make sure that Kibosh can deliver—and benefits from delivering—on everything we agree.

"Jonathan and I, we're on sort of the same side, because we both want you to succeed. But *my* job is to be your agent and advocate on a personal level, and *his* job is to make sure that the business we're gonna talk about is as profitable as we can make it, as soon as possible. Does that make sense?"

"Um." I scratched the back of my neck, then snatched my hand back, doing my best to suppress the fidget impulse. "What does success look like from your perspective, if it's not me running a successful business?"

"Happiness. Progression on your chosen Path. Social integration." She ticked off three fingers, paused, then ticked off two more. "Fulfillment on an intellectual level. Maintenance of your physical health and emotional health, above and beyond just being happy."

"All of those are, uh." I searched for the right word. "Fuzzy? Subjective?"

"Progression isn't at all," she retorted. "There's a set of ranges based on a bunch of variables, and it's all concrete and objective. As for the rest?" She shrugged in an attempt at nonchalance, but I could see the hungry tension in her eyes. "You could say the System grades me on my performance. A good enough job is worth a Discovery; I'm aiming for a *Feat*."

"That applies to all of us, Sophie." Jonathan's tone betrayed only a tiny hint of exasperation, but his words made the extent of his feelings more clear. "A year and a day, and we'll all receive anything from a drop in the desert to a river flood. Well, a year from today, I suppose. But it's not only that, and Kelly is doing Shem a disservice by implying we rely on the Divine Flame's evaluation—the Clerks have been very successful in creating frameworks to do these, and the System's expression of the Flame's measures are themselves the work of the Archmages, a majority of whom have always been Shemmai."

"Okay, okay." I held out my hands in a gesture for them to stop and, wonder of wonders, they did. "Kelly's on the side of me being my most actualized self, Jonathan is on the side of me being a productive citizen. I'm sure this will make more sense really soon."

Jonathan nodded sharply, resting his palms on the table. "I apologize for my tangent. To continue: in brief, there are five sources of revenue for an alchemist. Two of them—selling intermediates and patent license fees—are unlikely to be useful to you."

"Transportation costs for the first one," I said with a nod, "and the unlikelihood of my revolutionizing an industry already populated by a wide variety of intelligent, clever, diligent, or lazy professionals for the second."

"A *revolution* in an industry would be… surprising indeed." James cut in smoothly, apologetically. "However, that is the ultimate form of licensure, as most truly disruptive innovations are purchased directly by the Crown. Their Majesties have no interest in unmanaged social upheaval; such innovations are considered carefully and released in controlled fashion, with the attendant shifts in industries and lives ameliorated, over a span of no more than twenty years."

"Okay." I found myself drawing it out, hissing out a breath of emotions I couldn't really separate enough to grapple with. "That's… a lot of something. But even the little stuff, nobody actually expects me to come up with anything new in a tearing hurry. Right?"

"I do!" Kelly beamed as four pairs of eyes turned to her. "What? I do."

"Thanks for the vote of confidence." I was intending it to be mildly sardonic, but about one syllable into it that got lost in just how genuine she looked. "So, since Kelly thinks I can do it, how would it work?"

"I'd like to list the other three paths first, if that's quite alright. One of the remaining three is marginal at best; potions in the Basic Set are price-fixed." Jonathan didn't pause between the not-a-question and continuing his spiel, but he was obviously amused, and I couldn't be upset with the good cheer he was radiating. "It's price-over-cost, and the demand for them is constant, so there's no risk of taking a loss on them; but the profit is... small. That leaves two paths. Selling alchemical creations within Kibosh is one, whether to residents or those stationed here; the other is patent validations or challenges."

"Okay, I get the first two, the Basic Set and the local sales. That's what I expected I'd be doing; make fire resistance potions or whatever, or, uh, lubrication for armillary spheres, I dunno. What's the other?"

Kelly and Jonathan shot each other a look, like neither of them wanted to be the one to explain it. James and Judge Fatei shot each other a look, too, but it looked like the two of them were competing for which one of them *did* get to explain it, and James somehow won.

"Patents are a mechanism by which the State provides an incentive for trade secrets to be brought into the common knowledge." He looked at me, and I tilted my head and nodded. "Shemmai law provides a patent for one hundred years to an inventor, whose license is the larger of a flat fee or percentage of the difference between sale price and materials cost. Any derivative patents pay a partial fee to the patent of origin, which cascades up the chain in a somewhat complex formula. *However*.

"It does not benefit the Kingdom or the Commons for such knowledge to be entered as patents in an adulterated form." He leaned forward, expression for once breaking from its previous contented placidity in favor of something fierce and passionate. Given that he was talking about *patent law*, I was almost too filled with delight to hear the next thing he said. "We do not permit anyone to benefit from the protections of these laws while evading the responsibilities the laws lay upon them, no more than we would permit the responsibilities to be levied upon someone who does not receive the commensurate benefit."

"Amen," I murmured. *May it be God's will.*

That, or my obvious enthusiasm for what he was saying, got me a round of indulgent smiles as James reconfigured his face and body language back to normal. "The primary mechanism for ensuring that patents are viable—" he said *viable* like the term of art it obviously was— "is challenges. Anyone with a competing patent has an interest in demonstrating that a patent does not contain the details necessary to replicate the work. Thus, concretely, a competitor will provide you with the materials to execute a patent and a small additional sum of money. They will ensure that you have access to a qualified librarian, and they will provide someone certified as a notary public. The librarian will answer questions pertaining to the patent or its instructions, while the notary will ensure and attest that you are executing the patent's steps to the best of your ability.

"Multiple failures are grounds for an Inquiry as to whether the patent should be revoked; a high proportion of failures nigh-guarantees this as an outcome. As a result, a competing system has arisen. Patent *validations* are, effectively, a patent challenge sponsored by the owner of the patent. They, too, will provide the materials and a fee, though often a smaller one; and if your efforts fail, they will pay for your continued efforts in order to either demonstrate that your failure was a fluke or find a more reliable, reproducible recipe."

He stopped, blessedly, giving me an opportunity to digest. "Wow." I massaged my forehead, half grimacing and half smiling. It was maybe one quarter ridiculous and three quarters *absolutely fucking awesome*, "That's… a lot. A lot better than what I'm used to, I think."

"Take your time, of course. If you have any questions, please ask them!"

"Well, since you're offering." I grinned at Jonathan, headache fading by the moment. "What's considered the more prosocial choice, if both are on offer for the same patent? Because I'm guessing I can't take *both* of their money. Is it the challenge, since that reinforces the dynamic that guarantees the validity of the patents? Or is it the validation, since that means the inventor retains the patent while still, uh." I ran out of steam, casting about for the words that should have been obvious but were escaping me.

"You cannot, in fact, take both contracts." I had the feeling that Jonathan would be sticking his tongue out at me, if he had Kelly's level of self-control. "As for the… prosocial choice, that's not in my remit, but—"

"But it's in mine! And that's a great question and the answer is pretty much *always* the validator, if they have a contract open." Kelly looked around the table as if daring anyone to contradict her, which nobody did. "Some don't have a contract open, and that's fine, if they don't then you can totally take a challenge contract. But validator contracts still mean the record gets fixed, and if you get a failure it's part of the record, so if they messed up badly enough they'll get the patent yanked out from under them *anyway*."

"Okay, got it, got it." I grinned at her, and her look went sheepish as she realized how emphatic she'd been. "What about equipment? I'm guessing there's, like, a whole universe of *stuff* out there as far as tools of the trade."

"Anything that is expected to be consumed or destroyed, or that is so single-purpose as to be useless for any other purpose, is provided. Anything else is the purpose of the financial support that the Ducal Bank offers." Jonathan leaned forward, lacing his fingers together. "Which is my primary involvement here. As business or professional loans cannot be secured by personal liability, and as you have nothing to secure the loan, you fall under the standard baseline terms."

He paused at that, raising an eyebrow. I met his gaze calmly, maintaining a perfectly bland expression, and slowly performed exactly the eyebrow-raise he was leveling at me.

That got me the laugh I was going for, and he kept on. "The amount of money isn't *insubstantial*, but it's small; more than enough to get you set up with the equipment you'll need to make a Tier's worth of potions, but not much more. You have one year to make your first payment on your loan, during which year there are no taxes levied on your new business. After one year, payments are seasonal, and you deduct the payment from your profits before tax calculations.

"The standard loan term is fifty years, with the last year forgiven if you've made your payments; the—again, standard—payment plan is uniform, so one part in a hundred and fifty. And just in case the thought occurs to you, you do also have to demonstrate that you made that much in profit. No paying your first payment out of the loan itself."

"There's no interest on the loan?" I didn't even try to keep the surprise out of my voice.

"Sophie, the Duchy is already collecting your taxes. Some directly, some at a step removed, but if we want to tax you more, we can just *do that*."

I blinked at him a few times, somehow taking a bit to wrap my brain around that. "I absolutely cannot argue with your logic," I said finally.

"I should hope not," he responded tartly. "I've had this conversation more than a few times. So! Let's see, what else? You get basic equipment from the village, *basic* being defined as anything required to create the full range of the Basic Set. You get access to the first-level Library archives for effectively everything crafting, adventuring, and Guard related, and second-level archives for everything specifically Alchemy-related. You're obligated to make some amount of Basic Set potions every week, it may have changed recently, but I think it's four hours' worth—"

"Three hours."

"—three hours' worth, thank you Kelly. If you have more than some arbitrary number of accidents requiring medical care in any given season, someone who isn't me sends an occupational safety specialist who knows about Alchemy to see what's wrong. Finally, if you miss your loan repayments, we—in this case, that *would* be me—appoint you a manager who works with you to get you solvent again; they'd have the authority to direct what you work on until you *get* solvent, but they're judged almost entirely on how fast you're on your feet again. Any questions? Kelly, anything you want to add?"

"The equipment that you're entitled to in order to make the Basic Set is absolute shoatshit," Kelly responded immediately. "Like, the glass? You're entitled to glass with a compressive strength of five hundred of whatever the measure is, I don't understand it, and we don't make any here in the village with a strength under two thousand. So what you're getting from Hitz is a little better than the Basics."

"It is uneconomical to import and store such specialty goods for this purpose," James added blandly. "Items in storage require inspection and consume space. Kibosh declines to spend more effort simply to provide worse tools."

"The Duchy has no objection to Kibosh providing better equipment than the law requires."

"So long as these are provided at no additional cost, whether direct or indirect, the Law is appropriately fulfilled." Judge Fatei's response came right on the heels of Jonathan's, as though they had both said those exact words a thousand times before.

"There is a legal obligation," James said a moment later, more slowly, "that the village of Kibosh cannot fulfill. As an outer-ring village, and a new one, we are not in a position to provide you, Sophie, with an unlimited volume of subsidized reagents for the creation of Basic Set potions. Kibosh will require a waiver."

"*Sophie* has an obligation for three hours of Basic Set work a week." Kelly's voice was sharp, sharp enough that I had to fight the urge to jump in and de-escalate, which was ridiculous of me. "Doing more than that won't be in her best interests; she's not an apprentice learning the trade, but her obligation can't go beyond your ability to fulfill *your* obligation."

"In the unlikely event," James said dryly, "that we are unable to provide sufficient reagents for Sophie's time, we will waive her obligations to the extent we are unable to fulfill ours." He held up a hand as Kelly opened her mouth. "In writing," he added, and Kelly nodded, satisfied.

"Not the Duchy's business," Jonathan said after a moment's thought. "So long as Kibosh is able to fulfill its obligations with regards to its residents, the dungeon, and the Ward, that's an internal affair."

Judge Fatei nodded at Jonathan, then at Kelly. "Granted, Clerk Administrator. Anything else?"

The four of them looked at me expectantly, and I tried to think things through. It seemed like, well, an offer that would be too good to be true back on Earth. Financial support with basically no strings, social support, and even the banker incentivized not to milk me for fees but to make me successful. Equipment, a place to live, a place to work, food… and a safety net, if I fucked up, in the form of someone who'd come tell me how to run my alchemy business as a business.

Given that I apparently had Kelly genuinely in my corner, I even had reason to expect that the failure case was both unlikely and not a bad outcome, objectively. That didn't stop me from vaguely hating it, from hungering for an independence I'd never had.

"What's my out?" That got me a head-tilt from James and Jonathan. "What happens if I decide alchemy's not it for me, I'm closing up shop?"

Jonathan startled, eyes wide. "Oh! Right, of course. Well. Yes, you wouldn't know. I'm truly sorry, I should have covered this! The standard terms for a Ducal loan are, as I said, secured only by your business. If you should default and retire, we would collect any equipment purchased by the loan that has resale value higher than the cost of transportation, close your line of credit, and decline to offer a loan to you further."

"You would, of course, remain a citizen in good standing," James cut in to add. "Eligible for all proper support—food, housing, other necessities, training in your profession, security and safety, access to knowledge."

I nodded slowly as they went back to the expectant waiting. There were other things that I could ask, obviously but their time was—no, if I said something like *I don't want to waste your time*, I was fairly confident that would give actual offense. "I have… fiddly, low-level questions. But I suspect I'll always have more of those, and if Kelly doesn't know the answer, James will. Overall? It sounds… I'd say good, but it sounds *great*."

"Tradition and the law alike," Judge Fatei said softly, "suggest that the appropriate response is that this Inquiry should not rest until dawn rises upon the fullness of your understanding. But I admit, I have a substantial circuit, and it will be some years before my junior Judge can shoulder their share of the work. Nonetheless, you have the right to, in the scope of this Inquiry, have your questions answered."

Questions flickered through my mind. *How much transport am I allowed, and will I be charged a standard rate, and if so, is it the same rate the village pays?* "I'm good, then," I said anyway. *What's the lead-time on equipment? Are there restrictions on what I can make, who I can sell to, who I can buy intermediates and ingredients from?*

In the end, though, I was reliant on their good faith no matter what they gave me for answers. There was no use pretending otherwise.

There were nods all around. "I'm good with this, on my and Sophie's behalf," Kelly said firmly. "I know she doesn't know all of the fiddly bits, but I'm qualified to act as her agent on this, and it's in her best interests. And I'm *really* confident she can make her payments on the standard loan."

"The Village of Kibosh finds the specifics of this arrangement to our satisfaction."

"The Duchy likewise."

We all looked at Judge Fatei, who nodded briskly. "This arrangement is within the bounds of the law, and I find it to be equitable and in the best interests of all parties. Clerk Administrator Morei, do you have the appropriate forms filled out, and do you attest that they faithfully represent the arrangement that has been discussed?"

"With the exception of the waivers, which I will file today in a manner compatible with the agreement reached? I do, Your Honor."

"Then this Inquiry is concluded."

A pressure I hadn't even noticed eased off of me, and everyone's body language loosened up. My ears popped, and sounds from outside started to filter in, a lack that I had totally missed. *So I guess we're doing this.*

CHAPTER 2.18 - DINNER, AND OTHER UNRELATED COMMITMENTS

The moment the meeting was formally over, Kelly tackled me with a whoop and squeal of joy.

I was still in my chair when she did it, and I almost slid off entirely. Catching myself with a shift of my feet—and thanking Hephaestus for the workmanship of my boots when I slammed the side of my foot into the chair beside me—I hugged her back. I couldn't help but smile at the enthusiastic joy she was vibrating with, and—not for the first time in the past day—at how *nice* it felt to hug someone.

Judge Fatei and Jonathan left with only the briefest remarks, "I look forward to watching your Path prosper" and "James can reach me *anytime*, don't hesitate to reach out" respectively. By the time Kelly let me go and I untangled myself from the chair I'd been braced on, it was only the two of us left in the room, and she was urging me onwards and outwards.

"We're done in time, but only barely. Come on, we can't be late! It'll look real bad if we're late."

"Where are we going, that we can't be late to?" I allowed her to tow me out the door, though given how surprisingly strong she was, I wasn't sure I could have stopped her. "I hope it's not more meetings. I'm not sure I can integrate much more in the way of anything; my brain kinda hurts."

"Don't be ridiculous. Actually, no, be ridiculous more often, it's a good look." She winked at me, outrageous and exaggerated, and turned left on the ring road. "We're going to Fall, 'cause it's dinner time! And if I get you there at the start of first seating, we'll be showing respect for Thesha and her team! And the social context of the refectory, and the basket she gave us."

"Oh shit, the bask—" I stopped myself, looking at Kelly's other hand and the basket she was carrying in it. Feeling sheepish, I started picking up the pace to better match hers. "Thanks. I'd say I can't believe I forgot that, but I have a lot on my mind right now. You ate your share?"

"Yep!" She patted the basket, smiling at it. "It's funny you didn't notice. But I guess you've had a lot to think about."

"Yeah." I snorted. "I really have."

The sun was a lot lower in the sky than I'd have guessed. We'd obviously taken longer in that Inquiry than it had felt, which was a bit of a shock given that it had felt *long*, and possibly I hadn't internalized how long we'd walked from the Tower to the guardhouse.

The village in the evening was a model of ease. Children played in the gardens and helped with maintaining the plants, and adults walked around outside or sat and worked on what were obviously hobby projects. It was the first I'd seen of anyone else on the ring road, and Kelly slowed down to have a quick banter or ask a genuine question of nearly everyone we passed.

I just offered an *evening's ease*, and got them in return. Judging by the smiles and body language, that was fine.

Delays or not, we eventually made it to Fall. Judging by the trickle of people coming in after us, we were in good time for the first sitting, arriving well before they'd close the building and clean up before reopening for the second sitting. This was proper—dinner, especially, you expected people to come earlier. It wasn't quite a social obligation, but it *was* an expectation.

We passed through the door of the refectory in silence. The hall was... not exactly full, but certainly not empty; there were maybe thirty people there, half of them kids. The noise washed over me, more eyes than I could really deal with turning to look at me, and I distracted myself by studying a nearby mural. The vivid wildlife scene sparked a memory of Kelly telling me about what kinds of meat sources the village had, and I frowned in concentration as I looked for examples of what she'd mentioned. "Hey, Kelly. I see some birds, I think, in little wooden structures? On the wall mural, I mean."

"Yeah, those are the cotes, we call the birds cote-birds. Good memory and good eyes! Let's grab a side table. You look overwhelmed, and nobody's gonna judge you for wanting to eat alone, especially with how new you are."

"How about the other animals you mentioned?"

Kelly led us towards a table that, thankfully, was obviously a two-seater, and I followed her lead as she pulled out a chair and sat down. "See the bunch of little ponds about a quarter of the way down that wall?"

"Emphasis on little, but sure." I looked again, squinting. "The teal, those are fish?"

"Yep! And the four-legged thing with the ears near the top of its head just behind your shoulder, that's a rakin."

I turned, studying it. It was chubby, with over-developed hind legs and stubby little forelegs. There were a few of them in different positions, some of them in motion, so I could see that they mostly walked on two legs but went to four when eating or standing around. Eyes pretty close to the sides of their heads, sparse fur, and one of the rakins in the picture was climbing a little ways up a tree to get at a piece of fruit.

"Those sure are some talons, alright."

"They didn't breed 'em out, 'cause even in the village pens you can get birds and snakes and night-hunters like foxes. Yalad! How are you? How're you and Dana?"

I turned back around to see a young man—no, probably a teenager—placing a couple of long bowls on the table. He blushed, muttering something I couldn't quite catch in a rapid, accented deflection, and Kelly giggled.

"Thanks... Yalad?"

I'd obviously not quite gotten the pronunciation right, but he barely winced. "Yalad," he said with a little more *yuh* than I'd used, and I nodded as I filed away the correction. "I gotta go."

I watched him as he dashed off—not exactly running, but more than just walking. He slipped into another one of those mostly concealed doors down towards the opposite end of the building from us, and I turned to the long bowl in front of me.

It was some kind of stew, and after one taste I started eating it as fast as I could handle the spice level. We had glasses of something sweet and thick, like a pulpy juice with some yogurt in it; as my eyes started watering, I took a drink, savoring the way that the fat washed away the spiciness.

Initially, I couldn't place a single one of the flavors, other than something that vaguely reminded me of—of a plant that didn't exist here, I supposed, or didn't exist in any of the languages I'd been granted. By the time I'd worked my way through the bowl, I was fairly confident there was zucchini in it, and the beans were obvious; but other than that, I was absolutely clueless.

Moments later, a different teenager slid a second bowl in front of me and snagged the old one. She was fast enough and light enough on her feet that I didn't hear her coming, and she disappeared without a word immediately afterwards. I stared blankly at the order she left in her wake—dirty dishes collected and empty chairs slid forward under their tables, mostly—and looked over at Kelly with a question in my eyes.

"Tizpa." She shrugged expressively, a *what can you do* in body language. "Quiet little bird. Fast, smart, hard worker, gets along great with the dogs, but she says more words to one of them in a day than to anyone else in a week. The older kids like her and Yalad cycle through all the jobs around, even if the herder kids are almost always gonna go into herding."

I paused in my eating. "And it gets the food moving, and the dishes done."

"And it gets the food moving," she agreed, grinning at me, "and the dishes done."

Tizpa had managed to also switch out my nearly empty glass without my noticing, and I drank gratefully as I worked my way through the second bowl. Kelly chattered at passers-by in the meantime, having obviously finished with her dinner—not saying anything particularly of consequence, just... chatter.

It was surprisingly nice. Not much of it actually registered, especially since I didn't know a single person whose social lives she was detailing. I *certainly* didn't have the context of the centuries-old grudges and relationships that the stories she told relied on, and a lot of the social mores were foreign to me.

It was, however, acutely boring after a while. Maybe once I'd gotten to know the people, that would change; but as it was, I was visibly distracted and fidgeting, even while eating. Eventually, Kelly noticed, or maybe she'd noticed earlier and eventually she decided to intervene.

"Sophie."

"Kelly." I looked over at her, raising an eyebrow.

"If you're up for it, you know, you could take your Class. Now would be an appropriate time."

I blinked at her, then looked down at my empty bowl. "It would? I didn't—well!" I stopped myself from arguing, sticking instead to grinning. "If it's an appropriate time, it's an appropriate time."

I waited a beat to give Kelly a chance to tell me *actually, no, it's not*, and then dropped into the frame of mind to send a message to my System. This time, though, I was too excited to form a packet of words; instead, a wash of intention and desire carried me into that communion.

The world faded in that already-familiar way, and my sense of self faded along with it.

> *Your Divine Flame Heeds Your Will!*
> *To Transcend Is To Change.*
> *To Change Is To Transcend.*
> *Evolution Of [Worker] Into [Alchemist] Commences!*
> *Be Not Afraid. All Shall Be Well.*

I opened metaphysical eyes, and I saw the world in concepts and theory.

I saw a woman sitting on a bench, elbows propped on a table, breathing steadily. Each breath came in for three seconds, filling her lungs; the air was held for three seconds before it flowed out just as slowly, and three more seconds passed before she breathed again.

I knew she was black-haired and neither fair nor dark of skin; I knew that she was a paradox of clumsiness and carefulness, of clinging to a past and reaching for something that she at the same time rejected. For all that, I couldn't see her, nor could I hear her.

To her left sat a woman barely older than her who seemed much younger, a woman fighting to keep her face pleasant and happy despite a deep concern and doubt. To her right stood a woman who seemed old and was far older, gazing on the other two with a stern and commanding expression that covered every inch of her body language and went no deeper.

I was none of those women, inhabiting none of those bodies. I was cradled within the comforting arms and tendrils and fractal mesh of the Divine Flame, a thing of such vastness that I could not encompass its smallest facet, and of such intricacy that I could not see its largest component. I was encompassed within the shield of its consideration, and I communed nonetheless with the heat of it.

It was a pyre in which my humanity would slowly burn.

I knew that woman sitting on the bench. I was, I *had been*, the woman who inhabited that body; I would be again. That knowledge flowed to me from the Flame as it held me in its grasp, keeping me away from the material world. I knew from it that all which I once was, I remained, for all that I was becoming something more in its care. Power flowed from through it to the System and then to a hundred trillion points in the body, and I watched as that body *changed*.

It burns from within. I let the truth of that resonate within me, understanding perfectly why I could not inhabit that moment physically. *Its nerves scream to a brain that has no consciousness operating it.* Were I there, were that brain still a bridge to my Self, I would have gone mad as a multitude of small changes twisted and remade it on a fundamental level. Some of the lines on its face faded; skin that was loose tightened, skin that was tight loosened. *The body is no taller, and neither its curves nor its muscles are more pronounced or more defined,* I thought clinically, or perhaps the System observed on my behalf, *but a thousand invisible changes have left it more vital, more energetic. Where before it had seen the touch of a master sculptor, now it suffered under the care of something which worked at a far smaller scale.*

Not content with that, the power continued to flow, though only in a comparative trickle. Hundreds of thousands—millions, perhaps—of tiny motes of power sank into the body, hunting. They hunted things smaller in some ways than light itself, but even those things had orders of magnitude of size in their range, and there was not enough power to hunt every one of them. Still, most of them flowed gently away from where they lived or latched, oozing through pores or out orifices to then fade into a heat that was siphoned away.

It all took no more than fifteen seconds, fifteen seconds in which I watched the body I once inhabited—*my* body—be subtly refined. And then the Flame which had me cocooned in its warmth, shifted in an immaterial way.

I began to drift out of the liminal space, striving to return or, failing that, to observe the function and form of where I had been held.

It burns itself into me in an eternal present, a memory so vivid that it encodes itself forever as though I am living it in every breath. *I see it*, no, I see its *interface*, its mediating layer between itself and me, as everything fades into communion once more. It's a beautiful thing in its own right, a spark—no, a tendril of divinity, a symbiote that I've been drawing closer to me, wrapping around myself as I lean into it for comfort and strength. There's something in the distance, something vast and so far beyond my capacity to truly comprehend that I can only think about it in abstractions of abstractions, but I have a word for it nonetheless—and one blinding insight.

It—that Divine Flame which my own is the merest mote of—is a god, built by mortal hands.

Your Divine Flame Hones Body And Mind

Your Tier One Class Was But A Brick In Your Road:
[Worker] -> [Alchemist]
You Walk Your Path: Tier 1 -> Tier 2, Level 10 -> Level 1
Your Attributes Grow: *Hale Improved, Meticulous Gained*
Some Skills Consolidate: *Learn/Read/Study -> Comprehend, See/Inquire -> Observe*
Some Skills Improve: *Nothing Left to Chance, Chemical Calculation, Mechanisms*
Some Skills, Left Fallow, Diminish: *Endure, Cope, Weather the Storm*
Feats Deserve Mention: *To Glimpse the Divine Within*
Feat-Skill Earned: **[Fleeting Touch of Divinity]**

Manifold Are The Glories Any Mortal May Become! Learn. Change. Overcome. Rise.

For a moment, I opened my eyes in a stranger's body. Panic flooded me and I made as if to scream, but there was no oxygen in my lungs and no blood in my body, because *this wasn't my body*—and then it was. I sucked in a ragged breath, my heart beat wildly, and adrenaline coursed through my veins.

Slowly, my body began to relax. As though my consciousness were settling back into my brain, I started to feel again—or see, at first, a faint leavening in darkness. I almost panicked again before I realized my eyes were closed, and then more senses started to integrate, or perhaps my mind integrated with them.

I saw light, even through my eyelids. I smelled the dining hall, food and people and wood alike. I felt, I tasted, I heard.

There was a hand on my back, rubbing in slow circles, and a murmuring voice to my right, cold and precise. My mouth tasted of dryness and the remnants of dinner, and when a straw entered my lips, I sucked at it and swallowed water cut with citrus.

For a long moment, I tried and failed to open my eyes. It was like I'd forgotten how to turn the will to act into action itself; it was like I'd gotten disconnected from all of my nerve endings. I studied the impulse to drink and the way my diaphragm contracted and expanded, and then it clicked into place.

I opened my eyes to see a world a little richer, a little sharper. The murals on the wall distracted me with the glory of their colors and the incredible levels of detail that I could pick out, and as I breathed in I felt like I could separate every individual smell from the overall blend.

It was a nostalgic feeling. I'd worn glasses for almost two decades, until lasers reshaped my corneas into a more functional shape. I'd forgotten over the intervening years what it felt like to suddenly see that trees have leaves, the surprise at how sharp the world of vision is supposed to be.

"Well." I swallowed, fighting a tongue and mouth that felt unfamiliar. "That happened."

Kelly hugged me, laughing, as more than a hundred voices erupted in cheers.

CHAPTER 2.19 - AND THEN GOODNIGHT; SO PASSES A MOMENTOUS DAY

It seemed obvious in hindsight that going up a Tier would mean a party. It happened only twice in a lifetime, for nearly everyone in the Kingdom of Shem; once when they came of age, and once when they settled into their trade and lifestyle.

Not having put any thought into it, and not having prepared myself for it, I lasted about five seconds before I wanted to sprint for the door and escape. I managed to endure it anyway. It wasn't even that raucous or anything, and once I got over the fight-or-flight-or-freeze response—to which my answer was, as ever, *freeze*—I knew it wasn't even that many people.

It quite literally couldn't have been more than a hundred and seventy people, even if every villager was present. I'd been to bigger weddings; I'd been to bigger award dinners.

"We've got everyone but the duty." Kelly's voice was cheerful, verging on exuberant. "Duty in the evening's just inner watch, outer watch, and skywatch. Everyone else is here, just about; or was, or will be."

"Duty. That's someone watching the dungeon," I guessed, "a few people watching the outer walls, and someone in the Tower?"

"Two on the dungeon," she corrected me. "And one on each gatehouse."

"Seven people. Still leaves…" I grimaced. "This."

"Do you not like parties, Miss Sophie?"

Despite my discomfort, I smiled down at the tow-headed urchin sitting beside me on the bench. Aliza was five years old and possessed of an energy I instantly recognized from the torn knee of her pants and the patches of dirt on her face and calves. She was one of seven children who'd gravitated to me, all of whom I'd welcomed with relief as they formed a sort of shield against the party at large.

If it weren't for them, I would have bailed the moment my legs were working again.

"Do I like parties? Not really. I don't dance, and this is… not how I'm used to being social."

I didn't have to shout, at least; something about the hall's magics kept the noise down to just above a conversational level. There was that anxiety-inducing party energy, but none of the overwhelming wall of sound that I would have expected.

I shook my head, trying to clear it. *Getting distracted,* I told myself, *gotta stop that.* "I'm sorry." I smiled at the kids, leaning a little closer. "I was thinking about something and missed what you said. Can you repeat it?"

"Mom says that you're from far away. Like, really far."

"Like maybe as far as Hayir!"

"No, silly, like not even from Shem!"

"Hey, hey, let me answer, okay?" I held my hands up in surrender as the kids' words tumbled to a stop. "I'm from even further away than that. I'm not from Yelem; I'm from a place called Earth."

"Naaaaaah." Aliza drawled out the denial, smirking at me. "That's a silly name."

"As silly as calling your world 'World'?" I huffed, hands on my hips, playing it up for the giggling children. "Just because it's in the Old Tongue doesn't mean it's any less silly than Earth!"

"Maybe all names are silly."

"Oh yeah? What's your name mean, Aliza?"

It was one of the other children who answered, someone a little younger whose name I didn't remember. "Aliza said it means cheerful, but one of my grands told me it means playful." That came with folded arms and a grumpy sound, as though the kid was offended.

"I don't see why it can't be both. Anyway, I don't think that's a silly name. Unless you got that scrape on your jaw from sitting in a chair?" I grinned to take the sting out of the jibe. "And the bark bits on your feet are probably because you live in a tree, right?"

"She might as well. Are you having a good time, *tikti?*" The woman who'd approached us glanced at me once before focusing on her daughter—the family resemblance was obvious, between the dark brown skin and those eyebrows and cheekbones. "I think it might be time to go home now. Fun is important, but…"

"… but sleep is too." Aliza offered the response with the weight of ritual, scrambling to her feet. She started to turn away, paused, and turned back to me. "It was nice meeting you, Miss Sophie! I hope your name isn't silly."

"It was nice meeting you too, Aliza," I said to her retreating back. She disappeared with all the scampering grace and speed that I'd expected, her mother bestowing a faint smile on me in passing. Chuckling, I turned back to Kelly as the other children all disappeared in short order.

"Thank you," a voice said, one I didn't recognize.

"No problem." I replied on autopilot, then looked at who it was.

"I mean it. Genuinely." The newest stranger beamed at me, dapper in presumably impeccable fashion, bright colors bringing out the vibrant purple of his eyes. The cut of his clothes highlighted the softness of his features, and those clothes were damp with sweat. "You know how it is. You find a nesting partner—and then you wind up being fathers together, and you never have the time to dance with the man you adore."

"I don't, actually." I smiled back at him as politely as I could manage. "But I'm glad you enjoyed the party, and the kids were all delightful and perfectly well behaved."

"Ah." He seemed to find a puzzle of some sort in my response, frowning in thought. "I did indeed. Enjoy the party, that is. Must go, alas, to put the storm to bed, lest the moment pass." He glanced at Kelly, then back at me. "But before I do… I was wondering. Do you know—well, there's no reason you would. Kibosh has never had an alchemist before. Very little in the way of institutional knowledge past the books. Which," he added hastily, glancing at Kelly, "I am sure your First Friend has studied thoroughly."

"Get to the point, Tomas."

I raised an eyebrow at Kelly, and she colored slightly. It might have been the first time I'd heard her genuinely get waspish or snide with someone, and it didn't seem like he'd said anything that justified it.

"Miss Avara, will you be working alongside her?" At Kelly's nod, lips sealed against words left unsaid, he frowned deeper. "I would appreciate your both visiting my shop in the morning, after you break your fast. I won't trouble you for too much time."

"We don't—"

"Happily," I interjected. I glanced at Kelly meaningfully, and her face went neutral, controlled. "We'll be over right after breakfast."

"We can't stay long," Kelly said levelly. "The week's coming to its end, and Sophie needs to put in her hours on the Basics."

"Of course. Miss Avara. Miss Nadash. Again, thank you, and good night; I'm sorry you didn't enjoy the party as much as we did."

He wove his way out of the refectory, leaving a slight gap as he went. I hadn't even noticed the party getting rowdier and more crowded, as caught up with ignoring it as I had been; the music was in full swing, there were tables of snacks and sweets, and most of the chairs and tables had disappeared to open the floor up for dancing.

It was intolerable, especially without the kids around to distract me. Without checking with Kelly, without really considering whether it was proper or not, I got up and made use of Tomas's wake to escape into the night.

And night it certainly was. Between two bowls of dinner, taking my Class, and the impromptu party—during which I'd eaten yet more food, which was a bit of a highlight of it—the sun had long since set and a chill had descended with the darkness. It nipped at my face and ears, particularly when a breeze brushed by, and I tucked my hands into my coat pockets for warmth.

Warmth. The thought jogged something loose in my head. "You know," I thought out loud, "I hadn't actually considered the fact that despite it being high striving—possibly the warmest time of the year—I've been perfectly comfortable. I'm in a leather coat with multiple layers underneath; I should be broiling."

"Comfort enchantments. Yours is a masterpiece, a divine one, obviously." Kelly sounded like she was smirking; I hadn't even been sure she was walking with me. "They absorb light, ideally in the—you know that in a real sense, warmth is a kind of light, right?"

"Yeah." I studied the road under our feet, trying to figure out why I was able to see it in the darkness. *It's not actually lit up, and it's not illuminating anything...* "Infrared, visible spectrum, ultraviolet."

"Comfort enchantments, I don't actually understand *how* they do it, but they absorb light. Tuned to a specific kind, or a blend. Sunlight's most common." She yawned, a long *yah-hm-rum* sort of yawn. "What they do with it? Depends."

"You okay?" I looked over at her with some concern, abandoning my study of the ring-road. "You don't sound like you usually do. And you're... kinda stumbling."

"Guess I am. It's fine, I'm fine." She gave another jaw-cracking yawn. "Just... tired, been a long day. Not an everyday day. Party was nice, bit of a drop, hitting me now. Drank a bit, not drunk, jus' sleepy."

"Do we..." I stopped. I'd almost asked *do we drop you off*, but I didn't want the answer to be *yes*, and I especially didn't want to imply that I wanted that to be the answer. "I don't want to assume, but I saw the other mattress."

"Across the hall. 'm sleeping there. If it's 'kay."

"Come on. Lean on me, we'll get you there." I slung an arm around her back, doing most of the work of keeping her upright and steady. "Stay awake, yeah? Tell me about the road. What's up with it? Why can I see it?"

"Perceptual enchantment." Kelly waved her free hand in a sort of vague, half-hearted gesture. Her diction was over-precise, hitting every syllable as though doing so deliberately. "It's not light, it's... perceptibility. Road. Things on the road. 's standard."

"Neat."

We walked in silence for a bit while I chewed on that. The night wasn't exactly quiet, but it was a different sort of noise than I was used to, neither the city noise nor the countryside of Earth, and I kept noticing things about it. The birds and insects made distinctly different sounds, sounds that just didn't sound right, and the brilliance of the stars and moon were something almost alien to me.

A guard nodded to us from the walls at Tome's gate, and we saw a few people here and there inside the village. They sat on porches, balconies, the bridges from one building to another; they walked in their quint's vegetable garden, and every single one of them was half-listening for sounds from inside their homes.

None took any note of us. It felt deliberate, like there was something embarrassing going on—though to be fair, I had someone practically falling asleep on me, so maybe that was it.

And if she fell asleep, her weight would go from awkward to infeasible, so measures had to be taken. Besides...

"Hey, Kelly."

"Mmm."

"What's up with you and Tomas, anyway?" I glanced over at her, seeing her eyes flutter open a bit wider. "You two have beef? History?"

She made a grumpy *mnurgh* sound at me, rubbing her eyes with her free hand. "Now? Really?"

"Keeping you awake. I don't think I can carry you. And I want to know, and also I feel like I was super rude to cut you off and accept his invitation without consideration for your feelings."

"Mrh. No, that was right, actually. I guess."

She took her hand off my shoulder and shrugged my own arm off, plodding forward in silence. I kept pace with her, not saying anything—I was an expert in silences, and this one wasn't one in which she was falling asleep. If anything, she was more awake than we had been since we left Fall.

"We do have history. We... actually, I don't wanna, it doesn't matter. Really, it's... he's so..." Kelly waggled her fingers, visibly trying to muster enough wakefulness to answer the question. "Tomas is so *much*. Color match this. Cuts and shape and form and fabric and... ugh."

"Really."

"This is what you wear to this. Wear that to that. These mean something, those mean something else, it's like a whole language. And I know it's 'cause he's him, *Resplendent Tailor* or whatever. But I just. Just..."

She sagged against me again. With the long silences and steady pace, we were well past Tome and coming up on Rise. I was fairly confident in which shop-house we were looking for—which one was *mine*, now there was a wild thought—so I let her keep leaning.

"He just can't *not*," she mumbled eventually. "An' I don't care."

"I care," I said carefully, gently. "It took me a while to learn how to, but I care about how I look. About what people... infer and assume from how I look."

The silence from that got us all the way into the yawning emptiness of the store and up the stairs to the living space. It was only when she was leaning on the doorway to her room—and I had a bunch of complicated feelings about that—that she seemed to rouse again enough to speak.

I waited patiently, leaning back against the wall, eyes mostly closed as I cultivated the heavy-lidded feeling of sleepiness, letting the alertness and determination to keep moving drain away.

"You shouldn't," she said eventually, abruptly. "Shouldn't care. Shouldn't need to care."

"I know." I smiled at her. "Good night, Kelly. And thanks."

I didn't so much as remember stepping through the doorway, much less taking my boots off or lying down; and if I had any dreams that night, they had long since fled by morning.

CHAPTER 2.20 - INTERLUDE: KETKA

It was a beautiful day, and Ketka was killing a horrible goose.

"I'm not sure about this." She flipped one of her axes in her hand to reverse her grip, keeping her motion going even as the neck wrapped around her, immobilizing her. Despite the crushing constriction the monster was trying to apply to her chest, Ketka's voice was a low, booming alto. Her words echoed in the cavern like a chant or a song, one whose beats were in time with her movements. "It doesn't seem quite right."

She didn't want to let **[Flow of Battle]** drop, so even as she struck with a precision that belied her seven feet of height and the three-foot hafts of her axes, she was focused on what would come next. She had slashed open a fair number of muscles in that enormous neck, and as its grip loosened, she dropped to the ground and rolled to the side. A great leg pounded down on where she had been less than a heartbeat later, and shards of stone pricked at her bare arms as the floor beneath the strike exploded.

"If you get hurt trying to be funny," a carrying tenor voice snarled, "I will salt your wounds with acid!"

"I'm just not sure it's actually a goose, Deoro!" With her out of the way, blood exploded out of the wound she'd made as the Irontouch Mage got to work. That didn't mean Ketka was out of the woods; what they were fighting was almost ten feet at the shoulder, and exsanguinating it at a rate of under a liter per second would take—

"Why the *fuck* does it matter this thing is a goose or not?"

—between ten and eleven minutes, judging by how biologically grounded this particular beast seemed to be. "It's not polite to call something by a wrong name!" She spun lithely and severed a hamstring, her hundreds of kilos moving like water. It wasn't even her Skill doing it; training and practice were wonderful things, and her muscles sang with the glory of exertion. "I don't want to be rude."

"You don't—*lover of a thousand monsters*," Deoro ranted in exasperation, lapsing into their shared native tongue, "*I will fill your throat with vipers until you choke on their venom!*"

The blood kept flowing, richer and richer even as it slowed, and she'd gotten enough of the beast's attention—and crippled it to enough of a degree—to let Beyin get involved safely. *Safely* was important, since they were the team's best healer, but something this outright *big* was a problem that had no risk-free solutions.

The monster was already healing, after all. In the dim, shifting light cast by Iōanna's magic, they could see that it had mostly knitted its neck back together, though the hamstring was mostly still cut. The wounds were fighting Deoro's magic, but they would clot momentarily. Its iron might not replenish, which would *eventually* kill the creature if that were true, but a habit of extended fights was a death sentence when the sands shifted beneath your feet.

"Deoro!" Ketka's tone was light and chiding. She leapt to avoid a kick and cut a casual arc in the viciously clawed foot whose passing breeze fluttered her hair. Twisting in the air as she did so, she slammed feet-first into a wall and sprang off of it as the stone shattered. Swinging her weapons, she carved bloody furrows into the possibly-goose's back to slow herself on the way down. "Speak Shemmai, or speak Qatn. Only we two here speak Yaroba!"

"Mother of wretches," he spat in the tradetalk's pidgin, forming the iron he'd collected into spikes with a gesture that set his robes to billowing. Glowing red with heat, they shot up from below the beast, momentarily impaling it and immobilizing it. "You shit in your water!"

"Gratitude." Beyin was, as ever, a font of grace and civility, of gentleness and compassion. Their voice was suited to their manner: calm, soft, and soothing.

Beyin was Shemmai born and bred, Ketka knew. They could recognize Yaroba when someone was spitting imprecations in it, but they didn't speak more than the usual pair of languages—Shemmai, obviously, and the nearly universal Qatn. That meant that they had missed some of the implications, which was good; in Shem, the suggestion that you abused your children or fouled your community's wells could get someone killed in a heartbeat.

Conveniently, since Deoro would have drawn steel at an insult that vile even were it directed at Ketka instead of at himself, Beyin wasn't the foul-mouthed type.

"We are friends," they continued with a smile, after dodging an accidental tail-scythe. The admonishment was clear, but nonetheless kind. "We speak the shared language together, when we speak."

Beyin laid their hands, the healer-soft hands of a Propagation Biomagus, on their enormous foe's side for a brief moment. It seemed to sense them, but it was too late to stop the spell from being channeled. It turned ponderously as if it knew that vengeance was suddenly the only thing left to it, but Beyin—no fool, and besides, they'd practiced this—was already sprinting away.

Ketka blurred as she caught up, reaching out and hauling Beyin with her as she ran. She slowed and put them down only after they passed around a curve and through the scorching heat of Iōanna's blessing-shield. It was almost certain that neither of them would have had any problems even if *they* hadn't gotten through, but there was no sense in taking unnecessary risks.

"I think it had no crest," Ketka said thoughtfully. She wasn't making any effort to be quiet, but even so, the splashing sounds were audible in the gaps between her words as parts of the animal began to slough off or disintegrate. "Doesn't it have to have a crest to be a goose?"

"What? How does this matter?" Sayyad spat on the cave floor, scowling, her Shemmai a low growl. Ketka didn't take offense; the wanderer had brought her usual huge number of arrows, spare strings, and two spears, but all were used up or broken—or, in most of the arrows' cases, rotted during a previous encounter—and her **[Mystical Hunter's Spear]** was in abeyance.

Sayyad, Ketka knew, did not tolerate idleness well. Tolerated it least out of all of them. But even if she wasn't contributing to the fight, she would still have been listening, not just sulking.

"It always matters," Ketka said with a gentle smile. "To know is required to understand. To understand is power in its own right, but more importantly, to understand is to grow."

And to grow was to become divine. Immortal, powerful, unending—all of them had that same goal in sight, despite their varied origins.

"Still wrong." Sayyad switched to Qatn, striding out from Iōanna's protection. The sounds had died down, and the others followed her, reacting with various murmurs, whistles, and nods of satisfaction. Beyin had outdone themself—the liquified remains had settled into a puddle, and were solidifying. "Dishonorable."

"Dishonorable?" Beyin gave Sayyad a sidelong look. Two years ago, they might have had a different reaction; two years ago, they had not fought by Sayyad's side and seen how pragmatic a fighter she was.

"Offensive to the Gods, rude to the Dungeon," Ketka clarified in Shemmai, filling in the words that Sayyad hadn't known, and got a grateful nod for her efforts. "It is better to kill cleanly, and better to harvest than to waste."

"Truth is spoken. Loss of bounty is failure to honor." Deoro grimaced at what now looked like a pool that had been transmuted into stone, without a hint that it had ever been a living creature. With a furrowed brow, he tapped into **[Iron Calls To Iron]** and slowly pushed three small crystals out of the remains of the now-unidentifiable anserina—the best word Ketka had for it, now that the question of *duck, goose, or swan* was no longer answerable.

The crystals sat, balanced on thin spikes of metal, until Iōanna washed them in blue-white flames for a full thirty seconds.

"Skin, bones, blood, organs, feathers. All are gone."

"Better only crystals than death," Ketka said, and everyone nodded grudgingly.

They were adventurers in their third Tier, all five of them. They knew better than to take unnecessary risks for such minor gains. That didn't mean that having to have Beyin liquefy the monster sat well with any of them, and especially not with the three who could have died in just as horrifying a manner were the spell miscast.

"Deeper?"

Three pairs of eyes turned to Iōanna in emotions ranging from surprise to disbelief. "Miss Ba-Itar," Deoro said slowly in his rough Shemmai, picking words carefully, "that seems unwise. While we took no wounds from this beast, it was a near thing five times over."

"I will attend, and make our path one of wisdom." Iōanna's voice was placid, drifting and thready. Her eyes were clouded, and her hands shook as she lowered them. Those things might have been mistaken for weakness, by those who were unfamiliar with her; none present so qualified. "The sun falls once for each time it rises."

"Deeper," Ketka agreed simply. Her eyes were roaming the shadows; they had never stopped doing so. She flicked a glance back at the aged Thousandfold Adept, smirking broadly. "If you say it."

"Weaker apart," she responded without hesitation. "Stronger together."

"We grow," Deoro supplied in ritual response, "the five of us as one. Fine. Deeper, if you can shoulder it. Or if you want our rotting corpses to start a maggot-farm."

"She spoke the words." Beyin hummed, a sound of appreciation common in the Shemmai towns and cities. Of the five of them, they had found more amusement in the once-ironic phrase than anyone other than Ketka herself. "We fulfill their promise. Deeper, to grow."

Sayyad looked as though she wanted to spit again, eyes narrowed and shoulders set. "I hold to my word. Deeper. But we hunt in the Forest tomorrow."

"If the weather stays bright." Ketka's voice was idle, even somewhat distracted. "Rain means mud in my hair."

Sayyad nodded, though the other fighter couldn't see her do so. There wouldn't be rain in the Forest for a week, and everyone knew it; Ketka's codicil was less a practical concern and more a step in their social dance, a message about their relative position in decision-making.

And that was fine with Sayyad, Ketka knew. She hadn't brought up the Forest as a challenge. Sayyad had brought it up because she found the caves distasteful and cramped, and her own combat style needed more open space than she could generally find in them.

Motes of light gathered from around the room, most of them from the corpse—though it was something far past a corpse. They shaped themselves into the outline of a spear, which slid, glimmering, into place on Sayyad's back. Rearmed and able to fight again should she need to, a great deal of tension drained out of her stance, and she smiled like a razor.

Without further conversation, the five began to move. There was no light, but they had all long since learned to compensate. They could hear the walls, some of them, where others saw by mana vision, by the rays of darkness that appeared where there was no memory of light, or by other methods entirely.

Small things, subtle things, died without comment and with minimal effort. The weakest among them fell from barely more than the desire that they do so—a spike of iron growing suddenly out of the blood vessels and into the brain, or the spark of life drifting away from them to return to the Gods. These, they left where they lay, to feed the cycle of decomposition and the dungeon alike.

The cave, and the irregular stone of its walls, began to widen as they explored. They were all experienced enough to avoid the most obvious traps—friable footing, passageways that narrowed to impassibility, and pockets of dead air—even moving as quickly as they were. Still, they were not equal in those skills, and more than once Sayyad, the best scout among them despite her antipathy towards the close quarters, redirected their search away from a hazard.

There were places where roaring water rushed down a seemingly clear passage, sweeping away anything in its wake with its power. There were places where a cascade of rot had birthed some manner of magical plague, sustained by something that might seem like patience, were it capable of thought—but they knew that such plagues were simply the ones that survived, and not possessed of deliberate intent.

They heard the grinding and scraping of a vast body long before they came across it. Of the seven heads of the hydral elemental, one had already known of their approach, from some kind of metaphysical perception; two others spotted them as soon as they entered its line of sight. Those, Ketka knew to be air and shadow: the first to see the way even their cloaked presence shifted the flow of air around them, and the other to see the cloak itself.

She reached into her belt pouch and came out with a potion—of sorts, she thought to herself in annoyance. The Shemmai word was a category-word which encompassed many things, but the language of her homeland was far more specific. She had learned to avoid using separate words for ointments, elixirs, coatings, spikes, and more, but it was still utterly bizarre to her that a single word might describe both a thing one drank to heal wounds and an explosive.

These were a non-standard design, and one that she disliked. She'd still bought two dozen of them, when they'd passed through the city of Mevi; for the results these provided, she could deal with the awkwardness.

She pressed the cap down, twisted it a quarter turn, and pulled it out. The pouch of reactants tore, and oxygen flooded into the vacuum of the flask, disturbing the careful layers inside. She slammed the cap back down— she wanted the explosion, not the tongue of searing flame—and twisted it back to seal it.

She gave the situation a moment's consideration, despite the now-strict deadline she was on. Flashing a hand-sign for *fire*, she began to run forwards, Skills activating as she did so. **[Flow of Battle]** began its escalation, **[Primaeval Shift]** ate at her consciousness as her body came into alignment with the thousands of years of history she was an heir to, and **[Shatter Their Strength With Overwhelming Power]** infused the burgeoning cataclysm she held in her hand.

By the time she threw the flask into the flame-mouth of the elemental, the explosive had become something edging into the realm of the profane. Alongside that potion, Sayyad's grenades flew with casual ease, as did Deoro's tiny, compressed marbles of molten iron—explosives without explosions, thermobarics that would feed on the oxygen within the creature and expand, very briefly, its understanding of the word *exothermic*.

All of these carried blessings from Beyin, but those blessings would likely die in their fires. Still, it was best to invest in the attempt. Not all things could suppress the explosions—and of those, most were particularly vulnerable to the biological attacks which the iron, kept intact, would carry.

The moment before their attacks began, their foe preempted them. Seven attacks, each lethal to the party in its entirety, struck as one. Each enhanced the others; there was no interference between them, only synergy and amplification. Each was, alone, an attack that any of them might have dealt with, but even Deoro would have struggled to contain two.

Iōanna set herself in a balanced stance, back cracking softly as she straightened to her full, still-average height. Her eyes lost their rheumy tint, and her hands did not shake as she thrust them out, **[A Moment Beyond Mortality]** snapping her into focus in the world as though the room suddenly revolved around her.

Her shield permitted the attacks of her team to pass through. It consumed the attacks of their foe, transmuting them and repurposing them into a shell around the elemental. She contained and amplified the heat and shockwaves of the explosions, feeding more oxygen into the flames.

And with that, the fight began in earnest.

CHAPTER 3.1 - LET VILE AWAKENINGS NOT HINDER YOUR BANTER

On the second morning of my new life, I woke up in a state that could only be described as pathetically gross.

I made it to the bathroom in time to cough up the first glob of mucus and spit it cleanly, inasmuch as that could ever apply, into the toilet bowl. My throat seized up for a moment as the second one surfaced, and then I gargled up the third and hacked up the fourth.

I was dimly aware of Kelly's rapid footsteps, of a panicked tone to her voice and her hands pulling my hair back. I couldn't breathe; my throat was too locked, every muscle involuntarily trying to shove everything out for a totally unconscious definition of *everything*.

"**[A Daily Reference]**," I heard a voice intone, and that made it through my stupor.

Nothing else made it through, though. I could hear her speaking, but the words didn't arrange themselves into sentences, didn't parse into words.

The fifth wad lodged terrifyingly in my throat for a moment, too thick and broad to easily get out. My muscles redoubled, straining somehow as though I were birthing a homunculus of snot, and with one final heave it splattered into the dry bowl.

I retched, vomiting—blessedly, without nausea and without a hint of stomach acid—until finally the flow stopped.

I reached for a towel to blot myself free of tears and residue before realizing that my face was clean and dry. Feeling a sense of almost grudging joy at that, I opened my eyes, staring down at the pristine, polished stone of the bowl that perfectly reflected every drawn line of my face. I could breathe again, too, and I did so—slowly, steadily, willing my racing heart to calm.

"That," I said softly into the silence, "might have been one of the grossest things in my entire life. Nothing compares since the time I was shat out of my mother's vagina in a flood of blood and amniotic fluid."

"Back with me?"

I turned to look at Kelly. She was doing her best to smile at me, but I read a terrified concern in her body language. "Morning's joy, Miss Avara," I managed, smirking feebly.

A substantial amount of tension bled out of her. "Morning's joy, Miss Nadash," she responded gravely. "You seem to have been in a bit of a state, I must say."

"Yeah, well." I giggled, a weak and watery sound but still with an unexpectedly genuine mirth. "At least the *magical bathroom* handles the cleanup. What'd your Skill say?"

"My... you noticed?"

"It shook the world and wrote itself across my brain, Kelly." My throat burned a little, and my voice was a little bit hoarse, but I managed wryness nonetheless. "Hard not to notice."

She blinked a couple of times, humming to herself. "That's some strong attunement. Was that a blessing from one of the Gods?"

"Not that I know of? Skills activating sound a lot like my... patron, I guess?" I scowled at nothing in particular. "They sound like the goddess who sent me here, when she spoke with divine intent." I forced myself to stand up, which was a good decision. The burning feeling in my mouth and throat was fading fast, and everything was settling back to normal. "What'd you get from it?"

Kelly scowled fixedly into the distance. "Something that isn't *totally* useless! There's a set of attestations that Travelers who get the Adaptation spell can have, and I'm quoting verbatim here, *a variety of fleeting secondary effects as a new equilibrium is reached*."

"Not totally useless indeed." I was still wearing my clothes from last night, but there wasn't anything to be done about that, since I didn't have any other clothes. It all felt clean against my skin, but the thought was still gross; it would have been a lot grosser if there'd been any food or stomach acid coming up.

I'd taken my boots off. The need to put them back *on* was a titanic gulf my brain couldn't conceive of crossing; I got up anyway, walking over to my mattress. Acknowledging the vastness of the undertaking and the hopelessness of ever changing my immediate status quo for the better, I grabbed my boots and shoved my feet inside them.

"They don't say what the effects are, though, and I've *read* all of the records and books we have on extraplanar Travelers from non-adaptive settings! And okay, I don't remember everything, but if we had anything that expanded on it, I'd have pulled that up. So I think this afternoon, we might have to visit the Library and see about getting some texts transferred."

"Uh huh." I studied the buckles on my boots. This wasn't the first time I was putting them back on, but it'd been few enough times that I was still relearning the fasteners. They were close enough to ski boots that I could figure it out, though; ratchet, lever, snap, and the counter-tension kept the buckle closed. "You have your boots on?"

"No? I was *sleeping*. You woke me up! Not that I'm complaining, I was just worried."

"Well, get your boots on." The second buckle was easier than the first, and the third easier than the second. The fourth and fifth were just above the ankle, and then it was on to the second boot. "If the sun's through the window, breakfast is on, right?"

"Sun's—sure." I heard her walk a couple of steps away, and then her footsteps paused. "Sophie, are you… okay? Because you don't sound okay. Do you want to talk?"

"I want *breakfast*, Kelly." I laughed quietly, forcing my shoulders to un-hunch. "I want something to wash the taste of that out of my mouth, and something to give my stomach real flavor to focus on. And also I'm hungry enough that I'm probably rocking a malus again. But you know what else? I'll bet you a crown that Raphaella is at Rise right now, waiting for me to show up. May as well take advantage of that."

There was a moment of silence after I said that, and I tended to my boot fastenings. A few seconds after I was buckled up, wiggling my toes in wonderfully supportive footwear, I heard her stomping out into the hallway. Standing from where I'd been sitting on the edge of my mattress—it hadn't gotten old in those few days, and might never get old, that I could just stand up like that without using my arms—I met her half-scowling, half-curious look with a smile.

"Bit of a sucker's bet for me, isn't that? You don't even have the crown you're betting."

I smirked at her and fished one of the small coins out of my pouch. Flipping it into the air with a thumb, I caught it between two fingers and slipped it back into the pouch. "Face on each side, right? Both crowned. That's why you call 'em crowns."

Kelly didn't seem to know whether she was more interested in burying her face in her hands or glaring at me. Instead of doing either of them, she spun on her heel and started marching towards the stairs. "I'm not dealing with this right now," she groused. "Got woken up early after a dancing night, now she's making fun of me."

"When did you tell me that you had some coinage, Sophie? Because I don't remember you telling me that, Sophie! Is that what I hear you ask?"

"No, actually! I didn't ask!"

"That's right." We headed down the stairs, her determinedly not turning around to show the grin I can hear in her voice, me following in her wake. "You didn't ask, but also I don't rem—what's all this stuff?"

"Oh, these?" Kelly turned to smirk back at me as we reached the main floor, sitting gingerly on one of the dozens of crates that'd appeared overnight. There was still a wince in her expression, but her voice had some humor in it as she avoided answering my question. "Well, aren't you a curious one this morning."

"I will absolutely cough on you if you don't cough up some answers." I nudged the smallest of the crates with my foot, shifting it without too much effort. I could hear the contents sloshing as I did. "Are these reagents?"

"No, silly, the reagents are downstairs. This is from the village's stock of Basic Set potions."

I took one look at her smirk, which was wider than ever, and then tore my eyes away from the rows of containers and marched towards the door. "Reagents are downstairs, she says. No, you're being silly, she says. From the village's stock, she says they are. Bah!" I threw my hands wide as I stepped outside, taking a deep breath as though I were breathing in the sunlight itself. "Bah, I say! I can't deal with her nonsense until after breakfast."

"*My* nonsense?" Kelly lunged off of her seat and stomped after me, audibly slamming her hands onto her hips after she closed the door with deliberate care. "Oh, I see how it is. You can wake me up with—I don't even want to say it. I don't want to remember it! But it's *my* nonsense?"

"Sounds about right."

It was petty of me, petty of both of us, but we bickered loudly all the short distance from the shop-house—from *my* shop-house—to the refectory at the eastern end of the village. Far from being able to keep our faces straight, we were outright giggling by the time we were halfway there. We bumped hips with matching grins as we walked through the door to the dining hall, and I let her lead us to where the plates were stacked.

"Traveler."

"Rafa! What a coincidence to—"

"**[Diagnosis At A Glance]**."

The words slammed *through* me, hitting me with such perceptible force that I was surprised I was still on my feet a moment later. My eyes watering, I blinked a few times, expecting a follow-up—but she just grunted and started turning away.

"Ma'am?" Kelly was suddenly standing in her way. She'd moved *fast*, fast enough that I hadn't noticed her moving at all. She didn't say anything else, just stood there, hands clasped behind her back, perfectly composed and expectant.

"Hmph. You think that just by being polite, you can get me to work before I've had breakfast?"

"It's as you say, ma'am." Kelly's shoulders squared up just that little bit more, her eyes growing more intense. "My friend didn't have such a good morning. But you already know that. Ma'am."

"Ain't on healer duty today." There was a shift in Rafa's body language and a glint in her eyes as she turned to walk away, then paused. "You, girl!" She turned back to me, and though her eyes were stern, the muscles around them—eyebrows, corners of the eyes, and more—betrayed her more pleased mood. "Eat some oatmeal! Skip the sweets. Your respiratory system is more or less done fucking around, like you found out this morning, but your digestive system isn't by a long shot. Fats will give your system more time to chew on it—which you need, to be clear—and the fiber will bind it a bit. If you start getting skin itch, take a hot shower—it'll be because your skin's trying to shit itself out of your pores. And maybe don't look at what's coming out."

"Thank you, Doctor Raphaella."

She'd taken a couple of steps away, but at that, she turned and fixed me with a level glare. Her mouth opened and closed, and then she grunted quietly into the sudden, echoing silence of the refectory.

"I go by Rafa," she said eventually. "Pretty sure I asked you to call me that. Don't take particularly well to someone ignoring that."

"I apologize," I said with a faint smile. My voice was still contrite, for all the humor in the situation. "It's inappropriate of me to disregard your preferred terms of address. Morning's joy, Rafa, and may this be all the duties that come to you as a healer today."

Rafa snorted at that, but she did it with a sort of wistful smile, something easing in the wrinkles of her face. She turned and half walked off, half stomped off, like she was too distracted to properly pretend to be cranky.

"I like her," I murmured to Kelly. "I'm gonna dedicate my second bowl of oatmeal to her."

Kelly snickered quietly, looking mildly horrified. "Get your food, Sophie, and let's stop holding up the line."

I glanced backwards performatively, raising my eyebrows at her. "Yep. That's definitely a line of people looking really impatient. Actually," I mused, grabbing the largest bowls they had available, "there's surprisingly little food compared to yesterday."

"Yesterday, sittings were at Thesha's, so here we had the open table. *Today*, we are at the sitting refectory, the refectory where we sit and eat what they bring us, *before the first sitting*. They're not all the way ready yet."

"That's funny." I loaded up my plate with a variety of fruits, two kinds of juice, and a tall glass of milk. I added something halfway between milk and cream by thickness to the oatmeal, then did the same with some honey. "Why are you awake so early, anyway? You coulda slept in! Goodness, at the refectory before first sitting? Scandalous. Anyway, let's grab a table, since we're here."

I glanced over at her out of the corner of my eye, trying to be subtle. She caught me at it, turning her half-infuriated, poleaxed look into an almost-suppressed sigh.

"Come on." I looked over at her as I sat down, tasting my first spoonful of the oatmeal. "Wow, this is *amazing*. You gotta explain these fruits to me, and what the juices are!"

"Sophie."

"Yes, Kelly?"

"I'm going to have to find a way to get you back for this. You know that, right?"

"Yeah, I know," I said, starting to snicker. "But you'll—scuse me." I took a deep breath, composing my face for the critical moment. "Looks like you'll have to get up a whole lot earlier to do it."

She sat down a few beats later, cackling in laughter along with me, and we dug into our food with gusto, like we were two friends getting ready to take on a very small slice of the world.

CHAPTER 3.2 - ORDERS OF BUSINESS

"The first order of business is taking stock."

We'd finished eating the food we'd gotten ourselves and, since first sitting had started, I just kept going with the first and then second plates a couple of teenagers had brought me. The fruits I didn't already know were identified as rast—a semi-sweet, reddish-purple berry full of juice—and a tangy, dry apple. One of the juices was from that same apple varietal, while the other turned out to be a blackberry cider. That one made my brain stop for a moment while I sat back, eyes rolling back in my head from bliss.

"There's five crates of what I think are Basic Set potions, which means there should be enough furniture to put a representation of them up, and we need to see what reagents—"

"The first order of business is visiting Tomas," I said gently, cutting Kelly off. "I know you don't get along with him, and I have a feeling there's a history there, but I said we'd be there."

I got up in the moment of uneasy silence, looking for where I should be bringing the glass that was the last thing at my seat. Tizpa snagged it out of my hands a couple of seconds after I stood up, shooting me a genuinely aggrieved look that made me wince.

Guess that's a faux pas, I thought to myself.

"Tomas," Kelly said with a sigh as she got up. "Fine. You're right, and I'm definitely not going to tell you to spurn someone reaching out to you. Make friends with everyone you can. A load spread is the load most easily carried."

That had the sound of an aphorism, but it was a good one.

"And you're sure I should do that even if it's socially awkward for you?" I shot Kelly a grin to try to take the sting out of the words as we left the hall.

"Even," she said with a forced cheer, "when it's awkward for me."

"What if," I said, drawing my face into utter solemnity, "Matron Zeva decides to be friends with—" Kelly started giggling before I finished the sentence, and I couldn't keep a straight face once she did. "Okay, maybe not that."

"That would be a miracle," she said cheerfully. Her finger jabbed out, nailing me right under the ribs, and I squeaked in surprise. "A miracle! Worth a Feat on its own! By all means, do it."

"Does she not have any friends?" The thought was a little sobering, some of the levity leaving me. "She seems like an unpleasant old lady, but that doesn't mean she should be alone."

"She's not... *alone*."

Kelly frowned, and I gave her time to think. She was leading us south around the ring, and I could see within a few steps where we were heading—there was a sign with a spool of thread crossed with a needle, subtly done in relief on weathered wood, and that couldn't be anything other than Tomas's shop-house. In the meantime, I wasn't in any hurry and I wasn't bored at all. The morning was bright and sunny, the trees were gloriously vast, and everything I could see was beautiful to behold.

"Matron Zeva doesn't have any young friends," Kelly said eventually, once we were most of the way there. "She expects a level of deference that my generation, our generation, won't give, even to most people who deserve it. But she'll accept respect without deference from the older folks, and she's done a lot to earn respect. She's still kinda nasty, but she's not..."

"She's not socially isolated?"

"Yeah." That got me a nod. "Her immediate family's either come to the end of their Paths or left for elsewhere—or didn't come to Kibosh in the first place—but she's not isolated." We were at Tomas's door, but Kelly hesitated, face scrunched. "She manages the beans and fruit for three quints. They out-produce the rest of the village combined. And even if she didn't, even if she hadn't been worthy of respect in the past, we still wouldn't let her be shunned."

"That's... really reassuring, actually." I grinned at her, then jerked my head at the door. "Want to do the honors?"

She glared at me, then sighed. She raised her hand to knock—or whatever the Shemmai equivalent was—and the door opened smoothly before she could actually do so.

Tomas's high, fluting tenor rang out from somewhere inside, out of line of sight. "Miss Nadash! Miss Avara!" There was the tiniest hitch in it, one that was small enough I thought I might have been imagining it. "Please come in."

The public area of Tomas's main floor turned out to be surprisingly sparse. There were three mannequins, each with an eclectic mix of clothing in various styles—and similarly a mix of body types they were suited for, which was an interesting choice. There were a couple of racks with some more clothes which might have been organized by style or cut or something… and that was it, other than a bare counter.

"In the back room," Tomas called out. "Around the corner, I *think* the area is clear but I'm missing a needle, please don't step on it!"

Kelly reached a hand under the lip of the counter, frowning. "Tomas, you left the counter down and locked!"

"Oh!"

A few moments passed as we stood around, Kelly awkwardly and me inspecting one of the pieces on display, a broad-brimmed hat with a stiff, mesh netting hanging from the inner banding. It ran around three quarters of the hat, and the mesh was incredibly fine and gleamed in the light streaming in through the windows.

"Here we are, I do apologize for forgetting the flap, did *not* intend to waste even a moment of your… oh! Are you interested in a repelling hat? It's not something particularly necessary during striving, not until late Harvest."

"Sorry, I was just distracted." I turned back towards him, blinking a couple times as I took him in. "That's an amazing fusion of practicality and style, wow."

"Thank you! Please, follow me."

It was clear that he was preening at the compliment, but he deserved it. He was one step away from peacocking with his colors and possibly also fabrics, resplendent in vivid blue, purple, and red silk and shimmering cotton—or the equivalent. Still, everything was tight enough not to catch and loose enough not to bind, and he wore gloves that had reinforced padding in certain, no doubt critical places.

Also, he had a phenomenal ass in those tight pants. Gay as I was, I still noticed; and then I deliberately shifted my attention elsewhere.

His workshop was almost as sparse as his storefront. He had indexed—some sort of numerical shorthand written on their sides—waist-high shelves whose cubbies had small stacks, or often just one piece, of clothing. Those clothes were tightly folded and covered in sheets transparent enough to be barely visible, and everything was meticulously clean, colors contrasting without clashing.

The shelves were set out in rows across the space with just enough room to walk between, with one crossing lane in the center along with the one near the storefront, and Tomas wound through them as we bobbed in his wake.

"Miss Avara, I do not want to presume—"

"Really."

"—but," he continued gamely, as if she hadn't interrupted, "your measurements have not changed?"

Kelly opened her mouth to say something, then closed it. "Right," she said after a long moment, voice controlled and quiet. "My measurements haven't changed."

"Good! I took the liberty of preparing yours beforehand, as I said, don't want to waste even a moment of your time. Sophie, please stand on the, ah, feet around the corner, place your hands on the hands, and wait a moment. Leave your boots on, but doff your coat, if you please."

I nodded at him and stepped around the corner, blinking a few times. Tomas's actual *working* space was as cluttered and disorganized as the rest of the building was tidy. It was a wonder he'd only lost one needle; a vast array of tools and fabrics was splayed across three long tables, hanging from hooks, and stuffed into shelving and boxes.

The feet he mentioned were a pair of raised blocks next to one of the walls in the least-cluttered corner of the workshop, covered in chalk squiggles in a vaguely foot-like shape. There was a hook to hang my coat on, which left it brushing against three pairs of pants on one side and a bolt of cloth on the other; presumably this was fine, so I didn't worry about it, and put my hands on the hand-shaped squiggles on the wall.

What followed was... startling, in a sort of abstract sense. I got an intense feeling of being *observed*, one which was localized to a narrow band around my toes and which moved steadily from them to my heels and then up my legs. It kept going, like a computer vision version of elevator eyes, tracing every inch of skin from my toes to my fingers and scalp—and then my feet slid back, and the pieces of wood that my hands were on shifted downwards and rotated to face up.

Muttering imprecations under my breath and shaking my head, I let the measurement area guide me into being on my hands and knees. Various bits of me which could be described as *curves* hung down, which wasn't so much uncomfortable as it was embarrassing, and then the observation-or-scanning feeling once again passed over every inch of skin from my fingers and scalp back down to my head.

I didn't actually mind it all that much. I'd had more invasive bra fittings, and the bras I'd bought at those stores were by far the best I'd had, and I was resolute in not thinking about it any further than that.

The feeling winked out after the second pass was done, and I stood up as the *tack, tack* of Tomas's crisp footsteps heralded his and Kelly's approach.

"Nice," I said after a moment of consideration, nodding at Kelly. "Long sleeves, overlap, vents for a couple of pockets or pouches. Nothing trailing, nothing that'll knock something over by mistake, but it goes past the knees and covers the neck. Absorbent? How fast does it come off?"

Kelly looked like she was about to say something funny in response, then visibly changed her mind. "Fast, it's got a quick-release." She reached just into the overlapping panels in the front of the lab coat—because that was *definitely* a lab coat—and squeezed something. The coat dropped to the floor instantly, leaving her in the calf-length, sky-blue skirt and teal blouse she'd been wearing.

I looked at it as it pooled on the floor. It was the one piece of protective gear that even Hitz's workshop area hadn't had; it didn't seem likely that there'd be a lab coat in my starter kit. And even besides the fact that it was protective gear, well…

"How much? For two of them, obviously."

It was a *lab coat*. I wanted it, and both of us needed one regardless.

"My husband," Tomas said quietly, "is in the Guard. He has quiet days, but almost never quiet weeks; and say what you will about the diligence of Clerk Administrator James, he simply *cannot* ensure an adequate stock of the Basic Set. The available mandates aren't enough for a village this close to the Forest."

"It's the dungeon." Kelly saw my confusion before I opened my mouth to ask the question, and preempted me by answering it. "We need to hold a reserve sufficient for a Breach, which means our usable stock is lower than they'd want to use in the time between supply runs. Between the delving runs and the fighting Forest-side, the village goes through a *lot*."

Tomas had started rummaging through a bin that he'd pulled out from under one of the tables, nodding along to Kelly's answer. "I would rather see the Guard go through elemental grenades than universalized blood and rapid-healing elixirs, even if it takes many of the former to save some few of the latter."

I blinked at that a few times. "That's… obviously that's a thing. Right. Obviously those are all things. Things which I can make?"

"As long," Tomas said with a perfectly even voice, "as you can work. Mustn't be injured, can't work with hydrochloric acid burns, funny how nobody thinks about that when they write the books. Take the coats, Miss Nadash, Miss Avara. Your good health and safety are the safety and good health in turn of my husband, along with others."

"Looking out for each other," I murmured dryly, glancing over at Kelly. "And for the village, I think it was. So that everyone wins?" She had the grace to redden a bit at that. "Thank you, Tomas. And call me Sophie, okay?"

"Tomas," Kelly began before he could say anything—and then she stopped, as though she didn't know what to say. I looked at her, my face twitching against a grin, and we waited patiently. "Thank you," she eventually managed. "You've always been gracious, even though I can't seem to be."

"No regrets for the destination," he said quietly. "Not the easiest journey. **[Final Adjustment]**." He stood, wincing a little, and dropped a folded lab coat into my arms.

He caught Kelly's gaze, like he was challenging her, and she folded her hands at her belly and stayed quiet. They stood like that for a long moment, doing *something* culturally social that I didn't know anything about, and then it passed and left an even more awkward silence in its wake.

"Morning's joy, Kelly. Lock the counter on your way out, please. Morning's joy, Sophie. Find me sometime and we can see about more clothes for you."

The dismissal was obvious, and neither of us was inclined to argue about it. We made our way into the brilliant morning sunlight, burdened by the products of his kindness, heading home.

CHAPTER 3.3 - IN PURSUIT OF THE TRUST THAT PERMITS DISCUSSION

We made it about halfway to the shop-house in silence.

This was a tremendous feat for me, because I spent the entire way fighting my urge to say something rude or unkind. Every step seemed to emphasize the weight of the lab coat in my arms, and every step underlined how good of a call it had been to visit Tomas at his invitation.

"So."

It was Kelly who broke the silence, sounding awkward and almost nervous. I looked over at her, and was instantly distracted by the basket on her arm, which I hadn't remembered her having gotten. *I must not have been paying attention*, I thought to myself wryly. *There's a hint of irony in that.*

"So!"

"So… this morning, we should work on something from the Basic Set. Discharge your obligation, let you get used to your tools with something low-complexity?"

"Kelly, is that the thing that…" I paused, sighing. "Don't you think we might have something we should be discussing?"

"Planning's important." Her voice was a little strained, but she had it mostly under control. "I had a plan, I think it's a good plan, let's get back to it."

Okay, so, nice isn't going to work. I could still just let it go, and navigate around whatever her problem was. Multiple problems, obviously, everyone had multiple problems. *Or I could just… not.* "You're really bad at some of this, aren't you."

I almost regretted saying it the moment it left my mouth, even if it was true. It was *absurd* to want to reroll the dice on something that was basically functional. Sure, she had an obligation to me, but she was also my lifeline in a strange new world—and *hope* was a dumbass kind of plan, even if I was pretty confident in navigating this conversation.

Thankfully, miraculously, Kelly seemed more defensive and embarrassed than hurt.

"Sophie! I don't know what you're talking about. Why would you even say that?"

"Kelly," I said patiently, "we just walked away from a meeting you'd have had me miss because you don't want to hang out with your old flame. In that meeting, I learned vital civic information *and* we both got a high-quality piece of important personal protective equipment. You don't think there's anything to discuss about who else I might want to talk to?"

"Sure, but... none of the Basic Set calls for these! I mean, not that Tomas wasn't being kind in giving them, or that we should have refused, but—"

"Kelly." I cut her off, keeping my voice utterly gentle. "It's okay to not be good at things. I'm sure you're doing a great job overall. You've kept me in motion when I would be breaking down if I stopped for too long. You're keeping me fed, you helped me find a Class that I'm genuinely excited to start working on, and you've introduced me to some really nice, interesting people. It was obvious that using Hitz's workshop was a big thing, even if you played it down. I watched you casually take two problems and gently bop them together, and *poof*, a solution.

"But I swear by the seven sacred names of the God of my mother and father, that single sovereign power who was said to have created the universe: if you can't step back and acknowledge when you fuck up, I will drill it through your skull. Let my name be struck from the Book of Life if I lie."

I didn't stop walking as I talked, and Kelly was sort of dragged along in my wake, trying not to stare at the ground in a defensive hunch. I let the silence drag on—it was a useful silence, a pressure silence. I was a connoisseur of silences, though almost always from the other side of the conversation, and any—

"I *am* good at my job," she blurted out. "Empirically."

I glanced back, smiling a little at her. "I have no doubt."

Her face got redder at that. "I've gotten the absolute top end of the statistically plausible range for System Experience *or higher* every single time I've been assigned to anyone!"

"And I have no idea how impressive that is, but I'm sure the answer is *very*."

"Don't *mock* me!" Kelly's mood shifted suddenly—and predictably—to anger, anger at the pressure of the silence and at a half-dozen other elements of the situation. "Don't you *dare*—"

I stopped suddenly, spinning on my heel to make eye contact with her. My hands came up to shoulder height, palms facing hers. "Kelly, I would never mock you. Seal it with our palms if you want, I wasn't mocking you and *will never* mock you."

"I'm not an idiot," she spat. "Don't condescend—"

"Would never condescend, either. Name an oath to bind it, seal it however you want. I don't mock, I don't condescend, I don't do passive-aggression." My eyes bored into hers, deliberately drawing her up short. "I can be hard to be friends with, because I won't shy away from speaking my heart's truths. But I'll never use that as an excuse to be unkind."

"Then…"

She looked lost, and I wanted to hug her, tell her that she wasn't the one who was supposed to be lost, that was *my* job. I wanted to yell at her, because kicking her ass into gear *wasn't my job*, and why didn't she have someone else who could show her what she was doing wrong? If she was so good at her job, *why did this fall to me*?

I wanted to scream, because yet again, here I was with the shittiest job, the one only the new girl could do. Pointing out problems to—and with—my boss, even if she was also my coworker, agent, and social worker. Setting the stage for yet another stint of dysfunctional dynamics.

"You're very impressive," I said instead. "Really. You did a bunch of impressive things—like that one conversation with Kartom—and I think we're going to absolutely kick ass together."

"And you think I'm *really bad* at this anyway." The anger was mostly gone, replaced with confusion and the hurt that had fueled the anger in the first place.

"I think you're really bad at *some* of it." I paused, studying her face, gauging my words. My hands were still up, and I waggled them to catch her eye. "Listen, I was serious about… it's sealing it with our palms, right? We put our palms up like this."

"And we're sealing… what?" She put her hands on mine, despite everything she was feeling, despite the emotions so clearly on display. "That we'll be… I mean, that wasn't nice."

"No mockery, no condescension," I said softly. "We'll never belittle, never degrade or deride each other. No hidden meaning left as a trap for moments of recollection or reflection, no knives slipped in through pleasant words. Whatever we say to each other, it won't ever be that. Because I need you to know, always, that if I say you're impressive? It's because you are. So that if I tell you that you fucked up by letting *your* bullshit get in the way of *my* getting knowledge, social connections, and gear that I needed, you can listen without it poisoning the other stuff I say."

"Easy to say," Kelly murmured. I wasn't sure if she even knew she was talking out loud. "Anyone can say that."

"So seal it." There was a roaring in my head, a call somehow both overwhelming and muted. *How many times have I wished to be able to do exactly this?* "Tell me what vow, what oath, will convince you that I'm serious."

"That you're... no, that's not right." Her voice was soft, distant. Her eyes were unfocused, and her body strangely relaxed. "What you're asking for is an oath that seals us both, isn't it? So this isn't about me, when people ask about this kind of thing... it's about you, everything I know about people says this is something you want for yourself."

The denial stuck in my throat, refusing to come out. "It is," I heard myself say instead, which was entirely not what I'd intended. My hands were—no, *our* hands were warm where they touched, palms pressed together precisely as she'd shown me the day before. "My jokes have claws, and my praise can sound like jokes. And I grew up surrounded by that, so how can I ever trust in the jokes and praise of others?

"Everywhere I've been," I continued bitterly, "everywhere I've worked, a suggestion or even an observation was an insult and a challenge, so how could anything improve? And are you any different? If you can't look at something like our interaction with Tomas and accept that you made a series of mistakes, I'll have to either poison everything between us or compensate for you behind your back. Again, yet again, like every *single* time."

"They treat me like a child," Kelly said. There was a quiet fierceness in her voice, a wounded pride that was lashing out at those not present. Maybe there'd been the same tone in my own voice. Maybe my fingers were flexing against hers just like hers were flexing against mine. "Maybe some of them won't treat me that way once I've had my century's turn, but even those do it right now. No matter how fast I advance, no matter how well the System itself grades me on my work, that won't change."

"Won't it be nice?" There was a heat coursing through me, a feeling like I'd clasped a live wire with a third hand and the only thing saving us was standing on the thinnest of insulation. "No forced truths, no geas on our actions. We wouldn't have to be friends, even; maybe won't be, not for long, there'll be too much honesty and nobody's ever been able to handle me being honest about their work to their face without taking it personally. But we could trust. You could trust, I could trust."

"Sophie. This doesn't seem like you. None of this, my read on you was that you were conflict-averse and non-confrontational, my *Skills* told me the same." She took a deep breath, nostrils flaring. "Forge-fire and the wilds; are you manifesting—"

"I'm allowed to contain multitudes." I was grinning at her, but I couldn't feel most of it; only the tips of it, where my lips ended, where the muscles pulled until my face folded and ached. "I'm allowed to be conflict-averse and still throw down when I need to. I'm allowed to *want* to be non-confrontational and still force the issue. Besides, there's a part of me that's young and hungry and fey, and it's been in torpor or a coma for seventeen years. And this idea? I like it. Don't you?"

"Because you need this."

I wanted to shake my head. I would have, but my muscles were locked and immobile, and I was pretty sure so were hers. "I won't let you make this be just about me. I don't fully know why I'm doing this, why *we're* doing this, but this is about us. Both of us, independently, and the two of us together."

There was a tension in her fingers and wrists at that, one which rippled and almost forced our hands apart. Then she relaxed, bit by bit, until she looked like she was in the grip of some ethereal ease, a counterpart to my fey mood. "Each of us," she said, voice hungry. Her voice echoed, ringing in a way that wasn't physical; it wasn't *her* voice, not entirely, three-toned and too formal. "Each and both of us. May all Gods who have their eyes upon us be kind, in this pact we're forging."

"Artemis Daphnaia, Artemis Eurunomê." I called on her without preamble, without thought. It was the first time I'd spoken her name out loud since meeting her, and it was *different* somehow—and in Sylvan, because there simply wasn't a name for her in Shemmai, but at the same time her name and her two epithets weren't in *any* language. They were just… a pair of numinous Truths that stood alone, or rather as part of one broader Truth. "Goddess of women and girls, I call upon you. I know that you abhor that which is false; I know that you cannot abide the veil on an insult or a smile that bears a knife. Grant us this blessing, and the first works of cypress and laurelwoods that pass through my hands, I'll dedicate to you."

"I invoke Eichan the Striver." Kelly's pupils were ringed in steel and a brassy yellow. "Through this pact, may we take the world and set ourselves to change it. I invoke Midu the Enduring, the Unyielding. May we weather all storms that threaten the pact we now make, and never break it even if we grow apart or opposed."

"Hêphaistos Klytotékhnēs. God of artisans, of masterworks, of things made with purpose." Words were flowing through me in real-time; I had no idea what I was about to say, or where they were coming from. All I knew was that this was proper, that this offering of exchange was *right*. "What we build now, we build deliberately. Let every link of this chain be strong and light. Let it be, in the end, a thing of beauty; let it be not a shackle but a lifeline.

"Do this for us, and—" I flailed mentally for an endless moment, near to panicking. But there was a familiar smell to the air, one of heated metal; and there was a hand on my shoulder, a hand whose weight and strength were tempered only by an incomprehensible control and patience, and suddenly I had *time*. "Do this for us," I said after an eternity that lasted only a heartbeat, "and I will learn the truths of sand and fire and air. I will make from those, by my own hands, a tool of glass, of quality suitable to my work and usable in my craft—and that tool, and what it produces, I will dedicate to you."

There wasn't a flash of power, nor was there a burst of searing heat. We stood there, palms pressed against palms, and I realized that Kelly had wrapped her pinkies around mine in an awkward imitation of a pinkie swear—and that was it. No feeling like words were spilling out of my mouth, no jaw-shattering grin. No inability to turn my head, even if I wasn't looking away from her eyes, and the rings of color around her pupils.

No pressure from my System, like I was a channel for a bolt of lightning between it and the world.

In fact—

"Sophie," Kelly said with a voice of quiet terror, "I can't... I don't..."

"I can't touch my System either. Feels like it's just not there, like there's nothing there. Even when Kartom blocked me off and tested me..."

She broke eye contact, looking around wildly. She almost immediately stopped, staring at something on the ground with her eyes wide. "Sophie?"

"Yeah?"

"I… look at the ground, Sophie."

"Gods abounding," I murmured a moment later. "That's beautiful."

Patches of ash, like someone had turned a flamethrower to the ground. Frozen earth, like in each patch, every molecule of water had crystallized. Vines and weeds and grasses, like a thousand seeds had been a season in the ground.

Fire, ice, and life surrounded us in a thick circle made of complex, fractal whorls. They had no discernible pattern to them, blending into each other in irregular and partial ways, and there was a fourth element to it. It was a kind of conquest, where life thrust into ice to shatter it, fire turned life to ash, and ice choked the fire's supply of air.

"I bet," I said with a soft smile, "the second we step outside of this circle, we'll have our Systems with us again."

"Sophie, what the *fuck* did we just do?"

My smile widened. "I think we just swore a pact." For all that Kelly's voice sounded like she couldn't decide whether to be insensibly astonished or terrified, everything in me sang of a strange purity and rightness. "I think we just swore a pact before four gods, which is going to be really awkward for me come the Day of Atonement, because I don't actually have any regrets."

"I have no idea what that means." She started giggling. "I have no idea what that means but I know in my bones you don't care that I don't know, that you're not making a reference to something I don't know just to be mean, you just said the thing that you were going to say without thinking about whether I was in or out of it."

I shifted forwards—when had I sat down? we'd both sat down at some point—and put a hand on her shoulder. "Kelly, there's a critically important matter at hand. And we have to address it before we have the conversation."

She visibly strangled the giggling, shoulders still almost vibrating and chest heaving. I averted my eyes from that, though not in any particular hurry, and she tilted her head at me. "The conversation?"

"The conversation we were going to have. The one that started this? The reason we made a pact, because I said you were really bad at some things?"

"*That* conversation." She took a deep breath, then another. "I'm not panicking and I'm not mad. I'm—"

"*Kelly.*" I cut across her, putting my other hand on her other shoulder. "There's a thing!"

"Okay, okay." She breathed deliberately, deep and slow. "What thing?"

"See, there's a thing where I come from. There's a phrase, a self-assessment phrase, a phrase for a state of mind. Follow?"

"I follow." She nodded a couple of times, head bobbing up and down.

"It's a phrase that's a sort of tautology, because the word for evaluating the state is the word for the state; you say the word, and it inflicts the state, or maybe you react to it in the state that is the word." I locked eyes with her, pitching my voice low. I had no idea why I was doing this, but I knew the urge came within me—was boiling out from my depths. "And the word, and also the state, is… *spoon.*"

The silence between us lasted exactly three heartbeats, and then the moment shattered and we fell to the floor, howling in laughter with our hands clasped together.

CHAPTER 3.4 - A GIFT OF YOUR HEART'S TRUTHS

Our hysteria—left, no doubt, by the passage of divinity—didn't, *couldn't* sustain itself. We didn't try to make it last; we laughed until we wept, lying on the stone of the ring road with our wrists clasped, and let the moment pass in its chosen time.

"So," I eventually asked, tired of silence and still gripped by the last of the fey mood, "what was he like?"

"What?"

"Tomas," I clarified, glancing over at Kelly. I didn't bother hiding my smirk, or the glints of humor in my eyes. "Who was obviously your old flame. What was he like?"

"I…" She frowned, turning the question over and around in her head. "Different?"

"Well, obviously." I snorted. "Moments of revelation change a person, I'm fully aware of that. He has a husband now?"

"He always was attracted more to who a person was than to what body they had." She shrugged, sighing. "He changed. I didn't. The breakup went badly, in a way that was entirely my fault."

"Yeah. That much was obvious." I waved a hand in dismissal, the kind of gesture that normally would have made me socially terrified at the implications someone else might read into it. Not worrying about it came so *naturally*, in a way that couldn't possibly have been natural. "I guess it doesn't matter, since he's, like, his more actualized and real self now."

She boggled at me for a moment, shoulders shaking in suppressed laughter. "Thousands, Sophie, no wonder you needed a pact. You've got claws that drip poison!"

"Brutal." I giggled, turning my head to stare up at the astonishing clarity of the sky and the vast trees above us. They were planted at the corners of the four plazas, and—like the sequoias whose names the redwoods shared—they reached a literal couple hundred feet up in the air.

The trunks ranged from, at a guess, five to eight feet thick, and the average crown spread—width of the branches, more or less, though it was a little more complicated than that—was more than fifty feet from dripline to dripline.

You could stand at the highest points of the arched bridges that connected the two-story houses to each other and raise your hands to the sky, and you'd be somewhere between six and a dozen feet short of the very lowest branches.

"He could be nice," Kelly said abruptly. "Incredibly supportive of me as a professional. Wanted me to be the best person I could be, to present as the best person I could be."

"Oof." I winced in sympathy, a very specific sympathy. "Didn't like the way you dressed and looked? Suggested that you owed it to yourself to do better?"

"You too, huh?"

"From friends and coworkers alike, yeah. Take better care of your nails, Sophie. Dress more femme, Sophie." My voice was somewhere between wry and venomous, remembering those days. "Would it kill you to wear some eyeliner and lipstick, Sophie; don't you know that it's unprofessional to dress like that, Sophie? You're letting yourself down."

"Tam—*Tomas*," Kelly began, correcting herself almost in time, and then paused for a moment. "Tomas would say that I needed to stand up for myself, but that I needed to be gentler. That I needed to use my tools better—how I dress, talk, walk, touch, everything—to keep someone making the right moves, but that I needed to be less manipulative."

"Eh, it's not like you're subtle, and sure, there's stuff you suck at, but it obviously works for you. My shards had a whole lot of bad Paths and only a few good ones, and the one you pushed me towards was one of the best. Sometimes it's better to build on your base than try to change it."

"Claws," she murmured, almost inaudibly. "I'd be gutted by how casually you said that. It's not just that you think I'm flawed to my roots, but also I can't even fix it?"

"We mostly don't," I said, smiling up at the sky. "Change, I mean. We reify, bugs and features alike, and then we calcify, and then we deteriorate and die. If we had the luck of the Prophets, maybe at a hundred and twenty; but the median age at death was below eighty."

Kelly snorted. "You're not *really* an adult here until you've gotten your century. They don't count anyone under that as capable of fulfilling a required trade or position for a village, Third Tier or not. I'm going to see the other side of my threefold, my third century, unless something kills me first."

There was a blur in the sky, a ring reaching up, presumably from the circle around us that somehow didn't disrupt my ability to see the canopy of needle-like leaves high above us. "I guess you have time, then. So did folks at home."

"So?"

I wouldn't have insulted her by pretending I didn't know what she was asking, not even if we hadn't formed our pact. "I shouldn't have been able to bulldoze you on our first day. That whole thing led into a pile of little things that mounded up until we basically had a fight before the Thousand, and that only happened because you were too pissy to de-escalate."

"What, and that's *my* job, when it was you being an idiot?"

"Obviously." I smirked, even though I didn't think she could see my face, upturned as it was. "Are you not the older, wiser, more experienced one? The one who's integrating *me* here? If I'm a bitch about something, it's your job to find a way to get me to stop without me realizing that you're manipulating me, exploiting a power dynamic, or playing on my insecurities."

"Without you *realizing?*"

"Well, sure. You got me to back down and go along with you by showing vulnerability and pain, in a way that was, like, *transparently* manipulative, even if it was also heartfelt. And it worked! But also, it should never have come to that. You could have traded question for question—I love talking about myself, for the record—or just not let me sidetrack you. Which, okay, dumb of me, but very typical, just as a note for the future."

I heard her take a deep breath, then let it half out. I could imagine her picking words, stringing together sentences in her head, and then discarding them.

I gave her time. We probably had plenty of it.

"What else? Don't open up a wound and then leave it only half-debrided."

"The thing with the forehead-flick gesture, from back when we were having that argument." It was a hard thing to say, for completely inadequate reasons. "It felt like an implication of violence. I know you probably didn't mean it that way, fuck, there's a whole language of casual low-grade stuff that's not—" I stopped myself belatedly.

The first three or so things to come to mind were apologies, and I was absolutely *not* going to apologize about this, I was determined not to. I waited my thoughts out instead, letting them flow through and past me, and tried to marshal new ones.

"Where I come from," I eventually said, "there's a whole language of casual violations of bodily autonomy that are considered, culturally, not to be a big deal. Pain, discomfort, or humiliation, in a hundred different flavors. People don't think of it as violence, it was just... part of how people socialize. And you were a spoilsport and immature and unwilling to *get along* if you objected."

"The more I hear about where you come from," Kelly said thickly, "the more fucked up it sounds."

Her usual cheerfulness and pep was gone from her voice, and I hated it. I wanted to apologize to her for bringing it up, for burdening her with the traumas of my childhood and of an Earth she'd never see. I wanted to apologize for robbing her, even momentarily, of the spark that made her voice ring like chimes.

I waited, instead. I owed her the opportunity to choose... what, exactly, I wasn't sure. Whether or not to tell me to just socially integrate without letting my bullshit get in the way, maybe, and whether or not to pry about the history that left those scars.

"That gesture," she said eventually, "to someone Shemmai, it means a... a drop of wisdom, we're asking the Gods, not any specific God, for a drop of wisdom to fall onto your head. Maybe it sinks in, maybe it runs down your skin; it's, I don't know. It's asking for the opportunity to be given. But it's also like saying here, what I'm saying is a drop of wisdom, and you can let it sink in if you want."

"I flinched," I whispered, "and almost fell off the bench." I couldn't have said it while making eye contact; I probably couldn't have said it if I weren't in this strangely intimate mood and place. "Meredith, Captain Morei, she called it. I'm a flincher, it's absurd, it's idiotic, and I can't stop doing it."

"I'm sorry." Her voice was suddenly calm, professional. "I should have noticed. I *really* should have noticed, I must have been absolutely up in my own head. I fucked up there. I can say that, see? I fucked up!"

Well, maybe not entirely professional, I thought to myself, smiling despite myself. "Well done. I fucked up too; I should have trusted that when you said we needed to go, it was true."

"Yes! Because I'm a seasoned professional who absolutely knows what she's doing. Okay, so. I'm on grinder duty, and if someone needs to hold delicate equipment when things explode, I get to! What else?"

I blinked a few times at that. "You sound... all peppy now."

"I didn't become the youngest First Friend on record at any village by accident, Sophie. I admit, I fucked up a few times already with you, just like I've fucked up with all my clients, though admittedly I've never had to admit it to one. But even though I've never broken individual category records, every single job I've done was in the top decile for every measure of integration. I'm not perfect, and I do want to be better, but Tethyanne would have had you learning exactly the proper things at exactly the proper times, and Ellana would have you paralyzed with indecision.

"And instead you're an Alchemist—a Path that goes beyond your sight and into the unknowable future—and excited, and even if I had fucked things up with Tomas for you, he wouldn't have blamed you for it and everything would have been fine! Because I'm. Good. At. My job." Kelly paused, breathing hard as she audibly gathered herself, and when she spoke again it was slower and more deliberate. "I'm not without my own issues. I have an *entirely* inappropriate fixation on being treated with respect in my profession, because forcing the issue and making a point of taking offense when they didn't was the only way. I'm a conversational pushover who likes to go with the flow, and I'm a total gossip.

"But I like my job. It's an important job for society, it's an important job for the people like you I help, and I *like* my job. So if you need me to be your hands when things get loud? I'm gonna be your hands, and I'm gonna have fun doing it. And I'm gonna be *good* at it, just like I'm going to be good at... I don't know, warning you before something makes loud noises? We use air bladders for packing fragiles or volatiles, they make a loud wailing sound when they're deflating. Our firewood tends to sort of explode a little when we poke it, when it's burning, not dangerous but it is kinda startling. There's all sorts of stuff like that."

"I tend to lose track of people and then get surprised when they say something or move," I admitted, laughing softly. "Whatever's in my hands has a substantial chance of going flying. Why do you think I was so obsessive about making sure that everything was bolted down and secured, that anything I was carrying, I carried for as little time as possible?"

"And you still got to find out that our glassware is tougher than you thought!"

"That wasn't me being startled," I said primly. "That was me being clumsy. Related problems, but different."

"Noted!" There was a note to her voice, a contented joy, that set me on edge. "I can keep an eye out for ways I need to mitigate that, too. What else?"

"Kelly, not that I don't appreciate the thought, but…" I stopped, not quite sure what I was trying to say, like my words had run ahead of any conscious understanding of what I needed to say. I made myself walk the mental path again, more deliberately, reconstructing the impulse that had started me talking. "I wasn't really looking for solutions. I'm a grown-ass professional, who hasn't been even *socially* a kid in more than a decade. Sometimes, I'm just cracking a joke, or bitching because I want to be heard, not because I need a problem fixed."

"Well, that's gonna be awkward, and not for me."

"Hey!" I rolled onto my side to half-glare, half-stare at her. She was laughing, and I was mad about it and not mad at the same time. "Really? Come on."

"I'm a problem solver! I solve problems." Her voice was full of pep, eyes sparkling. "I'll solve this one, too! When you come to me with a problem you *don't* want me to fix, you can just say, hey Kelly, this problem's a comfort toy, please don't take it away."

"*Really* now." For some reason, I was laughing at that. "What if it's… a problem… that…"

She cocked her head at me as my words trailed off. "A problem that what?"

"A problem I want to fix myself," I said distractedly. "Kelly, who are the two people there next to Kartom? And why… are… Rafa and James…"

As my voice failed me, she took one look over her shoulder and blanched white. "Five Pillars sustain me," she whispered, "that's Cleric Veil and Magus Zrodne. And Kartom, it's morning, he works in the morning, why is he…"

Standing just outside the circle which the gods had burned into the road were five people. James, who was *Clerk Administrator* of Kibosh, was one of them. A flicker of seriousness crossed his face as I met his gaze—and then it was gone, but a coldness in my gut burned away the laughter and the happiness.

"Sophie, I have no idea why they're here." Something firmed up in Kelly's shoulders as she announced that. She drew her legs around herself, sitting cross-legged as color started flooding back into her face. "But we didn't do anything wrong, and even if we did, *you*, by definition, can't have done anything wrong. Whatever paperwork James throws at us, it's my problem."

"And uh." I drew myself up to my feet as the five people in front of us spread out around the four-element circle we'd been lying in the middle of. Kelly followed suit, and we bumped shoulders almost unconsciously—for solidarity, maybe. "You're going to be fine, right?"

"Oh, not even a little bit." There was a humorless laugh bubbling up in her throat, something that sounded like laughing at a joke that had never been funny. "Forget whether we did anything wrong or not. I'm going to get lectured so hard, the paperwork is gonna seem like a vacation!"

CHAPTER 3.5 - AN ORDERLY DISCUSSION, WHATEVER THOSE PRESENT MAY PREFER

It turned out that the four-element circle around us was pretty thoroughly muting sound from outside. I could infer this from the silent mouth-movements of the five people arrayed around us, but sadly, I couldn't read their lips.

Judging by the way her expression was growing more nervous, Kelly, it seemed, *could* do so.

We waited while the people outside had some sort of argument, body language suggesting there were three sides. Kartom and Rafa were on one, the former bending down to inspect the circle and the latter seeming vaguely dismissive of the whole situation, while James had a poker face and perfectly neutral body language. The two people I didn't know were standing across the circle from each other, in one case pacing and waving his hands in agitation and in the other case practically vibrating with tension.

The two agitated people won the argument, and they took a simultaneous deep breath. As they exhaled, one's face lined in concentration and the other's smoothing into something far less worried, the circle started to… sublime, I supposed, though I'd always preferred sublimate as the verb form. It had a far nicer aesthetic, and wasn't as easily confused with the term for a sublime moment, and—

—*and this distraction is external.* The thought flared through my head, and I opened eyes that I hadn't remembered closing. It was actively difficult to look at the person who was… who was not one of the three people I knew nor the Magus, and trying to do so was making my head spin. It wasn't my head, though, not per se—it was some sort of inner ear disturbance, though obviously here it could be magic, or—*no.*

I wrenched my eyes away, staring at the residue from the divine activity in our area as it started to vanish. The ash and ice went first, wafting away into the air; the vines went afterwards, crumbling into a dust that was reabsorbed by the road. Finally, as the Magus's hands came together in what was no doubt a thunderclap of palms, the road evened out until the deep scars and burns in it were no more.

The silence shattered the moment the road was fixed, and the sounds of the village—animals and insects, wind in its own right and wind in the trees, children at play in the distance and more—resumed. And with it, so did the sounds of our… interlocutors.

All of them at once.

"—waste of my time—"

"—I'll have them censured if—"

"—have not examined any precedents—"

"—fascinating, simply fascinating—"

"—quite literally blasphemous, even—"

Absolutely not, I thought to myself almost idly. I was already doing my best to acknowledge the pressure of the System without letting it take over my sensorium, and the cacophony was going to give me a headache in short order. *This won't do at all.*

"Gentlefolk, please!" I put a tremendous amount of carry into my voice, as much as I could manage. It didn't quite echo off the walls of the buildings around us, since there simply weren't enough of them, but I fancied that it might have. "One of you at a time," I said at a more normal volume, "starting with whoever's the bass and going up from there."

That got a moment of baffled silence, and disappointingly—there was absolutely no way that his mellifluous baritone was the lowest in the group, I'd heard someone lower—James was the one to break it.

"Miss Nadash, thank you; despite the oddity of your request, it had a salutary effect. Miss Avara, would you kindly… explain?"

"We made each other a pledge," I said, cutting off whatever Kelly was going to say. I put a hand on her shoulder, smiling at James and being a little surprised at how genuine and broad the smile was. "I know, I know. It's unheard of, absurd. Made each other a pledge! Unthinkable."

"This is no time for japes and nonsense!" The Magus—and it was definitely the Magus, if Kelly had identified him correctly; his robe made Kartom's look like a ratty bathrobe—was intensely unamused at my antics, and it showed. "Kelly, what *rank idiocy* drove you to sever this large of an area from the Kingdom's wards? Not that *any* size area would have been acceptable!"

"Using a divine intercession, no less." The androgynous figure had an equally androgynous voice, colorless and without affect. "We are disappointed in you, girl. The Greatmother is not to be invoked so trivially."

"Magus, Cleric, I think you misunderstand what—"

"This is an absurdity, and I want an *answer*, Kelly, not your charge's ravings. The risks taken here were utterly unacceptable, and you had no authority whatsoever to take them."

"We may not know how you came to misuse such power so ridiculously, but we will take whatever steps are necessary to ensure it does not happen again."

My eyes flickered between James, Kartom, and Rafa to see if they were going to speak up. They didn't, or at least they didn't in the moment I gave them, the moment before Kelly said something.

They shifted a little, though. Just enough for me to notice; just enough that they were perfectly between James and the other two. James, who was standing due north, flanked by... our friends? Well, that was a message in its own right; he was distanced and blocked from the new two.

"I didn't know," I remarked pleasantly, turning to my friend, "that it was considered polite here to ignore people. Good to know. Since that's the case, let's get a move on?"

"Sophie, I—" She took a deep breath, and then she *got it*, realizing what my intention was. With an act of will, she managed something vaguely similar to her usual sparkle in her voice, and I exulted in our being on the same wavelength without needing to speak a word. "Yeah! I mean, we learn something new every day, right? I grew up here and I keep forgetting that. What are we making again?"

"Grenades!" I laughed, grinned, and hooked my arm around hers. "Gren*aaaaaaaa*des," I sang to the sky, and together we took a step up the road. "Grenades! So that the Guard can use those, instead of universalized blood. Oh, James! Fancy seeing you here."

"Sophie," he said quietly, not getting out of our way, "I understand that the councilors may have spoken intemperately, but please take this *somewhat* more seriously. **[An Orderly Discussion]**. If you all please."

"Clerk Administrator Morei." I nodded at him, letting the false humor drop off. I felt *compelled* to speak, but that was fine; nobody else was talking, and James seemed to be actually listening.

Or was it fine? If I was being compelled to speak by the Skill that James had just invoked, would I know? Or would I just—no. It didn't, in the end, matter that much. Kelly was catching my eye, and she nodded at me, fractionally but somehow emphatically, and that was answer enough.

"As there hasn't been any rank idiocy, and as our relationships with the divine are necessarily *our* business, I'm inclined to let my previous answer stand. We made each other a pledge, a pact. It was witnessed and… I don't have a good word for it. Endorsed?"

James glanced over at the androgynous figure in the cowl. "Cleric Veil, if you would be so kind?" His tone didn't waver in the slightest, but there was a bite to it that I hadn't expected.

"Blessed," Veil said flatly. "A God blesses, nearly by definition."

"Thank you, Cleric Veil. Continue, please, Alchemist Nadash?"

"It was witnessed and blessed by four gods. On my part, by a goddess of nature and the wilds and by a god of craft and mastery, both of whom I've had dealings with before. I'd rather not speak for Kelly with regards to the two gods she invoked."

"The Striver and the Enduring," James said. "They are from Yelem, and well known to us. Kartom?"

"Yes, yes, that much was obvious." Kartom sounded like he was too distracted to bother being peevish. His eyes were fixed on where the circle had been, like he was tracing the whorls that the elements had formed until they'd vanished. "For all of Veil's pretenses, this was not an invocation of Sundered Namma's shards, unless Veil wishes to argue that the well-attested Risen are the separated flesh of a primordial."

"We will defer any such argument." James's voice was firm, and it didn't so much cut Veil off as give them no leave to speak in the first place. They looked weirdly calm about that, after having looked pissed off a minute beforehand. "Magus Zrodne, your assessment of any concrete, realized harm beyond the need to trigger the self-repair spells of the road?"

The man glared at me, Kelly, James, me again, and then Kelly again in succession. His hands smoothed his robes, lingering on some of the weird blue swirly bits that my eyes couldn't focus properly on, and his mouth worked silently for a moment. "Time away from our duties and the efforts of analysis," he said eventually. "No other harm done. The road, now that the homeostatic enchantments have run their course, is at a higher level of reserves than it was beforehand. The Ward stands and is unaffected."

"Thank you, Magus." Zrodne's face contorted furiously at something in James's voice, but nothing came out, and James moved on. "Cleric Veil, is there any business of your Pillar here?"

"An apology, and perhaps a request." Veil's speech was still in that atonal, affectless voice of theirs, but it came with a wash of emotion, like the feelings were being carried separately as metadata. "We were too quick to judge. We will address the reasons for that ourself, as we seek the truth of the matter without our undue haste, but we here express our awareness of it. We acknowledge the presence of Gods not accounted within Yelem's Thousand here in our demesne—as manifest in these shards through Alchemist Nadash here, neither their priestess nor their acolyte."

My mouth opened, but the act of speaking failed to manifest, which was a fascinating feeling and explained why Zrodne hadn't said anything after James cut him off. James glanced over at me and raised an eyebrow, and when I nodded at him, he nodded back. The lock, which I hadn't noticed in its own right until it went away, lifted.

"Do you, uh, want me to relay that?" My voice was carefully level, but I tried my best to convey that yes, this was a genuine offer.

"Not at this time, Alchemist Nadash." James's voice was, for once, a bit rough around the edges. "The village of Kibosh appreciates both your offer and your *discretion* with regards to repeating anyone's words to any Gods in *any* of their shards, particularly Gods they do not cleave to." He paused for a moment. "Raphaella?"

"Boy Morei," the healer—not Doctor, she'd been clear about that—grunted in acknowledgment, and I blessed the fact that I physically couldn't snicker out loud.

"May I ask your evaluation of—"

"They're fine." Rafa cut James off brusquely, making a show of turning to go. "Well, as fine as they were this morning. Better. Avara needs to do more flexibility work, and the Traveler's a disaster, but they're about a meal up each. Come, Kartom, we're leaving."

"Rafa, I—"

"The circle's *gone*, boy, and you've nothing to learn from the echoes. I'll give you an imprint."

A sort of gratified astonishment flashed across Kartom's face, leaving an undisguised glee and excitement in its wake. "Magus, Cleric, Alchemist. Avara, James."

"Breadth first," James admonished—and it was definitely an admonishment, judging by Kartom's reaction. "I want a preliminary report no later than the first dinner seating."

Kartom nodded after a moment's hesitation, and raced after Rafa—she'd strode off the moment she'd stopped talking, and he wasn't making up much ground on his spindly legs. Veil, bowing slightly, stepped away as well, every step emitting a ringing, soundless pulse of emotions—regret, abashment, curiosity, and patience—that was somehow *specifically* colorless.

"Kelly," James began, "I have a fair number of questions."

"Magus Zrodne probably has some too!" Kelly's voice was an almost insultingly cheerful chirp, which was probably deliberate. "Sophie and I might have some answers. But are we gonna stand around and talk?"

"I would, I admit, prefer otherwise." James waved a hand, and the pressure of his Skill vanished. He hadn't so much as winced or stiffened during its time running, but his eyes narrowed just the tiniest amount as it came off. "The village is not best served by unnecessarily wasting productive time."

"As we *just did*, due to these children?"

"Who is this Zro-bro joker, anyway?" I put a fair amount of exasperation in my voice, though internally I was mostly laughing that *bro*, of all words, had a perfectly insulting translation into Shemmai—not so much a jock as a *would-be* jock, someone who adopts the culture without having the talent or drive to actually succeed. "And why am I supposed to care what he thinks?"

"I am a councilor of the village of Kibosh, you…"

"Brat?" I smiled thinly at him.

"Sniveling *child*, have some respect," Zrodne spat. "If not for my office, then for the work I do to keep this village safe from the Forest! Work you put in jeopardy, regardless of a lack of damage *this* time!"

"I don't know much about that." My smile stayed in place, though it might have gotten a little thinner. "I landed in the Forest, and it seemed a nice enough place, but I get that it might not be; and I did come here instead of staying there. What I do know is that the first impression I have of you is that you yelled at Kelly like an arrogant idiot, and ignored me when I answered your question."

"Perhaps your *First Friend*," he said in a voice dripping with condescension, "might enlighten you as to who I am. If she can recall."

"Magus Zrodne," Kelly said softly, and without any of the animus I expected, "is the Tower councilor in Kibosh. His rank, formally, is that of Pillar. In his two centuries of service as a battlemage, he has served widely, including undertaking the Three Threshers: suppressing a Break, establishing a Low Road, and defending a Forest Claim. He is, in his present duties, personally responsible for the Ward-borders of the Kingdom near Kibosh, among other duties, as he was responsible for the Claim which expanded the borders to permit Kibosh's founding."

The Magus's eyes narrowed, something easing in his body language. "An adequate summary," he said grudgingly.

"Sounds like you do good work." I kept my voice even. "But none of ass-kicking, authority, or prestige ought to exempt you from treating other people decently. That's what I've always felt, even if it was different where I come from."

That seemed to hit home, and he breathed in, palms together, and breathed out after a moment. "Wisdom is to be recognized no matter its source," he ground out. "I apologize for my intemperate words."

I couldn't help my eyes going wide, and I blanked for a moment. "Accepted. And I apologize for my unwarranted insults."

"Kel—Miss Avara." Zrodne corrected himself, looking like he'd just sucked on a lemon, or possibly had a very uncomfortable chemical reaction go off inside his mouth. "Alchemist Nadash. May your work serve the community."

"Indeed, may it be as my colleague says." Veil's eyes bored into me. "And, Alchemist Nadash, on that subject? To call the divine by true name, whether in plea, prayer, or offering, carries more meaning than you know. Invoke no shards from beyond our Thousand within the Wards of Shem. If your First Friend's explanation of delineation does not fully satisfy you, any who attended upon you today might suffice. You will find us entirely willing to make sufficient time for a complete explanation—it is entirely within the realm of our duties."

I watched the two of them stride off, blinking. *I have very little idea what just happened*, I thought to myself, *and I don't like feeling that way*.

"Well!" James's voice cut through my thoughts, and he clapped his hands together, rubbing them briskly. "That went quite well. Sophie, may your morning be productive, and as Veil said, please delineate the space in which you perform any further divine invocations. Avoid the necessity of the Gods doing it themselves. Kelly, I expect you to call on me immediately after lunch. *First* seating."

"Paperwork," Kelly said to me mournfully, pouting, and we both broke into mad, cackling, *relieved* laughter as we started walking to the shop-house.

CHAPTER 3.6 - PAIN IS NOT WEAKNESS LEAVING THE BODY

Whatever else had just happened that morning, I was bound and determined to take Tomas's request seriously—even if he hadn't directly framed it that way. Everything else, all the revelations and troubles, could wait. The Guard needed tools to take fights without getting injured, the Basic Set included some of those tools, and I was going to make some.

Things were even *almost* that simple.

"So, just to confirm, you're okay with us *not* spending any time deconstructing, analyzing, or discussing in any way what just happened."

Kelly nodded at me. "It'd take us hours! Especially 'cause you'd get sidetracked every thirty seconds. And do you wanna make some potions, or what?"

I snorted, but it wasn't like she was wrong. "Okay." I glowered down at the slim book in my hands, and at the painstakingly neat writing on the third page. "The list of Basic Set combat potions looks like it has… no, elixirs and weapon applications are listed here in the index but as *preparatory*, not as in-combat. Grenades, Smokers, and a Flametongue Potion?"

"Yup!" I couldn't see her face, since she was busily lifting racks of bottles out of a box, but I could hear her smile. "Smokers aren't useful to the Guard, so if you're gonna make something for them, it's Flametongue or Elemental Discharge potions."

I didn't correct her, but I did have to fight the urge, since it would have been funny. *Helping anyone helps everyone* was something that she'd told me verbatim, and all of the Basic Set potions—a set of industrial, medical, and combat products, so useful that they were subsidized into being effectively free—helped… well, a lot of people, most of them.

But as critically important as quicktan and metalmelt might have been to Kibosh's industry, they apparently weren't in short supply the way the combat stuff was.

"Flametongue is…" I flipped through the book, eyes narrowing. The headache was getting in the way of reading, but it was hardly the first time I'd endured that. "Oh. Oh! Naphtha, quicklime, and resin. I *know* this mixture, or at least, I know what we called it."

"No naphtha." Kelly was surrounded by orderly racks of bottles and piles of the shock-absorbent material they'd been packed in. Every now and then she would lift a bottle out of a rack, read the label carefully under the light of the hanging orbs, and bring the rack to a shelving unit. "We haven't been storing it, it doesn't have enough general usage and it doesn't last long enough. Five days till we get some."

"That simplifies things. Okay. Elemental Discharge potions… elemental discharge my ass!" I blinked at the page I'd flipped to, with its diagrams and formulas. "These are just… grenades? This is pure mundane chemistry, with some optional magical reagents."

"Yes? I mean, you can make them elemental grenades, but everyone wants some pure mundane ones." Another rack went *clunk* into some very specific location on the shelves, as determined by some ordering she hadn't felt the need to share with me. "We used to use some sort of sulfur thing, I think, but it couldn't bind to the standard elemental-infusing materials, so it was a *big* change when the Discharge potion got adopted in the Basics."

"And I guess the magic ones are more complicated, but I want to make *something* magical after these. Okay. Nitroglycerin. Not actually the worst thing, but it's tetchy as shit to handle. This says there's two different methods of storage: frozen or diluted. Do we have one or both?"

"Something magic tomorrow, got it. Um!" Kelly put down, very carefully, the bottle she'd been studying the label of. She had seven books split into three stacks on the larger table, and she opened one of the top ones to about one third open with a *whump* and started flipping pages, searching. "Um, um, the ledger says… we have six standard diluted N-G, um, cross-referencing the definition just to be sure…"

I grinned down at the book in my hands. "You learn fast."

"It's not like you were wrong that I should be making sure! Okay. Yeah. That stands for… nitroglycerin." She sounded the word out slowly and carefully, mimicking my pronunciation. "Standard diluted cylinders of it, and we have six of them. And the Standards Appendix says… one point four three kilograms? That's… that's gotta be a number with a reason."

"Seventy percent nitroglycerin with thirty percent ethanol. We need to get the ethanol out, which will leave us with pure liquid nitroglycerin, with which we will *very carefully* not kill ourselves."

"Yes, ma'am!" Kelly looked over, humor in her eyes, and then sobered at the absolute seriousness in my expression. "Oh! That wasn't a joke."

"Nitroglycerin explodes if you heat it, freeze it the wrong way, shake it, poke it, or shine too much light on it. It doesn't just burn; it'll blow itself the fuck up in a vacuum." I didn't fight the scowl, the glower, or the flatness in my voice. "It is *not* to be fucked with, and we will treat it with deathly seriousness regardless of the supposed strength or thoroughness of our containers or safety measures. Clear?"

Kelly nodded once, firmly. "Clear." She paused, blinking at my continued stare, then nodded again. "We're going to treat it completely seriously and like none of our gear can possibly save us if we do it wrong, even though it's stoneglass."

"You do not ever work with these materials outside of a workspace rated for them, and you do not ever work with them unless you have competent, professional supervision. Nitroglycerin is not a toy or a novelty, nor is anything you make with it either of those things; it is a catastrophe begging to happen."

"I don't touch this outside of here or Hitz's labs, and I don't touch it without you or Hitz working with me. Understood."

My serious face broke, and I grinned broadly at her. "Right! Okay, so. I'm guessing the thing to do is for us to make the…" I glanced back down at the page. "Unaspected Elemental Discharge Potion, which is dynamite in a bottle."

"I'm gonna pretend," Kelly said with a grin of her own, "I didn't hear you say that. I'm gonna pretend that, 'cause you've *just* been on my case about being specific."

"True!" I nodded towards the books on what I was already thinking of as *her* table. "Go ahead and look up diatomite, or diatomaceous earth, I don't know which name it'll be under in the book. We need one part diatomite to three parts nitroglycerin, and there's a kilo of *that* in each of the cylinders. That'll give us a kilo and a third, which we'll split, once we have the dynamite mixed, into three grenades. Four-ninths of a kilo of product, one third of a kilo of actual explosive. And that's about two megajoules of total force, though some of it will go into shattering the... huh. What's M-S-T-G, Mile-Sand-Tango, uhh, Gyroscope?"

Kelly, predictably, had understood me perfectly the first time around. Still, she giggled at my distracted word search, so it wasn't wasted effort. "I dunno what a gyroscope is, but... looking!"

"Add it to the list of things I should show you," I said vaguely, rubbing my forehead as I read. "That's a really small amount of energy wasted in breaching the container. Huh."

"Added to the list!"

I glanced over at Kelly's peppy tone. "Is that..." I blinked. *Yep, that's a notebook.* "You have an actual list. Written down."

"Yes ma'am, miss Alchemist Nadash! This lady who's basically my boss, she told me I should write things down, 'cause if I don't, I'll forget 'em."

I giggled, a sound I usually hated, and I didn't have it in me to care in the slightest. "You know, nobody's going to take you seriously while you're smirking like that."

"Fine by me." She snapped her little notebook closed, tucking it away somehow under her blouse, and pointed to the two books she had open. "Metastable Tempered Glass. And *that* means that until you hit the right condition, it's just like the regular glass we make, but once you hit it, it's... frangible? What's frangible mean?"

"Brittle, shatters easily."

"Makes sense. Anyway, this note says that MSTG is also called grenade-glass, with or without a hyphen. That's all I've got. Lemme know if you need me to pull deep for it; my easiest Skill, I can't use again till tomorrow 'cause I used it this morning, but I've got more."

"Nah, that makes sense, or at least enough sense to work with. And the usual glass is, uh, rockglass?"

"Stoneglass. It's what we call the standard-strength tempered glass, glass that we heat-treat somehow, I don't actually know the details." She paused. "Sophie," she said in a careful, concerned voice, "why are you rubbing your eyes?"

"It's nothing," I said automatically. "So we need three—"

"No." Kelly's voice cut across mine. I glanced up to see her expression—worried and determined. "You said we cross-check everything even before we start, 'cause every machine is always on and every reagent is always open unless we *check*. Why are you rubbing your eyes?"

"It's not my eyes, it's my head. Rubbing my eyes doesn't actually help, it's just reflex, my head hurts."

"Your head..." Kelly's hands reached for a slim booklet, flipping it open to the second page. "Headache. No, no, no... your goggles aren't on so it's not that... *air poisoning*, says it's from fires—"

"—I don't think it's carbon monoxide—"

"—and smoke primarily. Should we step outside? Or can we test for it? How fast is it... a few minutes?"

"Kelly, it's not that, it doesn't even feel like a physical thing!" I waved a hand in vague frustration. "I know what carbon monoxide poisoning feels like, and this isn't that, even leaving aside the fact that we don't have anything that would produce it. It's just *pressure*, like an icepick from, like, *out*, in a weird not-spatial sense, like... it's coming from..." I trailed off.

"Sophie."

"Sovereign power," I muttered, face buried in my hands, "I beg you, sustain such idiots as I am."

"*Sophie*. Really? Really now!" There was an edge of humor in her voice, but also some real concern. "This isn't even the first time!"

"I know, I know! Okay, gimme a sec and don't break anything, I'm going to try something."

Reaching out to my System, that little sliver of an aggregate godhood that I was growing ever more connected to, I tried to express what I wanted. *Transparency* was involved, but it wasn't a simple concept. It was this complex mix of not taking over bits of vision that didn't need it, but ensuring enough contrast for the bits that did. It had gradients and color theory and I knew I wasn't getting it right, but I gave it a shot anyway.

Hey, System, I wrote, or maybe thought in a way that was in some ways like writing. *Try to be more like this, and let's resolve whatever you're poking me about. And I'm sorry about being so damn dense. We'll get more used to each other, but also I'll try not to have this happen again.*

Green text on black came into being like it was swimming into my field of view from a great distance—but this time, it only took up most of my field of view, and left me with peripheral vision.

Progress.

Your Divine Flame Whispers!

Feat Performed: *Spake Thou Unto Divinity, And Wert Heard Without Intercession*
Feat-Skill Earned: **[Divine Communion]**
A Skill Might Grow, Or Might Be Absorbed: *System Communion has been absorbed by Divine Communion. Your skill and Skill have been retained.*
A Skill Once Fallow Becomes Manifest Once More: *Endure*

You Dwell Ever A Mere Breath From Your Gods. New Again Is Yet New.

"Huh." The System message and its box faded from my view, and I looked over at Kelly, who was practically vibrating with anticipation. "What's it mean if I got a message that was, like, *archaic*? Not in Ancient Shemmai or the Old Tongue or whatever you call it, but archaic modern Shemmai."

"It… um!" Kelly looked lost, lost and absolutely delighted. "I have no idea! What did it say?"

"Uh, I… um. Let me write it down." I grimaced, suppressing the urge to laugh nervously. My pencil scratched its way across a page, transcribing what I'd just seen. "I… don't want to trigger this Skill in, like, vain."

"Huh!" She squinted at the page, humming. "You… talked to a God without needing anyone or anything in between. I can see why that counts as a Feat. If you were in the clergy, that'd be a Class Feat, but instead you're picking up a Tier-up Feat-Skill."

"That raises more questions than—"

"Endure." Kelly cut me off, eyes narrowed. "Sophie. You're hale now, by literal divine intervention and the System."

"… and?"

"If you." She jabbed me under the ribs with a finger, and I flinched away. "Are hurting." She jabbed me again, and I grabbed her finger, opening my mouth to protest, but she moved before I could. "There is!"

"Ow, fuck!"

Her other finger jabbed me again, harder still, not just startling but *hurting*, as her voice got still louder, a yell and a scream. "Something WRONG! WITH YOU!"

The force of her outburst sent me staggering backwards, hands raised in surrender. "Okay, okay! Don't *do* that!"

"Don't get upset because you're injuring yourself? Fine, I'll tell Rafa, if you'd rather! Make it her problem to stop you from stirring the oil with your hands! Maybe if you promise it to *her*, you'll actually *follow through*!"

"No, don't *hit me* and don't *yell* at me!" I stopped myself before I took another step away from her, forcing myself to stand up straight. I breathed, bringing my voice back under control; I'd trained my voice, and my shout had echoed deafeningly. "Don't hit me, and don't yell at me," I repeated quietly into the sudden silence, hands clenching and unclenching. "The rest you're right about. But don't *ever* lift even a finger in anger at me again."

The silence spooled out as Kelly sat down heavily at her table, breathing hard. I sat down on the floor, suddenly without the energy to get to a chair, but I—

"I'm sorry." Kelly's quiet, almost plaintive voice cut off my train of thought. "I... being worried about you, for you, doesn't mean that was okay. No amount of leaning into Skills that let me communicate better with you justifies not having my brain between the Skill and what I'm doing, and even *that* wouldn't justify me yelling at you or making you feel unsafe. Especially not after what we talked about, the way you opened up to me about... everything. I... betrayed that."

Forgiven, I wanted to say. It almost bubbled out of me, but I knew it was my history and my traumas talking. For all that I was still a work in progress, I'd gotten better at some things over the years. "I hear you," I said instead, just as quietly as she'd spoken, and then I somehow cracked a smile. "And you know, that raises yet more questions."

"You don't have to forgive me, not when this is the second time, not so—"

"Kelly." I cut her off this time, smiling a little wider. "Who said anything about forgiveness? I hear you; and if you're serious, you'll show me you mean it. Just like I'm serious about not breaking that promise again, which, by the way, I am." I collected my legs under myself and stood, not wobbly at all. "If it happens again, we'll figure something out. I'm sure there's coercive mind magic that can help the two of us have some semblance of self-control. Anyway, I don't have time for this.

"Feat-Skills, Class Feats, *tiers* of Skills, those Skills that let you communicate better with me that I know you also mentioned last night... I'm accumulating so many questions! And I'm gonna ask them, and you're gonna *answer* them, unless I get sidetracked and ask other questions first, which I probably will. But first! We have grenades to make, so that people don't die."

She nodded, smiling back at me with unsteady humor, probably understanding perfectly that I wasn't, in fact, totally joking, even if I also wasn't entirely serious. I pulled out the Journeyman recipe book for the Basic Set, she ran her fingers down the spines of the reference material, and we got back to work.

CHAPTER 3.7 - YOU CALL THAT A FUME HOOD?

"What do you mean, that's the fume hood? Where does… it vents into a *tank*?" I stared at the contraption we'd just assembled, horribly confused. "I'm supposed to vent a *mix* of *volatiles* into a single tank?"

"One segmented tank." Kelly's brow was furrowed as she cross-referenced whatever TSSCVG stood for. "I don't have the right book, why isn't this the right book? What am I even…"

I looked at the spine of the sizable tome in her hands as her voice trailed off in frustration. "Equipment Appendix: Support Trades. Any reason it'd be in a different book? That's four words."

"I know it'd be *in* other books, but it should be in this one too, 'cause it's all cross-published."

My eyes ranged over the books behind her. *Reagents*, no. *Products*, obviously not. "What's in the Installations Appendixes? Is there… there's one for—"

"Oh!" Kelly's exclamation of surprise was as delightful as she was delighted. "I was gonna run a Skill to find that, but you got it before I did! Thanks!"

"Um. You're welcome." I was not going to blush, I was *absolutely* not going to blush. *Especially not so soon after that little fight*, I thought to myself, and the rising heat vanished.

I missed it, the moment it did.

"So." I gestured to the book, which she'd rapidly paged through before coming to a stop. "Segmented tanks?"

"Tank; Segmented, Self-Cleaning, Volatile Gaslikes." She blinked a few times, then sighed, reaching for yet another book. "The Installations book says how it works, and that it's pronounced TISK-vig, but not what the names mean. I don't even know some of these *words*."

"Well, tell me how it works, once you're ready."

She was silent for a moment, though I could hear the pattern of paging through the book, pausing, writing something down in her notebook—she said she integrated information faster by writing notes—and then paging again. I went back over the list again in the meantime, nodding as I found myself able to recall everything we needed.

Cylinders of diluted nitroglycerin and a container of diatomite—diatomaceous earth—were the only two reagents involved. There was a fair amount of equipment, though, even leaving aside all the various clamps and stabilizers and hoses and gaskets.

A capillary with a stopcock—to put a carefully-controlled floor on the air pressure—would go into the basin that was apparently called a *soaker*, while on the other side of the apparatus the vacuum pump would work to keep the pressure down near the floor. There was a burner, because nothing made chemistry exciting like heating up a solution of nitroglycerin, and a condenser that would use water cooling to turn the ethanol back into liquid so that it didn't all go into the pump.

Add in the grenade-glass flasks, and the only truly mystifying thing was the fume hood, the only installation.

"Okay. Ready?"

I glanced over at her, a little mystified, and then remembered what I'd been waiting for in the first place. "Yeah. Dish the details!"

"Dish the... okay. So, the fume hood's rated at the tank rating, and the tank rating's in, um, hourly peak normalized volume per second, that's volume at one atmosphere—it's got some other number that it says is the same—and *standard temperature*, which, I don't know why it's zero, does it matter that that's where water freezes?"

"Hourly peak normalized volume per second." I stared at the fume hood. "I know what normalized volume is, and they picked zero because water ice is really easy to use as a standard for cooling things, probably. But hourly peak volume? The fuck does that mean?"

"Um. I think—no, I *see*, it's in the book, it means that it can take the rated volume every second, but over the course of an hour, it can only take that amount, which... oh! Oh, oh! It can be two numbers, but it's only one for this tank, so it's just the normalized volume per second."

My eyes narrowed. "So some tanks can take more than they can sustainably deal with, but they can store—why is the tank even rated in volume *per second*? It's a tank!"

"It's not just a tank! It's got a hundred little chambers, a separator, a bunch of tubing and stuff, some valves, and a runic web I don't understand even a little bit, but the book says that what it does is it pulls mana and heat from what you send in, and it cleanses itself, and it... *vents non-reactant, thermally excited gasses* as residue?"

"Hot nitrogen, probably," I said contemplatively. "Nitrogen and helium, and maybe argon. Carbon dioxide? How hot are we talking about?"

"Twenty-five degrees, and, uh, okay, a bunch of stuff that doesn't matter for us, it doesn't actually say what gasses, just says that they're non-reactant and safe to vent out the wall vents."

"Vent out the wall... okay." I took a deep breath, letting it out slowly. "Fine. Twenty-five degrees is fine, I don't know why that would even count as *thermally excited*. And if the best practice is to vent it into a tank and then outside, fine!" I stomped over to the wall, looking at it closely. "Where's the wall vent, anyway?"

"Here." This one, at least, Kelly seemed to know off the top of her head. A circle marked where I should press in with my hand and rotate a piece of the wall, and it slid down to reveal a completely normal-looking, mundane piece of piping. "There's seven along each wall, and seven around the cauldron-mount on the floor."

"Okay. And this just... turns any leakage of the ethanol, which will have trace amounts of nitroglycerin, into inert gasses."

"That's what the book says!" She nodded soberly at me as I caught her eye, visibly trying not to wince. "The book also says that the glass is fine if it goes off, but you said we're assuming it's not, right? So... if we don't trust the safety equipment, what do we do?"

"That's..." I sat back down, leaning back and staring at the swirl-patterns of the hanging light fixtures. "That's the right question. Good job asking it."

"I'll keep reading while you figure out the answer."

I glanced over to see her smirking—well, fair play, that, since she was right that I needed to think and had been in a way stalling.

In a practical sense, there was very little to be worried about. The likelihood that the gear I'd been provided was substandard was low, from what I could tell of Shemmai culture, and even if it were I had that Skill in my back pocket. If anything went wrong, the glass would contain the blast. There weren't even gaskets that could fail, since the tubing would be bonding glass-to-glass.

But safety was a matter of principle and habits. You didn't just blithely accept that you were going to be okay because your glass wouldn't shatter; you actively engaged in the practice of analysis and risk management, because the moment you stopped doing that you were inviting disaster.

What was the risk, on a concrete level? The fume hood was the thing whose possibility of failure was least clear. Even if it and its connections failed, though, and even if the apparatus was leaking—which it shouldn't— we'd smell the ethanol long before there was any danger... I was fairly sure. But only fairly sure.

"What are the failure modes of the fume hood?"

"I... the book doesn't say?"

I grinned at Kelly. "That's right. So use your head. This is a learning exercise; we're going to go through the whole experiment, and I'm going to walk you through the risk analysis. So?"

"Um." She frowned in concentration, chewing on her bottom lip. "The tank could rupture, or it could vent something unsafe. It could... blow air instead of sucking air? But we can't do anything about the tank, or the venting, right? And we can't look inside it."

"Yeah. Some risks, you can't really mitigate at their source; you can only mitigate their effects. What *can* we mitigate out of those risks?"

"The airflow," she said immediately. "Put a piece of paper up, watch to make sure it doesn't blow out instead of in."

"Clever." I had been thinking of something less simple, which spoke to how over-engineered my habits were and how used to ubiquitous electronics I was. "Okay, so that's the fume hood. You missed that it could ignite the ethanol that's heading into it, but we can't do anything about that, either; it's part of the internal workings. Next up, there's the actual blast shielding layer of the hood, which..."

"Which has a hole," she pointed out dryly, "for the vacuum pump, and your hand will be there."

"Yeah, and another for the stopcock, but think about *where* the vacuum pump is."

"... above the flasks?"

"Above and on the other side from the nitroglycerin," I said with a nod. "I won't need to configure the stopcock once we get started, so this means that I've got some distance from the explosive side. And you say a hole, but what's worth noting about the holes?"

She stared at them, blinking. "I... don't see anything?"

"They're apertures." I slid my finger along the side of one, following the stubby guide-bits.

"It closes!" She leaned in closer, humming thoughtfully. "And it stays a circle, because... I can't tell, actually."

"Something with the arcs and how they move." I slid it back and forth, opening and closing the aperture. "It's the same bond-glass, too, and that means..."

"Um. It means... that even if there's a leak and the fume hood isn't pulling... we won't be breathing ethanol?"

I nodded, smiling a little. "That's true. But even if there isn't a leak, there's still a burner there."

"There's a... *oh*." She leaned her head on my arm, groaning performatively. "So it brings in air through that vent, and it's got a flap, so if the pressure reverses it won't vent into the room."

"Good eye!" There was a heartbeat where I was worried about coming off as condescending. The next heartbeat, I realized with a feeling of glorious freedom that I *didn't have to worry about that*, and leveled my best, most praiseful grin at her. "There's two more major hazards: the soaker basin, and—"

"—and the flask that's collecting the ethanol? And, um, the bits of... traces?"

"The ethanol flask's gonna have traces of nitroglycerin, yeah. Only traces, but it could spark the ethanol, so it's a good thing there's going to be a near-vacuum; ethanol needs oxygen to combust. And what could go wrong with the soaker basin?"

"Too much heat," she said immediately, then paused. "Shaking? It... soaks unevenly into the diatomite, and pools?"

"That's a good start. Imperfections in the glass, too. Anything you can think of with the condenser?"

She stared at it for a bit. It was the least obvious bit of the apparatus, but even so it wasn't particularly complicated, just a tube running through some water. The gas would pass through it, cooling down in the process and condensing onto the sides of the tube, and by the time it passed through the narrow straw into the ethanol flask, it would be drips of liquid instead of gas... and it wouldn't get sucked up into the vacuum pump.

"What happens if the cold-pump stops working?"

"Good question! And I don't have a complete answer for that, because it depends on how it stops working, and I don't know how it works.

It's got a cycling piston, which I get is linked to the enchantment that… sucks heat out of the water?"

"What I'm hearing," Kelly said dryly, "is that I should go back to my books."

"Soaker, collection flask, condenser circuit. Let's work through all of the failure cases, try to figure out what the actual, practical risks are for them, and then come up with any mitigations like you did with the fume hood."

"Back to the books." She sighed, starting to walk over, then stopped suddenly. "I'm looking up answers you already know, aren't I."

"If you're going to be my assistant," I said, grinning, "you'll have to know all of this too."

"Back to being a student." She made a half-gargling, half-laughing sound. "The things I do for you, Sophie! The things I do."

She didn't turn back to let me see her face, but by the sway of her hips, she was entirely pleased; and with the way she focused intently on learning everything I had to teach, I was almost delighted enough to forget how fast things could go wrong.

CHAPTER 3.8 - QUANTIZATION OF PROGRESS IS SETTLED ART

In the end, after spending the necessary time on safety protocols and making sure everything worked right—and taking a break for a second breakfast, eating miniature savory pies with hands that shook at first—we made a single batch of grenades.

I tended to my more theological obligations first. A quick aside to Hephaestus, to acknowledge that the flame of the burner was a thing holy to him and dedicated as such; something not exactly a prayer to Hermes, an acknowledgement of the craft of alchemy being relevant to his domain. And one more prayer besides, drawn from my own history.

Blessed are You, I murmured under my breath, ad-libbing as I never had on Earth, *Lord and God of my forefathers, who smiles upon my renewed life, my sustainment, and my reaching of this day. Blessed are You, who created us capable of the act of creation.*

From Hephaestus, I felt the fire's warmth despite its distance and the fume hood in between. From Hermes, I felt a subtle feeling of curiosity.

The third blessing, as far as I could tell, was heard only by my own ears.

I made the first two grenades with a substantial amount of trepidation. For all that I'd been admonishing Kelly about safety the entire morning, and for all that we'd worked to enact any mitigations we could think of, this was *nitroglycerin*. Famously volatile, famously explosive—I'd worked with it several times in labs, but I had electronics to monitor every step of the process and safety protocols that had gone through weeks of iteration under the eyes of a dozen people.

Of course, most of those weeks of iteration had involved me trying to get someone, *anyone* out of those dozen people—the Principal Investigator who was theoretically in charge amongst them—to take even a cursory look at the protocols. Kelly, amateur though she was, at least paid attention and put in the effort.

I'd worked with worse, and with things that were more volatile, and in far larger quantities. And I was alive, and so was everyone I worked with, because even when we were doing scale-up experiments I was an absolute tight-ass. It was still terrifying to squeeze the bulb on the vacuum pump, and to watch the merry flames licking the metal heat-transfer elements of the soaker.

With the process proved out and two grenades loaded with slurry, I allowed Kelly to make the third. Every erg of my attention was focused on her as I watched her every movement like a hawk, but those motions were exactly as I'd shown her.

She told me afterwards that she'd had the option to, using a Skill of hers, mimic my *Meticulous* Attribute. She hadn't, because she'd wanted to see if she could do the job without it. To see, under my watchful eye, if she was good enough.

As relatable as that was, I didn't have it in me to admonish her. And besides, she had a surer touch than I did.

The moment the third grenade was properly capped, I felt a gentle pressure from my System connection. I checked the grenade caps anyway. They were clever things, easy to pull on purpose and basically impossible to pull by accident. When they were primed, the molecular structure of the glass would decohere in some way, propagating a shattering of the previously-aligned lattice.

It reminded me vaguely of magnets, something about atoms or molecules being lined up in the same direction. But I wasn't that kind of scientist, and I didn't remember it more than vaguely, so I just dismissed the thought.

Not long after I'd re-racked the grenades in their traveling containers—not exactly glass, some sort of transparent ceramic, and I made a definite note that I wanted to know how *that* worked—I saw Kelly starting to stir from the momentarily glazed look she'd gotten on her face.

"Was it good for you too?" I regretted saying it as soon as I opened my mouth.

Kelly, bless her, or maybe bless our pact, just smirked at me. "A full Discovery, and two crafts. More than I thought! Actually, I didn't even *hope* for more than crafting's worth, which. Well!"

"I have no idea what you mean, you know." I gestured at the rack. "Talk while we get this upstairs?"

"Ready?"

Her hands were under the grips on one side, and I stepped over to better grip the other. "Together," I said.

She beamed at me for a moment, then focused on the job. "Together," she repeated in the cadence she'd taught me, each syllable precisely equal. "We. *Lift.*"

The rack, too heavy for me to carry easily by myself, came up smoothly with the two of us. We started walking towards the ramp, and I averted my eyes from the floor carefully to avoid the sight of the false steps—something which I couldn't *believe* was standard.

"System progression's been quantified for the first three Tiers for hundreds of years." Kelly had her lecturing voice on, not at all marred by the carrying we were doing. "The first level at each Tier takes the same amount of growth, the same experience, and it goes up from there. The ratios are known: two-point-one, two-point-two-one, two-point-four-six. Ready for the turn?"

"Ready. What the shit kind of sequence is that?" I carefully hugged the wall of the ramp to make space for her to make her turn. It wasn't strictly necessary, but it let me brace, and it gave her more clearance. "Up by one-oh, up by two-five?"

"I dunno? I'm not actually good at math. I mean, I can do the basics, 'cause I've had to settle folks from out-Kingdom who didn't have a formal education, so I had to learn, but that doesn't mean I'm *good* at it. Clear to the front?"

"Clear to the front."

She led us, walking unerringly backwards. "So I know enough about shapes and angles and stuff to get by! And algebra, but everyone in Shem knows the basics of that, and I'd have to be Eichan come again to suffer through theorems. And, weirdly! Normals and adequals, you know 'em?"

"Uh. I know *normals*, if you mean the ones perpendicular to tangents."

"They're really useful, it turns out!"

"Yeah, all of the calculus—huh, Shemmai has the word, but it's a Qatn loanword, and Koshe has a separate word for it? I'm gonna swing around."

"I'm anchoring. Yeah, I don't know the Koshe word, obviously." It sounded like she was rolling her eyes at me, but I was too busy swinging the rack around, as carefully as I possibly could, until we had it parallel to the window instead of perpendicular.

The bit where I rammed my hip against the *other* rack we'd set up earlier, the one with the examples of the Basic Set that had been hauled out of storage, was fine. It was fine, everything was fine, because the rack with the grenades stayed absolutely steady.

"Ready down?"

I glanced around, making sure that the landing area was clear. "Ready down."

"Together," she said, to the same cadence we'd lifted to, "lo-*wer*."

The rack touched gently down. Not exactly feather-light, but it was a pretty heavy assemblance of stone and wood; we did the best we could.

"Anyway!" Kelly made a dusting-her-hands motion that was more like slapping her hands against each other in passing, three times in quick succession. "We use the Qatn word for calculus, 'cause it was Yaro, I mean it was some Yarovi, it wasn't the Empire itself, who pulled it all together."

"I… so, just to be clear. There's a political entity which you refer to as Yaro or *the Empire*, whose people are Yarovi. And a bunch of their scholars turned what was scattered knowledge into something more advanced and compiled, and the terminology came through via the trader pidgin as a loanword."

"Yup!" She beamed at me. "See? Simple!"

"… right." I sighed, leaning on the counter which had appeared, no note or notice, while we were working downstairs. "Can we get back to progression stuff?"

"I'm gonna write the numbers out for you, 'cause I know you're plenty literate and numerate. Actually, I already did!"

I glanced up at her smirk, then down at the piece of paper she'd pushed in front of me. "Alright. So… huh. Level one, ten experience to gain a level." *Levels. Experience.* It was just absurd the next day, distanced from my initial conversation with Kelly by a good night's sleep. "Level two, at my Tier, twenty-two, and then it's forty-nine. Crafts give your level's worth of experience each, Discovery gives five at first level and doubles from there. I… can kinda see how the scaling would get brutal at Third Tier, with a higher multiplier."

"Five hundred and sixty-three equal-leveled Discoveries." Kelly shrugged. "You get a trickle from doing your diligence, whether that's crafting or killing or services, but the System rewards novelty, mostly. And there *aren't* a hundred twentieth-level potions for you to get Discoveries for—there's only eighteen in the open books—so you try for Feats and you do what you can. Anyway!" She clapped her hands together, grinning at me; not the breath given to the future-her, but some other thing. "I got a half-Discovery for *you* getting your first Discovery, and another half for *me* making one with you. I won't get that again, but that was nice!"

"And your... two crafting credits?"

"I don't know, actually." She shrugged, frowning. "My System didn't tell me. I'm *guessing* that one of those was from working with you and the other was from making the grenades, but... I don't know. It doesn't matter much, anyway; I'd have to get thousands of crafts at full credit to make real progress."

"Got it." I glanced down at the paper again. I wasn't trying to commit the sequence of experience numbers required to level and experience provided per Discovery to memory, but I did want to get a sense for it, a basic feeling. "That's my cue, I guess. I probably shouldn't put off communing or whatever with my own little huggable metaphysical tendril."

"Your—Sophie, what—"

I grinned at her as she sputtered. *Alright, little Spark. You've been nudging me more gently, and I appreciate that, because I wanted to get things squared away before getting distracted. That's being Meticulous, right? Anyway, go ahead and send me that status update.*

The amount of effort it took to put the thought together and send it out was less than ever, and most of my field of view faded into black and green.

Recognition From Your Divine Flame!

To Discover Is The Essence Of All Artisanship:
Mundane Concussion Grenade, Unmodified (Level 4 Discovery, Basic)
Skills Yet Amorphous, Yet Latent, Begin To Form
Workshop Dedicated: *(Primary: Hermes, Secondary: Hephaestus)*
Experience Gained: *Discovery (40), Craft (8), Mentoring (2)*
Behold, Your Growth: *Alchemist (1, 0/10) -> Alchemist (3, 18/49)*

The Spark Of Invention Is Isomorphic To The Flame
The Use Of This Name Is A Suitable Thing
Discover. Teach. Learn. Actualize.

Power flowed through me like a warm cuddle on a cold night, relaxing and intimate. It washed through me like a breeze, flowing between cells and navigating a maze of molecules, and it latched onto its targets as it found them.

It wasn't the titanic-yet-subtle reshaping of when I took my Class. It was a few tens of thousands of molecules—or even individual atoms, in some cases—being gently, inexorably unbound and nudged out my pores and mucus membranes, evaporating into the air.

It was a tithe of... not toxins; *toxins* was a ridiculous word to use for this kind of thing, toxins were what the liver, kidneys, and colon dealt with. This was heavy metals and microplastics, it felt like, but that wasn't quite right; Hephaestus had reforged my body, and I doubted that he'd done so shoddy as a job to leave those. Well, maybe the microplastics—but he was a *smith*, he knew metals.

I didn't know what these were. I just knew that they felt, semiotically—or maybe metaphysically, or maybe both—like heavy metals, like microplastics; but also that they felt like they were *alive*, or had the potential for life, or had that once and didn't anymore.

They didn't like me. No, that wasn't quite right. They didn't like the System, and they were... out of place, or in the wrong place.

I shoved that thought aside, leaving it as a worry for another time. I'd been scanned by some sort of magitek runic gauntlet-looking thing by James, by a refectory manager who'd seen everything under the sun, and by a doctor who'd clearly seen even more. If this was a pressing concern, they'd have said something, or possibly incinerated me and atomized the ashes.

The power, in the meantime, ebbed and faded. It had left me a little bit more relaxed, feeling a little more like I could breathe, a little more like I could *move*. A tension eased in my wrists that I hadn't even noticed, probably caused by gripping too hard and trying to be too controlled with my movements, and I relaxed against the counter.

"Well?"

I looked over at Kelly, quite literally bouncing on her toes with anticipation. "It likes my nickname for it." I leaned closer, bringing up my left hand to the right of my mouth. "I nicknamed it Spark," I stage whispered to her conspiratorially.

"Sophie! No teasing me."

"The workshop is dedicated, now, and I've got a Latent Skill forming—"

"Sophie!" Kelly's glare was a thing of legend, marred only by the giggles she was barely suppressing and the smirk threatening to take over her face. "If you don't tell me what that gave you, I'll..."

"You'll pout at me?"

She snickered at that, any pretense to displeasure gone. "I bet that would even work! But no, really." She sobered, cocking her head at me. "What did you get for Discoveries and Crafts? I need to know, 'cause I need to compare it with what you *should* get, according to all the books. You did get numbers, right? Because if you didn't, that's a Numerant Shim problem, which means a James problem that becomes a Maintainers problem."

I couldn't really argue with that, in part because it would have required asking an already-impatient woman yet another series of questions—what was a *Numerant Shim*? An ad-hoc modification to something to show numbers?

That... might be exactly what it is, huh.

"Forty from Discovery," I said, realizing I'd been lost in my thoughts for a moment. "Eight from Craft, two from Mentoring. One Discovery—level four, basic. It took me to Alchemist 3, 18 out of 49."

"Perfect!" She started to lunge for me, then froze—I'd flinched, and before I even realized that I had, she was balanced precariously on one foot. "Um. I'm very excited, but I've been doing too much leaning on my Skills and not enough asking. Can I hug you, just 'cause I'm excited?"

"Kelly, I appreciate you asking." I resisted the urge to roll my eyes, and just smiled at her. "You can *always* give me a hug just because you're excited."

She had just enough self-control to finish her lunge in a way that didn't bowl me over, and we wrapped our arms around each other, grinning broadly.

After all, as absurd as the idea of *leveling up* might have been, I wasn't any less excited than she was.

CHAPTER 3.9 - A BRUSQUE ACCEPTANCE OVER LUNCH

We left everything racked and unsecured when we left the shop to head to lunch. It made a certain amount of sense. The village was tiny, the vast majority of the potions that we'd unboxed were Kibosh's stock anyway, and the few we'd made were in the Basic Set.

Free or next-to-free ingredients, miniscule profits.

It was still weird to leave the door unlocked. Folks would be free to grab a potion and drop a half-crown in the till, though it was more like a tin, but according to Kelly most wouldn't—it was more proper to come by when I might plausibly be present.

"So, Kelly."

"Sophie," she said with a totally false gravity, nodding at me. "Which question's answer would you like to have spiral out of any semblance of brevity on our walk over?"

"I can *see* your smirk, you know," I groused. "You're not hiding it at all."

"And?"

I wasn't hiding my grin either, so I let it pass. "And I absolutely have one of those. Is it a—" I didn't find the word I was looking for, not at first. There was a Sylvan word that felt etymologically similar, but it didn't mean the same thing. Instead of a social misstep, it was more specifically something that people ignored, as though forgotten. "Is it socially inappropriate to talk about peoples' Classes?"

"Um!" She blinked a few times, glancing around. "Do you want the short answer, the medium one, or the long one?"

I followed her eyes. They'd lingered on one or two of the other folks in sight, mostly people walking east along the garden paths. We were all headed to the refectory, I supposed, and the shop—*my* shop—wasn't far, so... "Short, probably? But I'll defer to your judgment."

"Okay!" For all that Kelly wasn't letting anything through to her voice, that was clearly the right answer. Her shoulders eased from the small amount of tension I hadn't even noticed, and her eyes stopped flickering between two particular people a little ways ahead of us on the path. "So, the short answer is, mostly yes. Um."

"Take your time. Or don't, you can just tell me you don't think we need to go more in depth."

"I just—no, this is good for you to know. Gimme a sec."

We walked for a bit more in silence. I was starting to recognize some of the social tells I'd been subliminally picking up in the previous days, the ways that people acknowledged that Kelly and I had a conversation going. I couldn't put it fully into words, but it was something with eye contact and expressions, and the alignment of her body language towards me.

Whatever the exact causes, it left us walking with everyone keeping a certain distance. They still acknowledged her, acknowledged us, and it was an interesting puzzle to figure out what they were doing with their body language to make me feel that way, but they weren't approaching or chatting us up.

"So," Kelly said suddenly, startling me, "it's not exactly an Edict of Paths thing. But it's kinda close, 'cause Paths are about who you want to become, and that's a personal thing, right?"

"Sure."

"Like, people maybe call you Alchemist Nadash, 'cause that's your *job*. Kan's a member of the Stone Team, and he quilts, right, and I'm one of Kibosh's two First Friends. And that kinda thing is known, talked about, 'cause what your job is, that's part of life. My Classes, though?

"It's not important what my Path is or what my Classes are, or it shouldn't be. What's important is that I can do my job, 'cause it's one thing not to have a job, but it's another—and real bad—to have one that I'm bad at." Kelly paused just as she started to get vehement, visibly reeling herself in. "Or, uh, that's how we say it should be, maybe."

"I guess that makes sense. Kinda like how if you can do the job, it shouldn't matter if your scholarly credentials are in this or that bit of the study of life." I paused, mentally checking over what I'd said—it worked well enough. "I guess there's an exception for, like, educational purposes?

Even leaving aside having to teach me about my Class options, Kan wasn't reluctant to share some of his own details."

"Kan's... not village-born, didn't grow up here, either."

"I mean, yeah?" We were almost to Levali's, and I slowed my pace to match Kelly's as she dawdled a little. "Kan said that he'd met Katana—"

"Ketana."

"Right, thanks. He said he'd met Ketana more than two hundred years ago. Kibosh didn't exist, right? And they specifically mentioned having met while working somewhere else, anyway."

"Sophie," Kelly said slowly, smiling, "I don't give you enough credit, sometimes. But Kaffar is a village, too—you just reasoned yourself to the right conclusion from absolute nonsense."

"I... hmph!" I spluttered as we walked through the doors of the refectory, going a little red. It would have been embarrassing and a little bit validating if she'd said that first bit the day before, but with the pact in place, knowing she was being truthful and honest... "I'm going to pretend you didn't say that."

"You have fun with that." She grinned at me, then started heading towards a table on the outskirts. It was small and unoccupied, clearly intended for someone who wanted to sit alone or with only a small group, and I hesitated before following her.

She caught it. Pausing, she turned to raise an eyebrow at me.

"I was thinking," I said slowly, "that if Jannea is here, I might want to talk with her?"

Kelly hesitated only a heartbeat, blinking. "Absolutely," she said. Her voice was almost perfectly controlled, with only the slightest hint of bafflement. "I see her."

We wove through the small crowd, nodding and smiling to various people, exchanging pleasantries and occasionally more substantial things. In response to inquiries, I mentioned that I'd started working on the Basic Set recipes, and people nodded in what I thought was approval; Kelly, meanwhile, was... not exactly gossiping, more collecting information and dispensing it.

A child's toy had torn. Someone had been surprised and gratified by a parting gift, and she was trying to think of an appropriate gift for when the courier found herself in Kibosh again. The Stone Team had been called in to fix a flaw in all five houses of a quint but that was fine; alas, wasn't it a shame that so-and-so's wall-hanging had been damaged in the process?

It was… instructive. A half-dozen little problems were taken to people who could solve them, not by people having to ask for help but by Kelly doing what was superficially indistinguishable from gossiping. And it wasn't indiscriminate—the looks of acknowledgement were clear, and so was the body language equivalent of *well, that's a shame, but it's not my problem.*

Not every problem would be solved, but a few would, in a way that seemed to be almost deliberately designed to avoid any social obligation or pressure.

"Zenith's blaze, Jannea, Tayir." Kelly smiled at them, and the two of them nodded back, mouths full of food, some kind of stuffed bread.

"Zenith's blaze. Jannea, Tayir," I echoed, and waited for them to have a chance to respond.

I took that moment to study them a little more closely. Jannea was a tiny woman, dressed in an earth-tones rainbow of loose, light clothes with that same palette in miniature in the thick strip of cloth tying her hair back. Tayir, on the other hand, was a mountain of a man in browns and greens, with his shaved scalp and clothes—shorts and a sleeveless shirt that left his belly bare—showing off an impressive set of muscles and dark brown skin with gray traceries whose patterns reminded me of… something.

Something I couldn't place, something mathematical. A specific kind of fractal, maybe; but as beautiful as I'd always found them, I'd never been good at that kind of math.

"Something need staring at, Nadash?"

I blinked a few times, and realized I *had* been staring, even if I'd been also waiting for them to respond. "Sorry," I said, smiling sheepishly. "I was, um, waiting to ask if it was okay for us to—"

"No."

"Ignore her." Tayir's bass rumbled out as he reached out to cover Jannea's mouth, giving her an unimpressed look. "Sit."

"Um. I don't—" *I don't want to be a bother*, I was about to say, but Kelly was already in her chair, and I followed suit a moment later, following her lead. "I wanted to ask for some work to be done on my house," I said instead. "An art—"

"Yes." Jannea pushed Tayir's hand away, though it hadn't impeded her from speaking regardless. "Show me after lunch. I'll do it tomorrow morning."

"Thanks, Jannea." Kelly shot me a complex look out of the corner of her eye. "I won't be there, but it's Sophie's project anyway."

"Two projects, actually. I was looking at the ramp, the one that looks like stairs, and I don't—"

"They like symmetry." Jannea cut me off absently, not looking at me. "Two stairs or two ramps, but they can't have it functionally, so they have it visually. Wrong, *obviously* wrong, everyone gets it fixed. Tayir, handle it."

"Ma'am."

A *thunk* interrupted me before I could ask if that was actually okay with Tayir, heralding the arrival of my food. I had two loaves of bread in front of me, round and squat enough to eat without cutting, and two tall glasses—water in one of them and some sort of juice in another.

The bread exploded with flavor in my mouth. Each was stuffed with garlic butter and paprika, some kind of salted meat, tomatoes, and at least two kinds of cheese. A crunchy vegetable that might have been a cousin to celery, something with a hint of bitterness and a medium crunch that could have been thin-sliced radishes, and fried pieces of fish all managed to put the breading front-and-center without having its dryness take over the meal.

Kelly was making contented noises and both the others at our table seemed content to relax and wait, so I focused mostly on eating.

Not that, being who I was, I didn't have questions.

"I know a few ways they might have stuffed the bread," I said between bites, "and that's even without Skills. But how do they fry this much fish for this many people?"

"Mmm. What difference has—what is the difference," Tayir began, correcting himself, "between cooking one and one hundred? A matter of tools."

"Mmm." I shook my head, chasing down the bread with a long slug of the berry juice—somehow both sweet and tart at the same time—and managing not to hiccup. "I don't get it. Are they using magic? That seems inefficient, given what I've seen from people and how much magic costs."

"To lower one fish into oil requires one tool. To lower ten, simply a different tool. To keep something fresh is a small magic, and even so, the…" He frowned. "Ma'am, what is in Shem—"

He said something I couldn't really follow the phonemes of, rolling and tonal and long. I caught a couple syllables of it that sounded like *aitoia*, but Jannea clearly knew the word, even if Kelly and I didn't.

"Humidity," she said. "And you switched the noun and preposition."

Tayir nodded at her. "The humidity is the greatest factor in freshness. For this, there are tools."

"And you don't mind doing the ramp to look like a ramp, instead of stairs?"

"From this, I still learn." He shrugged. "When I learn no longer, it will be an apprentice's turn."

I nodded at him, and focused on my food. Kelly, when she was done eating, took up the conversation with Tayir, talking about flavors he missed from his parents' cooking. They'd gone back to where they called home, and he'd moved to Kibosh, seeking somewhere where their memory didn't dog his steps.

He called the country Tagata—an abbreviation and translation of a longer name Shemmai speakers couldn't pronounce. A loose confederation of small islands, its people navigated vast distances through an intimate knowledge of the sea and sky.

"They lack the System, you see." He leaned back in his chair, closing his eyes. "And they do not build tools as we do here. Still, they may travel thousands of miles, and find an island by the change in the light of the clouds above it, or by the angle of sun and stars or the color of the seas. And they know more of the skill of cooking, without such aid as the System provides."

"And you didn't want to go back with them?" I asked the obvious question, and then immediately regretted it.

He looked at me, then closed his eyes, visibly considering his response. "To see one's children die of old age? To be still young when the body of one's wife or husband is given to the sea?" His voice was soft. "I will live as long as I may, and I would not trade that for the company of my parents, or to know what each manner of bird portends for the currents."

I didn't know what to say to that. I didn't even really know what to think about that, or how to structure the questions that I could feel forming under the surface. I finished my food in silence instead, and by the time I'd finished, Kelly and Tayir between them had found a more cheerful place to bring the mood.

Smiling at their antics and at their deliberately-petty arguments about the flavor profiles of herbs grown in different kinds of soil, I led the way out, heading for… well, home, I supposed.

CHAPTER 3.10 - COUNTLESS HOMES ON COUNTLESS HILLS

Kelly split off from us as soon as we were out the door, handing me a basket with a gently admonishing look.

Truthfully, I'd forgotten entirely that James had oh-so-politely required her presence to, as she put it, *attend to* the paperwork. I was fairly confident Kelly was joking when she told me that "Ward Disruption, Unplanned", "Ward Disruption, Unforeseeable", "Ward Disruption, Precipitous", and "Ward Disruption, Divine" were separate and overlapping forms, but... well.

I'd seen worse, and for less reason. Though I still wasn't exactly clear on what the Ward in question was or represented—and for once, instead of just telling myself that I would add it to The List, I pulled out a pad and a pencil.

Awkwardly, holding the notebook with the arm hooked through the basket's handle, I started writing. *What is the Ward* went after *what is a delineated space, and why is it important, what should I know about a second Class*, and *inquire about patent validations* in the notebook. After a moment of thought, I added *what is the nature of mana* and *is there a structured and empirical study of mystical environmental phenomena.*

On Earth, the positions of the stars and planets hadn't actually affected anything. Having your alchemical apparatus aligned north-south, chanting in Latin or Greek, and the time of day didn't change what you made.

Yelem, however, wasn't Earth.

Jannea and Tayir waited for me with different varieties of patience— one entirely zoned out, the other calmly attentive. They both followed me once I started walking, Tayir exchanging nods with passers-by and Jannea giving them no heed as she stared fixedly into the distance.

"I've got to ask," I said on impulse, "how do people know that you're not interested in pleasantries? It's one thing when Kelly and I are talking, there's a sort of social bubble effect, but when you're just walking?"

"I do not—"

"It's the eyes." Jannea cut Tayir off, then glanced at him. She waited for a moment, then shrugged. "The eyes and shoulders and hips. Tayir is working. He only glances and nods, eyes leave after the glance. Shoulders stay mostly forward, hips stay completely forward. Even stride, no turning, and neither hand open towards them, but that's marginal details."

"I… ma'am." Tayir frowned, forehead wrinkling. He visibly thought about that for a while as we walked. "I cannot claim this to be wrong," he said eventually. "It is not a matter to which I have put thought."

Jannea snorted, but didn't say anything in response. We were almost at the shop-house anyway, and I was digesting what she'd said and what it implied, so I didn't push until after we'd gone inside.

"Once you're done with this," I said slowly, "I would appreciate any advice you could offer about social norms and mores here. If not written down, then ideally with permission for me to take notes."

She didn't react to that or respond for a long while, leaning on a rack in silence. The potions in the rack would have survived being hurled at the wall and I knew we'd bonded the legs to the floor. For that thing to shift even a millimeter, she'd have to shatter stone.

I still had to control my reaction, turning instead to the handbook for the Basic Set and flipping through it to think about what I might work on in the afternoon or the next day.

"Give me a Feat," Jannea said suddenly into the silence.

"What?" I turned back to her, blinking. I'd managed to somehow forget that she and Tayir were even there in just a few short seconds. Clotting Salve, the page I'd turned to called it, and I was flashing back to the enzymatic cascades caused by clotting factors, with everything around me disappearing from my awareness.

"Give me a project worth a Feat." Her face twisted like she was biting into something sour, and she added, reluctantly, "I'll write it down for you anyway. But I want a Feat."

I took in a breath, letting it out in a long audible not-quite-sigh. "Let's go upstairs, and I'll do what I can." I found myself grinning suddenly. "I don't know if I can describe it, but—"

"Up." She cut me off and started walking. "I'll use a Skill, I don't want your words. Tayir, don't make mistakes you need my help fixing."

"Ma'am." Tayir looked like he had a half-dozen other things he wanted to say, but instead he walked over to the ramp, sitting down and staring at it.

"I changed my mind." Jannea stopped short to let me catch up, speaking with the same suddenness she'd been evincing. "Start talking."

"Sure." On one level, I felt like I was scrabbling to keep up with her sudden shifts; on the various other levels, I had plenty of experience with wild oscillations in expectations from literally everyone in my life. "Ideally, I was thinking of three multi-wall murals, one for each room. The glade with a pond and waterfall where I met the goddess who sent me here, a cityscape, and a cliff overlooking a mountain lake."

"I've painted lakes and cliffs." Jannea waved her hand dismissively as we reached the top of the stairs. "Pick something I haven't, or have Tayir do that room."

I stared at her for a moment, then shrugged. *In for a scepter, in for a balance.* "A different view of the same city, lit up at night, from a few hundred feet up."

She stared at me, half-glowering, half-considering. "Tell me more about both city ones."

I did my best to summon the images in my mind, conjuring not only the visuals but also the feelings. "It's a city of about a million people," I said slowly, leaning against the wall. "Hills everywhere. One shot is from the top of one of the hills, six hundred feet up, looking east over a few thousand buildings. Almost all homes, almost all three stories and split between two or three families; but there are temples to one god or another, spires rising above the roofs of their neighbors, and buildings vast by comparison to the smaller homes that have dozens or hundreds of families.

"And in the background there's a great wide bay." The image flooded my mind as a subtle song played just under the edge of audibility. "Ferries and cargo ships seem so small in the distance, but a hundred feet of ship is a feeder ship, not one of the seafaring, oceanic vessels that are the arteries of trade. And the far shore's another city, smaller but it's still a half million people, with fifteen-hundred-foot hills rising in the blurry distance, thirty and more miles away."

"**[Inscribe Perfected Vision]**."

Jannea whispered the words, and they echoed deafeningly. I fell to my knees, staring across the city of San Francisco from where I used to sit on Diamond Heights, eyes drinking in the thick splay of Edwardian townhouses, and my throat was thick with emotion by the time the vision faded and I saw the corridor of my shop-house again.

It took me a long moment, and a long drink from the water in the basket of dumplings, to get ahold of myself.

Jannea was weeping silently, crumpled in a heap in the corridor. I stepped hesitantly over to her, but she waved me off, shaking her head; a few moments later, she'd at least sort of uncrumpled. Tears still running freely down her face, she sat against the wall, eyes closed, smiling.

I took out my notebook in the meantime, not particularly feeling like I wanted to just stand around. *What determines if something is worthy of a Feat*, I wrote. *What is the difference between a Class Feat and a non-Class Feat? Can Feats be upgraded? Are there constraints on the merging of Skills or Feats? Can—*

"What a terrible beauty," Jannea murmured suddenly. "How did you breathe?"

"Not as well as I do here," I replied with a sad smile. There was a long line and a squiggle where I'd flinched from the voice of someone whose presence I'd forgotten.

I put the notebook away. Writing down more questions could wait.

"One in six people had breathing problems, medical conditions in the lungs. And that was far from the worst city. Actually, I think it might have been one of the best ones."

"Which room?"

"The empty one." I nodded to the room at the end of the hall. "Kelly's will get the aerial night shot, and I want the glade."

She took in a shaky breath, then rose and walked on unsteady feet to the room. She had a disc in her left hand, and she slowly, reverentially placed the disc on the floor just inside the room. Tapping it twice, she nodded, satisfied by something, and walked the few feet back to me.

"The glade now."

"Are you su—"

She cut me off with nothing more than her glare, incandescent despite her body's shakiness. "The glade," she said softly. "And then I'll rest. Start talking."

"I was wandering off the path in the Greek woods," I began, smiling at the memory. "There were glimmers of mist rising from the creek, and a waterfall in the distance. And I shouldn't have followed it, because I wasn't equipped to go trackless, but what did I have to lose?

"There wasn't anything special about any given piece of it. The trees were just trees, the mosses were just mosses. There were other fish in the world just as colorful; there were other waterfalls bigger, louder, quieter, splashier, any attribute you want."

"Sublimity from the ordinary."

"Yeah. Exactly. Everything was perfectly within the statistically plausible, but it all came together to make something utterly perfect." There was a pressure building in the air, or possibly building between us. "It was just a forest glade, but it was like it was the archetypal forest glade, the ideal all the others were—"

"**[Memory, Grist And Source]**." The world shook. "**[Reify Recollection]**."

"—made from," I whispered. I couldn't see; not my home's corridor, not the glade, not even a darkness beyond my eyelids. "Every sound was an instrument in a symphony, and every thing that lived did so to its own ends, but the trees sought the sun and the air and the soil, and they walked up the cliffside and reached into the air…"

"**[That Our Art Might Be A Glimpse Of Divinity]**."

Everything shattered. I saw a thousand goddesses, each of them Artemis, speaking to a thousand people. A hunter, a shrine priestess, a traveler, a hiker; a mortal, a spirit, an animal, another god. And then she looked at us, and her eyes fastened on Jannea.

"Lady." The artist's eyes were calm, her voice a whisper. "For the art's sake. Please."

A thousand responses flooded into us, into *her*; I only got caught by the penumbra, and it somehow hurled me out of the vision, slamming me bodily against the wall of the corridor. I half expected Jannea to be gone when I managed to get my eyes open, but she was on her knees just inside my room, tapping absently on another one of those discs on the floor.

She smelled like a waterfall, like the spray of water and the thunderous noise, and I somehow knew that her pupils were shaped like arrows, despite not being able to see them.

"Well. Uh." In lieu of anything remotely sensible to say, I reached for the basket of food. I'd expected to feel bruises all up and down from my body, but to my surprise, I felt amazing; relaxed and singing with the potential to move, though I was... *right*. A bit hungry, which was why I'd reached for the basket.

I hope Kelly is gonna get fed by James, I thought to myself, and then laughed softly. *If she doesn't, she can just gossip at someone and fix it. She'll be fine.*

"Jannea." She didn't respond to my voice, but I saw a way to take the basket apart into two halves, and slid one of them towards her. "Take your time," I said gently. "Let's eat. Food is fuel, you can't do art without fuel."

"Food is fuel," she repeated in a dutiful, distracted tone. She popped a dumpling into her mouth, chewing mechanically, not looking away from the disc on the floor.

I settled onto the floor, pulling my legs into a cross-legged pose with each foot up on its opposite thigh. Savoring the euphoric feeling of being able to just *do that*, a flexibility target I'd never expected to reach in life, I pulled my notebook out, popped a dumpling in my mouth, and kept writing down questions.

CHAPTER 3.11 - AFTERNOON'S CONTENTMENT

I pushed a lot of thoughts away until we'd gotten the third mystery disc in place. Jannea took much longer to recover from the aerial shot than I did, and much longer than the first time she'd used her Skill, which I was guessing inscribed the memory onto the disc; while she rested, my mind wandered.

I'd expected to be shaken—or Godtouched, for that matter—and for very little time to have passed. Jannea was non-verbal and barely present, still smelling like an ever-shifting, slowly fading piece of nature, but I... wasn't.

I was, however, hungry enough that at least a couple of hours had to have passed. Even so, I wasn't able to internalize the amount of time I'd lost until I stepped outside and saw the sun, which had moved about a third of the way down the sky.

Stepped outside, because Jannea had emphatically kicked me out of my own home.

Tayir declined to come with me. Jannea, he told me with a sonorous voice and a fond smile, would forget to go to dinner without a reminder; and he wanted to finish his own work as well. So it was alone, and feeling it, that I let my thoughts spin as I stood on the edge of the ring road.

It felt... weird. I'd had the occasional quiet moment in my first few days in Kibosh, but they'd been just that: moments, interstitials bookended by diving into learning something, meeting someone, acting, or sleeping. I had nothing planned until dinner, no access to my house, and complete confidence that Kelly would find me when she was done no matter where I wandered.

I was, in short, at entirely loose ends, and it was... really quite nice.

Still, delightful as the lack of pressure and expectations might have been, I didn't particularly want to spend it standing alone on the side of the road. There was a library I could visit if I walked south along the ring road, one with an absolutely implausible number of books given the number of people living in Kibosh; that would do for a destination.

Not long into my walk, though, I was drawn inexorably off the ring road onto the quint paths. Someone had just the most amazing alto laugh, carrying and full of an uninhibited joy, and something was nudging me to go investigate.

I stopped for a moment, looking down at the path I'd stepped onto, and tried to sort of relax into the feeling and interrogate it. It was a System feeling, I decided, coming from either *Observe* or *Comprehend*, or maybe some mixture of both.

Fascinating, and reassuring, since if I couldn't trust the System, I was fucked regardless.

There wasn't much to distinguish the quint I was walking to from any other, to my eyes. Sure, the ornamentation and art was unique, but they were *all* unique, and I had no idea what the particulars meant or implied. The color scheme of the houses was primarily reds and purples, with flowers and vegetables painted onto or maybe somehow integrated into the stone itself, but the five houses spread around the central garden plot all interpreted that in their own way.

I had no idea what any of the flowers were. That wasn't an unfamiliar feeling; I could vaguely identify a rose from a non-rose, but that was about the limit of my understanding. Most of the flowers I saw as I walked down the path towards the garden even looked perfectly mundane, things that I wouldn't have been surprised to see at the Conservatory of Flowers or the Botanical Gardens.

Most of them. The one that looked like a more elegant pitcher plant with a symmetrical pattern of seven nectar pools that had reinforced ribbing and thorns, pictured in the middle of skewering something that looked like a cross between a flying ant and a wasp? That didn't look particularly mundane.

The vegetable garden itself was interesting enough to make me stop, no matter how alluring that astonishing alto sounded. Fruit trees bracketed terraces of vegetables—leaves of tubers or other root vegetables poking out the soil, low plants that looked vaguely like some kind of lettuce, and then beans and maybe tomatoes on scaffolding. There was no way that there should have been light getting to all of them, but I supposed that was what the magic was for.

Shadow spilled out in every direction from the vegetable garden, dark and thick. The light was being collected at a thousand little points, redirected to supplement what would otherwise have been inadequate sunlight in the dense vegetable forest. And it was *dense*; the individual plants were huge, and they were packed in closely enough that I was surprised their root systems weren't one conjoined system.

Though, after all, that was entirely possible. Who was I to declare otherwise, in a world of magic?

The path took me under an arcing planter, no less dense with vegetation, and into a thicket, a maze of greenery and life. The smell was astonishing, too dense with odors of food and herbs for me to make out any individual thing other than the overall earthiness of it all. I shivered in memory as I came to a tiny gurgling brook, hearing in my head the whispers of the waterfall that I'd followed not much more than two days ago, and then smiled.

I needed to find cypress and laurelwood, and make arrows from them, which would take a teacher and a fair bit of study and practice. I'd need to learn to shoot a bow more seriously than as a way to flirt with other women at a Renaissance Fair, and find people to take me on hunts. But I'd just seen a woman take three memories of mine and inscribe perfected versions, and I had my own three-thousand-square-foot house whose rooms would bear that art.

A damn good deal, I thought to myself with a grin as I continued down the path that bridged the water, following the laughter.

The path took one more turn before opening up into the central part of the garden, and suddenly the conversation that I was dimly hearing snapped into focus. A moment later, in the middle of saying something about iron in thickly accented Qatn, I came into view and the speaker cut off.

"Um. Hi!"

I might have flushed under the sudden gaze of seven people, but I was too busy marveling at the chairs and benches. They were all obviously carnivorous plants—a set of chairs styled after that sevenfold pitcher plant, a couple other chairs that were some variant of plant-with-teeth, and a couple of benches that were made to mimic long, barbed-and-glistening fronds of some sort.

"Be welcome in this place! Please, come join us as a guest."

My eyes snapped over to the speaker, the owner of that glorious voice that'd drawn me here. Once I'd looked at her, I couldn't understand how I could have been looking at the chairs and benches in the first place, or at least not for more than a heartbeat. Easily overtopping seven feet, she looked like her *rest* days involved carrying boulders across the ocean floor in sprints—broad-shouldered and with thigh muscles that looked bigger than my head, she practically radiated power.

I *knew* her, or at least recognized her. We'd worked side by side, after all, in that vision where I'd seen the future I might have had as a Production Alchemist.

Absolutely not, cut that out, I thought to myself dimly. *Down, girl. She's probably not even into women.*

"Thank you," I managed to say to her without stammering, accepting her invitation. Someone else had said something about bread and salt, and my hands came up to catch the piece of flatbread before my eyes caught up to the throw.

I'd caught thrown pieces of challah at the Shabbat table for almost twenty years. They were complicated memories, invoked by the act of making the catch, and I had to very deliberately not burst into tears.

I ate the salted bread instead and smiled politely at the titanic powerhouse taking up an entire bench on her own, and then at all the others.

Well, the kid determinedly trying to climb a trellis got a grin from me. But the others—two men in very different kinds of robes, two women in very different kinds of armor, an ancient-looking lady, and a scowling clerky type—all got a smile.

There was a shifting around of body language, looks traded around. Six of the people were sitting in some manner, and five of them were glancing towards the sixth seated person. She was *old*, old in a way that eclipsed Kibosh's Matrons or Thesha, and she turned rheumy eyes towards me and beckoned me closer with shaking hands.

"Elder," I said as I approached, "I am—"

"Sophie." Her voice was soft, but it was clear and carrying enough that I didn't have to strain to hear her. "I know you, Traveler, and your Gods; not for hundreds of years have their shards within our Thousand dwelt on this side of the Wardline, may it stand."

My heart was beating loud in my chest, and there was an utter silence from the others. I knew that silence; it was the same silence I'd heard with

Thesha, the silence of someone suppressing sound and being obvious about it.

It was the silence of *privacy*.

"What is—"

"Three thousand and more in full array, behind those who touch still this soil—and there are Gods in that number whose shards outnumber the sands. Tell me, will you bring them all?" Her hands grabbed mine, firming up around her no-longer-gentle grip. "Will you overtake the world as a channel for their divinity? Will the Five shatter the lands and the Forest spread primeval over Kingdom, Principate, and Sarkārat alike, and then onwards?"

"No?" I tried to pull my hands away, but her grip was like steel; I tried to look around for help, but my eyes wouldn't leave her suddenly-clear ones. **Channel**, the world whispered to me, and my brain stuttered as something slid between me and the world, leaving it somehow dimmer. "I have no idea what you're talking about, but that sounds bad, and I'd rather not?"

"Ah. Well." She let go of my hands and leaned back in her chair, eyes clouding over and hands shaking until they landed in her lap as sound caught up with us again. "That's good."

I blinked at her, mind still not remotely caught up with whatever was going on, though whatever she'd been doing to my perception faded away. "I'm… glad, Elder…?"

"In this time—no, in this place, I am called Iōanna, and I am a Delver registered in the Kingdom of Shem. Be known to Alchemist Nadash, children."

A spate of introductions followed, and I managed to actually pay attention despite now having multiple additional major categories of inquiry and some absolutely blissful preserves spread on a thin slice of hard cheese. I nibbled at it, tasting something very similar to cloudberry, and attended as best I could, trying to project the feeling of being *present*.

Deoro was the man in the sand-colored robes that covered everything but his face and hands, and Ketka was the woman in the leather-and-steel armor which covered only her vitals and sang somehow of magic. Between the two of them and Iōanna, they were three out of a five-person delving team, taking a day's rest between outings before they struck out for the Forest to hunt… something. I wasn't entirely clear on the specifics, but apparently they routinely brought back a range of materials, reagents, food, and more from Kibosh's dungeon and the Forest areas surrounding the village.

Deoro didn't speak much in the way of Shemmai, but he was fluent enough in Qatn for all that he had a fascinating accent full of gutturals and rounded vowels. Iōanna didn't volunteer anything about herself, but she'd been speaking Shemmai earlier, and Ketka spoke *eleven* languages and visibly preened at my impressed and somewhat stunned look.

The others seemed almost faded by comparison. Aliza, whom I'd recognized as soon as she turned around, was one of the kids I'd used as a shield in the party the night before, dark-skinned and with light, wild hair escaping its braids. She applied herself diligently to ignoring me in favor of continuing to try to climb the trellis, which I approved of, laughing off the occasional fall and marking with chalk every time she got even a little higher.

There was, I noticed, quite a lot of chalk, and it started very low.

Shafta, the young woman in robes whom I'd initially thought was a man, was reserved—not shy, but distant and controlled, quiet while still being firm when she did speak. She was the Clerk-Adjutant to James and Meredith, and she'd dragged along the scowling, clerky girl who turned out to be Shuli, Kartom's apprentice—a sorceress, rather than a wizard, which was a distinction lost on me. Tseizal, the Guard in some kind of armor—kinda like a breastplate over a leather jacket, with gauntlets and a helmet at his side—with a spear resting next to him, joked that it was so that they could both be notionally social while still having someone silent around; he, on the other hand, was just happy to be on *downshift*, which meant he was equipped and alert but not engaged in any particular duty.

Oddly, as things shifted back towards conversation instead of introductions, I found myself talking mostly with Deoro. Iōanna was quiet, possibly asleep, and Ketka was *attentive*, but Deoro obviously loved to talk and needed practice with Qatn. Shafta spoke Yaroba and contributed by translating whenever Deoro's Qatn wasn't good enough, but mostly Deoro was able to make himself understood.

He was a good storyteller, even in pidgin, but while I was polite and nodded along, I wasn't actually that interested in the story I'd interrupted by my arrival. Some birds had done a favor to a king, and made a bad choice as to their reward; they wound up being so insufferable they didn't have friends, left to make their own community, and got caught in a sandstorm and died.

He kicked it over to Ketka, who stretched, muscles flexing, and shook her head. "If two have heard my story," she'd said, "then there are three more who have not heard Sophie's."

So I settled down and, a little bit haltingly, started to talk. About hiking and the dullness and colorless life that drove me to seek solitude in nature; about the decision to follow the creek, and the encounter with Artemis. I named no names, remembering Veil's request in the aftermath of my and Kelly's truth-oath, and saw Iōanna's eyes narrow in recognition regardless—but I carried on, pushing aside my curiosity about her reaction.

I told them about my having asked her to make sure my mother knew of my fate, and the realization that, dressed in hiking gear, she'd mistaken me for a man; I told them about her domains as a goddess and about theoxenia, the hospitality laws that her father enforced. About the way her social mask had come off as she offered me a new chance as a gesture of evening the scales, and about the way her half-brother, a god of crafts and craftsmanship, had stepped in to reforge my body in the process.

And then I told them about how I'd seen the beauty of the forest and the majesty of its trees, and then after some time left it to make my painful way to Kibosh; and at that, Iōanna stirred.

"Ah. Either way you went," she said softly, "it would bring glory to them."

"I... don't understand." *Again*, I didn't say, but I certainly thought it.

"Sent here," she said, switching to Ancient Shemmai, "bear you those ancient Olympian foes of ours, and a conduit to them all you are, even within the Warded Kingdom. If took you the path to the cities of the Forest, you would have been oracle and Priest unto them—and for a hundred years not an inch of land may we have dreamt of taking."

CHAPTER 3.12 - A SPECTER OF THE BAD OLD DAYS

"I... what are you—"

"Ah, I tire." Iōanna smiled at me, switching back to modern Shemmai. "I think I will retire. Deoro, child, will you help an old woman to her bed?"

"Miss Ba-Itar." Concern and worry flashed across his face, but he didn't say anything else. He offered his shoulder, and she put her weight on him.

"Wait, please!" *A conduit to them all*, she'd said. *Even within the Warded Kingdom.* "I need to know—"

"Need?"

"—am I a danger? A conduit to your foes. Am I an explosion waiting to be set off?"

Iōanna's smile didn't waver, and there was no surge of power or aura of ominous intent. The hairs on the back of my neck went prickly nonetheless as she paused, considering my words and leaning on Deoro.

Everyone else's gaze was blank, though not with the same flavors of blankness; Shafta and Ketka were keeping a straight face, while the other three present looked lost. Iōanna had switched languages specifically—and I *knew* this to be so, without being sure how I knew—so that at least one person couldn't understand her, for the same reasons that she'd used her bubble of silence earlier. And that meant that there were parts of what she'd said I couldn't discuss with at least that one other person present.

I wasn't an idiot. She'd handed me at least a partial answer to both of those questions, so when I asked, I did so in the same dead language she'd used.

"A children-question." She turned away, taking careful steps with Deoro's help. "Is it not so, that all who live are blade and balm? Impossible it is, to *take* personhood from another."

I kept my eyes on her as she walked slowly away. *All who live are blade and balm.* Not as reassuring as I might have liked, but… in a way, it was just something I'd already known. As a chemist, and in particular a process and scale-up chemist, I could have done a ruinous amount of damage in any number of ways, and that was with only mundane means.

The fact that the gods whom I'd been having dealings with were opposed to Shem in some manner? Given that I wasn't and wouldn't ever be a puppet of theirs? She was reminding me that once I was familiar with the form that the mystical alchemies took in Yelem, which I didn't expect to take me long at all… well.

It would have been very difficult for a chemist, no matter her talent and resources, to do more than kill everyone in an entire watershed. At most, a few tens of million people in a nation of ten times that amount. Armed with anything even remotely like the Law of Sympathy…

"You are thinking heavy thoughts." Ketka's booming alto shattered the quiet and wrenched my head around to look at her. "Share them!"

"I am a cataclysm waiting to happen," I said, switching unconsciously to the modern Shemmai she'd used, and then blanched.

I went from blanching to blushing as Ketka started laughing boisterously. "Oh, to introduce you to Beyin! They are so soft, and nothing but smiles. They are kind and full of love and joy."

"But you mention your Beyin." Tseizal broke in with a small smile, but his fingers were fidgeting with his spear. "And you mention them for a reason."

"A clerk kills with a pen; a magus kills with mana and arcana. Deoro kills with sand and iron, and I kill with axes, potions, and my fists." I half expected her to flex at that, but she just leveled a calm gaze at me. "Beyin kills with sickness and plague, with the smallest things that live and things even smaller. Beyin kills by turning against you that which keeps you hale, kills by some arcane art of a spreading change to how tiny things inside your head are folded.

"Not a day ago, we fought a creature which we could have bled for dozens of gallons, one which healed a neck cut through and muscles severed in moments. Beyin touched it, and we fled behind Iōanna's shield as though frightened children."

I swallowed, my throat dry. *Prions. God of my forebears, let it be that no person should die from such a thing.* "And then what?"

"It was a pool upon the stone," she said brightly. "And then all it became stone, everything that once was the creature, save only for the mana crystals near its hearts."

"That sounds," I croaked, "very hygienic."

"With a sufficient application of heat, indeed so." Ketka smiled, and somehow there was genuine warmth and humor in it and in her eyes. "Beyin is not a cataclysm waiting to happen, because they would die before killing another person. But they doubt themself and doubt themself; you were making the same face they make."

"That's... surprisingly reassuring. I don't think it should be, but it is."

"I don't find it reassuring," Tseizal said dryly. "I prefer sources of death I can hit with a spear before they kill me. I'd go to my end more satisfied."

"My teachers." Shuli surprised everyone by cutting into the conversation, it looked like. "They could too. No System? Still could."

"Shuli," Ketka said gently, "I know you respect Kartom, but—"

"Resonant link to the sun through a metaphysical binding," she snapped, tightness in her voice giving way to a controlled anger. "Sympathetic link from a pressure chamber to the heart of the Great Volcano. Cascading conversion of oxygen in the air."

"Cascading how, without subatomics?" Shafta tilted her head at Shuli, frowning. "Ah. Not a violation until cast. Once cast, difficult to reverse."

"Couldn't you cast, like, semiotically-driven alert and prevention spells?" That got me two measuring looks and two confused ones. "A spell that says hey, your intent or the predicted effect of the spell you're about to cast is a cataclysm, we're alerting an Archmage?"

Shuli nodded and Ketka smirked; the other two still looked confused. "Action is a form of communication," the young sorceress said. "It exists. It is *known*."

"And so it can be avoided or evaded; but for each spell known, other spells may hide in the shadow of its presence." Ketka shrugged. "Magus Zrodne would know of a hundred spells for each one I do, and why should he know of more than a tithe?"

"Dying, an Archmage takes a hundred secrets into darkness," Shuli said. "Bound to stone, current, idea, or law, a spell lasts until its substrate is dust."

"That sounds like a recipe for…" I paused, looking for the right word or phrase. *Destructive interference? Constructive interference? Two spells triggering off of each other due to prognosticated intent?* "I guess… complications?"

"Not wrong," Shuli said. "Archmage problems."

We sat for a bit in silence, leaning back in our respective chairs or benches. Shuli and Shafta seemed to relax as the quiet moment extended, and Tseizal's fidgeting stopped, but Ketka was gazing expectantly at me and I had a question kicking around in my head.

Not a question I knew how to ask, though.

There were too many variants on it. *Why did she say that* was too open-ended and also too obvious; she spoke to influence my future behavior. *Why didn't anyone tell me there were cities in the Forest* could have any number of answers, and Ketka might or might not know them, but between Kelly's careful—and occasionally not-careful—comments and Captain Meredith's own disposition, I knew I was missing a fair amount of information because Meredith just… hadn't told me despite it being her job to do so.

And, I thought to myself dryly, *I should maybe not speak in the modern tongue when I ask the question.*

"Upon what," I eventually asked in Ancient Shemmai, "shall I need to speak not of around Deoro? Why, and who else?"

"From a culture long of spoken memory, does Deoro come," Ketka replied, her broad grin confirming that I'd guessed right about what questions to ask. "Before Yarovi, before Scholars of history and of Gods, do not say that you bear the Gods of Olympus, who are also the Remnant Gods that in the Forest dwell; not that you bear them and not that a conduit to them you are."

"Enough it is, for me, to know that Ióanna trusts." She sobered, grin fading away. "But not very much more has passed than a thousand years between the War of Olympus-of-the-Forest and now, and the memory does not fade of your patroness's shard-sister and the rivers of blood she her Forest watered. A God, that Forest became, grown on the blood of every ilk of kith and kin who came to our aid. Bargain with strange Gods through their foreign shards as you may, and none will gainsay you for it; but should there come forth word that through you, Arês Enyalios and Aphroditê Encheios might bring sword and spear to Yelem anew…"

"They would kill me, I suppose." I didn't even shiver at the thought; it was something alien, too absurd to even engage with, but at the same time it seemed obvious. Like a piece of math, maybe, describing a reaction that defied conceptualization, much less visualization. "To avoid the risk that I'll bring back their old foes, and the… rivers of blood."

"What? No!" Ketka looked genuinely offended at the notion. "For one to do such injustice as *they* might have, so that they might not rise anew? Even in Yaro it would not be done so, if without struggle you submitted to being bound and severed from them. For what purpose would we kill you, when instead the Archmages could render you separate from them forever?"

"That… makes a surprising amount of sense." I tried to meet her gaze, but failed; I wasn't even sure why. "Forgive me. Unfair, that was, to you and yours and all they who dwell here. Was there more I must know about this?"

"There's always more," she said, switching to modern Shemmai. "But I've answered your question. Rude to shut out our companions, is it not? Even if the opportunity to practice is not so easily set aside."

"So practice," Shafta said dryly.

I twitched in surprise, having genuinely forgotten anyone else was around in the intensity of my focus on Ketka. Shafta was broadcasting a tremendous apathy, Shuli was faking the same with a tremendous lack of fidelity, and Tseizal was…

"I'd rather you stopped." Tseizal was twitching, fingers curling and uncurling around the haft of his spear. "Down to my marrow, I feel like what you're talking about is trouble. I don't want any of it, and I'd *really* rather you didn't make me party or complicit to it."

There was something about the way he was moving, the specifics of what he was saying. I could feel something kicking in, feel the way there was a give-and-take with my System—with Spark. It wasn't something conscious, not yet, but… "You have a Skill," I guessed, and saw his eyes narrow fractionally. "Some sort of problem-sense that was going off, a kind of gut instinct?"

"*Storm Warning*," he said. "It's pretty standard, but… who told you about it without telling you its name?"

"Nobody." I shrugged. "*Comprehend* and *Observe*, or just one or the other. Plus the way you said it, and the way you were grabbing at the spear."

"Then we give regrets to the moons, and perhaps you will tell us more of your life's tale?" Ketka glanced over at Shuli and Shafta, the former of whom looked annoyed and the latter flustered. "Lovers," she clarified. "The two moons that became one."

"I've done a lot of talking," I said, staunchly not addressing what she'd said for the sake of the two introverts and their obvious discomfort. *Interesting saying, though. Two moons that became one? That's worth asking about.* "Besides, Kelly isn't here, and it would be both weird and kind of disrespectful-feeling to tell you a bunch of stories I haven't told her. Which I know makes no sense! It just feels that way."

Ketka gave me a level look with a raised eyebrow, and I almost checked over my shoulder to see if my First Friend was standing back at the entrance to the seating area, smirking at the back of my head. I didn't, though; Kelly was a lot of things, but she wasn't light on her feet, and she was neither patient nor that kind of subtle.

Instead of looking to confirm her absence, I pulled out my notebook. *What are the standard, expected-to-be-known Skills of different archetypes and professions*, I wrote on one line, and then *what's the deal with Ketka using 'the two moons that became one' as a reference for lovers* on the next.

"Taking notes?"

I looked up at Tseizal, who at least wasn't fidgeting with his spear anymore. "Kinda? Writing down questions to ask, when I get a chance."

Shuli's head snapped over. "Ask one."

"Huh?"

"A question," she said impatiently. "Ask it."

"O...kay." I flipped back to the first page. *Shuli's apprentice to Kartom. That means she's Tower, and involved with arcane stuff, and this... was a Magus Zrodne thing, and that means Shuli might know. Okay.* "What's the Ward?"

"A zone-defining enchantment, both a tactically-defensive and strategically-offensive encirclement of the Forest God and the Remnants that live there." She tilted her head. "You weren't informed."

"Not in the least, not in the slightest. Someone implied that it's not surprising Captain Meredith didn't see fit to tell me."

"Mmm." Shuli could do a pretty solid *no comment* noise, it turned out. She leaned forward, and I realized that this must be her version of fully present and intent. There was a pressure to it, like watching an ocean wave on the horizon and wondering whether it would break or swamp the beach. "History and teaching. How far back will you still listen?"

"How far back... Shuli, if you start at the beginning, I'll hear you out even if it means we have to talk through dinner."

She smiled at that, the first real smile I'd seen on her, and her body language loosened into something approaching fluidity. "Then attend," she said. "This story begins some thousands of years ago, when all Yelem rose to war."

CHAPTER 3.13 - FOR THEY WERE RIGHT BASTARDS, THE LOT OF THEM

This is the story of the Olympian Wars. I heard it from Shuli, whose name means *peace* and who was growing fast into Historian, which she was going to use for her Third Tier breakthrough. She heard it from Kartom, and given his personality, he probably validated that it was true using divination.

And so from Kartom to Shuli, who was studying war under Magus Zrodne. The irony of *that* wasn't lost on me.

Anyway, the story of the Olympian Wars, as Shuli told it to me.

It starts like this:

About five thousand years ago, which was about four thousand years before the Theurgist's whole deal, twenty-seven Gods led something just under a million people to war.

Yeah, I know, a million people was ludicrous. Or maybe it wasn't; there were armies being thrown around in Earth's ancient times that were north of a half-million even without magic. But this wasn't some sort of all-out invasion or a best-effort deployment. This was just a raid writ large, a bunch of marauders heading out from Ipeira—the name for the continent that's now Alqar, the name for the continent that Shem's on.

There were a hundred and fifty-nine on-the-record Olympian divinities of some sort kicking around Ipeira. They had the whole place to themselves, and when the internecine bloodletting got too much, their Gods and Goddesses of War would link up with the Sea Gods and take the pressure off. They'd done this for a while—how many centuries, nobody was exactly sure—and as far as they were concerned it was a stable arrangement.

And then, about five thousand years ago, they did something obscene even by the standards of war to a God almost vile enough to deserve it.

Ipeira was almost eight million square miles back then, and nobody knows how many people lived there, but it couldn't have been more than a couple hundred million, and not for any lack of fertile land. There were seven billion people all told living on Yelem when the Olympian Pantheon killed the God Shĭ-Onde, by comparison—and rather than try to grapple with that number, I stopped trying to second-guess the story and just went with it.

There were a million people on that raid, and all of them were warriors. Soldiers, in a way; as disciplined in battle as they were mad and vicious outside of it. They were broken in heart and inflamed in spirit, for all that they cultivated a sense of culture and literacy and an understanding of magic. They could fish and hunt, they could make camp, clean, and repair. They could use the traveling forges they brought with them; they could build siege weapons for those fortifications they could not bring down through their Gods and spells; and they could build monuments, testaments to the destruction and butchery they wrought.

It was their practice, when they sallied, to raze to the ground any city which they deemed to fight only insufficiently against them—and only those cities, and their Gods, sparing those who they found worthy. Kill enough of them, kill one in ten of them or one for every ten of you they killed, by the time they had killed nine in ten of your soldiers, and they would call peace. They would flood through your city, trading for food and trinkets, laughing as your merchants fleeced them; and they would kill in an instant anyone who tried to settle the score.

It was their practice, when they left, to tithe to your War Gods, and to whatever Gods were domain-siblings, as they called it, to their own. They would leave a bounty of blessings, spells, and precious metals with those they left with child—and a vast array were those—and they would take with them in their wombs the seed of every consenting survivor who'd killed an Olympian soldier.

And then they would go on, and on, until finally they had glutted themselves on killing and fucking and the horrors they called glorious war.

And then, one year, they killed the God Shĭ-Onde.

He was not a beloved God, or a great one. He was a vile, vicious cretin, and they took particular offense to him, because as he was venerated in the city of Hŏgal, he was everything they despised.

God of the broken promise and the knife in the back. God of lies and deceit—not for the sake of victory, but for the thrill of the infliction of pain. God of deals forsaken which would have enriched you both, God of the responsibility spurned and the obligation pressed.

God of envy, of burning the book that you cannot read or do not own. God of rapists.

The citizens of the city fought, once the streets began to run red with the blood of Shǐ-Onde's priests, once his sanctums began to fall and his altars began to burn. The Olympians said they fought because Shǐ-Onde was beloved to them, but it cannot be known if that was true; maybe they fought because he was *theirs*, because he was being killed by an army that had laughed and called truce and was now shattering their own promises in turn.

Hŏgal burned, and Shǐ-Onde did not manifest—though he was risen anew—to defend them or face the Olympians. So too did the next city, without any quarter offered, and the next, which had swelled tenfold from the armies that awaited the Olympians. And on the pyre of *that* city, the last tens of thousands remaining from the raiding army of Ipeira bound and summoned the God they were hunting and killed him, binding him to his shard of Godhood, his metaphysical anchor within the world of Yelem.

Their Gods who rode with them still numbered four, and all four spurned the power in that shard and called it tainted. They cast it—God and power and divinity alike—beyond the bounds of the planet, and until Shǐ-Onde fades from the memory of the world there will be one God of the Thousand who suffers in the endless void, and on Yelem there will be nine hundred and ninety-nine.

For that, as much as for any of the other violations and excesses, within twenty years, every major nation of Yelem had committed to the destruction of the Olympian Gods. They had been party to that ultimate act of sacrilege, deliberately destroying a sacred piece of the future—a wellspring of that energy which defied entropy itself—for no reason other than to fully express their spite. Thirty years later, the first fleets set sail, and three hundred Gods sailed with them.

Poseidôn was incarnated on Yelem in those days, and three Gods who called themselves the Children of Póntos, and Amphitrítē Ketos and five of her children. They and a dozen others whose names were lost to or cast into the dark stood against the Gods of the Evgōméng Fleet, that grand coalition who'd united to break a continent gone warglory-mad to avenge the worst of the worst.

If the Fleet's Gods had needed to defeat the Olympians, they might still have failed; Olympus was mighty beyond reckoning, and these seas were their home. But for two days and two nights, mortal sailors strained at the ropes and navigated their ships between swells, and the Gods of wood and cloth held their ships together even as Gods of the air gave them shelter from the storms. They gave themselves to the Gods of dream and nightmare in shifts, sleeping in their embrace as their bodies worked tirelessly, and their muscles pushed to the breaking point but never further.

The waters were still contested when six in ten of their ships made landfall, and only one in ten of their Gods had been slain; and none of those were so dead as to be unable to return, reforming within the temples the Evgōméng would construct. This was so even when the ferocity of that landing battle rent the shores before and below them and reshaped the coastline of the continent, and what ground they took, they held.

It was a war of annihilation—not of cities, not of peoples, but of Gods. They would put to the torch a thousand temples and put to the knife a hundred priesthoods, and they would wield magics of every shade and stripe to rip the beating heart out of every community of practice, every tradition of worship that those Gods fed on.

The Evgōméng did not last. It could not last; after the seventeenth fleet, after over fifty years of war with ever-diminishing support, it collapsed. In its place, the Severed Kingdoms rose in the continent of Alqar, as they renamed it. But the Severed held their alliances with each other for thirteen hundred years, and even after that time they remembered the purpose of their founding, as did their Gods.

By war and by subterfuge, by assimilation or by simple *departure*, through weariness of being hounded or being rent asunder, the facets of the Gods of Olympus which were among the Thousand of Yelem were sundered from the world. New Gods rose in their place, and pressed them further. Chief among them was Naga, who smiled back at Aphroditê Tymborychos and held her close even as the grave opened beneath them, and then closed again. She defied the Gravedigger and her own death, and rose to kill also one of the divine attendants to that facet of Aphrodite; and this was repeated a dozen times over, a hundred times over, as Gods were born and slain and reborn and reshaped.

Time and again, the Severed Kingdoms fell to infighting; and time and again, as the Olympian cities fought to reclaim their lost ground, the Severed Kingdoms made common cause once more. Time and again, the Kingdoms fought to the gates of a city, only to be opposed by horrors divine and mundane. But even the hearthfires could not sustain the scourging flames of Hestia Potheinotáti, beloved of mortals and Gods alike, when the siege of a city lasted long enough to drain the vitality from the soil.

And though the centuries were long, the memories of Gods and Heroes were longer, and one by one the cities fell or surrendered, leaving their faiths behind and keeping their lives.

Eventually, the Severed Kingdoms developed their own identities, something beyond a mission colored by their particular choice of divinities. Yaro sprawled across more than a million square miles of desert, ravaged by vicious sandstorms; the Kings and Queens of Deshanna ruled, immortal, over the peaks and valleys of the central mountains. Sudh, Payazh, Bithydä, and other nations lost to time, war, and politics grew and changed, and over the thousands of years, their languages and cultures changed with them.

And eventually, nothing was left of Old Ipeira but those—Gods, Heroes, and mortals—who had fled into the Forest, where once nobody dwelled but two Goddesses and their retinues.

Eight armies followed them. Two and a half million soldiers, veterans led by Heroes and Gods, they numbered; and not one was seen or heard from after they crossed into the Forest. From that gruesome harvest, there arose a God of the Forest—of the Forest in its entirety, a God that was one and the same with the air and soil, with the water and stone.

It birthed, either in the process or as an attack, the dungeons whose products and threat alike remain central to every nation of Alqar, from Payazh in the southwest to Yaro in the northeast, for all that they undergird only the land of Shem. The toll in blood was unimaginable, but the nations survived, and when the remaining Olympians pressed their attack, they were met by the fury of the new Kingdom of Shem and its Magi.

Met, and stopped.

Shem burned. Its Magi died in droves, and its armies were massacred wherever they stood. The Fortress-Cities fell one after another, each exacting its vicious tithe, until the waves crashed against Basathon, last of the bastions of Shem. The architect of that city stood, protected by Emmna, on the walls; and he bled heartsblood for seven hours, six hours more than any other city had won, and his walls stood against Gods, siege weapons, and magic alike.

Basathon, who builds; Basathon, whose city, named after him, held long enough for the armies of Alqar to arrive.

Of all the Olympian Gods who had sallied in their last great blaze of glory, only one left the battlefield that defined the Forest War. Haidês Agesander put to rest all the unquiet dead of that day, and when he left he took with him the shards of Athênê Axiopoinos and Apollôn Karneios, leaving on the field of battle those others who fell; for he had come not to fight but to do his duty, and none raised a hand against him. So died the last God who had taken part in the end of Shĭ-Onde—and so ended the war waged against Olympus by the nations of Alqar.

Many were the Heroes and Gods who died that day, and just as many rose. The two Kings and three Queens of Deshanna were lost, and their daughter Najjara took the throne as Regent in their name and rules still. The Praetor of Sudh was there to witness the death of the Prince and Princess, and the Praetor returned home to butcher their way through civil wars that arose in their absence and to then shock all Alqar by refusing to take the throne themself. The Yarovi fed their sandstorms with the Godhoods of the sundered, and Payazh did the same to the very land beneath their feet, and that land now sails the Yelemi seas.

And the Kingdom of Shem built its cities anew, for peace and learning instead of war; they honed every citizen as though they were each destined to be Heroes, as though every carpenter and singer and Magus were to someday face down a God.

The Theurgist was alive in those days, and his hatred of Gods had only grown from the Forest War; and Emmna was alive as well, who wished nothing more than to defend Shem as she had Basathon. When the Ward rose, she was the anchor and the keystone of it, and she became a Goddess—Emmna who shields.

The Theurgist, we know, could have ascended as a God in his own right. Even without the shard of Godhood he held from the War, he could have ascended; but instead, he drew the Forgotten God in its entirety through that shard and slew it, or perhaps the God came to him and bared its chest of its own volition. With something that was thus far more than a shard, he built a wonder which had not been seen before him, not in Yelem nor in any world that any of the Thousand were present in.

He called it the Divine Flame, and it burns still, nurtured and guided by those Archmages of Alqar who dedicate their retirement to that work. And the Ward burns still, too, resonating with Emmna's determination that Shem should prosper; and the Wardline advances, one step at a time, even as the Five fade and their names are forgotten. The Forest of Artemis Hêgemonê spills the blood of armies always and of lone travelers rarely, and the dungeons below the surface of Alqar give way in places to the Low Roads of legend.

And that was the story of the Olympian Wars, as told to me by Shuli, Apprentice Mage whose teachers are Kartom and Zrodne. I had no reason to believe that anything in it was inaccurate, and Ketka's nodding along suggested she didn't find fault in it either.

And that was why, as the truth of it and the vastness of it settled into me, I found myself vomiting what little was in my stomach, heart hammering, shaking uncontrollably.

CHAPTER 3.14 - STOP MOVING, AND EVERYTHING CATCHES UP

It had taken stopping for a history lesson for it to *really* sink in that I was in a different world.

Gods, friendly strangers, baffling social norms and mores that I had barely started to adapt to, and a civic status quo that felt impossibly sensible? Spells, enchantments, impossible construction with impossible materials, mystical alchemy, and a structured system of magic that could have been pulled out of a video game if it weren't obviously an entity in its own right, bombast and all?

All of those, I could handle. Handle them at a trudge, handle them at a run; they were tractable, they were task-based, they could be grouped in the quadrants defined by importance and urgency. I could stave off thinking about or internalizing the reality of the ones that were too absurd, and focus on the somehow radical notion of surplus capacity even *existing*, much less it being used for the common good.

I couldn't handle… this, whatever it was, I couldn't even think about it. My mind was racing to think about literally anything else, but at the same time it just kept circling back to that utter void of horror, to the desolation of history that they built a peace out of and which had settled into my mind with a divine attestation of its truth from my own divine patrons, if patrons they were.

I threw up again and again, trying to control my breathing, trying to get my heartbeat to slow down and steady up. Every time I thought I had a grip on myself, a different facet of the truths in Shuli's story hammered into me again. They resonated along every one of the metaphysical pathways I'd established, a resonance that *insisted* on confirming, intrusively, every single piece of the story as my mind *kept coming back to it*.

The worst of it, and the least of it, was that I could tell myself it wasn't *my* Artemis. That *my* Artemis was a shard—a divine fragment, no more the fullness of a god than was the Artemis of Yelem—who had faded from Earth along with her Pantheon rather than rage against the tide, and had never stepped foot on this new-to-me world. That *my* Artemis had passed me to something like a sister, and I'd left that sister's domain and struck out for civilization.

I could tell myself that Hephaestus had never forged weapons or armor for the Yelemi Olympians, because no shard of Hephaestus had ever *been* here, which I somehow knew in my blood and bone. I could tell myself that Hermes was a trickster god, and that he went where he pleased and always had.

None of it changed the fact that if I listened too closely to my pulse, I could hear the drums of a thousand divine shards calling for war, each a facet of a hundred different gods. None of it changed the fact that I now understood *why* Veil had told me not to invoke them, and why Zrodne had been so livid—I had, in a small way, *brought their enemies here.*

I was making an utter, grotesque fool of myself. I knew this to be true down to my marrow, and it didn't matter whether it had any factual basis. I was a mess, I was pitiable in the worst of ways and I was sweating and cold, dizzy and weak, and the ground…

The ground was so close, and so *gross*, and someone had been holding my hair out of the way but now I was falling into the amber-colored vomit, thinking *there goes the cloudberry, that sucks, it was tasty*—and then I wasn't.

There were words being spoken at me, soft words murmured gently and soothingly. I couldn't make them out; all I could hear was my own heartbeat and my panicked breathing. I was being held, I was trapped and someone was holding me, and I got a hand free enough to connect with an elbow, but the arm around my waist just tightened. A heel strike, my head slamming back; I twisted in a panic and managed to foul my own footing, and I fell onto my back with my head barely missing the ground.

There was a hand cradling it, gently, and that same voice. It was telling me to breathe deeper and more slowly, telling me with a thrumming reverberation of the world, and my body obeyed; it was telling my heart to beat with a steady rhythm, and my body obeyed.

I heard the words behind the words when she told my stomach to steady and my blood vessels to loosen. I couldn't fully understand them; they might have said *Influence,* or *Nudge,* or *Ease,* or *Support.* They might have said all of those things, but when I opened my eyes, trying to blink away tears and ignore the snot, Kelly was lifting me up to a sitting position and the dizziness was starting to fade.

"Can you wipe your face?"

Her words preempted mine, which was probably for the best—I had no idea what I was going to say, anyway. I reached for the handkerchief she was offering, trying to make my hand stop shaking, and then let that hand fall to my side.

She wiped my face, and I could *see* again.

This wasn't an improvement. Deoro was gone, and Shuli and Shafta were focused on each other, something beyond Guardsman Tseizal's own not-seeing—they were lovers, the Clerk-Adjutant and the Apprentice Magus. I'd somehow missed the physical signs until that moment, for all that it was so very obvious once I saw it, for all that I'd been *told* they were. But Ketka, Ketka of that glorious alto voice, Ketka of the six and a half feet of stunning muscle, Ketka who looked like she ran marathons underwater with rocks tied to her back for fun…

Ketka was looking at me with concern and worry and no small amount of pity, and I was absolutely mortified. Kelly was a lost cause; Kelly had seen me with my heart beating in my eyes staring at Hitz's lab and had seen me tithing mucus to the throne. But I'd hoped to retain some vague semblance of dignity in Ketka's eyes, for a variety of reasons.

My mouth opened, and words failed to come out as anything other than a hissing croak. Kelly all but shoved something into my mouth, a hollow reed of some sort, and I sucked at it and swallowed warm water cut with lemon and honey. It was a relief that had me almost break into tears again, but instead I breathed in, deep and slow, and smiled faintly at both of them.

"You held my hair," I said to Ketka, in lieu of a thousand other things I wanted to say.

"It needs washing," she said in her accented Shemmai, "but some things are not the proper solution to that problem."

"Did… was…" I stopped, marshaling my words on purpose. Everything was still hazy and floaty, with a feeling like there was cotton filling my brain, so it took a bit longer than usual. "Did you just make a chemistry pun? You absolutely did. Why do you know enough chemistry to make puns?"

"An axe is nothing without the body to wield it," she said in what was obviously a rehearsed answer. "A body is nothing without the mind to guide it and understand its purpose."

"So you're a scholar of some sort," I said slowly, trying to wrap my malfunctioning brain around it, "because it makes you better at hitting things."

"You cannot answer a question which you do not know how to ask."

I squinted at her, then shook my head. That turned out to be a mistake, and in the grips of the renewed dizziness I almost vomited again. There was a hand on—one of Kelly's hands was on the base of my neck, massaging a tense muscle, and the nausea faded. "I don't think I can deal with you right now," I said, grinning weakly to make the joke obvious. *A question you don't know how to axe, huh.* "But thanks. That helped."

We lapsed into a moment of quiet. Kelly more or less pulled me onto the bench; I straddled it with my head tilted up, staring at the stylized plant-teeth on the back support and canopy that looked as though they were going to snap down onto us. Her hands kept returning to one muscle in particular, somewhere vaguely in my neck region, and it made me feel…

… I wasn't quite sure. Warm, yes, and it was pleasant; my muscles were struggling to tense themselves even as I focused on Kelly's touch and deliberately relaxed them, from my calves and knees all the way up through my back and fingers. It was making the nausea ebb away, making my inner ear feel less like the world was spinning; it was slowing my heart and lungs back down to a normal rate even as my skin started to prickle.

"It's called the levator scapulae." Kelly's breath tickled the back of my neck as she leaned in, putting a little more weight into her thumbs. "You're already spending a lot of time looking down and forwards, between the books and your notebook. Rafa said I had *a Clerk-tight neck*, when I went to her one day while I was settling Hitz, helping them with the accounting for the transport fees. So I looked it up."

It felt extremely nice, and I wanted her to never stop. "I need you to not lean forward like that," I heard myself say.

"Got it." The pressure of her breasts against my back and the tickle of her breath against my neck both went away. "Better?"

"On one specific axis," I said. *No, in other words, and I hope you understand that.* Her fingers resumed, at least, working their way down my neck to the muscles just below my shoulder blades, and I hissed out as a wave of tension rippled across my muscles.

She kept going, bless her; and I kept working on my body's reaction to being touched.

"It's funny," I said with an affectedly idle air. "I hadn't actually realized how ragged you were running me, or that it was on purpose."

"You napped." Kelly snorted at her own tone of voice, recognizing how evasive it was. "I did my best to keep you in motion whenever you were awake," she said after a moment. "We'd dial it down slowly, that's the general idea, and you'd use the morning's labor as an anchor, and you'd look back a few months later and it would hit you. Not in a bad way, but you'd go *oh*, this is a new world, I've built a new life."

"Instead of being hit in the brain by the life that I'd left behind. And on…" I took a deep breath, momentarily lost for words. "History," I said vaguely, for lack of anything more coherent. "A whole new world."

"It's a lot."

Kelly's hands stopped, and I resisted the urge to whine or push back against them to get them to restart. I turned, instead, seeing her glance with narrowed eyes at each of the others present. "I probably needed to know," I murmured suddenly, pitched quietly enough to hopefully evade Tseizal's ears. "Not just that I shouldn't name them. I needed to know the context, *before* I started talking about how great the—that pantheon is, even if they're a different set of… shards from the ones I've encountered and made deals with."

That got a round of awkward half-laughing from Kelly, and a soft, rumbling chuckle from Ketka. "I do not choose to guess what the Priests will decide about your Gods, little Alchemist." There was a look in the delver's eyes that I couldn't decipher, but it wasn't a *bad* one. "Perhaps the records of Shem might instruct a woman of the axe as to when previously anyone had dealings with Gods not counted within the Thousand?"

"Not even a James question." Kelly was smiling distantly, distracted by some thought. "That's a question for our senior Librarian. Have you met him, Ketka Fasjum?"

"My people have not styled ourselves so for many years," Ketka said. It was mild, but Kelly winced—clearly a rebuke, then. "My interest in our friend here is in her trade, not her Gods. I am content enough with mine; with the sand that flows, the wind that scythes, and the oasis."

Our friend, huh. I smiled as best I could at Ketka, my professional smile, the one I wore to interviews. "I'm always happy to do business. Is there anything in particular you're interested in?"

"So soon after your distress, you wish to…" Ketka trailed off, brow furrowed. Her hands twitched at her sides, then clenched as a flush started creeping up her neck. "I… how does one say it in Shemmai, to put aside pleasantries and bring out the knives?"

"That's how you say *let's talk shop*? What kind of…" Kelly shook her head. "Yaroba! I'd heard people talk about it, but that's *ridiculous*."

"I'm very good at compartmentalizing things," I said to Ketka, ignoring Kelly. My spine straightened, and my overall posture shifted into *let's make a deal*, a message in body language that I couldn't have put into words for the life of me. "Let's bring out the fire and ice, since I'm sure you'll go to someone else for knives. What are you looking for?"

"*Haruna*," Ketka murmured. "You have a resilient strength. Well, none are surprised that Friend Avara chose well in guiding you through the path of motion." She settled herself, sliding down to sit on the grass so that our heads could be on more or less the same level. "What have you made so far that is of interest?"

"Made a Brightly Burning Mist Potion," I said. "For my professional qualification, in order to Class up. Other than that, just the Basic Concussion."

"I have no need for Basics," she said, waving dismissively. "An alchemist in Mevi sells explosives better than I expect from someone new. But tell me." She leaned forward intently. "Brightly Burning Mist?"

I smiled brilliantly at her, and matched her posture with mine. Hungry with anticipation for something—I wasn't quite sure what—I pushed everything else away and considered carefully.

"So," I began, "you're aware that the stonework of Kibosh's walls is… robust."

And with that, and my smiling pause, I had her complete attention.

CHAPTER 3.15 - DIFFERING STYLES OF NEGOTIATION

Ketka did not wind up buying my Brightly Burning Mist potion.

It wasn't dynamic enough, she explained. A fight against a monster in the dungeon, or a swarm of them, was either a wild, fast-flowing dance where a misstep meant death or an instantaneous kill with all the team's might. Something that built up slowly, and which needed to be held while doing so, just wasn't useful.

"I will teach you how to bargain with Yarovi," she told me, smiling. "There are three of us here now—Sayyad, our Mystical Hunter, speaks Yaroba well, but she is not of the sands—and Deoro does not use the products of alchemy. And so you will sell to Elaneir, who is a singer and chanter and who uses potions which grant easement of the throat; but also to those who will come in time."

"There's tea involved," Tseizal interjected. "Tea and tiny plates of food."

He, unlike Ketka, was very obviously interested in my magical, stone-melting pepper-spray. There was a whole dictionary involved in the way he touched the spear he always kept at his side—tapping, clenching, rubbing with a thumb, it was all different moods. This one was *impatience*, I was pretty sure, and that boded well for the usefulness of the potion.

Still, he was playing along, or that's how it felt to me. There was a layer of social nicety involved, something that made it important or necessary to give space to Ketka and encourage her rather than getting down to business.

"The Guardsman speaks true. Where did you learn?"

"In school." He visibly bit back something pithy, pausing to pick what were probably more diplomatic words. "Village Guard isn't about policing, like it is in the coreward rings. Kibosh doesn't need more policing than the Clerks."

"James? Really?" I couldn't control my face, something between a snickering laugh and a look of surprise. "He doesn't seem the type, and Shafta—well, you don't either." I gave a head-tilt and a bit more volume on that one, and let a little more laugh into my voice.

It was mostly cover, though. It might not have been *fair* of me to have such a strong reaction to the idea of police in a fantasy world, especially one whose civic institutions were so emphatically reasonable thus far, but…

Well, traumas weren't so easily ejected, and I had a *lot* of reasons to have negative responses to the police.

"I file papers," Shafta said in a carrying voice. "Boss fixes problems."

"Paperwork *also* fixes problems," Tseizal said to me, also loudly enough to make it clear he was talking to Shafta. That got a huff, and he shook his head in… fondness, maybe. "Anyway, coreward is settled land. *We've* got Forest-spawn, dungeon lobes, adventurers, and Delvers who think they're adventurers. I don't carry this spear around for people, I carry it for bloodmoths, spite packs, and the occasional blinker or phaser smart enough to need handling."

"I have no idea what basically any of that means," I said. I almost asked for an explanation, but stopped myself just in time. Judging by Kelly's reactions to my constant jumping from one train of inquiry to another, that might be something best avoided, as best I could, when I was talking with people who might be less… tolerant. "You were saying, about school?"

"Cultural insight training." He shrugged. "How people do business, make friends, make enemies, flirt, break up, settle down, move on. Fighting styles, faiths, what gives offense and doesn't. Languages, dialects, differences in how they speak Qatn."

"Thorough," Ketka said approvingly. "Even for Yaro, which trades not even our sand?"

"You send Delvers." His expression went intense for a moment, before smoothing out. "All you types need more managing than we can do blind, to keep you pointed in the right direction and *alive*. Yaro, Sudh, and Deshanna, mostly."

"Are there no Payazhan who come to Shem in these times?"

Tseizal snorted at that. "*They* don't need our help, and they stick to the towns. The most junior Primo is more firepower than anything we need in a village, dungeon or no. Can't even bribe 'em to help with a Breach, though I've heard they'll chip in on a Wildlight run."

"Excuse me." I raised my hand. "Primo, Breach, and Wildlight?"

"Primos are Payazhan water mages," Tseizal said. "Tiny water jets that can cut through anything, big jets that can shatter basically anything, that kinda thing. A Breach is when you break through from a living dungeon to the Low Roads, and a Wildlight is…"

"A godspark comes to rest within a dungeon of the Forest," Ketka supplied, "and the God of the Forest permits it to take root. It is a great trouble to cut a path to there, and once it is reached, the dungeon must be killed as the godspark is sundered. To kill them apart is to have one be reborn in the other."

"That sounds *fascinating*," I said, shivering, "but all the same let's not have that happen. How do we not have it happen?"

"Nobody really knows, I think." Tseizal shrugged. "That's why we have so many powerhouses in the outer ring villages. One Primo might be worth more than Ketka and the three other kids put together—"

"Strong words, from someone not in his double."

"—but *that* lady is something else." He nodded towards the path Iōanna had left on, ignoring Ketka. "She's, what, triple-high Third, refined?"

"One apex and approaching a second in her twice-refinement."

"Emmna's Shield." Tseizal whistled, obviously impressed. "I'm glad I didn't ask that to her face. I forgot that Sudha folk refine more than once."

I, on the other hand, did not understand well enough to share his reaction. "I have no idea what any of *that* means either," I said crossly. "And I wouldn't turn down an explanation."

"Apex is the very tippy-top of a Tier," Kelly said, startling me. I managed to not fall off the bench, but it was a close thing; I'd somehow forgotten she was there. "It goes low, high, and then apex. You pick up a Class when you hit 'high' for your Tier, which is level fifteen for Third Tier, and then apex is twenty."

"Another Class." I blinked a few times, trying to remember. "I… knew about that. Kan and Ketana have three Classes. Which means they're… in high Third Tier, at least. Like Iōanna, except that she's higher than that." Kelly nodded, and I rubbed my head, gazing over at Tseizal and Ketka. The two of them were having some sort of nonverbal conversation, pure body language and eyebrows, which suggested I could ask about the other half. "And refining?"

"Hit your apex in all your Classes in a Tier," Kelly answered, "and merge 'em into one instead of tiering up. You go back to level one, and all the stuff you've done, you're not getting credit for any of that again like it's your first time! So it's *hard*, it slows you down a lot."

There was absolutely a *but* there. "High cost for commensurate gain?" She nodded in a remarkably confident and familiar fashion. *Personal experience, then.*

"I undertook my second refinement not long ago," Ketka interjected. There was a sort of stunned silence pointed at her, and she smirked, exuding confidence and smugness. "One in my first years of adulthood, to take a..." Her smugness gave way to a sort of slumped frown, and she sighed. "Shemmai names, I forget, and our growth of power is not the same as yours—not in word nor in the charted path through the purposes of our power."

"So it's not just one overcomplicated piece of quantified nonsense," I muttered. "It's one for every country. Words, sure, but... purposes? Like what Kan talked about with learning as opposed to making connections and doing stuff?"

Kelly nodded at my guess. "The Archmages—they keep all this stuff running, make changes, that sort of thing—they don't think uniformity is important on this, or maybe even good. They do feel pretty strongly about some level of commonality, though. So the Yarovi Ranks aren't the same as the Realms that we grow through, just like Hitz's aren't, but they're the *equivalent*. The best translation we have into Shemmai would be to call them by professional qualifications—Apprentice, Journeyman, Expert."

"Then were I a Scion of the Desert, I might have been given such instruction as a child as to enter adult life as a... Journeyman." Ketka sounded out the word carefully, nodding slowly. "And then refined to an Expert, and entered Third Tier more advanced than I did. But we are born only once. Instead, I began as an Apprentice and refined in the dawn of my adulthood."

"So leaving aside the cultural details, you were an Apprentice Fighter," I said, trying to follow despite her own struggles with the language we were speaking, "and a Dancer or whatever. And you merged those into a Journeyman Dance Fighter, kinda like I'd be a Journeyman Alchemist where you come from, and—you're smirking." I tilted my head at her, then started grinning. "You were a dancer, without the whatever. In a way that's amusing, and makes you smirk."

"And you are blushing," Ketka retorted, smirking wider, "because you know the manner of dance I studied. This speaks to your cleverness, which is good! You will be quick to learn how to brew tea as we Yarovi brew it, I think, and to know which things to ask of your food-halls for preparing the small plates and the flatbread."

"But for now," Tseizal said impatiently, "can we talk about that potion, instead of this knot of string masquerading as a conversation?"

"You sound aggrieved, Tseitchik!"

"*Don't* call me that, Avara. Even when we were kids, I couldn't stand it."

The playful tone left Kelly's voice, and she nodded once. "Sorry, Tseizal. I'll bear that in mind. Five balances."

"Five—oh, come on! This is a non-standard, we don't even know if it'll work out. And even if I trust the description, we'll have to discharge the first for testing to get a finer measure. One balance for a fresh one, and that's because I want to encourage Sophie's innovations."

"Hitz put the half-discharged one on ice, pull the pin again and you'll get your measure. Four and a coronet—"

"Get off, nobody calls a half-balance that—"

"—for the second one I made with Hitz, and I'll throw in the half for another one and a half."

Tseizal seemed to give that some real thought, chewing on his bottom lip. I felt something brush my hand while he did so, and Ketka folded my fingers around a piece of flatbread. It tasted of nuts and oil and, well, bread; and I nodded at her appreciatively as she slid a bit closer, grinning.

A scepter for a meal, I reminded myself. *Ten scepters to the crown, ten crowns to the balance. So she opened by asking for five hundred meals' worth of money.*

"In Yaro," Ketka murmured to me, "we would speak more of what this coinage could afford us, or afford the other. Perhaps I would accuse her that she wishes the city to fail, if five balances were standard for such a potion. Madness, for the work of a day! And of course I would speak glibly of the potion's flaws, of the uncertainty, of the labor and risks in testing it."

"And she," I murmured back, "would presumably say something about how I have loans to pay, and it's not the work of a day, it's the work of a day after twenty years of study and training—and if the Guard can't handle testing the potion as part of their routine? What an interesting thing that would be, a Clerk might be interested to hear about that."

Before Ketka could say anything else, Tseizal shook his head firmly and broke the momentary quiet. "We don't know if it's better than a Flametongue yet or not. Width and time of application, how it faces up in terms of resistance, and the mist can be as much downside. I'll pay you five crowns for the partial on my own call, and if the Captain is game, two balances for the full one."

"Most of this is going back to Hitz for ingredients and using their lab. Five and a half for both, coin on the counter. Then again, I mean, it's you." She shook her head, grinning impishly at him. "I'll take a verbal agreement."

"On behalf of the Guard? Fat chance, but five crowns on the test and I'll commit us to three balances for the full one *if* it passes muster. Anything past five crowns and I'm not risking being out of pocket, and besides, Hitz goes easy on you; they'll do flat cost."

"I would *never* ask that." Kelly glared at him, and there was a bit of genuine edge to it. "Five crowns for the partial, and four and a half balances on the full when our claims bear out. That only gives Sophie five crowns of profit all told, and we could get more than that if we sold it in Hayir."

"Five crowns? Shoatshit, that should give you a balance and five—"

"The lume was from Hitz's presale stock, we didn't pluck it from a tree. And tax hasn't been paid on it."

I'd finished the flatbread, which was more filling than I'd expected. Ketka must have noticed, because she passed me a waterskin of some kind, and I took a swig from it. I almost spat it right back out; there was a *kick* to it with a spicy sweetness underneath the burn. Surprise notwithstanding, though, it was damn good. I took another swig before handing it back, savoring the warmth pooling in my belly and shooting down to my toes.

"Five crowns of profit is a fair amount, if still generous," Ketka murmured to me as we waited in a momentary silence. "For a day's ordinary labor in a skilled trade, it would be overmuch by perhaps threefold; but this is a sale of a potion, not of your labor." I nodded slowly at that. "Wouldn't a more experienced alchemist with more supporting infrastructure be able to make more of them, cheaper? Buying commodity goods at artisanal prices doesn't make sense for the village."

"Were this a township, it would be so." Ketka smiled at me, and the warmth I was feeling redoubled. "But we pay for transport, here—and even with all the Shemmai magics and the sponsorships of the Crown, there are too few couriers and drovers. A potion bought for testing is a complication, one which supplants a potion that is known to be of value and function."

Tseizal interrupted us with some sort of grunting thinking sound, grimaced, and then finally let his shoulders slump in defeat. "Fine," he eventually allowed, "if it's from the dungeon, not Forest-cut. Helps explain things, I guess. But you gotta know those five extra crowns—*and* the sourcing problem—are awkward if you're looking for a money-maker."

"Not really price-relevant to this sale, and Hitz *has* a stock. Besides, Sophie's not going to be going into repeat production anytime soon, she's got better things to do."

"Five crowns for the test and I'll back you on the four and a half." He held up his hand when Kelly opened her mouth to object, forestalling her. "Yeah, I can commit us to it, and it'd be fair. But if Meredith isn't gonna be fair, she'd have my ass for getting in her way; and you don't *need* us to be fair, you'll sell it coreward if we offer a scepter less."

Kelly gave that a slow nod. "Not wrong," she eventually said into the silence. "Five crowns, you back us on the four and a half, *and* you commit the Guard to giving an attestation on the test either way."

"Done, done, and done," Tseizal said immediately. "With James and Shafta both working out of Tome, that's easy enough. You'll get a copy of the Captain's due diligence. May Zuqeh seal it."

"Sealed," Kelly agreed, "and—"

"—**witnessed**," they said in unison. Their words danced across my fingers, clenching them around a pen that didn't exist; I smelled a waft of ink and heard the *slam* of a stamp.

"Shemmai," Ketka murmured in disapproval from next to me. "So straightforward. No artistry."

"I guess." I grinned absently at a spot near the two bargainers. If you drew a line between them, and then drew a perpendicular line at the midpoint, you'd wind up with an equilateral triangle, with the two of them being vertices… and the third point being where a tiny speck of power had momentarily manifested. "Zuqeh. Huh."

CHAPTER 3.16 - QUESTIONS OF REFINEMENT

After the bargain was sealed and some parting pleasantries were exchanged, we all made ready to split off. Ketka suggested she host me two days from then, just after lunch, to start teaching me how the Yarovi bargained; I agreed, and then caught her smile and the knowing—and approving—look from Kelly.

I blushed bright red, but I didn't take it back.

"Always good to learn things," I'd said with a total failure to be blasé, and they'd agreed.

Aliza was long gone, left when I wasn't paying attention, having managed to reach a handsbreadth higher on the trellis than her previous high-water mark. Shafta and Shuli had already disappeared on us as well, and Tseizal followed Ketka on her path, both of them heading for Tome and the Library.

I'd have liked to be heading there myself, and when I suggested it to Kelly, she gave it some visible thought and then agreed.

"We'll swing by the shop first, pick up the half-full Mister and take it to the guardhouse. It won't be much out of our way, and it'll get that moving."

"We are *not* calling the potion a Mister," I said flatly. "And I'm not letting Tseizal call it that, either. That's terrible."

"It is!" She beamed at me. "Do you know what's the best way to get people to come up with good names?"

"That strategy can *really* backfire. You wind up with names like *Thedas*." We wove our way around a very picturesque rock pillar in the middle of the path, one that spiraled up to become part of the supports for the overhead trellises and paths. "Mist-torch has a really awkward phoneme pair. What about Brightmist?"

"Better than a Mister," she conceded.

"So." The path took us around in wild greenery and flowers in a riot of colors, and I noticed for the first time that some of the wooden supports were actually *trees*, for some reason disguised as carved wood. "You're refined, like Ketka was talking about. What's it like?"

Kelly's stride hitched, but she recovered almost fast enough to hide it. "I did tell you that's a rude question, right?"

"No, I asked if it was a rude question and you gave a partial answer, and then we got to the refectory." She shot me a narrow look, and I shrugged. "Okay, yeah, the partial answer was mostly in the *yes* direction."

"Good!" Kelly clapped her hands together, the two of us walking out of the garden and into the late-afternoon light. "*Don't* ask any of the herder folk a question like that, unless they bring it up first or you have a genuine need to know. I mean it when I say it's rude, at least to them and most folks you'll find in a village by primary choice."

"But not to... people who got assigned here or came to work here for non-cultural reasons?"

"Yes! And that's the Delvers, the Guard, and a handful of Hammer folks, but half of all *those* are village-born. So who can you ask?"

"Basically nobody, it sounds like," I said after a moment. "You, Kan, Ketana, any of the obviously visiting types."

"Almost nobody in Hammer's refined. I mean, Hitz, but don't ask them about anything until you're at least high Third Tier, they think we're all babies. About a fifth of the Guard, about a third of the Delvers."

"Why does nobody in—wait." I saw the look in Kelly's eyes, and stopped myself just in time. *Try to solve it*, that look said, and she wasn't wrong.

What was refinement, exactly? It was an expenditure of short-term power and medium-term growth cadence in exchange for long-term power and maybe medium-power too. A first refinement required hitting the apex of Second Tier, which felt like something I could pull off in a few years; why wouldn't it be common?

Well, there was the fact that I wasn't typical. I was going into my profession as a professional already, starting Second Tier in whatever Connection meant rather than Earth; plausibly it could be harder to pull that off starting lower in Realm. Though it wasn't like the lack of short-term power was a particular hindrance, here in Shem. Given what I'd been told the day before in the Inquiry, that a village had better be able to support totally non-productive citizens...

… but at the same time, and by the same token…

"Shem," I said slowly, "is a culture of… moderation? Of, like, being chill and not stressing about things, and especially not making other people stress about things. Especially in the villages, or maybe mostly or *only* in the villages." I glanced over and received a nod and a half-suppressed smile. "So if you don't *need* to do it, it's sort of… trying too hard, and putting social pressure on other people?"

"That's part of it!" That was the brilliant smile, the full and exuberant one that—even before the pact—I'd never taken for condescension in its celebration of me. "Another piece is that people who grow up in the villages feel like it's not taking proper care of yourself, if you do that. Relax, the logic says! Don't get caught up in the search for power! Live a good life, eat good food, have friends, help the place run."

"And someone who fights might need the edge, but someone who doesn't…" Shem made ridiculously high-quality glass, even in the villages like Kibosh where the manufacturing infrastructure was relatively lacking. If that wasn't something that relied on the Skills of the glassblower, which it couldn't if the edge was irrelevant, it had to be something else. "Do the, uh, Hammer folks use enchanted equipment, magical ingredients, or both, for making stuff like rock—sorry, like stoneglass?"

I took a couple of steps before it registered that Kelly had stopped in her tracks. She stood there in the middle of the path, hands on her hips and head cocked quizzically at me. "Did I miss the part where you were talking with a glassblower?"

"No?" I scratched the back of my neck, confused. "It just seemed like a reasonable question. I know Kibosh does a bunch of ingredient extraction, right? And if someone who's making stoneglass doesn't need the edge from refinement, if it doesn't make a substantial difference…"

"Well." Her smile had an edge, one that I found delightfully and wistfully familiar. "I'm *not* used to someone else being the clever one."

"You're way better with people," I said, shrugging. I started walking again, and heard her footsteps behind me. "You said *another piece*, not *the* other piece. So there's more?"

"Time and experience. See if you can figure it out."

Time and experience. Still absurd, but come on, I can take this seriously. I let my feet take me down the path towards the ring road, letting thoughts percolate through my head freely. The trees were as stunning as they'd been the previous day, the construction of structures and roads just as impressive, and I took them in with newly sharpened eyes.

What would looking at the world be like when I reached my third tier, or if I refined? As I climbed through the levels, how would the world change?

Climbing through the levels. *Ah.*

"Three hundred years," I said softly. "How many Discoveries will it take me to reach the apex of Third Tier again? Six hundred?"

"About that, if—."

"—if they were equal-level," I agreed absently. "Which they aren't, like you said. But... how long will it take me to go through a validation or challenge bounty, getting a Discovery the easy way and making a profit while I'm at it? How many of them are multi-day pieces of work?"

"They're almost all single-day, maximum sixteen hours including sitting time. Some of them manage it through intermediaries, and some of those are products too. But some are longer! We just won't get them here, 'cause it's a team thing, you can go as long as you need with three alchemists and three notaries."

"Huh." We were about at the house; lost in thought, I leaned against the wall, not really looking at anything. *If there's even a hundred of those total...* "I could easily do a couple of those a week, and then there's Feats and mentorship and bulk production." *Can't remember the numbers for Tier Two, but it was something like two point two, and Discoveries double; so that's one point one to the power of fifteen for the final push, that's like four-ish, base of two, eight Discoveries to go from level fourteen to fifteen.* "Kelly, what's—oh, right."

Kelly having stepped inside to get the potions, I ran through the rest of the math in my own head, approximating it as best my memory could handle. This turned out to be *way* more tractable than I remembered; I was pretty sure my Spark had to be involved with that, probably through my new *Meticulous* Attribute, but *Comprehend* might also have been in play.

"You need to hit fewer than seventy additional Discoveries if you refine in Second Tier," I said to Kelly as she walked back out the door, potions in hand. "It's nowhere near enough to make a difference in Third Tier, especially since those are all low-level stuff. It wouldn't move the needle at all. Though I guess refining *in* Third Tier would take a while. If I can spend ten percent of my time working on self-funding potions and work sixty hours in a fortnight, and they're sixteen hours each, that's three fortnights to a Discovery.

"If I need a couple hundred of them just to finish that last level, that's *decades* of work right there. And that's just the one level, right? I could spend a century on it, to have refined twice like Ketka—wait, fuck, how *old* is Ketka?"

Kelly blinked a few times, gears almost visibly turning in her head. "I'm not exactly sure," she said after a few moments. "I know she's not a double yet—not past her second century. Somewhere on the younger side of that, but that's all I can tell you."

"I am suddenly feeling very conflicted about her flirting with me," I muttered.

"Why? Did you think she was older, to be twice-refined?" Kelly started walking down the ring road, and I pushed off from the wall of my house to follow in her wake. "It *is* impressive. She's a prodigy; everyone on that team is. We're lucky to have them here."

"No, that's not it." I carefully didn't say *it feels predatory, since I'm so much younger*, because that wasn't the reason I was feeling conflicted. "There's a taboo, where I'm from, about dating or even hooking up with people with a big age gap. A couple of decades qualifies, twenty percent of a long lifespan. I guess I'm worried about the difference in… life experience?"

"Well, that seems ridiculous. You'd have to limit yourself to just your cohort! I mean, some do, it's cute, they usually take a name-pair like Kan and Ketana have. I didn't know Vala and Shuli were so close, but I'm gonna have to get them a pairing gift!"

"I—why Vala, is that—wow." *It doesn't matter right now*, I told myself firmly, *why Vala is a diminutive for Shafta, if that's even what's going on*. "I feel like every time we're getting even remotely close to having covered a subject, suddenly we open up a bunch more."

"I'll just pretend we didn't get distracted, then." She shot a look back over her shoulder at me, grinning impishly, then sobered. "There's one other thing, and it's a big one. Without refining, you can't hit Fourth Tier, can't become an Immortal. And it's *so* much easier to refine in Second Tier, like you just figured out, so if you don't? If you go straight to Third? Almost guaranteed you're going to die of old age as a triple, and it's not like you'll stay all the way hale until then.

"And the old guard, the traditionalists? That's *good*, they say. It's proper, it's important, you can't have a functioning society—and they mean a *Shemmai* society, they mean you can't have Shem the way it has been, the way they want it to stay—with a *lot* of immortals running around, they say there's a threshold where it'll break down."

"That's…" I felt myself slowing down and shook my head, speeding up for a moment to catch up with Kelly. There were people around, but not all that many; something in Kelly's body language had them not even glancing over, anyway, so we walked in a bubble of notional privacy. "That's a lot. I don't even know where to start with that, and this isn't even the first time I'm feeling like that *this afternoon*."

"So there's this pressure," Kelly said in an *I-am-not-listening* tone, "to not refine, 'cause doing it if you're not in a combat job where you're probably gonna die before getting there—Guard in the outer ring villages, Delve, Tower folks who fight—is a statement that you want to hit Fourth. And it's not like most people even *can*; taking three Classes to apex in Third Tier isn't easy, you're almost always going to wind up with overlap and slow yourself down. And the higher Realm you are, the harder you have to work for *everything*, including your Feats, so you shouldn't expect to get *more* years of life out of refining."

"Doesn't get balanced out by higher effectiveness, huh?"

"No, and not the point! The point is, socially I—" Kelly stopped in her tracks for a moment, shot me a dirty look in silence, then started walking again. "Balanced. Right, Technician was in Balance. Moving right along, socially I *shouldn't* have gone for refinement when I hit the apex of Second Tier. And by not asking, everyone gets to pretend they have no idea, when *obviously* I'd have tiered up by now otherwise, instead of still being in Second. Kinda like going to study in the city, instead of in a town or just using the books and correspondence, but almost nobody actually holds either of those against me personally—to most of them, it just means I'm living a different life than they chose."

"And that's the long answer that we didn't have time for, when we were walking to lunch."

"It's… sure," Kelly said. "Sure! It's the long version."

"So." I kept my voice casual, with some effort. "You want to live forever, huh?"

"What—I—Sophie!" Kelly spluttered, spinning around and laughing while she made faces at me. "You can't just *ask* someone that! And in public, too."

"Yeah, well." I grinned at her—well, smirked, more accurately. "Everyone's pointedly ignoring us, because everyone already knows. Am I right?"

"Probably!" Kelly shook her head and spun back around, laughter fading into chuckling and then nothing as we started walking again. "It's pretty great, being alive," she eventually said. "We don't really know what happens after. And even if we did know... there's so much neat stuff. I could live a couple more centuries and not even get tired of new people, one at a time. Seeing them settle in, grow, make friends? Learning their stories... I love their *newness*.

"And even after that! There's more to life than villages. There's more to life than Shem—more to life than Alqar, even! Hitz said that if I make Fourth, they'll send a letter of introduction I can take to Kandaq, which, like, the *Queen* can't visit without one of those." She stopped in the middle of the road—we were in Tome, at the guardhouse, and I hadn't noticed. "I'm gonna have to visit Tagata before I make it to Third Tier, though. You die, otherwise; fall into sleep, don't wake up."

"I can *tell*," I said with a mostly-mock glare, "that you dropped that on me once we got here on purpose. And I just want to be clear—"

"Oh?" She raised an eyebrow at me, smirking, as I paused for dramatic effect and to let her interject.

"—that I appreciate your candor and answers," I finished with a grin. "C'mon, let's go close out my first sale."

"*Your* first sale? Excuse me?"

"Come on!" I was pretty sure her hands were on her hips, but I was already striding towards the building. "It'll look bad if my minion is late, even though you did a better job negotiating than I could have done."

Spluttering, laughing, Kelly raced to catch up, and we walked through the doors side by side.

CHAPTER 3.17 – FOR BEHOLD, SHE HAS STILL MORE QUESTIONS

We wound up leaving Meredith's office—not the one she shared with James, her *formal* office, all of two doors down—empty-handed.

Tseizal, when we walked in, had a haunted look in his eyes which was easily explained by Captain Meredith's banked blaze of irritation. It was too late in the day, she'd pointed out calmly, to be doing any sort of testing on unknown munitions, and for that matter there wasn't a safety protocol worked out *or* a measurement protocol for this particular potion.

Come back tomorrow, she'd said, obviously fighting to avoid being dismissive or heated. Do paperwork and work out the protocols in the morning, and then run the tests in the afternoon. If, that was, we were competent enough to get the paperwork filed that quickly.

We still left both potions, along with the five crowns which we owed as tax for the reagents we'd used. There was no point in carrying the full one back, after all. And besides, we weren't going far, at least not at first.

There was still an hour left before dinner's first seating, and I had a mildly burning question for James.

"Clerk Administrator. Can I get a moment of your time?"

"Alchemist Nadash." James smiled at me from behind his desk, pairing a perfect customer service face with his impossibly engaging baritone.

A baritone whose undertones I was beginning to hear. They wove a subtle song of power, and I couldn't hear any of the lyrics; but it sure helped explain things.

"Actually, before I ask," I said on impulse, "is that the right thing to call you? Or do I use your name, or some mix of title and name, and what's the deal with last name as opposed to first name?"

"Perhaps," he said gravely, "it would be best for you to ask the question you arrived with first, and then I will answer them both."

"Right, that makes sense. I was wondering—" I turned my head, distracted, as Kelly made a murmuring noise.

She looked like she had stars in her eyes, like she was having some sort of epistemic rapture event; I was about to ask *her* why when the answer hit me, and I closed my eyes, biting back laughter.

At least seeing her pick up on what James was doing let *me* spot it. *Conversational Sophie-wrangling; apparently a Skill that our Clerk Administrator has.*

"Kelly's revelation aside," I said wryly, "I actually had two questions. Both... hopefully simple?

"The first is: why wouldn't I have been well advised to start with Technician, in the Realm of Balance, and then learn enough to pick up Alchemist at that same Realm and refine into something that could be implausibly powerful and well-suited? And second, is it, like, a standard practice to not talk about the actual mechanics of stuff like refinement and Class management to Travelers before we pick our first Class, or was it just Kelly wanting to keep my momentum going and there not being enough hours in the day?"

"The first is simple enough, and easy to answer. A refinement at your Tier incorporates elements of both Classes, and sets you upon a Path that is true to each individually and the two together." James paused, then gave a somehow-chiding smile. "And so?"

"Um." I hadn't realized this was a *the rest is trivial, and is left as an exercise to the reader* kind of situation. "Um, well, after refining, I wouldn't be on the Path of the Mystical Alchemist. I guess I'd be on some kind of... Alchemist who's also a Technician; Replication Alchemist? Validation Alchemist? Or, no, it would be a Technician who's also an Alchemist, right?" My gut churned at the thought. "That... I don't like that idea."

"Classes are not simply a tool, not simply a gathering and exercise of power. Classes are an expression of the natures of who we are and of whom we wish to become; first as people and then, as we begin to transcend our once-impassable limits, as something more."

"I'd have burned out," I said softly. "Even if I'd refined away from Technician, even if I'd made it that far, I wouldn't have had as clean a break as I've had. Not a break at all, really. The stuff I'm trying to get away from would be equally at the core of me."

"I have no doubt you would have achieved the Third Tier, and in time perhaps recovered, if only through what became of your further Class. Hedonist, perhaps, might have been a Path towards healing." James's voice was gentle, and his eyes had the perfect amount of humor to provoke a snicker even bringing up something I had *very deliberately* not thought about. "But, your second question! Hm. I... it *is* a simple question, or should be."

"I'm hearing," I said, intrigued, "a *but* there."

"But I have no answer for you in simple memory. Kelly?"

She shook her head. "Nope! I mean, I know why I didn't go into it, especially refinement; she didn't need to know yet, she needed to keep moving, and there just weren't enough hours in the day. She's still learning all kinds of things she needs to know, though, hey, how to ask you questions is one of those things! And obviously I was going to have the conversation with her when we started talking about her next Class, because that's when it would be relevant. But I *don't* know why it's not in the, you know, standard style."

"Standard style." I closed my eyes, thinking things through, and they gave me a moment to do it. "Someone said that you worked in the *orthodox* style," I said, opening my eyes. "Which I'm guessing is the momentum thing, only telling me things when I need to know them? And then there's the *standard* style."

"Rafa likes the standard style." Kelly was scowling, and I had to work hard to suppress a smile. "Study outside-in. The Thousand, the world, the System, the continent, the nation, the village. For what? You won't make better decisions for *yourself*, you'll just have wasted—"

"Not everyone has your skills, Miss Avara, much less your Skills." James's voice was almost prim, despite having interrupted her, but his face was the most serious I'd seen outside of the previous day's Inquiry. It was a pure Clerk face, the face of the Clerk Administrator. "The standard style is *standard* for good reason; it is a path that any and all might tread. The law does not require that you adhere to it, for all your displeasure that the law *did* require you to demonstrate your grasp of the subject."

Kelly flushed, and she opened her mouth to say something that I knew in my bones was going to be something intemperate. I put a hand on her shoulder instead, squeezing gently to cut her off. "Kelly," I stage-whispered, "I think he just gave you a compliment."

James waited a beat, performatively not-seeing the way that Kelly's indignation turned into a flush of embarrassment and happiness. "Well. My memory is far from perfect. We may yet have a simple solution… **[Query Local Records]**." The words twisted underneath their plain sounds like a wildly forking, branching path, and then he shook his head, standing up from his chair. "I see. Walk with me, if you would?"

"Walk with… sure?"

"To the library. I may inquire of those records we have stored here, but our Senior Librarian may cast that inquiry further. You asked with regards to modes of address, Sophie?"

"I did, yeah." We were going to the *library*. It struck me suddenly as incongruous that I hadn't gone there, that it had been almost two and a half days and I hadn't gone to the library. "Still interested, for the record," I said absently.

"Formality is a departure from the personal." James started walking down the hall, Kelly and I in his wake. "The most personal form is the intimate name, a name chosen and spoken only between those so close as to have entwined their lives."

"Lovers?"

He shook his head at me. "Those wedded, or those who choose a different form of life partnership. Lovers, not always; a lover can be…" He scratched his chin with one hand as he led us out the door and into the evening sun, heading across the road. "I should say that *sometimes* a lover is one such, but a lover can be transient, just as a friendship can be."

"Got it. So from there, the next one is just… someone's name?"

"Just so. From your name, Sophie, if one of us were a child, I would move to Miss Sophie; but as one adult to another, you would be Miss Nadash. Someone in your trade might say Alchemist Sophie, or a fellow scholar call you Scholar Sophie, as a means of saying that you speak as colleagues and peers, which is perhaps the same degree of formality as to call you Miss Nadash within its own context.

"From there, one says Alchemist Nadash or Scholar Nadash, with… perhaps somewhat arbitrary rules, if the context is formal but purely social, or if the speaker wishes to assert that the two of you are *not* peers; and from there, the address becomes simply Alchemist or Scholar. In the utmost formality—the utmost distance from the personal, and fallen entirely out of style some hundreds of years ago—you would be styled Alchemist Kibosh." He turned to smile at me as we arrived at the library doors. "Does the Alchemist understand?"

I nodded. As a person to another person, then, he'd be just James; but since I was there to ask something more formal, it would be proper for me to use a title. And since he'd just referred to me as *the Alchemist*... "Clerk Administrator," I began, and then I paused. "I understand, though I'd point out that there's a lot of different formality levels for how I refer to *myself*, and some of those are... hierarchy-based? Like, there's *this one* and *this Alchemist*, there's *the Alchemist* and there's *I*."

James's carefully constructed social facade cracked momentarily as he snickered. "We would never," he said in the controlled tones of someone trying not to burst out laughing, "use either of those first two. Not to a child, not to a Clerk, not to a God, and not to the Queen."

"That's not true!" Kelly's eyes danced with humor as she poked James under the ribs. "It would just be *super* sarcastic. Like when Matron Zeva told me that I was disrespectful and arrogant, and I said *this one has no recourse but to agree*."

"As I recall," he replied with some sternness and a whole lot less formality than he had been using, "Zeva brought a formal complaint to my desk about that implying you were agreeing in fear of violence. Which would have been malicious slander."

"Which was an act of violence, because—"

"She brought the complaint against your mother," James clarified, and Kelly's words slammed to a halt. "Because Zeva had neither authority nor capability to in any way compel your agreement, so why would you debase yourself other than to avoid the ire of someone who *did*?"

"I... didn't know that. I thought..."

"Well, nobody told you." James waved a hand almost dismissively, and his voice shifted back into its previous mellifluous state. "I mention it only to caution our Traveler, who does not know our ways: there is a point at which even for a pointed quip or humor, it is inadvisable to imply that there are onerous expectations when there are none."

"That... seems kinda fair," I said after a moment's thought. "And it might build a culture where you can raise those concerns more seriously when they're actually happening?"

"Many of us believe this to be so." He inclined his head and reached for the handle on the door, a long piece of wood that looked like it was the spine of a book, growing out of the stone. "Shall we?"

"Wait, no, one question. About that answer," I said hurriedly at his raised eyebrow. "A clarification. You say that when we move towards formality, we move away from the personal, right? So why were we using first names at the Inquiry?"

"Ah." James's hand fell away from the door, and he frowned unhappily, which I was pretty sure I had *not* seen his face do before. "Well. In a setting so formal... there is very little need to cultivate additional formality. There is already a sufficiency of gravity and a sense of importance. It is said that by shifting our forms of address towards the more personal, we remain more aware that we are people speaking with and upon people. That by doing so, we shift in some manner towards justice, rather than merely the law."

"You... don't sound super convinced."

"I am not." His voice firmed up, and he smiled at me again, probably genuinely. "I do not find the position well-supported by the data we have available. But it is a matter of discussion, and many are the experiments and endeavors which bore slow fruit; it may yet be so, in the twenty years to come."

"A twenty-year public policy experiment?" I didn't know which was more surprising—running a deliberate experiment within the legal system on that kind of timeframe, James's obvious willingness to go along with it despite disagreeing, or that this kind of thing was subject to optimizing in the first place.

"Twenty years *remain*. Twenty-nine years have passed since its inception." There was the tiniest hint of smirking in the muscles around his eyes as I sort of boggled at him. "Still, I should expect that those who are in need of the reminder are the least likely to heed it; and that their resentment outweighs it. Perhaps before the experiment runs its course we might sit a time and discuss it in the detail such a thing deserves. It is well known that statistics too often show that which the analyst sets out to demonstrate."

I shot Kelly a glance, and she nodded, tiny little rapid-fire head-bobs. "I would be delighted to," I said to James quietly.

He didn't say anything—just turned and, putting some flair into it, opened the door and gestured us inside. We walked into the library without further ado, James smirking, me lost in thought, and Kelly grinning from ear to ear.

CHAPTER 3.18 - RECORDS KEPT AND REFERENCED THOROUGHLY

Kibosh's Library, the civic institution, was embodied in its two Librarians: the Library Associate, who mostly did notary work, and the Senior Librarian, who was in charge of the records. It was the most mundane, the least magical of the institutions, because magic came with maintenance and power-draw requirements. Even stable substrates that had information magically encoded into them, like memory-crystal—whatever that was—were considered less than ideal, because the art of reading them and repairing them might fade.

Books, in the Shemmai way of thinking, were forever. So Kibosh's library, the building where that civic institution lived, was a thing of wonder.

I'd seen it from the outside, of course, and I'd had no doubt that it would prove to be as beautiful on the inside. And that wasn't a statement without its share of weight; a library shaped like an open book was a great style, and not one that I'd ever seen before. The way the five wings of the building jutted out from the central spine, their stone—dark gray, with white mortar—gorgeously decorated to look like pages?

Well, it made me want to grab a seat by one of the windows and curl up with a book for a while.

Stepping inside was… well, it was something alright. I stopped in my tracks, Kelly bumping my hip as she stepped up behind me, and I just—

—well, frankly, I just ogled. The floor drew my eye first, some kind of presumably nigh-indestructible glass with just enough opacity to reassure; or maybe what drew my eye was the floor *below* that, maybe eight feet down and much the same. There were two floors up above us, too, and all four levels had wall-to-wall bookshelves with a spiraling central array of *more* shelves.

The ground floor entryway was simple—just a large round room that opened into five halls, where the pages of the architectural book were—but it still had eight-foot-high bookshelves along a wide arc of wall and a set of long tables covered in gigantic... probably reference or catalog books, if I had to guess.

I'd seen bigger libraries, and fancier ones. I'd spent years studying and then working somewhere with a library system that held a couple hundred thousand books, all told; the main library had places where the walkway ended and the floor fell away into the depths. In those places, there were walls of books whose access platforms were dwarfed by the size of the room. You could imagine their absence, picture the book storage as traversed only by motorized platforms on rails, packed in a density only the professionals could navigate.

That would have been an OSHA violation, though. And besides, everyone knew how you designed a library, and how you made it beautiful—which you did with intricate frescoes, apparently, and those really weren't my thing.

But this? This was... it was ludicrous to call it the most stunning library I'd seen. It was vastly smaller than some, by orders of magnitude, and it lacked the Library of Congress's titanic veranda or the overwhelming weight of knowledge that I used to feel like I could taste.

And yet, I thought to myself... and then, shaking my head, I stepped into the building to let Kelly and James come inside.

"Clerk Administrator!" There was a pattering of footsteps, and a young-seeming woman—she looked twenty-five, and for all I knew she was fifty years old—dashed down one of the corridors towards us. She was preceded by a stack of books held in her arms, which she dropped unceremoniously onto a small desk off to the side of the room; the stack landed messily and visibly unstable, but it stayed upright.

Barely, but barely upright was still not falling over.

"Hello, welcome, oh!" We were only a few feet away, but the moment the books were out of her hands, she was back in motion in what looked like a nearly uncontrolled burst of speed. "It's our Traveler!"

"Um, ye—"

"Welcome to Kibosh!" She'd skidded to a stop, stumbling and barely avoiding slamming into me at speed; the pause she'd taken to recover her balance was the only reason I'd gotten a word and a half in edgewise. Clasping her hands together vigorously in front of her, she beamed at me.

"Hello, welcome! Oh, I already said that. Zqar will be so excited, this is wonderful."

"Associate Safra," James said, and the girl practically snapped to attention. "It's good to see you. It will be good to see Senior Librarian Zqar as well."

"Oh, yes, of course! I'll be right back. Clerk Administrator, Traveler, Miss Avara, please don't go anywhere!"

I watched her sprint towards the stairs and practically fly down them. "Is she always…" I started to say, and then stopped for lack of any coherent description, and also because as she ran down the stairs, she *disappeared*.

"Yes." Kelly grinned at me as I glanced over. "She's always. It's her charm, or it's maddening, depends on who you are!"

"She is… distractible. Prone to neglecting the filing of her forms."

"James," I said gently, distractedly, "you're not supposed to say that like it's a catastrophic moral failing."

He gave an exaggerated sniff. "Nonsense," he said, winking faintly at me. "I am a *Clerk*."

"I… was that a j—I'm not going to ask that. Are the floors actually transparent? How'd she disappear?"

"Look closely."

James sounded disappointed, and I tried, mostly successfully, not to feel crushed at that. I studied the level below us instead, looking and trying to figure out what James was talking about. There were bookshelves, sure, and they were full of books, and towards where the spinal central area of the library split into the different corridors, there were what looked like workshops full of all sorts of stuff. Benches and storage areas were full of crystals and tools, the odd book or two in probably the process of being repaired, and papers fluttering about—

—*ah*. "The floor filters out people, but leaves the stuff they're affecting?"

"Only that which they incidentally affect remains." I glanced up to get a small smile of approval from James and an ear-to-ear beaming grin from Kelly. "Should one among us be writing or reading, these things, too, would be removed from sight. It functions on a reading of the soul, I am told, and on the notion of intent."

"Huh." I walked further into the room as I processed that, glancing at the tomes on the tables. The first one was just labeled *Basic Books,* and the second was *Basic (Detailed) Books of Learning, Vol 1 of 2*. There was a third one on my side of the table, lying open to a page about a third of the way in, and I glanced over the page.

The text was... small. Tiny, really. I almost by reflex squinted and peered closer, but then I realized that I could actually read it, small as it was. *Responsibilities of the Maintaining Archmages*, it read, and there was a ledger next to it of names and dates, each with either the string *LAS* or *SLZ*.

Archmage Miyyon Ktav's seventh edition of this work dates back to four hundred years after the Enkindling of the Flame. It has since then been revised twice, by unknown persons; this revision has affected, each time, all but one copy of the book. It is comprehensive and has no known inaccuracies. The perspective of the writing is openly Shemmai, but it is consistent with the histories and policies of all other polities of Alqar. For these reasons, there are no competing volumes, and the Second Revised Seventh Edition Miyyon is the seminal work of the subject.

"Unknown persons. Eheh."

"Ayah!" I spun around at the unfamiliar voice, chuckling dryly from just over my shoulder. A gentle hand on one wrist stopped me from overbalancing, and I very deliberately did not hyperventilate as my heart hammered hard and fast.

"Mmm. Apologies. Did not intend to startle. Wished to allow reading to complete."

"Um." I took a deep breath, letting it out slowly as my brain shifted from *oh fuck oh fuck* to actually paying attention to my environment. "Hi. Sophie Nadash, Traveler and now Alchemist here in Kibosh. You must be Senior Librarian Zqar."

"Mmm." He didn't say anything else for a moment, holding my hand lightly, eyes flickering across my body. "Would not care to disagree."

I took the opportunity to look at him, taking him in as thoroughly as he was taking me in. He was short—*really* short, a few inches shy of five feet—with his starkly bald, remarkably shiny head a bit below my chin. His hands had that kind of papery, brittle feeling that I associated with old age, and those thin, knobbly hands were covered in... well, if he were white and they were dark, I'd have called them liver spots, but he was a sort of vaguely olive-undertone light brown and the spots were a faded yellow.

"Um!" Safra had come back while I was distracted; she was fidgeting, eyes glancing towards the stack of books. "I don't want to rush anyone. It's just that if we're going to stand around being weird and quiet, I have ledgers that I'm... supposed to update and it's by hand because I'm learning and..."

I hid a giggle as Zqar turned to look at Safra with a single raised eyebrow and no other noticeable expression on his face. Once she'd trailed off, fidgeting harder and blushing a bright red, he turned back towards James and nodded firmly. Safra took a step back as he did so, grabbing a ribbon out of somewhere—I didn't see any visible pockets, but that didn't mean there weren't any—and pulling her hair, frizzy and wild, back into a ponytail.

I wanted to study the way she was winding the ribbon around her hair, since I was terminally fascinated with different hair styles. *Well, maybe later, even if my hair isn't like hers*, I thought to myself wryly, and looked back to James and Zqar as the former started talking.

"I was hoping, Senior Librarian, that you might have room in your afternoon for a catalog query. I committed those efforts I could to finding the information, but I'm afraid it eludes me."

"Mmm." Zqar's face went from expressionless to extremely *present*, intensely focused. "Standard local record search?"

"It was, yes."

"Have kept two queries. Had an urge, always interesting." He walked with slow, tiny steps towards the table that was nearest the desk, farthest from the bookshelves. "Not a Skill, not an oracle, but sometimes get an urge. Tell me."

"The orthodox method of social and System Integration of Travelers," James said, "has the First Friend push the new arrival to make their necessarily manifold choices rapidly, from the heart and in conjunction with the First Friend's judgment. The standard method involves the Traveler learning about a great variety of things, and the Neo-Mazaran framework involves a series of what are effectively apprenticeships, ones far more intense than would normally be socially appropriate.

"None of these methods involve taking care to inform the Traveler of many specific dynamics of the System—refinement in particular, though as First Friend Avara says, that particular piece of knowledge only becomes entirely relevant some time after a first Class is selected. However, the Neo-Mazaran recommends actively denying the Traveler access to this information through apprenticing them exclusively to professionals not inclined to discuss the matter until the *apex* of Second Tier."

"Mmm." *I hear you*, I interpreted Zqar's murmur as meaning.

"Leaving aside the... *proximity* of the Mazaran approach to a violation of the Edict of Paths, I had expected, when Alchemist Nadash brought the question to my attention, for the answer to *why* this is the case to be within the Books of Learning for a First Friend. To my knowledge, we have all of those works within your records, though of course I defer to your expertise in the matter."

"Yes, certainly." Zqar looked away from James to run his index finger along the spine of a tome whose size was… well, my grandfather, may his memory fade from all worlds, once *confiscated* a dictionary weighing about fourteen pounds from a woman in what they called *his* community.

This looked substantially bigger, to the point where it was quite obvious that magic was involved in the binding.

"Come, come," Zqar said. Nobody moved, and he turned just enough to shoot me a glance. "A book is to be shared, a Traveler should know these things. Look here, yes?"

I jolted forward, dashing with almost as little grace as Safra had shown. "Sure, what am I looking at?"

Instead of answering, he reached out and slid something sideways on the table that I couldn't see. The flat surface shifted, with a pair of wood leaves—in a more literal sense than usual, since they were shaped and etched or engraved in some way to look like leaves—coming up to form a book cradle. The book unfolded, opening to what seemed like a random page about a third of the way in, and he glanced at me and then at the book.

I took it as an invitation and stepped forwards, hands behind my back, peering at the text. Peering, where I previously hadn't had to even for writing that was maybe a tenth of an inch or smaller; and for *this* text, I could barely make out the letters no matter how I squinted.

Iatzak Arabe—Translation of Liturgical Shemmai Humor Into Modern Syza, 2Ed, GCNP

"A book ledger?" *Those lines are smaller than four-point font. Twenty-five to an inch, at least? Three hundred to a foot, six across, order of three thousand books per page. Maybe two thousand pages.* "A ledger for six million books?"

"Pages not all filled. More than five, yes? This is the *standard* reference." He turned and smiled at me, with so much joy that it was palpable. "Quick eyes, a reader's mind. Ask the next question, yes?"

"How many books of reference," I said obediently, smiling back at him, "are listed in that book?"

"Ahhhh." He shook his head. "A more interesting question. A less *real* question. Thousands; certainly thousands. Ones incomplete, ones flawed, ones old, ones overlapping. Every revision, every edition, every author. But for the ones which hold for us the Books Known? Thirty-four."

I could do the math, but the number didn't actually make emotional sense. "A couple hundred million books," I breathed.

"And each day there are more." He touched my wrist ever-so-gently with his fingers, eyes hungry. "Sit with me soon. Tell me of the books of your world, when time permits, and let us bring them into this one."

"I don't—" I shook my head. "It hardly matters if I don't remember them word for word, does it? I'm sure you have magic for that."

"Not I, not in Hayir." He stepped back, un-skewering me from the intensity of his gaze. "But there will be visitors, if you allow it. Even from Bayirah; for a literate Traveler and the tales of her decades? Possibly the Lady."

"Zqar," James said from behind me, "I would hesitate to suggest that the Mistress of Tomes herself would find the time to travel the length of Shem, to a village in the outermost expanse. But even if she might be inclined, perhaps the query, before we distract our Alchemist unduly?"

"Yes, yes." Zqar waved a hand in something like a dismissive gesture, but in that moment he looked more torn between sheepishness and impatience than the intense Senior Librarian he had a moment before. "The question of Travelers and of refinement. And, mmm. The answer, if there is one to be found."

CHAPTER 3.19 - TO BRING KNOWLEDGE FROM AFAR

"So." Zqar's sheepish expression faded into a distant musing as he let the moment pass—as though it was just an ordinary thing to bring books I didn't even remember across the bridge of worlds. "The purpose of the practice, perhaps," he murmured, "or the history of it—or its siblings in other practices, and references... mmm."

"So broad?"

"Clerk Administrator." Zqar narrowed his eyes fractionally, straightening to his full height, and even I knew James had misstepped with that question. "My skills, ah, and my Skills. A Clerk knows them better than a Librarian, surely. He must. Yes?"

"I apologize," the Clerk Administrator said with immediate, intensely formal sincerity. "The Senior Librarian knows his art, and knows it far better than any report might teach."

"Mmm. Well. Don't suspect there will be another call tonight, bit late for that, would interfere with dinner. First... eheh. Traveler, numerate, not just literate. How do you search for knowledge, hmm? Sit, sit."

"Eh? Oh." I could have sworn there wasn't a chair where he was pointing, but there it was, gliding easily across the floor as Kelly pulled it out. I sat, doing my best to think fast. "I'd probably start by ruling out categories. A policy matter shouldn't exclusively live in fiction, right?"

Zqar sat in a chair across from me, which I *also* hadn't seen any sign of until he sat down. "And if it did?"

"Then... I mean, I don't know how information magic works. But if you were using the kinds of computational resources I had access to, you'd be... okay, not exactly fucked, but a couple hundred million books. That's order of... a hundred thousand words per book, so order of ten trillion words. Average characters per word, about five; a hundred trillion characters, a hundred... okay, I used to have a word for this. This isn't counting metadata, but that's probably a rounding error anyway.

"I honestly don't know much about how data can be organized to make it easier to search through. The word *index* vaguely comes to mind, but uh, I guess if you're using magic, for all I know you can get down to thermodynamic efficiency, but I have *no* idea what that is." I stared into space glaring as if I was looking at the physical representation of the question. "Can you do associational queries? Is there a fundamental quiddity that a word has, is there a linguistic equivalent of qualia?"

"Quiddity. Qualia. Think of purpose, ask a question."

I took a deep breath, then let it half out. Thinking better of that—I was going to want to fit in, after all—I pressed my palms together and breathed in. Letting myself drift for a moment, I tried to think of myself as handing that breath forward, and then breathed out.

It didn't really do anything for me, but at least it was me performing the right thing.

"Can you use magic," I said after a moment's thought, "to ask a body of work, 'return me this word and all other words that embody the same meaning?' And can you chain it, so that you only get results for two of these in the context of each other?"

"Synonym rings, yes. Good to know not to simply ask for synonyms, good. Why?"

"Languages change." I leaned forward, grinning. I hadn't gotten a chance to *have to* think about this kind of thing in a while; I guess it'd been too long, and I hadn't even realized how much I missed it. "Geographically, languages change; and across time. Hitz said that the language they grew up with uses different words, and I *know* Ancient Shemmai isn't anything like Modern, except superficially. If the decision was made five hundred years ago, would it still be the same words?"

"Troubled, hurt, but sharp." He got up and walked past me without explanation, patting me on the shoulder. "Not broken, this is good. So. Mmm. Hope for luck, prepare for the Forest. Might be, *should* be, in the Integration or First Friend works, yes? In its history, in its formation. In policy, or in stories told and not told. Not in the Books, the girl knows her work, wouldn't be in the Books."

None of us responded, which seemed right. He paced across the room and then back, nodding to himself and muttering under his breath as if none of us were there.

"So." His voice firmed up, cadence shifting subtly, and I noticed that I wasn't the only one whose posture straightened and whose attention focused. "There is a policy, for a First Friend to Travelers, of allowing them ignorance of refinement—but in the paths permitted, this policy exists only in what is unsaid, in which intricacies of the System are left unspoken.

"From where comes this policy... no, no. *On what grounds, and with what discussion, was policy made that has this outcome?* **[Query Composition: Deep, Yet Narrow]. [Remote Query: Central Archives]**."

The two Skills between them formed a single clarion call on a horn—one to compose the note, the other to cast it into the distance.

No response came back. Not an echo, not an answer.

"Senior Librarian," Kelly broke in, "if that didn't work, if you're going to—"

"Yes, yes, girl's right, should sit." He put his hands on the top of the table and hopped up to a seat on top of it without any noticeable effort. "Always clever, often diligent, well suited. You two, give me your hands. Yes, you, girl, no hiding." He beckoned to Safra and James, and a moment later he was grasping their hands, fingers wrapped around their fingers.

Blink and you'll miss her, I thought to myself, *blink and you'll miss it*. I hadn't even remembered that the Library Associate had existed until Zqar had called her over. I saw James murmur something that I couldn't hear, and saw the Senior Librarian murmur something back; I made a note to ask Kelly, whose eyes narrowed, and then things started to go emphatic.

"**[Authorized Draw]**," murmured James in a rumbling foundation that firmed underneath us.

"So, we begin. **[Through Bonds, We Draw Strength]. [Knowledge Calls To Knowledge]. [Every Gap, Bridged—Near And Far Become One]**."

Zqar's voice was a clarion call, a moving, shifting stacked chord that started pure and grew in complexity, not becoming cacophonous or discordant but *tense*. It shook the world, hammering me apart and holding me together with undertones and overtones.

I wanted nothing more than to hear that single chord forever; I wanted nothing more than for it to resolve.

"*Twinned concepts*," he said. His voice was normal, but it wove within the sounds of the Skills he was invoking, or maybe it was just dancing around them. "Refinement and Traveler. Traveler and Refinement. **[Query**

Composition: Every Last Grain Of Sand]. Oresh, path-lighter… **[Synset Query]**."

It was everything and nothing I'd been yearning for. It was that same horn call, responded to by a hundred different horns, some higher, some lower. Their calls were short notes sharply separated from each other, their calls slid up and down in pitch, their calls were one long, steady sound; their calls were all of these things.

I recognized some of those calls, because of course I did. I'd craved, as a small child, the ability to make them. One of the few genuine moments of affection my father—may his name diminish—ever showed me was tied up with that craving, because while his approval for my excellence in my studies and the connections I was making were his *legacy*, the ram's horn he prepared and carved himself?

That was his own time, his own zealously-guarded, precious-to-him time, spent with a child he saw as more a vehicle for his own ambitions than as a person.

Of course, he took it from me before I left. I never stopped wishing I'd stood up to him on that.

Why am I dwelling on this? My thoughts echoed in my head, filling the deepest silence I'd ever heard with maudlin memories. Something in the nature of the moment was trying to pull at things that didn't *have* answers, and so many of those were things I'd rather leave buried and in the past.

A thunderbolt of sound, the result of the Senior Librarian gently clapping his hands together, shattered the soundless void. "Well! Answer given, passing strange, so it goes."

"What—"

Zqar cut me off as though he hadn't paused in the first place. "On you go, better to give this girl something to eat before we try to walk, feed the Clerk, hmm?"

"I—" Safra sagged where she stood, face ashen. Her body language, which had previously been so vital and almost hyperactive, contained nothing but exhaustion; Zqar's hand on her fingers seemed to be the only thing keeping her upright. "Right. Yeah."

"I confess," James said raggedly, "to some curiosity. To what end this… endeavor?"

"Question asked, answer given." Zqar hopped down off the desk he'd been sitting on. He didn't stumble, but he did take a deep breath in and then out after landing. "Not in the books, not in the Knowledge. Not in stories, not in training, reports, or in policy. Can't help you past that, not a question for a Librarian."

"A thousand years of Travelers coming to Shem." Kelly's hands were on her hips, expression full of doubt. "A thousand years of refining being a thing and more than zero Travelers not knowing about it when they went up to Second Tier. And *nobody* even wrote down *this is why I didn't go out of my way to tell her about it*? Was the information suppressed?"

"A thousand years of Travelers, yes. Of refinement? Hmph. Any Librarian knows better. Mustn't judge the children, rude to judge the children. Not hard to look up how knowledge passes out of the Knowledge." Zqar turned away, slipping his hand under Safra's elbow. "Evening's ease."

James shook his head at Kelly as she opened her mouth to say something more heated in response to Zqar's pointed dismissal. "We will be in good time for first seating at dinner, and I will undertake to inquire further. I am not unaware of the process he spoke of."

"Then let's go. Evening's ease, Zqar, Safra." I nodded to them, Safra turning her head to give me a dead-eyed stare and a murmur of acknowledgement.

"Sophie," Kelly hissed at me, "what—"

I shook my head at her. "Didn't you see Safra? Don't you see James? We need to get some food into them. That's more important than following up on this, *way* more important, even though I *also* have no idea what his parting shot means."

"I can *hear* you, young miss."

The Clerk Administrator's dry look was marred by a wince and a certain amount of unsteadiness, which, given that it was *him*, was more worrisome than if he hadn't tried for it at all. I gave him a dry look right back and stepped out the door, James and Kelly following close on my heels.

It was as beautiful an evening as ever. I'd gotten a bunch of answers to questions that I'd asked and some that I hadn't even thought to ask, and seen a gorgeous library. I let these things fill me, and tried to cultivate the joy of them within myself.

I found myself smiling, which probably meant that I was doing okay.

Realizing that I'd forgotten something, I glanced back at James as we walked. "Thank you for your help this evening," I said quietly.

"It went to unexpected places," he mused. "I should like to think that the mystery will do well for me; I have had few of those, of late, and little more to stretch myself to discover."

"You *should* like to think?"

"Well." He smirked, eyes crinkling. "Let me settle myself around a meal, and I will feel entirely gladdened by the evening's endeavors. Singer Tayama! I was unaware of your return. Welcome back to Kibosh."

The woman walking towards us on the ring road laughed as James called out to her, a delighted sound that sounded like a wild, skirling run of bagpipe notes. She accelerated into a jog and then a run as her target held his hands up as if to ward her off.

It was to no avail; she grabbed James, slinging him up and around as she spun, laughing. Her joy added a drone under the bagpipes, turning it from just a melody into something with counterpoint, and I realized it wasn't her laugh at all; it was just the sound of her, the music of her presence. It cascaded off of her in waves, and I found myself moving with it, foot tapping as I swayed.

"James, where's the little boy who used to call me Tammy? James!" She put him back on the ground, putting her hands on her hips and leaning first one way and then the other, peering at him. "You look like shit!"

"Yes, well." He stepped to the side, making as if to pass her; she shifted back into his way, and he didn't quite suppress his smile in time. "I expended a fair bit of myself just now supporting Zqar in a query, and I was on my way to the refectory. Will you be joining us?"

"Will I *ever*!" She spun around, assessing us with the fastest, most intense look-over I'd ever been subjected to. "Kelly Avara, you look *good*. Teal and sky blue, only you, honey. I can't stand wearing a darker top over something lighter, personally. Traveler, wow, those dyes, how did you get a red that stunning and that many blues with non-magical dyes?"

"I didn't." Her music had crested over me after her question, taking two beats to recede, and I couldn't help but wait until the opening to talk. "I got sent here by a goddess. Between her and her half-brother, they reworked my clothes to something that wouldn't draw as much notice."

"You have a good ear." She'd stopped moving entirely, eyes rapidly cycling between my hands, lips, eyes, and somewhere around my collarbone. Whatever she found must have satisfied her, because she just nodded and looped an arm through Kelly's. "Kelly! I'm only here for the night. Catch me up on *everything*."

"It's been seven years! I'll have to talk fast."

"You are Kelly Avara," the new woman declared as she swept off with Kelly in tow. "You'll manage."

Five feet and two inches of bubbly blonde strode rapidly around the curve of the ring road, my First Friend in her wake, leaving me still reeling from her force of personality even after she disappeared from view.

"That," James said in a distant tone, "was Singer Tayama. Tammy."

"She doesn't look much older than Kelly." I left unsaid *and she says she knew you when you were a kid*.

"She looks to be on the cusp of a double. Just over or just under, as she chooses. In this time, she is also known as The Chord That Sweeps The Grasslands, and also as simply another woman of Shem."

Looks just under or over a hundred, I thought to myself, *and that makes her look a bit younger than me, even if she's more weathered. With an epithet, and having known James when he was a kid. Just another woman of Shem. Right.*

I didn't have anything to say to James in response, so we just kept walking in silence towards the refectory while I listened to the music she'd left in her wake.

CHAPTER 3.20 - THE CHORD THAT SWEEPS THE GRASSLANDS

When we got to the refectory, Singer Tayama was working her way through her crowd of fans.

The adults of Kibosh were scrupulous about pretending that there was nothing special going on. Sure, a woman was passing through whom they hadn't seen in a while, but that was hardly an unheard-of occurrence. Some of them might stop by and have a word, or catch up for a moment, but it was just as one adult to another—she wasn't a *celebrity*, just a beloved friend visiting for the night.

The children felt no need to inhabit that social life, and in the large open space near the door, they were absolutely mobbing her.

"Come on," she said. I couldn't see her face—while she wasn't turned all the way away, she did have a kid on each shoulder—but it sounded like she was grinning. "One line. You know, I spent the occasional night at your bassinet, singing a six-line lullaby over and over again for three hours? I bet you don't remember that song, but do you know any of mine?"

The dense mass of kids erupted in a cacophony of insistence that even if *she* didn't know a song, or wasn't willing to sing, *they* knew the songs, and *they* could sing them. Tammy—I couldn't think of her by any more formal name, not as intimately engaged with the kids as she was—just raised one hand in response, and in a sudden ripple of quiet, every kid around her dropped to the floor with a hand up, sitting silently.

There wasn't the slightest hint of magic involved, just charisma, the expectation, and presumably some degree of that being *practiced* expectation. In the silence and the now-clear sight lines, I could see that it was always-quiet Tizpa that Tammy was cajoling, squatting a bit to put herself on the same level as the girl.

"One line, kiddo. Young Miss, nowadays, coming into your growth as you are, lemme hear one line from you. Close your eyes if you want, yeah? It can be just me and you in the room. Nobody else around, the two of us alone. Or tell me no, and I won't embarrass you any further. I release you from your promise, but I would love to sing with you, even if it's just one line."

Tizpa closed her eyes, swaying in place. I could hear the faintest echo of a soft hum, and a moment later I could feel the Singer's aura of sound shift into the opening chords of a song, played on a hand drum and some sort of wind instrument.

"*In the grasslands,*" Tizpa sang in a high, pure voice, "*the birds alight, the rivers flow, and over all the sun shines; and I walk, and dance with the wind, and my troubles pass me by.*" As she got into it, her voice firmed into something more confident, stronger and more vibrant. "*For there are no words that speak to rain and river, and no words have they for me; only show them joys and sorrows, and watch them flow or fade and die.*"

"*Will you not bide with me in the grasslands?*" Tayama's voice joined hers, perfectly matched and perfectly blending in harmony. "*Match my stride, drum each our drums, and let the wind sing our dancing song. Will you not bide with me in the grasslands? The Forest strides, the dungeons rise, and we will fight and die ere long.*"

The words and melody of the song flowed past me not leaving much of a conscious impression; the shared beauty of their voices had drawn me too deeply into the moment. Tizpa's verses and their combined choruses rang out, and all I could do was rejoice in experiencing it. And then it was over, and a ringing quiet pooled for long moments as we all swam out of our reveries.

The silence was broken by a sudden wave of shrieking adulation from the other children as they swarmed—with a careful distance—around Tizpa and Tammy as the two of them hugged. About a third of the refectory slammed their fists against their shoulders or their tables, and the herders in the refectory broke into ululating cheers.

I swallowed a sudden rush of homesickness, feeling my throat go thick. They'd cheered me, my vast extended family, lifting their voices to the sky in a manner not so unlike this. It had been with a love contingent on my being a person I wasn't, but those memories… well, they were buried a lot deeper than my ability to be all that rational about them.

Distracted by homesickness or not, I raised my voice in chorus with the herder-folk. Theirs wasn't the same as mine, different vowels mostly, but

I matched their rhythm and tried to blend; a woman threw an arm around my shoulder, hugging me, so I must have done well.

Tizpa vanished in the chaos of the praise directed at her, Tayama disappearing as well. By the time the room had settled down enough for me to hear myself think, James and I were sitting with Kelly, Jannea, and Kartom at a six-person table.

I glanced over at the empty chair with some degree of bafflement, something tickling at my brain, like a repeated phrase just barely loud enough for me to sense without actually hearing. There was nobody there, and I glanced back down at my place and took a bite of—

"A fry-up! I picked the right day to swing by Kibosh."

I chewed steadily, determinedly paying attention to my food. The vegetables were crunchy on the outside, breaded with something salty and eggy; on the inside, they exploded with flavor. "You did that on purpose," I said once I'd swallowed, looking back over. "How did you tell when I stopped paying attention?"

"It's rude to interrogate me while we're eating, you know." Tammy mock-glared at me, stabbing at a slice of... root, probably, of some sort. "That's why they're not doing it."

Kartom gave a sniff at that. "Pay no mind to Singer Tayama on that matter. *I* am performing, as a pretense, an active disregard for her presence."

"That's 'cause you think she's got too big an ego."

"And am I *wrong*, Avara?"

"Nope!" Kelly grinned at Kartom, and then swung the grin around the table. "I mean, she's got a hundred people here who can't make themselves call her by her name, but who does she sit with? Someone who doesn't care that she exists, someone who pretends the same, a sister-by-choice, a nephew likewise, and someone who doesn't know who or what she is."

"Don't be ridiculous," I said around a mouthful of fried peas. I swallowed and washed it down as pretty much everyone gave me some sort of raised eyebrow or equivalent expression, and shrugged. "It's the other way around. The big ego goes for the praise; she's probably sitting here either because she doesn't want to be fawned over or because she likes you."

"And here," the woman in question said softly, "I thought you were going to *say* that you know what I am."

I turned, looking at her and tilting my head to the side. *Say, rather than show*, I thought to myself. "You don't look like that thought bothers you," I mused out loud. "Actually, it seems like you didn't just expect me to guess, you *expected* me to be right. And you're obviously an immortal—sorry, is that rude to say?"

Her music roused itself, some sort of chimes and bells. "Only in public," she said with a grin. "But it's tremendously rude in public."

"Right, only it can't be that simple, because that's too obvious." I frowned. "Also, like, you're too *grand*. All the other Kiboshers I might put on the list of They Who Should Not Be Fucked With—" I did my best to give the words their capital letters, and did a good enough job to get a few snickers— "are pretty contained, or they shove people away, or both. And you've got the music aura thing going on."

"You hear that a *lot* better than I expected. It can't be System-side; James barely hears me, and he's got perfect synch and, what, a Tier and a half on you?"

"Right, and that's the funny thing." I tilted my head to peer at her, then closed my eyes. I knew neither diddly nor squat about music theory, but I was still picking up *emotion* from what she hadn't denied was an aura of some sort. "Your music sounds like *Skills*. It sounds like the System when it acts through someone, and it sounds like the undertones of—of the divine." I stopped myself from saying any names, figuring I maybe didn't want to do that in public.

There was a rippling stillness around the table, broken immediately by the sounds of Jannea's determined chewing. She was still tuning everything out, and the incongruity had me giggling.

"Tammy," James said over my and the Singer's laughter, "did you manage another step?"

"I'm on the brink of it. It's still coalescing. I'm too broad and too narrow at the same time; don't ask me how that makes sense, I don't know myself. But I can feel it, it's *right there*, I just need to step over the threshold. Speaking of which, Sophie, can you do me a favor?"

I blinked, distracted by trying to figure out what James meant by *step*. Was it the same as Realm? "That… depends on the favor, but probably?"

"Sing me a line."

I gawked, staring at her. *Sing, after that performance? Me?* I opened my mouth to say no—

"Two notes. I mean, a line would be better, but I'd take two notes? Please."

I almost said no even after that, but something about her music had shifted and drew my reluctance away. It wasn't the same as the transcendental religious experiences I'd been having; it was just… nice, just a background sound that was like a hug, like a chord that wrapped arms around me and didn't ask questions.

My mind scrabbled for purchase, thrown off-balance by the baffling, unexpected turn the evening was taking. Mustering my courage, I sang the first thing that popped into my head, wincing even as I did so.

"*Come we have to banish night,*" I sang. "*In our hands are fire and light.*" The words flowed from me, line after line, for all that she'd offered to take two just two notes. "*Flee now darkness, from our sight. Flee now, before the light.*"

It wasn't exactly right. There was a symmetry and variance missing, there were so many things lost in the spur-of-the-moment translation. But at the same time, it was… right enough, or maybe too right.

"Well that's interesting." The not-exactly-vocal chords and harmonies that she'd been manifesting shifted into something more along the lines of a hand drum and a fiddle, something in a familiar minor key. "Again?"

"*Come we have to banish night,*" I sang again, and this time she sang with me. Her voice twined around mine, lifting me up on a note I must have been flat on, reducing the amount my pitch was sliding. It sent chills through me, a warm tingling from my toes to my scalp. "*In our hands are fire and light.*"

My eyes prickled, and I focused on my breathing and my control over my voice as we sang together. *I am more than my history*, I reminded myself, *and more than my father's child. I will not mourn what I might have become. I will not weep for having left those congregations behind, the ones which once sang with me and made holy my meager voice like she just did.*

"You really are from another world," she murmured. "Reaching for something you can't touch, and it should be as close to you as your own heart, as a twin. No wonder you think about them that way."

The bitterness rose, and it leaked into my voice despite my best efforts. "Well *that's* not cryptic at all. Is that why you wanted me to sing? So you could be vague at me?"

"I'm sorry," she said to me, giggling. "That was rude of me. It's just… you are *very* different, even if you're also very much like we are. Anyway, right, okay." Her tone went suddenly formal, all of the bubbliness gone in an instant. "Sophie Nadash, Traveler, Alchemist, I thank you. I've caused you some distress with the favor I asked of you, a favor I profited from."

I opened my mouth to say something like *you're welcome* or *it's fine*, and both Kelly and James put a hand on my shoulder before I said anything—Kelly visibly aborting a jab under my ribs with her elbow in the process. "I hear you," I said instead.

"You haven't started sync exercises, I'm guessing, Sophie?"

"Given that I don't know what those are," I said in what felt like a too-familiar litany, "probably not."

"I'd like to do you a favor in return." She looked squarely at me, her music settling into a three-note bagpipe drone, a chord that was relaxing and tense at the same time. "I can't tell you what it is before I do it, or it won't work; and it involves me using my music and my magic. But I'll give oath that it's nothing other than helpful, and that if you knew what it was, you'd want me to—well, that I can't think of any reason you wouldn't want it."

I glanced around the table, taking stock of everyone. Kelly's expression was hungry, and James's placid; Kartom was curious, and Jannea... well, she was paying attention, and that was a departure from the normal in its own right.

"I'll take that oath," I said. "If Kelly and James both think I'm wise to take the favor—"

"Yes," they both said in immediate unison, cutting me off.

"—okay. I'll still take that oath, but okay."

CHAPTER 3.21 - INTERVENTION UNDER OATH

Apparently this was going to be a bit more involved than Kelly and Guardsman Tseizal exchanging an oath to Zuqeh about a potion transaction.

We finished eating in mostly silence, everyone apparently racing to eat so that we could get to whatever was coming faster. Everyone had their own excuses, most of which were entirely unsurprising—Kelly to support me, James to make sure everything was in order, Kartom because there was something magical or magic-adjacent going on.

I hadn't expected Jannea to care, but that was absolutely on me. *There might be something worth painting* was obvious in hindsight, because if a woman was going around being called The Chord That Sweeps The Grasslands? Chances were pretty good she'd be doing something interesting from time to time.

It still took us a bit of time to finish dinner. Tammy—she'd turned her gravitas off again, and I couldn't think of her in any other way—went through three servings of food while chatting with every kid that swung by, but she'd finished them before I'd finished my second serving of dinner. We had a sort of apple-honey-cake kind of thing that was spiced too strangely for me to properly appreciate, and then in a rush we were all heading out the door before I was really aware of it.

I'd been expecting to wind up somewhere meticulously kitted out for ritual spellwork. Instead, we gathered in a sprawling garden behind the refectory, with the air redolent of herbs and spices. There were a bunch of freestanding structures haphazardly—or *seemingly* haphazardly, and probably very intentionally—scattered around, and a bunch of trellises covered with fruiting vines between herb patches.

We wound up inside one of those structures. Roofless and with four short eighth-of-a-circle arcs of vine-bearing trellis serving as abbreviated walls, it was warm even in the fading light of evening, and had room enough for all of us... and an almost completely unadorned circle of chalk.

"Not very artistic." Jannea scowled at the circle. "Sloppy."

"Nothing we are performing requires intricacy in our measures." Kartom gave one of those sniffs that I had rapidly come to expect from him, glowering at Jannea. "We have need of a buffered delineation, and only that. To do more would be both wasteful and increase the chances of complications."

"I appreciate," I said with a smile as I stepped between them yet again, "that you care about the look of it, Jannea. This is hardly what I associate with *magic circle*. Is this all that delineation means? A circle drawn with chalk?"

"Divinity is a state of being and a wielding of the Self," Tayama interjected. "Well, mine is, at least. The act of creating the delineation is all we need; you could do it with grass stems or inlaid in metal and it wouldn't make a difference."

"That would be foolish." Kartom didn't sniff or scowl. This was apparently too serious for either of those; he went cold, instead. "By your grace to Sophie, I infer you have gained an insight which you have not yet integrated. Sophie herself may not possess mana control, but her mana may yet react in unexpected ways; as well, she interacts with divinity in unusual—"

"Okay, okay!" Tayama raised her hands in surrender. "I cede the question of the ground to the expert, you're right to have a buffer."

It seemed like there should have been something to say after that. Kartom huffed, sure, but then it was just... silence, as we all stood around awkwardly, until James cleared his throat.

"Some formalities present themselves, and I am grateful for the forbearance of all present," he said. "Singer Tayama. Do you attest that you have no reasonable doubt that, were Sophie informed of what you propose to perform and what the range of outcomes are, she would both consent without reservation and consider it favorable in its own right?"

The Singer had settled down into a cross-legged seat on the ground, music tamped down to a quiet single-toned hum. "Yes," she said simply.

"Do you attest that you have briefed both Kelly and Kartom as to both your proposed action and its range of outcomes, and that you believe them to fully understand both of those?"

"Yes."

James turned to a smiling Kelly, his own face an impassive mask. "Friend Kelly, do you attest that you fully understand both the action and range of outcomes under discussion, and that you believe it to both be in Sophie's best interests and something she would consent to, had she the information?"

"Yep!"

"Magus Kartom. Do you so attest as well, with regard to all those matters?"

"I do."

"For my part, while I do not understand the action itself, my understanding of the outcomes is such that I endorse this for you, Sophie. However, I wish to emphasize that if you have any discomfort with the notion or don't wish to accept the Singer's proposal, you have, of course, no obligation to. This is *not* a matter of a time-sensitive threat to your life."

"This is kind of a lot," I said cheerfully. "In a way, I'd have been a lot less worried if we'd just gone, like, oh hey, step into this circle and Tammy's gonna do some magic to help you with something."

"No doubt you would." James was smirking, because of course he was. "However, you find yourself in the company of quite emphatically the least likely assemblage to take such an approach."

"Wrong," snapped Jannea impatiently. "Do it already."

"The least likely, Jannea excluded," I amended on James's behalf, and then I stepped into the circle with Tayama. "So, what do I do?"

"Sit down however's most comfortable," she said. "Close your eyes and open your ears, and focus on how my music makes you feel without analyzing the music itself, as much as you can."

I pulled myself into the full cross-legged seat that I'd never been able to do in my life on Earth, feeling a rush of joy at how my body could just *move*, how it could bend and take weight without pain. "Alright," I said, and with my eyes closed, I committed myself to listening.

It was easy enough to just focus on how it felt. I knew basically nothing of formal music theory, anyway. I'd had a childhood and four years of... well, there wasn't a word for it in modern Shemmai, but the Ancient Shemmai *seminary* wasn't wrong, but I'd left all of that behind at the age of twenty-two when I moved to California.

Having abandoned—or having been abandoned by—the congregations whose traditions were my heritage, I'd made no effort to seek out a replacement. I might have said, had anyone asked, that I wouldn't accept a substitute that had severed itself from the thousands of years of history that *defined* our shared faith; but I had lost that faith, and I was busy rejecting the cultural traditions that were, to me, inseparable from it.

And so in the fifteen years that came after, I neither sang nor studied music, neither orated nor engaged in debates. Those, after all, were part and parcel of what I'd left behind.

Maudlin, I thought to myself. *Introspective, but maudlin.* The music shifted as I realized the mood it was... not so much putting me in as drawing me gently towards, and the pull shifted with it. Aware of the effect, I could be more conscious of its direction and I could identify the burgeoning mood faster and more accurately.

The music shifted steadily, forming emotional cycles. Mostly she hummed, and whatever her aura was served to provide a drone that gave a foundation for her humming; but she broke into song here and there, or had the music shift into instruments of various sorts.

The effects slowly started to describe a cycle around a mood of calmness and connection. The song was a slow-moving sequence of chords, each evoking a subtly different emotion, gradually building and then releasing tension. And then it changed, and something *clicked*.

I reached out, hungry for the intimacy the song promised, and grasped my Spark—my System, my interface to the Divine Flame, my little symbiotic shard of a vast, diffuse godhood. It curled around me, eager and delighted, hungry to interact with me, and I studied it and its... mood.

I hadn't thought about the fact that my Spark had moods, about the fact that presumably the god beyond it had moods. Obviously it *did* have moods, or something very like them; it didn't just follow my directives, we'd had a back-and-forth about bombast and some learning experiences around appropriate alerting and field of view.

Drifting in a trance, I didn't so much think about what that implied as come to a set of observations. I'd been taking my Spark lightly, and everything about the System lightly by extension. Sure, I'd had other things to do—social things, mostly—and it had *really* not been very much time, but...

Well, I could see in myself that a week from now, I still wouldn't have been looking up what the Class Feats were for a crafter. I still wouldn't be cross-referencing Classes and figuring out what my selection strategy should be for refining, which I was absolutely going to do. It just all felt so *silly*, so pointless; I'd say it felt childish, but I'd spent a party at which I was the guest of honor surrounding myself with children rather than picking the brains of my crafter peers.

There was an imbalance there, rooted in my disinterest. My Spark loved me, and there was *something*, a closeness and attention from the god that I could hear only three echoes of, humming in the distance. *Or maybe mine's an echo of those*, I thought to myself in amusement, feeling like I'd caught myself in a moment of deep, deep hubris. *Theirs is a mountain to my hill, even attenuated by distance. And yet.*

I had options, of course. I could do nothing, and let our relationship—because that's what this obviously was in some sense, if my Spark had emotions and things it wanted—develop however it wanted to go. Alternatively, I could act; and I knew that I could draw it to me and use the magic and pseudo-divinity to push it one way or the other.

Which I might or might not do, because not choosing? Just letting it ride, and seeing what happened? That was a valid choice too. *But what are the other choices?* I looked around, studying everyone else's… synchronization, probably, since they'd used the word sync in reference to it. Drifting in the calmness, seeing through the lens of magic, music, and divinity, I saw and I understood, all at once, that—

—Jannea was simple and straightforward. Oil coated her fingers with a rainbow sheen and rested in her hand in the shape of a paintbrush. It was eager, hungry to create. It wanted to be used to bring art into the world, to create something that had never been seen before or that evoked emotions someone had never felt. In that way, they were one and the same, but also a team of specialists: Jannea as the vehicle and designer, the Brush as the means, and the fusion of them as the will to create. It didn't matter that Jannea was in ascendency and the Brush was a tool, because its goals were hers.

—Kartom's eyes burned with a fire that was layered over his brain in uncountable spatial dimensions, or so it seemed. He hungered to know and understand; his Sight took in everything we were doing with a deep satisfaction, and I realized that it wanted to *see*. They worked in tandem, vision providing the opportunity for comprehension and comprehension unraveling the universe and its underlying frameworks to make the opportunity for deeper vision.

—James breathed, and with every heartbeat the fire flowed. From his lungs to the mind and then to his fingers, and then to the quill that rested loosely between his fingers; and back again to the heart and then to the lungs. The fire was his ink and his ink was his mechanism, his trade and his craft. With every stroke of the quill, he wrote Law into the world; and with every stroke of the quill, he interrogated the Law and asked, *could this be better?*

—Kelly danced, still as her body might have been, with an ephemeral and ever-changing wisp. She led and she followed and they danced together, in every conceivable range of motions. Even when something repeated, it was a repetition that became something different by what led into it and what it led into. The *context* could shift, not just the steps of the dance, and alongside her Novelty she moved with a hunger for everything new. I knew that the intuition I'd had was correct, that it was the newness of who I was and what was between us that drew her to me, and I was... relieved.

—The Chord That Sweeps The Grasslands sang, perfectly contented and one with herself even as she kept me centered in the moment. There was nothing but her sitting there, but she was *more* than the others, like there were reflections layered on top of her. She was precisely who she was, and so was her Song, because she and her Song had melded and merged to the point where there was no distinction between them anymore. The connection between her and the Divine Flame, that god that was behind the System, was gossamer-thin and nearly empty; with one more step, once she figured out how to take it, those connections would lift in a goodbye thrumming with joy.

I could have done anything, including nothing at all. I could have consumed the interface, incorporated the bridge and its connections into myself, and drunk from the firehose, if I'd been enough of an idiot to think that was a good idea. I could have taken a shortcut to the destination I was heading towards and turned my Spark into a tool, a program that possessed a sort of pseudo-intelligence but still served only to execute my desires—a flame or a tome, a quill or a still.

But I wasn't a child anymore, and I had learned enough of myself to know what I feared and what I needed; and I wasn't my father, may all his rulings be overturned except for the one about it being necessary to get vaccinated.

While my father wouldn't have thought twice about it, my mother knew the truth—we have a duty to nurture what we bring into the world. And besides, I was never a pet kind of person. Company worth having was the company of *people*.

Something flowed into me from the music that surrounded me. For a moment I was afraid that, despite all of the assurances, it was going to change *me* somehow; but it flowed through me instead. It sank into the largely undefined bundle of potential that had been nothing to me but a bizarrely-hammy mechanism, reshaping it, and when the song faded it was something far more.

I held out a mental arm and Spark settled against my metaphysical side with the faintest, but still deeply comforting, thrum of a note I decided to call the Friend.

CHAPTER 3.22 - SO ENDS ANOTHER DAY

When I opened my eyes, perceptually seconds after Spark and I settled into our new equilibrium, it was twilight verging onto dusk.

Unlike the other times I'd interacted substantially with divinity in some form or another, I wasn't delirious or high. I *was* tired, possibly on the far side of exhausted, but it had been a long day, so that was only to be expected.

Jannea was already gone, and so was Kartom. I could hear his footsteps on the path and the seeming urgency in his fast walk, and I cracked a smile around the group. "They had to go write things down, didn't they," I mused.

"Each wishes to imbue a device with the record of his perception," James said. "Nothing so information-sparse as the written word will do for this matter."

"Kartom'll also write it down." Kelly giggled quietly. "He says that the act of trying, um, how did he say it… *to attempt to imbue mundane lettering with the meaning of arcana is instructive in its own right.* That's what he said."

"I can quite literally imagine his very cadence and tone of voice." I stood up smoothly, glancing down at my shins and knees. They were immaculately clean, because of *course* there wouldn't be any dirt or even dust in the… pergola, arbor, whatever this was. That felt weirder somehow than the fact that I wasn't sore or stiff after all that sitting. "I guess the delineation worked? Can I just… leave the… there's no circle anymore?"

"Matters sometimes are as simple as they are said to be." James nodded at me. "Kartom removed the delineation once it was no longer necessary. He wished to return to the Tower as rapidly as possible, but he is diligent in his duties. How do you… feel?"

"Tired." I stifled a yawn, forcing myself to put words together more coherently. "Impressed, because I really like your driving principle? Actually,

I like everyone's... engines, I don't know. Purpose, tool, companion, whatever."

"C'mere, Sophie." Kelly smiled at me, and I obediently wandered over and accepted her arm under my shoulder, leaning on her a bit. "James, Tammy, are we done here? She needs to sleep. Invoking the divine and leveling would have been a big day, and that was just her morning."

"In a moment, Miss Avara." James glanced over at Kelly, returning immediately afterwards to Tammy. "Singer Tayama, might I impose upon you a moment further before we go our separate ways?"

"James," she murmured, and opened her eyes. She didn't exactly look haggard, per se, but I knew that look and that voice. She'd pushed herself to her limits and maybe beyond, both in song and energy, and if she were a cantor—*huh, score one for the Shemmai lexicon*—back on Earth I'd expect her voice to be less than serviceable for a couple of weeks.

"I know that your travels demand your imminent departure, so I will be brief." He nodded to her, and she nodded back, some sort of social recognition thing that I could notice but not understand. "Do you attest that you have performed as described to—" James interrupted himself with a jaw-cracking yawn and a head-shake. "I apologize. As described to us? And do you attest that Sophie has maintained a continuity of personality and consciousness, and that any changes made to her were by her own hand, unfettered and uninfluenced by any external force or means?"

"Yes, yes, and no, did you *intend* that one to be a trap?" Tammy stretched carefully, bending forward, back, and then side to side with her arms high. "Uninfluenced isn't a coherent attestation, James, and we both know it. Her piece of the Flame influenced her, and being calm influenced her, and *seeing you* influenced her. That one surprised me, even after hearing you sing, Sophie. You're a fascinating girl, and I look forward to the woman you become."

"Hm. Which of those qualifies as an external force or means, rather than the internal perception or an externally-induced state of calmness giving her information and emotional stability?"

"Oh." Tammy frowned, rubbing her head. "Yeah. Okay. It's a good thing I'm not performing tomorrow or practicing Tizpa's song with her, I'm gonna need to rest for a day. External force or means, her... you know, it *should* be just something I could call an Ember with a straight face, but it was already too developed for that. It's why I'm tired, I had to—sorry, I'm rambling."

James went to rub his forehead with his fingers, stopping himself and steepling them in front of him instead, nodding like he was hanging on to bureaucratic dignity by a thread. "Her connection to the Divine Flame can be considered external, and it, strictly speaking, possesses both force and means. I apologize, Tayama. That attestation was malformed."

"I attest," she said with a tone striving to be dry, "that Sophie made the changes without *me* putting any ideas in her head or making any changes myself. The only thing I did was give her fuel, vision, and the ability to stay in the emotional state she wanted to be in for the duration."

"That... will do, I suppose? Ah." James turned, raising an eyebrow. "Kelly?"

"Are you really looking," Kelly responded acerbically, "for me to give you a second-guess on *Tammy*? If she wanted to compromise my charge, I wouldn't be able to tell. I'm taking Sophie home. She's had too much excitement today, and we deliberately don't try to magically shove more sleep into people for a *reason*."

We started walking, Kelly supporting about a quarter of my weight and me giving James a helpless shrug. *Hey*, I tried to communicate with body language, *don't ask me, I just work here*, and it seemed to work well enough that he didn't give more than a mild sigh.

"Let's try," I said with tired firmness, "to have a few nights where neither of us is leaning on the other for support on the way home."

"Let's."

We walked in silence for a few steps, tuning out the conversation that was happening behind us. "So," I said after a couple of moments, "Tizpa's song, with a possessive?"

"Tammy's an aunt of hers of sorts. Way I heard it, she used to sing to the kid, and one day she's swinging back around to visit and she hears Tizpa singing, well, *that*, more or less? So Tammy promises to turn it into a full song with her, and Tizpa promises to sing what's written with her every time she visits."

"And that was seven years ago?" I gave Kelly my best side-eye, which wasn't very good even when I was in top form. "Last time she visited, I mean."

"Tizpa takes a herd out farther than anyone else does. Far enough that she overnights; sometimes more than once."

"So Tammy sweeps by." I blink, then snicker at my accidental humor. "Sweeps. Heh. To sing with Tizpa in chords."

"It's good that you think you're funny," Kelly said, and that set me off to laughing properly, and her to giggling.

"There have been so many..." I propelled myself off of Kelly's shoulder so that I could gesticulate. It wasn't particularly hard to stay upright; even before I became magically hale; I was used to operating more tired than this at the lab.

I still couldn't find the right words, though. Say what you will for 2AM lab work, it came with checklists and a lack of verbal communication.

"A long day," my companion said eventually. "Lotta surprises. Not just for you, too."

We'd arrived at the house—at *home*—so I busied myself for a moment with the door and with the important task of not tripping over the threshold. I didn't head for the stairs, though. Instead, I leaned on the counter, and Kelly leaned next to me, waiting patiently for me to say whatever was on my mind.

Tayir fixed the ramp, I found myself thinking uselessly. *It looks like a ramp now, instead of fake stairs.*

"I don't like to think of myself as special," I said eventually, once I'd gotten myself back on track. "Thinking of yourself as special leads to trouble. I'm good at some things, sure, but here, a place like here, it seems like being surprising takes being special."

"Most people don't, for reasons that depend on the person."

"Isn't the whole, like, *thing* here that everyone's special?"

"No? Or..." Kelly trailed off, and I looked over at her to see a frown. "I don't like to think of it that way," she said after a moment. "Being the best at being yourself isn't special. I'm great at my job, but I'm not *special*, special is..."

"Special is Tammy?"

"Tammy is special even for special." Kelly giggled, an overtired giggle, too loud and too long. "Special is Ketka and Tizpa. Special is Farmer, but only because they're so busy *not* being more than just special. And you."

I giggled, despite my reluctance. "I sort of got that impression about Farmer. I got the same sort of vibes from them that I did from Hitz and Rafa, in a way."

"Hitz is special," Kelly said with a nod. "Rafa's better at not being special than Farmer is, and doesn't work a tenth as hard at it."

"And, uh..." I blanked for a moment, coming up with the name eventually, along with a shudder of remembered emotions. "Iōanna?"

"Not on Tammy's level." Kelly hugged me from the side, as careful as handling a flask of volatiles. "But she's... well, I'm not sure her story's mine to tell?"

"So what even is being special, then? Because Hitz and Farmer, they're immortals, right? And they're both just special, but Iōanna is more than that, even though she's a Tier below them."

"Um. I'm... not sure how to put it?"

"Eh." I shrugged, pushing myself off the counter into a standing position. I kept a hand there for stability and balance, which was definitely a good call, but I was steady within a few seconds. "We're tired. I'm way past tired. Can always ask you again in the morning."

"It's about how wide you are." Kelly pushed off in what had to be a deliberate mimicry of me, one that might have seemed mocking a day ago. "Rafa's exactly only what she is, and that's something that other people are, too."

"Even if she's really good at it," I said slowly, "that doesn't make her special. But Hitz is a lot of things, and Iōanna... is a Delver?"

"It's the people she's taking with her, if that makes sense."

I turned the thought over in my head, rotated it one way and then the other. "Not really." I snickered, starting to walk up the stairs. "But maybe it will in the morning. Tell you what, though."

"Hm?"

"I wouldn't complain," I said, taking the steps one at a time and with an abundance of care, "if I went, oh, at least a week without a day like the last few."

Kelly giggled at that, but she didn't say anything—just followed me up the stairs, turning when we got to the doorways to the rooms. She hesitated there, then drifted forwards a few more steps to stand in the doorway of the third room, the one room which Jannea had finished painting.

I stepped up to her and leaned against the door, taking in the view of what was once home. Taking in my new friend, and the intensity of her exhausted gaze; taking in how troubled that view made her feel, how drawn and repelled she was by the city that I'd loved.

"Night's slumber, Sophie," she murmured as if I wasn't there. "Breathe deep, here where the air is clear and the plains are endless."

I blinked a few times before I could formulate a response to that. "Night's slumber, Kelly," I finally managed to say, and then the only thought left in my head was a hope for pleasant dreams.

The raven might have had other ideas, but there was a kindness in it, at least tonight. It coasted past me, high above, its claws forming a cage around me—but the cage was as protective as it was a threat, at least for now. The sun was high, after all, and the heat beat down in the desert day, and I bound my wounds and staunched the flow with the long shadows it cast over me.

Not everything is a trick, it told me.

Everything is a trick, it told me.

I told it I already knew. Obviously, I already knew. Godhood was a trick, a matter of reprogramming yourself to see the stack instead of just the operation. Nothing more than a change in dimensionality, a perspective switch, a shift in reference frame.

You should ask me a question. I always tell the truth, it told me.

You should never ask me a question. I always lie, it told me.

I knew that already too. What kind of Trickster couldn't do both of those at once, couldn't provide a prophecy that fulfilled itself while also rendering itself false? But there wasn't any point in saying something like that. So instead of getting into a wing-measuring contest when all I had was a couple of Paridae, I leaned against a tree and watched the dawn peeking through the canopy, here and there.

It's a nice world, it told me. *I might visit, if you'll have me.*

I'm dreaming, I said. *Trying to make binding agreements with me while I'm dreaming is bad form.*

We're not in the desert, I said to it, *so don't expect me to wash your feet.*

Be bound by the obligations of a guest within my mind as also within my home, I said to it.

It smirked at me. *Good talk, good talk,* it said. *You won't see me for a bit. I think you're up for some really normal days, but I'll be watching when things get interesting again.*

That having been said, it flapped its wings at the buffalo it was riding, and they rode off. I waved, but it probably wasn't paying attention. Impossible to tell, though. It was a Trickster powerful enough to prophesize. I wouldn't make the mistake of underestimating it in such mundane ways.

And then I slipped deeper into slumber, and true to its word, I saw nothing of it in the eleven quiet, perfectly imperfect days that followed.

CHAPTER 3.23 - INTERLUDE: JAMES

James Morei, Clerk Administrator of the Dungeon Village of Kibosh, liked to call himself an ambitious man. It was one of his many jokes, in the manner of his favorite kind of joke—a way of lying, amusing, and telling the truth all at the same time.

Of course, no fellow Clerk would be misled by the claim. They understood, even when nobody else did, the truth of their shared ambition.

And yet, he thought to himself. His wife raised an eyebrow, and he smiled at the reminder of just why he'd murmured it out loud. It was the barest of vocalizations, a habit ingrained from a century of marriage—and in particular, marriage to someone who could hear, crystal clear, a subvocalization across the room.

"I've grown complacent," he said out loud.

"If you say so."

"And if I don't?"

His wife glanced over just enough to make obvious her smile at the old joke. "Then make it true, and you won't have."

That, he thought to himself, *was different*. Different enough to make him give it some thought and consideration. "The wisdom of your own path," he said eventually with a smile.

Captain Meredith Morei smiled back indulgently—or, well, in a way that *he* understood as indulgence, as a man who knew every fractional shade of meaning to her blade-thin smiles. She left it at that, as he knew she would. Her life, her philosophy, was not his own; she walked the Theurgist's Path, openly defying the expectations and strictures of society, System, and Gods alike in her pursuit of an apotheosis taken, rather than grown.

She had no interest in the gentler means of being defined by a single Truth, no matter how socially appropriate or fundamental to who she was. Since before James was born, she'd been hungry to remain *herself* even while wrenching away a seat in the Heavens… and she'd been furious that, once she had moved into open defiance of everything in her way, the barriers she'd faced faded.

The Theurgist's Path was fundamentally *proper*, where mere flouting was not.

He thought, as he long had, that she would have to let go of that fury in order to move beyond where she was. It seemed beneath a Goddess, too petty of one, to begrudge that those who *could no longer* stop her might stop trying—but he'd been wrong before, when it came to her. And since she could read him so well as to nearly know his thoughts…

"I performed a review—" James cut himself off, smiling faintly at the expected sour glare. "I reviewed," he said, "all five Traveler integration strategies, even knowing Kelly would pick her twist on the orthodox approach. She doesn't even know two of them *exist*, you know?"

"*You* know I killed one of them, right?"

He boggled at her, surprised briefly into discomposure. "You what?"

"One the strategies. Also one of the Travelers." She looked up from her own paperwork, glaring intensely at the wall behind James's head. "Everyone was *real* clear it wasn't okay, before. Probably my last step off the road."

"I didn't realize that was… well, of course I didn't. There's no suggestion of who wielded the blade, only the ruling that—" he stopped suddenly, looking at her. "Really?"

"Wrong order. They issued the ruling after I killed him." She smiled, that flavor of smile which was best described as *they fucked around, and I was right all along.* "Him and seventeen others, all told. Mala intervened, kept it quiet, put the real story under seal. Clever girl, asked me why, then asked me what she could do to make it so that I had to kill the fewest more."

James consciously didn't say any of the first few things that ran through his head. On many subjects, ranging from her casual, dismissive attitude towards the Queen to her uncompromising ideals, he deliberately didn't engage with her.

"If I never considered what all five strategies might have been missing," he asked instead, "what else have I overlooked?"

"You're not un-diligent," she said dryly. He winced, looking back down at his papers, and she soon relented. "You're a fish in the ocean. What were you missing?"

"The water," he murmured, and with a shift in perspective that was both a narrowing and a broadening, his world shifted into unreality.

James Morei sat still at his same desk, laden with the same writing tools and papers. His wife still sat at hers, for all that his mind's eye passed over her without a thought; and that was the limit of the similarity.

With a bare act of will, a stream of books and papers flew out of the notional, endless bookshelves of his mind. If he were conducting a review of his *Archive of the Mind*, those shelves would exhibit organization and true structure; with his current purpose, he was content to draw on the information itself through the Archive.

Shem integrated a wide variety of new citizens through the First Friend program. In the cities, there were other means available to immigrants—directed apprenticeships were common, in some ways the living heir to the Mazaran approach, but most came to the cities already grown and settled into their trade. The vast majority of those needed nothing more than language lessons, introductions to others in the community, and a helping hand with the bureaucracy; a Clerk Associate would suffice for them, within the Realm of Earth though that worthy might be.

Tagata, however, was... unusual.

It wasn't the only unusual nation whose citizens might choose to spend some years in Shem, of course. There were Forest-folk who had no particular ties to the Remnant Gods, and there were a scattering of other Yelemi nations with a visitor on record here or there. Each for their own reasons either understood the System and its ways—in their own manner, a manner which was often wildly different from Shem's, of course—or had no need to do so... save for one.

Tagata. They bought metals and chemicals, though only ones that could stand to be drained of every trace of magic, and they freely welcomed as tourists those who could talk their way into a Navigator's boat and who could survive the effects of the Confederation's oceanic dominion. In turn, they sold seedstock untouched—*untainted*, as they said—by the System, and collaborated on matters from the mathematical to the chemical with others everywhere upon Yelem.

And they sent their children, in no small number, out into the world. They were curious and hungry to travel beyond the vast bounds of the Ten Thousand Islands, and they had a stunning capacity for language and stories and art in all of its forms. They could navigate any sea, any river, any ocean; and a Navigator was welcome in any port, no matter whose flag flew from the masthead of their ship. Such a ship might make port in Yaro, Sudh, or Shem, in harbors where no other ship would survive.

And such a child, an adult by the reckoning of that Confederation of sub-centenarians, might undergo a System Integration wherever they settled for a time, and might need the help of a First Friend.

It took James, meticulous Clerk Administrator though he might have been, seventeen minutes and fifty-four seconds to identify and assemble the few relevant reports that had ever crossed his own desk or made their way into Kibosh's systems of record. Of the three remaining once one stripped away the duplicates, pointless responses, unnecessary commentary, and implementation details, two were aggregated data, structured according to what had seemed like perfectly reasonable metrics.

In the third, drawing on those damnably affable lies, a single sentence stood out starkly.

We therefore observe, read the report's conclusion in a dialect that had died before he was born, *that the Tagatan-born are most socially compatible with the herder communities; as such, and to avoid the accumulative problems involved in certain hypothetical Paths, we suggest here a largely familiar protocol for their integration.*

A slow fury began to fill him. He had been young enough when he began participating in the Discourse that the memories of the memories were nothing but haze. He had spent every year since—or so he had told himself—honing his ideals and the reification of them on the whetstone of his peers, his elders, and the generations that had come before him; and in time, he had added the younger generations to that list, as they sharpened themselves on him. He had found rot in the foundations... but that had been long decades ago, decades that had simply slipped by.

He had grown *complacent*. Oh, he had maintained the central creed, to see not simply that something works but how it works, for whom, and at what costs to others. Still, was that all he was, now? Gone, clearly, was the man who had taken to the histories to find the very roots of every judgment and decision before giving voice to what he believed should be done; absent was the meticulous drive which should have had him asking who collected that information and what other things were written only when their quill was dry.

It was a mercy that Tayir had been assigned Ellana as a First Friend. He had not been harmed by the steady study of everything there was to know about his decisions before making them, and more importantly, Kelly had never had to study the supplemental documentation for his integration.

She would have sought the reasons underlying the protocols, as he should have; and she would have read every word of every book, message, and judicial decision, just as she no doubt had for Sophie's.

Embed them into the herder communities. The Clerk who penned it simply asserted social compatibility, having chosen statistics that supported that assumption, and established the Tagatan-born exclusively amongst those who saw immortality as an act of violence against the broader context of society. Settled next to the Kennas, the Theshas, and the Theodoras, the new citizens chose to forego refinement at far higher rates than those from elsewhere, which retroactively justified placing those who came after them in settings where that was the prevailing choice.

And as those new citizens disproportionately chose to remain mortal, it further justified the policies that Clerk had proposed. Their choices must have been voluntary, the Clerk no doubt wrote—must have been because of *social compatibility* and *ethos*. Nobody had lied to them, after all, and they'd had access to all the information any new citizen had access to. And so, the Shemmai social and civic landscape avoided even the possibility of an accumulation of those who had been raised in a land that opposed the very mechanisms underlying Shem as a nation.

James didn't know what would have been worse—Kelly believing the honeyed lies, or the firestorm she would have done her best to summon if she'd understood what lay between them.

The answers to the question he'd *begun* with were no closer to hand than the full details of the discussions which had led to the Tagatan addenda within the orthodox integration recommendations. Travelers were few enough in Shem that their integration was a rare event, and the standard protocols avoided this problem by exhaustive study prior to any commitment. But Kelly was not the only person who took a different approach to their duties as a First Friend, and though the deeper rationales for the choices and recommendations might have been absent, the surface ones were... plausible, and a starting point for proper research.

Someone had clearly adapted the Tagatan protocols. Some centuries-gone Clerk had done it, faced with... what, exactly? A Traveler on hand, with an impatient First Friend whose inclinations towards momentum demanded an immediate production of civic guidance? A disaster down their line of reporting, or a hypothetical exercise done for its own sake?

In whichever case, they had either failed to properly identify the disquieting motivations of the protocol or had... agreed with them. The latter would have been an act of malfeasance, but that was hardly unknown; what *was* unknown was such a thing passing without notice, when millions from children through grown adults leapt on every published change to argue them back and forth in the refectory and in the fields, in their shops and in their gardens, in the Hall of Writ and between Clerks at their duties.

With a twist of will, the necessary paperwork assembled itself. He could go through the Senior Librarian, of course, but for a request of this scope… better to send a formal request for the documents. To ask for copies of everything relevant to a Matter Of Writ, no matter how trivial, was quite welcome even were he not a Clerk at all, but there was no urgency. A simple letter to the Central Archives of Writ, along with an accompanying storage crystal, would be most proper and would ruffle no feathers.

To file such a request in person would be a statement in its own right. A Clerk's firestorm in the making, and one more efficacious than mere public opprobrium.

He shunted his mind almost entirely out of the unreal and back into the real, laying the concept of the filled-out forms on blank paper. The two melded, and he smiled at the now-real writing. Glancing at what he called his *ghostwriting* inkwell—mostly embedded into his desk, and still three-quarters full even after that draw—he signed the papers, filled a message slip with them, and sealed it with the most basic of Clerk seals.

"Tagata," he said, sighing. "You were right. They formulated—they based the Traveler recommendations off of the Tagata ones, and those were flawed."

"I… what?"

James looked over, raising his eyebrows. "You told me to think about what a fish misses. Was that not telling me to look at Tagata? Only they, of those who integrate as adults, know nothing about the System and a great deal about the world at large."

"You know," his wife said, standing up and walking over to him, "this is my favorite side of you."

"I don't—"

She kissed him, tilting his head up by grabbing the back of his head. It was a long kiss, softening from its rough, forceful start, James's hands wrapping around her back as her hands twisted gently in his hair. They were smiling when they broke off, smiling with a fondness that had only grown over their long marriage.

"You take me seriously, and then at the same time you do something absolutely, ridiculously Clerky. I keep being surprised by you." She kissed him again, a certain tension going out of her shoulders. "I'm glad you found the fire again. I was getting worried."

"That obvious?"

"Only to me," Meredith said. "You haven't had that expression on your face in a couple of decades, since you called the Taqein Accord *de-escalation theater*. But to everyone else, you're Clerk Administrator. Show them your fire, love. Remind them why they prefer you at a distance."

"I'll have time on the way to do a review of my decisions in the past ten years or so," James said softly, unsurprised at her being a step ahead of him. "I have an obligation to Kibosh, and I need to make sure I was doing right by everyone here. No unchallenged assumptions, no carefully massaged reports used as a base a century ago for policies today."

"Sophie's not long for the quiet; I give it two weeks before she makes you and that banker boy eat your words about not coming up with something new. You know how *I'd* handle the noise."

"All the better to make this trip now, then." He smiled, wide and fierce—Meredith and Kelly had been right, and he and Jonathan had been wrong to dismiss the possibilities that Sophie brought with her. "When the letters come, when a thousand voices cry that she should be made to stop, or that she should be made to move to this town or that city, I'll have a thousand arguments to dissect, deconstruct, and refute.

"And I look forward to all of the different ways that I will tell them all: no."

To Be Continued in Book 2
Coming in 2024

ABOUT THE AUTHOR

Aaron lives in California, working as a software developer while muttering enviously about the superiority of walkable communities and countries with vastly better support for raising children.

Having had the Path of the Writer unlocked by the mid-life acquisition of an awesome rainbow hat, Aaron is now trying to inflict thirty years of arguing about civics and public policy at the Shabbat table onto readers seeking fantasy novels. Rumors that the devastating smirk masks a series of deep, dark secrets are entirely unsubstantiated—all such secrets are all-too-shallow and prone to being shared at the drop of a pin.

Follow the author:

Newsletter: aaron.sofaer.net/newsletter

Discord: discord.gg/XhnA8wyHRC

Follow us:

riverfolkbooks.com

Facebook /riverfolkp

Twitter /riverfolkp

Instagram /riverfolkp

If you want to discuss our books with other readers and maybe even the author, join our discord server using the link on our website

Made in United States
North Haven, CT
09 December 2023

45342009R00205